He softly chuckled, then let go of her hand only to capture her chin between his fingers. "Miss Knight, have I told you lately how happy I am that I hired you?"

She stared at him, once more transfixed by his amazing eyes. "I think you have, from time to time, communicated your appreciation."

When he chuckled again, she couldn't help wincing at how starched up she sounded.

A silence fell over the room, broken only by the occasional pop of the embers and the slow, steady rhythm of his breath. And perhaps he could hear the thrumming of her heart, which was beating so hard she wanted to press a hand to her chest. It seemed impossible to move, even though she should be scrambling to put distance between them.

His gaze slid down to her mouth, and then he tilted her chin up to bring her closer as he leaned in. He was going to kiss her, and she couldn't do a thing to stop him.

Correction. She didn't *wish* to do a thing to stop him, even though stern warnings were writing themselves across her brain in big, black letters.

His warm breath whispered over her face. "Och, lassie, I don't believe I've shown my appreciation quite enough."

It was the brogue that did it, by adding a rough, husky note that seduced her as nothing else could have. Her eyelids fluttered shut, her entire being waiting for his kiss. . . .

Books by Vanessa Kelly

MASTERING THE MARQUESS

SEX AND THE SINGLE EARL

MY FAVORITE COUNTESS

HIS MISTLETOE BRIDE

The Renegade Royals

SECRETS FOR SEDUCING A ROYAL BODYGUARD

CONFESSIONS OF A ROYAL BRIDEGROOM

HOW TO PLAN A WEDDING FOR A ROYAL SPY

HOW TO MARRY A ROYAL HIGHLANDER

The Improper Princesses

MY FAIR PRINCESS

THREE WEEKS WITH A PRINCESS

THE HIGHLANDER'S PRINCESS BRIDE

AN INVITATION TO SIN
(with Jo Beverley, Sally MacKenzie,
and Kaitlin O'Riley)

Published by Kensington Publishing Corporation

The Highlander's
PRINCESS
BRIDE

VANESSA KELLY

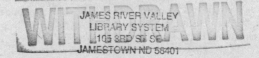

ZEBRA BOOKS
KENSINGTON PUBLISHING CORP.
http://www.kensingtonbooks.com

ZEBRA BOOKS are published by

Kensington Publishing Corp.
119 West 40th Street
New York, NY 10018

All Kensington titles, imprints, and distributed lines are available at special quantity discounts for bulk purchases for sales promotion, premiums, fund-raising, educational, or institutional use.

Special book excerpts or customized printings can also be created to fit specific needs. For details, write or phone the office of the Kensington Sales Manager: Attn.: Sales Department. Kensington Publishing Corp., 119 West 40th Street, New York, NY 10018. Phone: 1-800-221-2647.

Zebra and the Z logo Reg. U.S. Pat. & TM Off.

First Printing: November 2017
ISBN-13: 978-1-4201-4113-9
ISBN-10: 1-4201-4113-9

eISBN-13: 978-1-4201-4114-6
eISBN-10: 1-4201-4114-7

10 9 8 7 6 5 4 3 2 1

Printed in the United States of America

To Debbie Mason and The Piano Guys—
thank you for helping me find the heart and soul of
The Highlander's Princess Bride.

With grateful thanks to my agent, my editor, and
all the wonderful folks at Kensington
who do such a splendid job with my books.
You're the best!

Chapter One

"I never meant to kill him. Not for the most part." Victoria Knight hesitated, because honesty compelled her to make the hideous admission. "For just a second, I probably *did* wish him dead," she added.

When Sir Dominic Hunter and Aden St. George exchanged knowing glances, Victoria grimaced. "I know that makes me an awful person. I wouldn't blame you for marching me straight to Newgate and washing your hands of my very existence."

Chloe, Lady Hunter, patted Victoria's hand. "Nonsense. Fletcher was obviously a villain of the first order. No sensible person could blame you for defending yourself."

Victoria and Chloe sat on the silk chaise in the back drawing room of the Hunters' London town house. The late afternoon sun filtered through the sash windows, casting a soft glow on the cream- and rose-colored carpet and the elegantly papered yellow walls. An elaborate silver tea service sat on the low table in front of the chaise, but the generous plates of little sandwiches and iced teacakes were mostly untouched. Apparently, Victoria wasn't the only person in the room lacking appetite.

"I do blame myself," she said gloomily. "If I'd thought about it, I'm sure I could have found a better way to manage the situation than pushing Mr. Fletcher down the stairs."

"But you didn't have time to think, that's the point," said Lady Vivien St. George. Perched opposite Victoria on the edge of a Sheridan chair that was as graceful and dainty as the lady herself, Vivien gazed at her with earnest concern. "Besides, Lord knows how many people Aden has killed over the years. It's not like the tendency doesn't run in the family."

Victoria blinked, unsure how to respond to that startling declaration. Aden had served for several years under Wellington's command in some vague capacity she had yet to understand. It apparently involved dispatching large numbers of people. As she eyed his tall, powerful frame and his austere, intimidating air of competence, she could well believe it.

"For God's sake, Vivien," Aden said from the wingback chair beside her. "That is hardly a helpful observation, nor is it germane to this particular situation."

Vivien shrugged, unmoved by his scold. "I'm simply telling the truth, dearest. And, by the way, your cousins are just as bad when it comes to piling up dead bodies."

"My goodness," Victoria said. Those cousins were hers, too, and all illegitimate sons of royal dukes. She'd never met them and was beginning to think she preferred to keep it that way. They sounded much too exciting.

"The blackguards were all deserving of their fates," Aden said, "as you well know."

"As was the man who attacked Victoria," his wife replied. Then she flashed an apologetic smile at Victoria. "Forgive me. I mean to say, Miss Knight."

"There's no need to apologize," Victoria said, smiling at the charming, willowy blonde. "After all, we are . . ."

"Sisters-in-law?" Lady Vivien finished.

"Yes, I suppose we are," Victoria said, feeling awkward. She'd been introduced to Lady Vivien only this morning.

Like Aden, Victoria was an illegitimate child of the Prince Regent. She'd met her half-brother for the first time last year, and had only seen him once since then. Aden's mother was a wealthy dowager countess, whose husband had accepted her son as his own. Victoria's mamma, however, had been the unmarried daughter of an innkeeper. While he was a fairly prosperous innkeeper to be sure, Grandpapa had spent his life waiting on members of the *ton*, not socializing with them. To the lords and gentlemen who'd passed under the lintel of the Royal Stag Inn, Rose Knight had been little better than a barmaid—good enough for a romp, but certainly not marriage.

Aden was a powerful man, with a position at court and a wife who was the daughter of an earl. Victoria was only a governess and an unemployed one at that. She would never presume on her relationship with the St. Georges, despite their kindness.

"Indeed we are in-laws," Vivien said with a warm smile. Then she tilted her head. "Although we look enough alike to be sisters. I always wanted a sister."

"That's very kind, but no one could ever think so," Victoria protested. "You're so elegant."

She winced as soon as the clumsy words had passed her lips. But they were true, since Vivien was a diamond of the first water. Victoria, on the other hand, was entirely ordinary—perfectly neat and pleasant to look at, but no more than that.

"You're both delightful young women and, Victoria, you're as much a member of this family as Vivien," Dominic said. "As I've said on more than one occasion."

"And look how I've repaid you," she said with a sigh. "I've handed you quite an awful mess."

"I've dealt with far worse, as has Aden. We'll get you out of this, never fear."

"Lady Welgate said she would see me hanged for murder." Victoria pressed a hand to her chest at the memory of her former employer's rage.

Chloe wrapped her in a comforting hug. "I'm sure that was simply her grief talking. Please remember that you were defending yourself from a monstrous attack."

"I wish Mr. Fletcher's family shared your view," Victoria said.

Dominic went to a sideboard that held a number of crystal decanters and matching tumblers and wineglasses. "You may be sure I will be telling Mr. Fletcher's family exactly how to think about this matter," he said as he brought her back a half-filled tumbler.

Victoria hesitantly sipped the brandy. It made her throat burn, but she welcomed the warmth that soothed her shaken nerves.

"We haven't wanted to press you, my dear," Chloe said, "since you only arrived last night. But the more we know about the incident, the more we can be of assistance to you."

Dominic and Chloe had insisted that she relax after her precipitous arrival in London. They'd had a quiet family supper and then spent an hour playing with Chloe and Dominic's little boy. Victoria had been almost pathetically grateful for their sensitivity, welcoming the small break from the nightmare of the last few days.

"Aden and I can wait in my library," Dominic said, "so you can speak freely to the ladies."

Victoria had known Dominic since she was a little girl. He'd never been anything but kind and supportive, especially after the death of first her mother and then Grandpapa Knight a few years later.

"I have no secrets from any of you," she said. "If my account of that horrid day can help, then I'm happy to tell you more. I promise I will not succumb to the vapors."

"That's the spirit," Aden said. His easy acceptance of her was a surprise, and quite wonderful.

She returned his smile, then absently rubbed the plain twill fabric of her sleeve. "I hardly know where to start."

"Perhaps by telling us about Mr. Fletcher," Chloe suggested. "After all, he's the cause of this dreary state of affairs."

Dreary hardly began to cover it. "Very well. Thomas Fletcher was Lady Welgate's brother. I met him shortly after I took up my duties as governess to the Welgate daughters. He often visited his sister's household."

"I attended school with one of Lord Welgate's sisters," Vivien said. "I found him to be a very kind gentleman. Lady Welgate, however, is a rude, sour-tempered woman. I was surprised when Welgate married her."

"He didn't have much choice," Dominic said. "Welgate's father was a gambler and a spendthrift who all but destroyed his legacy. Serena Fletcher's father, however, built substantial fortunes in shipping and tobacco. Her dowry saved a distinguished family from ruin."

"No one in *this* family would hold Lady Welgate's background against her," Chloe said. "Most of us have what can only be described as mixed parentage, at best."

"True," replied Dominic. "But Vivien is correct in her assessment. While I have a great deal of respect for her husband, Lady Welgate is another matter entirely."

Dominic had counseled Victoria not to take the position, but the lure of working for such a well-regarded family that could give her excellent recommendations and a good salary had been too enticing. She should have listened to him.

"Her ladyship was not the easiest person to please," she said, "but I'd been managing it without too much trouble."

While Lady Welgate had been something of a harridan, Victoria had grown up in a houseful of brusque, sometimes-difficult women and was versed in dealing with the type. She'd made a point of performing her tasks with alacrity, and she'd never contradicted her mistress. Fortunately, her two charges, surprisingly well-mannered girls of six and eight, had taken a shine to her.

All in all, life in the sometimes-volatile household had been perfectly satisfactory until Thomas Fletcher had slinked onto the scene.

"Clearly her brother was not as easy to manage," Aden said.

"He was not. I made a point of never being alone with him. Unfortunately, he became . . ." Victoria hesitated, groping for the right word. Even now it seemed ridiculous. She was the last sort of woman for any man to pursue with such single-minded focus, especially not a roué like Thomas Fletcher.

"Obsessed with you?" Chloe said.

Victoria winced. "I suspect he saw me as something of a challenge. The more I avoided him, the more determined he became."

In the weeks before the incident, Fletcher had all but moved into his brother-in-law's household. It seemed that every time she rounded the corner of a quiet hallway or went to the library to fetch a book, he would be lurking about, waiting to catch her alone.

"I'm grieved you had to endure such a dreadful situation," Vivien said, her voice tight. "Before I married Aden, I found myself in similar circumstances. One feels enraged and helpless."

Victoria nodded. "That's exactly how I felt."

"But you took action even before Fletcher attacked you," Dominic pointed out.

"Yes. When he insisted I become his mistress, I knew I could no longer manage the situation." Victoria shuddered, recalling the way he'd backed her against the door of her bedroom and put his hands on her. Fortunately, a maid had come along, allowing her to make her escape. "I spoke to Lord Welgate immediately, who promised to instruct Mr. Fletcher to leave me alone."

"And yet the bounder did not obey," Chloe said in a quietly furious tone.

"For a few days he did," Victoria said. "In fact, he made a point of ignoring me if Lord or Lady Welgate were nearby, or if I was with the children. But it was evident he was very angry that I'd gone to his brother-in-law to complain."

When she was out on the terrace, playing with her charges one day, she'd glanced at the library's French doors and caught sight of Fletcher standing there. The look on his face, a horrible mix of hatred and lust, had almost stopped her heart.

And his hand had been on his groin as he'd watched her play with his two little nieces. She could hardly imagine how any man could be so depraved, and it had frightened and infuriated her in equal measure.

"Did he threaten you?" asked Dominic.

"No, but he made his intentions clear," she said quietly. "There was no misunderstanding them."

Dominic looked grim, but nodded for her to continue.

"I decided to write to you that evening of my intention to return to my family in Brighton until I could find new employment. I was going to inform Lord Welgate of my plans as soon as he returned from his short trip to London, and then leave immediately thereafter."

Victoria would rue that delay forever. She should have packed her bags immediately and walked back to Brighton if she'd had to. But Lord Welgate had always treated her with kindness, and she'd not wished to show him even the slightest hint of disrespect. So she'd taken the risk that Fletcher would not have the nerve to attack her in his sister's household, with two small children sleeping just down the hall. It had been a monstrous miscalculation.

"It was stupid of me to wait," she said with a grimace.

"You did nothing wrong, Victoria," Aden said firmly, "so, get that out of your head right this instant."

"Your brother is right," said Chloe. "The fact that you were not safe in your employer's household is a reflection only on Fletcher and his sister."

Victoria gave them a shaky smile. Most people would think her the guilty party, either for putting herself in harm's way or for "casting out lures," as Lady Welgate had put it. Life was often precarious for female servants, even in the best of households. She supposed she'd been lucky to reach the advanced age of twenty-five before finding out for herself just how ugly things could become.

"Thank you," she said. "In any event, that very evening, Mr. Fletcher took advantage of the fact that Lady Welgate was attending a dinner party at a neighboring estate." She huffed out a bitter laugh. "I'd assumed he'd gone with her."

Relieved that she'd made the decision to leave, she'd celebrated with a small glass of sherry from the bottle she kept in her room—a present from one of her uncles the previous Christmas. Victoria only ever indulged on her half day off— one glass in the evening, as a treat.

She drew in a breath, steadying herself for the next part of the story. "It was quite late. The children were asleep in the nursery, and the staff were downstairs in the servants' hall or gone early to bed. I'd borrowed a few books from the library, and I thought to return them while I was thinking about it. I was coming down from the nursery wing, which has a separate staircase to the first floor. Unfortunately, Mr. Fletcher was coming up that very same staircase."

"Did he have any cause to be coming up that particular staircase?" Aden asked in a chilling voice.

"He did not. That part of the manor is reserved for the children, the two nursemaids, and me."

"So the lout was deliberately seeking you out," Vivien said with disgust.

Victoria would never forget the horror that had surged in her when she saw him on the landing. Although she'd carried only one candle, a full moon had shone through the large window above the staircase, illuminating the flare of lust in Fletcher's eyes. He'd clearly been on his way to her room.

"When he saw me, he laughed," she said. "I told him to get out of my way, and that I would scream if he came any closer."

"Surely someone would have come to help if you had," Chloe said, her normally serene features pulled tight with distress.

"Yes, if they'd heard. But it was mostly an empty threat, which he knew. The door at the top of the stairs was shut, and I was too far from the servants' hall for anyone to hear a call for help."

"If the bastard wasn't already dead," Aden growled, "I'd rip out his throat with my own damn hands."

The look on her brother's face suggested he'd have done exactly that and not lost a moment's sleep over it. Victoria supposed it was rather awful of her, but his outrage partly dispelled the chill that had settled around her like a casket of ice since that terrible night. That Aden *could* do

something like that wasn't a question. That he would do it
for her was nevertheless rather amazing.

Dominic crossed his legs and rested a hand on his
knee. "A laudable if rather gruesome sentiment, Aden.
Fortunately, it's an unnecessary one, since Victoria ably
extricated herself from a very dangerous situation."

She choked back a spurt of nervous laughter. "That's
one way of putting it."

"It's the best way to put it," Chloe said. "So, Fletcher attacked you on the stairs, and then you struggled. I hate to
embarrass you, my love, but did he injure you in any way?"

Victoria pressed her eyelids shut as she flashed back to
the awful interlude. "Not really. He ripped my bodice and
scratched me a bit, but that was the worst of it."

Aden breathed out a rather shocking oath as even Sir
Dominic's calm expression disappeared under a barely contained fury. Victoria was exceedingly happy that both men
were on her side. It was unlikely that anyone on the receiving end of such intense fury would remain in one piece for
very long.

She managed a tight smile. "Fortunately, I was able to
give him a sharp elbow to the chin as he took me down
to the floor. He fell to the side instead of on top of me,
which enabled me to scramble to my feet. He was so furious that I resisted. At that moment I thought he actually
wished to . . ."

She couldn't say the words, momentarily swamped by
terrifying memories that flickered through her mind. She'd
been mere moments away from a brutal assault and possibly even death. It had taken every particle of strength to
push back against a fear that had threatened to turn her
limbs into leaden, useless appendages.

"It's all right, dear," Chloe said, taking her hand again.
"He can never hurt you again."

"Yes, I saw to that, didn't I?" Victoria's little attempt at insouciance fell horribly flat.

"You don't have to finish if you don't want to," Vivien said in a warmly sympathetic voice.

Victoria mentally shook herself. The deed was done and she *was* safe, at least for now. There was no point in indulging in self-pity or guilt.

"No, I'm fine," she said. "Fletcher grabbed for my legs, but I was able to step back and give him a good shove with my foot. The next thing I knew he was tumbling head-over-heels down the staircase."

It had all happened so quickly. A few moments after she pushed him, Fletcher lay in an inert heap on the tile floor below, his head and neck at a hideously incorrect angle. Victoria had suspected instantly that he was dead, but had run down in the vain hope that he might have survived the fall. When she crouched over him and saw the fixed, lifeless look in his eyes, she'd come to the wrenching real-ization that she'd killed a man.

A vile one, to be sure, but still a human being, one whose life she'd ended.

"And that was it," she awkwardly concluded. "It was over so quickly I could hardly believe it had happened."

"You did what you needed to do, Victoria," Aden said gently. "Never second-guess yourself on that score."

"Aden is correct," Chloe said. "It's a perfectly dreadful story, but we're all grateful you were able to overcome him. Some women are not physically strong enough to defend themselves, or would have been paralyzed with fear."

"I almost was paralyzed," Victoria confessed. "But I had the advantage of growing up in a coaching inn, where one does learn to deal with unruly or drunken males." Her grandfather had insisted that she learn to defend herself, and she would bless his memory every day for that lesson.

"After you ascertained that Mr. Fletcher was deceased, what did you do?" Dominic asked.

"I ran upstairs to the nursery and woke one of the nurse-maids. I told her Mr. Fletcher had suffered an accident and asked her to fetch the butler and housekeeper. Then I went to my room for a shawl to tie around my bodice." She grimaced, recalling how disheveled she'd looked. "For all the good it did me. The nursemaid made a point of relaying her impression of my appearance in the most lurid terms to anyone who would listen."

"Did either the housekeeper or the butler set any store by the girl's description?" Dominic asked.

"No, but others in the household were only too happy to listen."

Lady Welgate had certainly believed the nursemaid. Her ladyship had been all too happy to listen to the girl's version of events, one that had grown more salacious with each retelling. That particular nursemaid had never liked Victoria, accusing her more than once of "putting on airs." It was a common complaint about governesses. They were often looked down upon by their employers and often resented by other servants for their somewhat privileged role in the household.

"Lady Welgate arrived home shortly afterwards, did she not?" prompted Dominic. "And Lord Welgate also returned from London that evening as well?"

Victoria nodded. "Both came home to a total uproar, I'm afraid. Two of the footmen were carrying the body upstairs to an empty bedroom when her ladyship arrived. She immediately fell into hysterics."

By that time Victoria had managed to change her dress and brush her hair after giving the butler and the house-keeper a quick recitation of events. Mercifully, they'd believed her. The senior staff had disliked Mr. Fletcher, although they would never have openly expressed such an opinion. When it came to running the household, Lady Welgate ruled the roost, and she'd been devoted to her brother. Complaining about his unfortunate proclivities would have only resulted in finding oneself out of a job without references.

"You told me, however, that Lord Welgate kept his head," Dominic said.

"Yes. He convinced his wife to lie down in her room, then he sent for the magistrate. Lord Welgate made it clear to him that Mr. Fletcher had importuned me in the past, and that he did not consider me at fault in the accident."

Chloe let out a relieved sigh. "I shudder to think what might have happened without Lord Welgate's support."

"I owe him a great debt of gratitude," Victoria said. "Initially, the magistrate was not inclined in my favor, since Lady Welgate was so insistent that her brother's death was a deliberate act on my part."

"How did she arrive at such a ridiculous conclusion?" Aden asked.

Victoria glanced down at her folded hands, a mortified heat rising in her cheeks. "She accused me of trying to seduce her brother in the hopes of luring him into marriage. According to her, when he refused me, I murdered him out of spite."

"That is insane," Vivien exclaimed. "Why would she invent such a tale?"

"Lady Welgate was several years older than her brother," Victoria said. "Their mother died when Mr. Fletcher was quite young, and her ladyship all but raised him. She was devoted to him and devastated by his loss."

"Her grief is understandable," Chloe said in a clipped voice. "But that's no reason to accuse you of murder, against all evidence."

"It could have been worse," Dominic said. "Despite his wife's accusations, Lord Welgate allowed Victoria to send me an express, asking for assistance. That was quick thinking, my dear," he added, giving Victoria a warm smile.

"I didn't know to whom else to turn," she confessed. "My family wouldn't have any idea how to help me in a situation like this."

Actually, they would be mortified by her predicament. Her mother's family held a degree of affection for her, especially Aunt Rebecca, who'd essentially raised her. But they also found her existence rather an embarrassment, and would not welcome being pulled into the middle of a scandal.

"I was happy to help," Dominic said.

Thankfully, he'd arrived at Welgate Manor less than a day after the incident. Dominic and Lord Welgate had disappeared into the study, along with the local magistrate and the surgeon. They emerged with the agreement that Fletcher had been the victim of an unfortunate fall, and that Victoria was free to leave with Dominic. Lady Welgate's shrieks of rage had all but rattled the windows, but Lord Welgate had stood firm. It was clear he wished to avoid the scandal resulting from a public inquest that would expose his brother-in-law's sordid behavior.

"Then everything's all cleared up," Vivien said with a relieved sigh. "Splendid."

"Not entirely, according to the letter I received from Lord Welgate this morning," Dominic said.

"Fletcher's father arrived at Welgate Manor last night, and apparently, he's very unhappy with the magistrate's decision," Victoria said, trying to sound calmer than she felt. "He and his daughter believe I should be arrested for murder."

Aden scowled. "Well, that's not going to happen."

She smoothed her palms over her skirt to mask the trembling of her hands. "It's difficult not to worry, though."

"And I will repeat what I told you this morning, Victoria," Dominic said. "Leave Mr. Fletcher to me. The only thing you need think about is what you want to do next."

Victoria had been pondering that question a great deal when she wasn't envisioning a trip to the gallows. "I must find another position, although obviously I cannot depend on any references from Lord or Lady Welgate."

She'd been counting on another few years of employment to support her plan to establish her own school for girls. Her dream of independence had just receded farther into the distance.

"Are you sure you wish to return so quickly to work?" Chloe asked. "We'd be delighted if you stayed for a nice long visit."

Victoria was tempted. Chloe's serene, comfortable household could be the perfect refuge from her troubles. It had always surprised her how quietly she and Dominic lived, with very little ostentation. Most of the nobility enjoyed flaunting their wealth and extravagant lifestyles. Such was not the case with Sir Dominic Hunter, even though he was a powerful magistrate who had the ear of the Prince Regent.

The Prince Regent.

She'd never met her father and he'd never shown the slightest interest in knowing his daughter. Nor would he, of that she was quite certain. After all, Mamma had been nothing but a glorified barmaid. Victoria had long ago realized the folly of indulging in the belief that she had any place among the privileged classes, other than as a servant.

"Thank you for your kind offer," she said, "but I should find another position as quickly as possible. The sooner I can put this terrible incident behind me, the better."

Chloe wrinkled her nose. "Are you sure? There's no need to rush."

"Absolutely not," interjected Vivien. "You could visit with us, too. What you need is rest and a little pampering from your family."

"You are all incredibly kind," Victoria said, "but you mustn't think I'm unhappy with the idea of seeking another position. I love teaching. My greatest fear resulting from this horrible episode is that I won't—"

Her throat suddenly went tight. Teaching was the one thing that truly gave her a sense of purpose, challenging both mind and heart. There was nothing more satisfying than the look of joy on a little girl's face when she read a fairy tale or nursery rhyme all by herself for the first time. It was like having the opportunity to discover the world anew through fresh eyes every day.

Chloe picked up the half-empty glass of brandy from the low table and handed it to Victoria. "That will never happen, my dear," she said. "Dominic and your brother will not allow it."

"Certainly not," said Dominic. "But I would like to get Victoria away from London as quickly as possible."

Aden nodded. "Out of sight, out of mind is the best way to quell the gossip that might result from this situation."

Like them, Victoria knew that even the slightest hint of scandal would be a deathblow to her dreams of opening a school. Her sterling reputation was her most precious asset. If she lost that, she lost the future. Given that she was illegitimate, even with royal blood, she was already fighting with one hand tied behind her back. If Fletcher's death were to haunt her, she was finished.

"Then where will I go?" she asked. "Unless you have knowledge of an available position, Sir Dominic, I will have to advertise."

"Surely that won't be necessary," Vivien protested. "The

last thing you need is to be pitched into another uncertain situation with a family that cannot be trusted."

Dominic studied Victoria with an intensity she found slightly odd. It was as if she were a vexing mathematical equation he was trying to solve.

"As a matter of fact," he said, "I do know of a family in need of a governess, and I think you will fit the bill. Tell me, my dear, how would you feel about spending the winter in Scotland?"

Chapter Two

When a bounce jolted Victoria out of a fitful doze, she barely managed not to topple off the heavily padded seat. If Captain Alec Gilbride's luxurious carriage survived the beating from the rough road without breaking an axle or wheel, it would be miraculous. Since getting stranded in the remote Scottish countryside held no appeal, she hoped for that miracle.

His brawny frame barely moving despite the jostling, Alec flashed her a rueful grin. "Sorry, lass. I was hoping you'd be able to catch a bit more sleep before we arrived at Castle Kinglas. But that bump almost knocked my teeth out, too."

Victoria swallowed a yawn before securing her bonnet more firmly on her head. It seemed like years since she'd gotten a decent night's sleep. But there was little point in complaining, particularly since Alec and his family had fussed over her in the nicest way possible. It was no one's fault but her own that guilt and anxiety continued to plague even her dreams.

"I'm fine. Truly," she said.

She brushed aside the curtain. The views had grown in-creasingly wild on their trip north, with craggy mountain peaks looming on the horizon and rough, scrub-covered hills rising around the isolated road. "I just dozed off for a bit, which is a shame. I'm missing all the best scenery, I'm sure."

"The area around Loch Long is certainly dramatic. And I do hope you're suitably impressed, Miss Knight, especially with our fine Scottish roads," he said with a wink.

She gave him a reluctant smile. "I'm sure I'll find the views impressive once my brain stops rattling around in my skull."

They'd set out early this morning from Captain Gilbride's manor house just outside Glasgow. Within a few hours, they'd left the civilized Lowlands of Scotland behind and approached the first range of mountains that signaled the entrance to the Highlands. Ever since they passed through the village of Arrochar and left the well-traveled main road, conditions had worsened, rattling her bones as well as her brains. Victoria was tempted to walk the rest of the way to Kinglas, despite the cold.

"We'll be there soon enough, Miss Knight," Alec said. "And then you can have a nice cup of tea and a rest."

"I look forward to that more than you can imagine. And please call me Victoria. I feel certain we've achieved a degree of informality—not to say a camaraderie born of hardship."

Alec laughed. "True enough. It's been years since I traveled in these parts. Many people go by boat when journeying up the west coast, or farther north. You can certainly see why. I think I lost a tooth when we hit that last rut."

"It was so kind of you, but you truly didn't need to play escort. I'm perfectly capable of traveling by myself, as I told Sir Dominic. I feel terrible that you had to meet me in Glasgow, much less travel all this way to introduce me to the Earl of Arnprior."

Victoria feared she'd made a dreadful mistake when she

left London, now more than a week ago. Aside from the constant cold, the long days on the road, and her perpetually damp boots, she couldn't shake the growing sensation that she was running away. Disappearing so suddenly couldn't help but reflect poorly on her—as if she *had* done something wrong. To outsiders, it would appear she was fleeing the scene of the crime.

If her reputation was her greatest asset, why wasn't she standing her ground and telling the truth to whoever would listen?

She reminded herself again that Dominic and Aden had insisted they could manage the situation more effectively without her, and that her only task was to maintain a steadfast silence about the incident. The quickest way to snuff out gossip, Dominic had reiterated, was to deny it fuel in the first place. Still, her instincts were telling her that a happy resolution to the situation wouldn't be quick or easy. Whenever she was tempted to think so, she had only to recall Lady Welgate's shrieking demands to have her charged with murder.

Alec braced one booted foot against the rise of the opposite bench as the carriage drove through a series of bumps. "I'm happy to escort you, Victoria. And if you think this weather is bad, I'm afraid you're in for something of a shock come January."

She wrinkled her nose. "That sounds rather alarming."

He waggled his brows. "We'll toughen ye up soon enough, Sassenach, I promise ye. After a nice dram of whisky and some good flannel, all will be right in tha' world."

She couldn't help chuckling at his exaggerated brogue. Alec Gilbride, despite his formidable appearance, was no rough Highlander. He'd been a captain in Wellington's army and was heir to a Scottish earldom. An intelligent man who spoke at least four languages fluently, he was also her cousin, though she'd known nothing of his existence until shortly before she departed London.

She was collecting new relatives at a rather precipitous rate.

It had been awkward when she first arrived in Glasgow, but Alec hadn't blinked an eyelash after she haltingly explained her situation. Dominic had sent an express to him outlining her dilemma, thus sparing any need to go into uncomfortable details. To her relief, Alec had patted her hand and said Fletcher was lucky to die with so little fuss. If Aden or Dominic had gotten their hands on him, Alec had said, things would have been much worse for the rotter.

Alec's sanguine attitude was another interesting—if rather alarming—insight into her larger-than-life royal relations. That she was out of their league, both in temperament and station, was entirely evident.

Still, they'd all welcomed her with open arms.

"You've all been so generous to me," she burst out, feeling the need to thank him once again. "I truly don't know what I've done to deserve it."

Alec gave her a quizzical smile. "You don't have to do anything, lass. You're family."

"But you barely know me, and yet here you are, leaving your wife and family to go on a wild goose chase with me."

"Oh, I have a habit of getting on my poor wife's nerves. She's delighted to get rid of me for a few days."

Victoria eyed his sincere expression, but noted the twinkle lurking in his gray gaze. Her cousin was not only a very handsome man; he was both kind and charming. She found it hard to imagine that any woman in her right mind would find him irritating.

"Is that really true?" she asked.

"That I sometimes irritate Edie? Absolutely. That she wants to get rid of me?" The satisfied smile that curved the edges of his mouth conveyed the opposite. Like Aden, Victoria suspected that Alec had a very happy marriage.

If not for the fact that her goals did not include the wedded state, she might be a tad jealous that her brother and cousin had both secured the sort of family life a woman like her could only dream about. Illegitimacy was never an easy obstacle to overcome regardless of one's sex, and it was doubly hard for women. Like mother, like daughter, was the standard way of thinking. Tainted from an early age, a girl was likely to follow in those sinful footsteps, rendering her unfit for marriage to a respectable man.

Thomas Fletcher had certainly thought so.

"I'm sure your wife hates that you have to play nursemaid to me, but I'm grateful for your escort." Her comment was punctuated with yet another bounce through a dreadful rut, sending a rigorous jolt up her spine.

"The ride will smooth out as we get closer to Kinglas," Alec said. "The earl has been working hard to improve the roads on estate lands, after his long time away. And you're not to worry about me one bit. Since I know Arnprior, it makes perfect sense that I facilitate the introductions. Can't be easy for you to land on a stranger's doorstep, asking for a job—even if it's the doorstep to a castle."

His jesting words pricked her anxiety about her new assignment and her mysterious employer.

"Is the earl not a particularly welcoming person?" she asked cautiously. "I know so little about him, or what he expects from me. Dominic didn't tell me much." It had struck her as rather odd, but it had been such a rush to get her on the road that there hadn't been time for a full discussion.

Being cooped up with her thoughts for the last week, without her music or work to distract her, had been more of a challenge than she'd anticipated. Playing the pianoforte, in particular, had always been an escape and comfort for her, one she'd been denied for almost two weeks. Victoria swore her fingers were starting to itch with the need to play, and even the oldest, most out-of-tune instrument would suffice at this point.

Alec's genial expression remained unchanged in response to her query, but she had the impression he'd come to alert.

"Arnprior's a capital fellow," he said, "so no need to worry about that. But what exactly *did* Dominic tell you about him and your new position?"

"I know Lord Arnprior served in the army for several years and was away from home for most of that time. He has five half-brothers who are quite a bit younger than he is. The youngest one needs a teacher who can provide instruction in both music and deportment." She frowned. "I do find it rather odd that the earl would wish to employ a governess rather than a tutor. Wouldn't a male teacher be more appropriate for the boy? And I don't believe his brothers are still in the schoolroom, are they?"

Alec frowned down at his gloved hands, which rested loosely on his thighs. "From what I remember, Arnprior's half-brothers range in age from fifteen to twenty-five. I served with Royal Kendrick, the oldest. He's a good man, like the earl, if a bit rough around the edges. Royal will not be looking for any schooling in deportment, although he could certainly use it," he finished after a short pause.

"Oh, dear, is Mr. Kendrick an unpolished sort of person?"

Alec shook his head. "No, just gruff."

When she eyed him dubiously, Alec shrugged. "Well, very gruff, if you must know, although he wasn't always that way. He suffered a severe wound at the Battle of Waterloo and has not had an easy recovery. According to Arnprior, the poor lad has a tendency to fall into black moods."

"Ah, what exactly did he mean by 'black moods'?" she asked, trying not to sound rattled.

Alec's brow cleared and he gave her a reassuring smile. "He's not dicked in the nob or bad-tempered, if that's what you're worrying about. Royal is as good a man as you'd ever want to find. It's simply that the war turned him a bit gloomy and grim. He wouldn't be the first to have that happen. I'm sure he'll recover soon enough, since returning home to the Highlands will do him a world of good."

Alec almost sounded as if he was trying to convince himself as much as her. Thankfully, she wouldn't have to worry about Royal Kendrick. He was obviously a man of the world and certainly not in need of a governess.

"And what about the others?" she asked.

Her cousin went back to wrinkling his brow. "The twins are in their early twenties. They were too young for a commission when Lord Arnprior and Royal joined the Black Watch. The earl wouldn't have allowed it in any case. He didn't even want Royal to join, but the lad was old enough to know his own mind. The twins, however, were little hellions, without the maturity to manage life in the military."

"And do these hellions have names?"

"I'll be confounded if I can remember them," Alec said cheerfully. "I told Arnprior there were simply too many Kendricks running around the Highlands, stirring up trouble. I can't keep them all straight."

"And what did his lordship say to that?" What in heaven's name was she walking into?

"He agreed with me. But, again, I'm sure the twins are splendid lads when it comes right down to it. No doubt Arnprior keeps them under control."

"Thank God I won't be teaching them, either," she said. "I assume they've already been to university and are no longer in need of instruction."

Alec's gaze went to the window. They'd just entered a large stand of tall conifers with dark, feathered branches brushing against the bare limbs of leafless oaks. Her cousin studied the view with the concentration of a botanist.

"I think that's true," he said. "Can't be totally sure, though."

Victoria let go of the carriage strap, finally able to plant her feet firmly on the carriage floor because they'd hit a smoother stretch of road. It must signal they were nearing their destination.

"They must have had tutors," she said. "Surely Lord Arnprior would not expect me to take on the teaching of two young men of that age?"

Alec's gaze swung back. "I'm sure you're right. That would be ridiculous."

She eyed him for a few more seconds before letting it go. No one in their right mind would ask a governess to tutor adult males. "Alec, do you know *anything* about my assignment? Sir Dominic was so vague about the details."

He shrugged. "That's Dominic for you. Loves to keep us in the dark. Actually, I believe young Kade will be your primary responsibility. He's only fifteen. Arnprior had the lad in school, but he struggled, from what I understand."

She repressed a sigh. This assignment, far from helping reestablish her reputation as an educator, sounded like it could be a disaster in the making. "Kade is not academically inclined?"

"Quite the opposite. According to Arnprior, he enjoys his studies and is a gifted musician. One of the reasons Dominic recommended you was your reputation as an excellent music teacher."

Her tension unspooled a bit. This, at least, was familiar ground. "That makes sense, I suppose. But I can't help wondering why the boy struggled at school."

"He's sickly," said Alec in a somber tone. "Almost died from a lung infection a few months back. That put a proper scare into Arnprior, so he decided to bring him home and find a teacher who could work with Kade on his music."

"Poor boy," Victoria said. "Now I understand why his lordship would wish to hire someone like me."

Under the circumstances, a fragile, sensitive boy might be more comfortable with a female teacher because she would treat him more gently than the average male tutor. And since music was one of her specialties, it seemed a logical fit.

"But that makes only four brothers," she said, wishing to get the entire family sorted out. "Who am I missing?"

"That would be . . . Braden. Yes, that's the lad's name," Alec said. "He's not yet twenty. He attends the University of Glasgow. An exceedingly bright lad who wants to be a physician, from what Arnprior told me."

"So, my only pupil will be Master Kade?" Even Dominic's vague description had intimated that she'd have more than one. Something wasn't adding up.

"It does sound like that," Alec said in a cheery tone. "By the by, Dominic says you'll be setting up your own school once you get this Kendrick lot sorted out. I have no doubt you'll do a bang-up job of it, too."

Victoria crossed her arms and gave him a level stare. "You can't distract me with flattery, you know. You're being only slightly more helpful than Sir Dominic—which is to say, not very helpful at all. Is there something you're not telling me?"

Alec's eyes rounded in a credible pretense of innocence. "Haven't a clue, lass. I'm just telling you what I know. It's not like Dominic takes me into his confidence."

She allowed her expression to convey her rank skepticism. When he responded with a bland smile, Victoria shook her head with disgust. "You are not fooling me for an instant, Alasdair Gilbride. It's immensely irritating that you won't come clean. I've a mind to box your ears."

Under normal circumstances, she wouldn't dream of speaking so bluntly. But she was tired, cold, and heartily sick of spending day after day cooped up in a carriage. If she were a better person, she would apologize. Victoria was beginning to discover, however, that she was not quite the person she'd always imagined herself to be. It astonished her how the act of killing a man altered one's vision of oneself.

Alec didn't seem the least bit put out by her flash of temper. "You sound exactly like my old village school-mistress. She was a tartar, that one. Scared the wits out of me."

"I'm sure I don't scare you in the least. And you *are* fibbing, aren't you?"

He held up his hands to signal surrender. "I'm mostly in the dark too. I do know that Arnprior needs a governess for Kade and possibly a little help with the twins. Just in maintaining a good example in the household," he added hastily. "There hasn't been a lady in residence at Castle Kinglas in years, and I think Nick believes that having an educated, genteel female around the place will provide a good example for everyone."

"Lovely—a houseful of ill-mannered Highlanders, ones I'm expected to tame by virtue of my saintly presence. I can only hope Lord Arnprior fails to discover that my previous employer accused me of murder."

Alec pressed her gloved hand. "You'll be fine. And I promise I will not leave Kinglas until I'm certain everything is to your satisfaction. No tossing you onto the front steps of the castle and heading pell-mell back to Glasgow, I swear."

She gave him a reluctant smile. "I would certainly hate to have to chase after you for my bags."

His expression grew serious. "You'll make a splendid impression on everyone, Victoria. But I will repeat Dominic's advice that you're not to discuss the events of the last few weeks with anyone. Not even Lord Arnprior."

"It wasn't really advice," she said dryly. "More like an order."

"I can well imagine. But Dominic is wiser than any of us, so it's best to do as he says."

She couldn't help wondering if the rest of her life would be premised on a lie. It wasn't a very appetizing prospect. "I promise."

He gave her an approving smile. "Good. Then there's no need to speak about Fletcher or any of that dreary business again."

His tone signaled that the discussion was over. Alec was a genial, easy-tempered man, but Victoria was beginning to think that, in his own way, he could be just as bossy and overprotective as Dominic and Aden. Since she was used to making her own decisions, she didn't know whether to be touched by that or annoyed.

"And now," he said, brushing aside the half curtain from the coach window, "We're almost there. You might want to snag a look."

She followed his pointing finger. As the carriage emerged from the woods, the sun broke free of the towering gray clouds that had shadowed most of the journey. The starkly angled light illuminated a dramatic landscape of craggy outcroppings and steep-sided hills covered with fiery autumn foliage rising to the jagged, snow-dusted peaks. She blinked, momentarily disoriented by the blaze of color. It was beautiful but strangely unnerving, as if the landscape had gone up in flames.

"It's quite something, isn't it?" Alec murmured as he stared at the vista. "By the time I returned from the war, I'd

almost forgotten how amazing the Highlands are. I felt like
I was waking up after a long sleep."

"Yes, it's lovely," she said politely. It was also rather . . .
portentous was the word that came to mind, along with
remote and *wild*. She'd spent most of her life just outside of
Brighton, in a comfortable, bustling village that was none
of those things.

"We should be able to see Castle Kinglas after we round
this bend." He pointed again. "We're coming up almost par-
allel to the loch. Kinglas is at the base of the glen, right on
the water."

The carriage jostled through the curve, then straightened
out and ran smoothly along a surprisingly well-maintained
road. As if sensing the end of their journey, the horses
picked up the pace.

Victoria craned a bit and she saw it. "Goodness. That's
quite like . . ."

"Something out of a fairy tale?" Alec said with a grin.

"I suppose so," she said with a ghost of a laugh.

But Kinglas was not like the ones portrayed in the happier tales, where the handsome prince swept his bride off to
a lovely white confection with elegant spires and rose-laden
bowers. No, this particular castle, while imposing, was
grim and gothic, with smoky-colored stone and a tall tower
house surrounded by guard walls and battlements. It was
no home for a fairy-tale princess or happy endings, of that
she felt sure.

Then it's a good thing you're not really a princess, isn't it?

Victoria couldn't hold back a wry smile at the thought.
It was fine with her. As long as the rooms weren't too damp
or the chimneys didn't smoke, she would be satisfied.

"It's not exactly Sleeping Beauty's bower," Alec said,
echoing her thoughts, "but it's comfortable enough. Things
were rather neglected while Arnprior was away during the
war, but he's working to correct that. He's a terrifyingly

efficient man, so you'll not be living in a groaning old pile of stones."

"That's good to know," she said, smiling.

A few minutes later, they were bowling through a set of scrolled iron gates and past a neat-looking gatehouse. The horses trotted up a graveled drive lined by tall conifers and bordered by open lawn. There were no ornamental gardens as far as she could tell. The lawns ran in broad sweeps around the castle and down to the loch, its whitecaps glinting in the late afternoon sun. The dramatic and severe view seemed entirely fitting for the tower of gray stone that brooded over the landscape.

The carriage slowed through a wide archway in the outer wall of the castle. When they passed abruptly into shadow, Victoria shivered.

Alec frowned. "Are you cold?"

"I'm fine. Just a bit nervous, I expect."

He pressed her hand. "You needn't be. Highlanders are famous for their hospitality."

A moment later, a groom opened the carriage door and set the step. Alec hopped out and then handed her down to the cobblestones of the inner courtyard.

Victoria paused, taking a sniff of the bracing air. "It smells like the ocean, but that's impossible."

"This particular loch is salt water," Alec said. "It runs directly down to the sea."

She squeezed her eyes shut for a moment as longing swept through her. She'd spent her childhood near the sea and missed it when she'd been at school in Lincoln and then in positions in country manor houses. The familiar, tangy scent felt like home, and something inside her seemed to breathe a sigh of relief.

"I've always loved the . . ." She paused when Alec held up a warning hand. Behind her, she heard the firm tread of boot heels on the stone.

"Ah, there you are, Arnprior," Alec said.

Mentally bracing herself, Victoria smiled as she turned to greet her new employer. Her smile then wobbled on her lips as she took in the tall man, garbed in well-fitting breeches and a dark blue riding coat.

Arnprior was muscular and broad-shouldered, and seemed at first glance as grim and imposing as the keep in which they stood. His long-legged, athletic stride devoured the space between them, and he came to a halt directly in front of her. Victoria was rather tall herself, but she had to look up to meet his gaze. When she did so, all the moisture in her mouth evaporated, apparently taking flight along with the air from her lungs.

The earl's eyes were a startling, steely blue, made all the more piercing by his tanned complexion and hair so dark it looked black. She had a vague impression of slashing cheekbones, a high-bridged, Roman nose, and a hard but sensual mouth. But it was his gaze that held her attention. It studied her, seeming to strip away her defenses and expose her for the pretender that she was.

After all, she *was* pretending to be an ordinary English governess and not the by-blow of a barmaid and a future king, as well as a woman who just might end up in prison or swinging from the gallows if things didn't go her way.

Given its history, she supposed Scotland was as good a place as any to be a great pretender.

For a long, magnetic moment, she and Arnprior stared at each other. Then his gaze moved to Alec. Victoria mentally staggered, as if she'd been held captive by some invisible bond and then suddenly released.

"Arnprior, it's bloody good to see you," Alec said, thrusting out his hand.

The earl didn't exactly smile, but the severe cast to his countenance lightened a shade. "You had good travels, I hope? I'm pleased you were able to reach Kinglas before nightfall."

His voice was deep and rather rough, with a slight Highland burr. As a musician, Victoria was well attuned to voices. Something about Arnprior's appealed to her greatly, though it made no sense, given the brusque manner in which he spoke.

"We were happy to hit Arnprior lands." Alec winked at Victoria. "As were our backsides."

She blushed, but his jest pulled a slight smile from the earl's lips. "We've been working on that road for several months."

Then his gaze moved back to Victoria. She felt more warmth come to her cheeks under his perusal.

"But you'll not be wanting to stand out here in the courtyard talking about estate improvements," he said.

"I'm forgetting my manners," Alec said. "Arnprior, may I introduce your new governess, Miss Victoria Knight."

The earl nodded. "Welcome to Castle Kinglas. My youngest brother is looking forward to meeting you."

His manner wasn't rude. Not precisely, anyway. But despite his words, it wasn't exactly welcoming, either. Mentally shrugging, Victoria descended into a respectful curtsy. "Thank you, Lord Arnprior. I'm eager to meet your brother and take up my duties. Please accept my sincere thanks for the wonderful opportunity you've given me."

When his eyebrows arched up, she ground her teeth. She supposed she did sound a tad obsequious, but that was the result of nerves.

"We'll see about that," he replied rather cryptically.

Rather than leading the way inside, he fell to inspecting her again, this time with a frown. She had to resist the temptation to scowl back at him.

"Perhaps we should be getting inside," Alec prompted. "I'm afraid Miss Knight might be catching a chill."

"Oh, no, I'm fine," she said in a sugary voice. "I'd be happy to stand out here all evening."

Arnprior's dark eyebrows arched up again.

Lovely. She'd just been rude to her new employer.

"This way, Miss Knight," he said, waving her forward.

She didn't miss the rather long-suffering look he cast at Alec. Clearly, she and the earl were off to a less than stellar beginning.

Sighing, she headed toward the enormous oak door, held open by a footman dressed in plain black. An elderly gentleman loomed in the doorway and then stomped out directly in her path, forcing her up short. His thick, snowy eyebrows bristled at her, as if they had a will of their own, and his stare was more hostile than welcoming.

"Och, so herself has arrived, has she?" the man growled.

"Obviously," the earl growled back as he came up beside her.

"Just what we dinna need," the elderly fellow said bitterly. "A spoiled little Sassenach telling us what to do." He spun on his heel and stomped back the way he came.

Victoria was certain Arnprior cursed under his breath as he took her elbow and led her inside.

Chapter Three

Too pretty, too slender, too pale.

Miss Knight forcefully reminded Nick of one of the porcelain figurines his stepmother had loved to scatter about the drawing rooms. And like those Dresden misses, this woman appeared ready to shatter with the first bit of rough handling.

Just like Janet had shattered.

Gritting his teeth, he steered her toward the tower house. When she stumbled on the cobbles, he tightened his hand to steady her.

As a first impression, Miss Knight didn't look like she'd last a week at Kinglas. Not unless they put meat on her bones, color in her cheeks, and dosed her with a physic three times a day. Nick had never had cause to doubt Sir Dominic's word, but how in God's name was this weedy, pale-looking girl to manage the disaster that was the Kendrick family? Even he couldn't do that, and he'd tried everything, including knocking heads together in desperation.

He slid his hand up her arm. Sensing the delicacy of Miss Knight's frame even under the sturdy fabric of her wool traveling dress, he firmed his grip as he guided her up the steps of the stone porch that fronted the entrance of the great hall.

The girl shot him a sharp, sideways glance, her cornflower-blue eyes frowning a question. Their gazes locked for an instant that seemed oddly intent. Then her focus darted down to her feet again, and a sudden blaze of pink stained her cheekbones, highlighting a complexion so clear and delicate as to be almost translucent. With that hectic blush, the lass almost looked like she was in a high fever.

A string of oaths pushed themselves to the tip of his tongue. The notion of having the care of another delicate flower made his gut tighten with dismay. He'd been down this road once before and vowed never to do it again.

Get a grip, man. She's only a servant.

He could always send Miss Knight packing, but the fact remained that he needed her. As Braden had so trenchantly pointed out a few weeks ago, the family couldn't go on as it was. Kade needed the sort of gentle handling Nick couldn't possibly give him, and his other brothers had been running wild for far too long, wreaking havoc on the countryside. His next step might be to lock up his idiot brothers in the castle dungeon and throw away the key.

Even that likely wouldn't work, since they'd probably find a way to burn Kinglas to the ground.

Miss Knight, obviously a genteel lady, might be able to do his brothers some good if she survived their initial on-slaught. After all, Nick's stepmother had been a dab hand at managing the lads, including him, and she'd been a truly gentle woman. One sad look or quiet word from her and the Kendrick men had stumbled over themselves to fall into line. Because masculine influence wasn't working on them, he was desperate enough to hope that a woman's civilizing guidance might do the trick.

Sir Dominic had thought so too. That was why he'd

recommended Miss Knight. Now all Nick could do was hope the girl didn't die of consumption before they had the chance to put their plan into place.

Angus, stomping in ahead of them, spun to a halt when they entered the hall. With his bushy white hair, ancient leather vest, and even more ancient kilt, he was the very image of a deranged Highlander, albeit a decrepit one. Angus glared so fiercely at Miss Knight it was a miracle the lass didn't run shrieking back to the carriage.

Nick shot a glance at her perfect profile, framed by her no-nonsense bonnet. She didn't appear the least bit intimidated by Angus, instead inspecting the old duffer with a haughty regard that almost made Nick laugh.

"Arnprior, perhaps you'll introduce us to this pleasant gentleman," Alec said as they halted in the middle of the cavernous stone hall. He punctuated his sarcasm with a genial smile that fooled no one.

"This is my grandfather," Nick said. "Mr. Angus MacDonald."

"Yer step-grandfather," Angus shot back. "My daughter was the old laird's second wife, from the MacDonald clan. Arnprior is the son of the first Lady Arnprior, who was a MacFarlane. That Lady Arnprior died when the laird here was just a poor, wee lad."

"Thank you for clarifying," Nick said dryly. Angus had a tendency to bore visitors with the minute details of clan and family history.

Miss Knight appeared rather flummoxed by the explanation, but Alec looked like he was trying not to laugh. Like all Scotsmen, he understood their frequent obsession with family lineage.

Angus had a slavish devotion to clan ties and proper ranks. Nick didn't give a hang about any of it, and would have preferred to be called by his military title of major. But the old man was unbending when it came to the dignities due the title, and he invariably pitched a fit if some poor fool referred to Nick as anything other than Laird, Lord, or Earl.

"Mr. MacDonald is also my estate steward," Nick added. "He looked after the castle, the land holdings, *and* my brothers while I was away for many years."

Unfortunately, when it came to the boys.

"And did a splendid job of things, I have no doubt," Alec said, extending a hand toward Angus.

The old man blinked, then hesitantly took Alec's hand. "Thank ye, Master. I did my best for the laird, God knows."

Miss Knight frowned, likely puzzled by the old-fashioned form of address. As heir to the Riddick Earldom, Alec's courtesy title was Master of Riddick.

"Please call me Captain Gilbride, or Alec, if you prefer. I don't stand on ceremony."

When Angus vigorously shook his head, his wild white hair fluttered like dandelion puffs on the wind. "Nay, Master. That wouldna be proper."

"As you wish," Alec said. "And now allow me to properly introduce Miss Victoria Knight, Kade's new governess. Miss Knight, Mr. MacDonald."

The young woman dipped into a slight curtsy that conveyed appropriate respect for an elderly man and a family member. Nick fancied it also suggested a wee bit of superiority and disdain, if he wasn't mistaken—as if to say that she was well aware of her own worth. He'd never realized a curtsy could say so much, but hers communicated volumes.

The burgeoning scowl on Angus's face meant he'd heard the message loud and clear, and had no intention of backing down when it came to challenging the new governess.

Not that the old fellow was particularly agreeable when it came to any of Nick's plans. In fact, they'd been fighting since the day Nick sold his commission and returned to Kinglas. His grandfather's resistance to change, whether new ideas on crop management or renovating their crumbling castle, was just one of many problems he faced daily.

"Now that we've all been properly introduced," Nick said, "why don't we—"

A shrill yapping and the scrabble of nails on stone floors echoed through the hall. A moment later, the entire bloody pack of dogs—all five of them—tumbled into the hall like a gigantic, ill-kempt mop. Bruce careened into Bobby who bumped into Tina, which set off a horrific yowling that reverberated off the stone floors and timbered ceiling. The din was unbelievable.

Once the daft mutts had untangled themselves, four headed straight for Miss Knight while Bruce peeled off and charged for the luggage the footman had just carried in. Before anyone could say a word, the benighted animal lifted a leg and anointed what looked like a man's traveling kit.

"Bloody hell," yelped Alec. "That's my bag."

The other hounds from hell continued their charge at Miss Knight, who let out a startled squeak. Swiftly, Nick wrapped his hands around her slender waist and lifted her straight up—she weighed about as much as a thistle—and plopped her down safely behind him. He barely heard her strangled gasp over the commotion.

"Stop right there, ye bloody great fools," roared Angus.

The old fellow was the only one the dogs ever listened to. They came to a sliding halt at Nick's feet, bouncing into his boots and tumbling into one another. That set off another round of yowling. When two of the idiots tried to charge around Nick to get to Miss Knight, he turned sideways and thrust out a restraining leg, all while keeping a firm hold on her.

"Lord Arnprior, please unhand me," she said, trying to pry his arms from about her waist.

Nick had noticed right off that she had a lovely voice, cultured and feminine but with an appealing note of down-to-earth warmth. Right now, though, she sounded a bit screechy. The poor lass must have been convinced she'd stumbled upon a madhouse. There were many days when Nick felt the same. Unfortunately for him, there was no hope of escape.

"My lord, *please*," she said through clenched teeth.

"Forgive me," he said, reluctantly letting her go. He stood in front of her, just to be sure.

"If you think I'm afraid of dogs, you are sorely mistaken, my lord," she said in a voice that could freeze the bullocks off a bull. "Although this particular pack does seem exceedingly ill-behaved."

Fortunately, Angus had more or less gotten them under control by now. Three had plopped down in front of Nick, wagging their tails and panting like they'd run a marathon. The other two had rolled onto their backs in front of Alec— including Bruce, who'd disgraced himself with the luggage. Alec didn't seem to hold it against the dog, though, since he was rubbing the idiot's belly.

"That's better, ye daft beasties," Angus said in an approving tone. "No more larking about like ye dinna ken yer manners."

Nick didn't bother to hold back a snort. Miss Knight was correct—they were exceedingly bad dogs that took their cue from their ill-mannered master.

The governess peered around him. "What sort of dogs are those, if I might ask?"

The tone of her voice suggested she wasn't very impressed. It was understandable, since they'd obviously been rolling around in the mud. Thankfully, they hadn't gotten into the stables or paddock. If they had, they would have smelled a great deal worse.

Alec rose to his feet with a wry grin. "These fine specimens are Skye terriers, an ancient and venerable Scottish breed. One of their ancestors was with Mary, Queen of Scots at her beheading, hiding under her skirts. Loyal to the very end, he was."

"Really?" Miss Knight said. "They look rather like ragged dust cloths to me. Not that I know much about Scottish dog breeds," she hastily added.

When she gave Nick an apologetic grimace, he shrugged. He shared her view, preferring larger breeds like the deerhound. But these dogs were the descendants of his stepmother's beloved terriers, and were particularly cherished by Angus as a connection to his daughter's memory. Nick didn't have the heart to farm them out to his tenants, who could have used them as ratters or even as guard dogs, since they loved barking their fool heads off.

Predictably, Angus had bristled at Miss Knight's insult to his darlings.

"That's no surprise," he said with a sneer. "Coming from a blasted *Sassenach*."

"And here we go," Alec muttered, shaking his head.

Miss Knight went stiff as a poker, throwing daggers at Angus with her imperious gaze. The battle lines had been drawn before the girl had even taken off her bonnet. As for his grandfather, at the moment Nick would be happy to haul him up to the top of the battlements and throw him off.

"That's enough, Angus," he said sharply. "Miss Knight is our guest."

"I'll no have her insulting my bairns," the old man growled back. "They're just trying to be friendly."

"They can be friendly some other time," Nick said. "Such as after they've been bathed. Now, please get them out of here."

Grumbling, Angus began to round up the dogs. Nick was about to order him to also find the housekeeper when Mrs. Taffy finally came hurrying from the back of the house.

"Forgive me, Laird," she said. Her wrinkled face was flushed, and a few strands of snowy white hair had escaped from under her tidy lace cap. "We had a bit of an upset in the kitchen," she added, scowling at the dogs.

Nick sighed. "The pantry?"

"The cold room," she replied tersely. "I apologize, sir, but dinner may be a wee bit late."

Obviously, the dogs had made yet another raid on the kitchen. Nick's cook, although a good-natured soul, was not particularly competent, either at cooking or managing her kitchen. She had yet to poison anyone, but dinner frequently arrived cold, late, or occasionally not at all, depending on what particular crisis had developed belowstairs.

When the housekeeper narrowed her irate gaze on Angus, he blushed. There was only one person at Kinglas who could corral the old man, and that was Taffy, who'd been with the family for decades.

"I'll take care of it," Angus muttered. He stomped off to the kitchens, the dogs trotting happily behind him.

Quiet finally returned to the hall. Nick didn't think he imagined Miss Knight's sigh of relief.

"This is Mrs. Taffy, our housekeeper," he said. "She'll take care of all your needs."

Taffy gave Miss Knight a kind smile and bobbed her head. "It's a pleasure, miss. I'll do my best to make your stay here comfortable."

Miss Knight gave Taffy a sweet smile in return. It seemed to light her up from within, turning her porcelain features from pretty to beautiful. He registered a slight shock at the realization before forcing himself to shrug it off. He had no interest in her looks, only in her abilities.

"Perhaps you could escort Miss Knight to her room to set aside her things," he said more brusquely than he intended. "Then she can join us in the east drawing room for tea."

When Taffy grimaced again, Nick sighed. "Is there some difficulty?"

"I've had to switch Miss Knight to a different room," she said. "The chimney in the blue bedroom started smoking."

Nick frowned. "It's never done so before."

If there was one thing he and Angus agreed on, it was the importance of keeping the chimneys and fireplaces clean and in good repair. Winters in the Highlands were cold, damp, and long. Winters in a drafty old castle on a loch were even worse. Without reliable heating, the household would be miserable for months.

"Something seems to have got caught in the flue." Taffy's tone told Nick everything he needed to know. Something hadn't got caught. Something had been deliberately placed in the flue with the intention of causing mischief.

He had a good idea who the guilty party was.

"I apologize," Nick said to his guests, resisting the impulse to gnash his teeth. "This seems to be a day for domestic calamity at Kinglas."

"Might I suggest, sir, that you have tea while I see to a new room for the lady," Taffy said. "The maid will unpack her bags, and we'll have everything set to right in no time at all."

"That sounds splendid," Alec said in a hearty voice. "I'm famished, and I'm sure Miss Knight would relish a cup of tea."

"Or a sherry," the governess muttered in a barely audible voice. Then, no doubt realizing her slip, she blushed an enchanting shade of pink.

Despite his foul humor, Nick couldn't help smiling. "I'm sure sherry could be arranged. Or even perhaps a stiff dram of Scotch. I wouldn't blame you for needing it after our less-than-stellar welcome."

She gave him a smile that finally reached her eyes, calling notice to the fact that they *were* a rather spectacular shade of blue.

"Thank you, my lord, but a cup of tea will do just fine."

"I'll send Andrew in with the tea things," Taffy said. She bobbed a curtsy and hurried off to the back of the house.

"This way," Nick said, nodding toward the central stone staircase.

Robert, the castle's youngest footman, scurried from his position by the front door and preceded them to the first floor, turning right to the east wing and the main drawing room. After bowing them through the door, the lad went off to fetch the tea tray.

"What a splendid place you've got here, Arnprior," Alec said, taking in the spacious, Queen Anne–style drawing room.

This wing was hundreds of years newer than the main tower house, and had yet to start crumbling around their ears. The scrolled walnut furniture and the red and gold fabrics were rather dated and too grand for Nick's taste, but the sixteenth-century tapestries on either side of the stone-surround fireplace, with their depictions of royal hunting parties, were magnificent. Taffy had managed to fill several tabletops with late-blooming mums in warm yellows and deep reds that matched the tapestries.

The best part was the view of the loch. The ornamental gardens behind the castle and the lawns running down to the water were already steeped in shadows as evening approached. The last glimmers of sunshine danced across the loch, making the whitecaps glitter like crystals flung from a giant's hand.

Miss Knight headed straight to the windows. Although her slim build emphasized fragility rather than strength, she carried herself with a graceful confidence Nick found reassuring. Most ladies that tall often minced, seeking to minimize a characteristic considered unfeminine.

"This is a breathtaking vista, my lord," she said, casting him a quick smile over her shoulder. "I had no idea Castle Kinglas was actually on the water."

"It's our constant neighbor," he said. "One that is much more accommodating in the summer, I might add. The winter storms on the loch can be fierce."

"I won't mind," she said. "I miss the ocean, and am glad to be near water again."

The door opened and Angus stomped in, followed by Robert and Andrew. The footmen lugged in the tea things, along with a tray loaded with cakes and pastries. Cook had managed to pull off a decent tea.

"You grew up by the ocean, Miss Knight?" Nick asked politely.

She returned to join them in the center of the room. "Yes, in Brighton. My cousins and I spent as much time by the seaside as our parents would allow. It was always a treat."

"Och, Brighton," Angus said with contempt. "Where Prinny and those bloody royal dukes lark about with rakes and ladybirds, spending money they dinna have. I ken we'd be better off if they drowned in the Channel."

Miss Knight paused in the act of pulling off her gloves, her features freezing in offended lines. Even Alec looked irritated, but his natural father was one of the royal dukes, although that wasn't widely known. Nick was surprised, however, that Miss Knight was so thoroughly starched up, since the Prince Regent and his brothers were generally reviled. Angus's comment was crass, but the sentiments were hardly uncommon.

Then again, Miss Knight seemed something of a high

stickler, which was one of the reasons Nick wished to employ her.

"Careful, Mr. MacDonald, or I'll have to arrest you for treason," Alec said dryly.

Angus flashed him a grin. "Why, I'd be doin' the country a service if I took the whole lot down myself. The prime minister would probably give me a medal, and any good Scotsman would be filled with pride."

"I hardly think the prime minister or anyone else would thank you for expressing such a distressing opinion," Miss Knight said tartly. "I find that sort of remark deeply offensive, as would any person of sense."

Robert and Andrew froze in the process of setting up the tea tray, staring at Angus with something akin to alarm. Like Nick, they knew exactly what was going to happen.

Angus spun to face the girl, a gleeful smile creasing his wrinkled face. "Of course ye would. What else would anyone expect from a Sassenach? Ye like nothing better than grinding yer boot heels in the faces of good Scottish men and women. Well, let me tell ye, lassie—"

"No, Angus, you will not tell anyone anything," Nick interjected. "And we can leave the discussion of Scottish nationalism for a time when Captain Gilbride and Miss Knight are not a captive audience."

He regarded the Prince Regent as a disgrace to his family and his country, but he'd served under the Duke of York and had found him to be a fair and capable commander. And engaging with Angus was asking for more trouble than it was worth. Still, the governess had to learn to deal with the old fellow sooner or later. Nick wouldn't always be around to come to her defense.

Nick's grandfather scowled back at him, and for a few moments they waged a silent struggle. Finally, Angus grumbled his surrender and subsided into his favorite chair by the fireplace.

"Thank you," Nick said. "Miss Knight, would you be so kind as to pour the tea?"

She ignored his request, continuing to glare at Angus as if she might storm up and bash him on the head. What the devil was wrong with her, anyway? Angus had certainly stepped out of line, but her response seemed exaggerated.

"Miss Knight, if you have finished arguing with my grandfather, I repeat that I would be greatly obliged if you would pour the tea," Nick said in the voice he'd used on insubordinate junior officers.

She flinched, and her gaze jumped to meet his. Her cheeks flushed a pale pink, but then her frown smoothed into a polite, bland expression—the one that the best sort of servants adopted when what they really wanted to do was throttle their employers.

"I beg your pardon, my lord," she said calmly. "I certainly didn't wish to offend you or Mr. MacDonald."

"Of course ye did," snipped Angus.

"No, Mr. MacDonald, she did not," Alec said sternly. Then he looked at Nick with a cool, warning gaze. "I trust you realize that as well, Arnprior."

Something was going on here that Nick didn't quite understand. While Alec knew better than to take grumpy old Highlanders too seriously, his friend clearly felt a high degree of loyalty to Miss Knight. If he didn't know Alec was absolutely devoted to his wife, he might even think the two were romantically involved.

That was nonsensical, of course, but something about Miss Knight was definitely off.

"It's perfectly fine, Captain Gilbride," she said. "Please, if you'll all be seated, I'll be happy to serve tea."

She glided over to the tilt-top table where Andrew and Robert had set up the tea, giving them a sweet smile that prompted the footmen to grin back like besotted fools. Nick made a mental note to remind Taffy to give the male staff a stern warning when it came to Miss Knight. The last thing he needed were his men tripping over their own feet as they mooned after some winsome English lass. It would be hard enough keeping his brothers Graeme and Grant from flirting with her.

As if on cue, the door flew open, and the twins charged through. Unshaven, and garbed in kilts, leather vests, and muddy boots, they looked like younger versions of their grandfather. All they needed were dirks in their belts and tams on their heads to complete the picture of wild Highlanders.

In truth, they were simply boisterous lads, a little lost but trying very hard to be men—good men, if Nick had anything to say about it. But thanks to a combination of factors, one being their grandfather's influence, his brothers were kicking over the traces with disastrous results. It was why he'd been desperate enough to reach out to Sir Dominic for help. The wily magistrate had sent him Victoria Knight by way of reply, and Nick sincerely hoped she had the temperament and fortitude to do the job.

Graeme swaggered into the room with Grant following closely on his heels. They came to a stop a few feet in front of the governess. Since the twins were well over six feet, she had to tilt her head back to look at them.

"We've come ta meet the new lassie," Graeme said, in a brogue so exaggerated Nick wanted to either laugh or murder him. "We heard she was a rare beauty, even if she is a Sassenach." He punctuated his comment by waggling his eyebrows in what he obviously thought was a flirtatious manner.

I'll definitely have to murder him.

Miss Knight's dumbfounded expression transformed into one that mingled horror and outrage. If Graeme kept it up, Nick predicted that the first act of their new governess would be to box her pupil's ears.

Grant dug his elbow into his brother's side, obviously wanting in on the fun. He was never the lead, but willingly followed in Graeme's reckless footsteps.

Making sheep's eyes at the poor woman, as if he were about to launch into a serenade or a love sonnet, Grant pressed a hand to his heart. "How lucky can two fellas get ta have such a bonny teacher? We promise ta be the best pupils ye ever had, and mayhap we can even teach *ye* a thing or two."

Miss Knight's only reply was a choking noise that sounded like someone was strangling her.

Chapter Four

Victoria's breath caught as she realized the magnitude of the task looming before her. Both Sir Dominic and Alec had been deliberately vague in describing her new duties, and now she knew why. To live in a remote Highland manor with a family of brash men would be daunting. While the earl was obviously a gentleman, though grim to the point of unwelcoming, Mr. MacDonald was another matter entirely. Unwelcoming couldn't begin to describe his behavior.

But it was now also clear she was actually expected to *teach* the Kendrick brothers—well, something. And, good Lord, who knew what other ghastly surprises were in store when the rest of the brothers finally surfaced?

"These must be the twins," Alec said, stating the obvious. The young men were the proverbial peas in a pod.

Her cousin had stood and inserted himself between her and the strapping young brothers, as if to protect her. At the moment, however, the only people needing protection were the twins. She was sorely tempted to box their ears for behaving like utter cads.

The earl rose, looking rather like Zeus, with thunderclouds roiling about his head and lightning sparking from his noble brow. "Yes, I regret to say these sorry specimens are my brothers."

He stalked over, crowding the twins step-by-step toward the fireplace. By the time the young men's shoulders hit the edge of the mantelpiece, their mischievous expressions were more those of sheepish boys in a great deal of trouble.

"We were just excited to meet the lassie," the twin on the left said, the obvious leader. "We meant no harm at all, Nick."

"Aye," chimed in the other one, nodding his head so vigorously his unkempt red hair flopped in front of his eyes. "No harm at all."

"First of all, you will cease using that absurd brogue," the earl ordered. "You were raised in a gentleman's household, and you will speak and act like gentlemen. Is that clear?"

"Yes, Nick," they said in chorus. Their almost incomprehensible accent had already diminished, now simply coloring their voices with a hint of the Highlands. Victoria suspected they'd been putting it on, probably to annoy her.

Who in his right mind could expect her to tutor these grown men? That was *not* what she had agreed to in coming here.

"Secondly," Arnprior continued, "you will not refer to the lady as either *lassie*, *Sassenach*, or any other disrespectful term. You will address her as either Miss Knight or ma'am. Is that clear?"

Two red heads bobbed in unison. "Yes, Nick."

Arnprior nodded tersely and took a few steps back. The twins' shoulders came down from around their ears. They were obviously a handful, but it was clear they respected their older brother—perhaps even feared him.

Victoria shifted in her chair, suddenly uneasy. The earl was a stern man who demanded respect, as she would have expected from someone who'd commanded a military regiment. But she hoped he wasn't cruel or angry, because she'd had enough of that to last a lifetime. Even the lure of money or a sterling recommendation couldn't compel her to stay under his roof if such was the case.

Arnprior propped his hands on his hips, perusing his brothers with a look that now spoke more of resignation than anger. "And I suppose you were so eager to greet Miss Knight that you couldn't take the time to change instead of coming here looking like unwashed field hands?"

"The lads were just muckin' about with a bit of honest work," said Mr. MacDonald. "There's no need to be naggin' at them."

The old man had been surprisingly quiet the last few minutes. Perhaps even he'd been startled by the earl's fury and had thought better of getting involved.

Arnprior shot him a hard look. "And where, pray tell, have they been mucking about? More to the point, were you mucking about with them?"

"Aye. I took them to old MacBride's. He needed help with some of his sheep pens, and the lads offered to lend a hand."

"Repairing sheep pens?" Arnprior said sardonically. "That doesn't sound like the lads. Normally, they're getting into the kind of trouble that requires me to make financial restitution to some unfortunate soul."

"Nick, old man, there's no need to embarrass us in front of the lady," protested one of the twins.

"Gosh," said the other with a comical grimace. "You're making us look like a pair of jingle brains."

The earl snorted as he took in their pleading expressions, then flicked a glance to the stone-faced Mr. MacDonald. A fraught silence stretched out, broken only by the crackle of flames and the hissing of resin in the grate.

The twins, now rather red-faced, peered nervously at their grandfather. Clearly, there was something amiss, something Victoria thought the earl was trying to puzzle out.

"Let it go, Nicholas," the old man finally said. "At least for now."

Turning from his grandfather, Arnprior lightly cuffed the nearest twin on the shoulder. "You're both daft lads. And you'll be the death of me yet."

His brothers grinned at him with affection and relief. "We know, but you love us anyway, don't you?" said the cheekier one.

Arnprior let out a short laugh. "God knows why. Now, come meet Miss Knight properly, and remember your manners."

When he turned back to her, the storm had fully passed and a glint of humor now lightened his gaze. The gleeful smile the twins exchanged behind his back, as if they'd just pulled one over on their big brother, also went a long way to relieving her concerns about Arnprior's temperament. She suspected his stern demeanor was necessary to keep his chaotic household under some semblance of control.

Since Victoria also hated chaos, she sympathized with his desire to impose order.

"Miss Knight, I would like to introduce my brothers. This is Graeme," the earl said, gesturing to the brasher of the two. "And this is Grant."

Graeme's bow was the more flourishing, as was the smile he flashed. He would be the bigger problem, since he clearly fancied himself a charmer.

"Good afternoon, Miss Knight," he said. "It's a pleasure to meet you."

"Yes, ma'am," said Grant. "We're quite looking forward to our lessons with you. Nick—I mean, the earl—has told us we must work very hard and absorb everything you have to teach us."

Victoria was rising from a quick curtsy, but those words practically locked her knees in place. "Lessons? Surely you're both much too old for a governess," she said with an uneasy chuckle.

"Too bloody right," muttered Angus, scowling at her.

Victoria was growing quite tired of his ugly scowls. There would have to be a reckoning with the old man, but right now she had other concerns.

"We're twenty-two, Miss Knight," Graeme said. "But Nick says we still need tutoring."

"Not that we necessarily agree with him," Grant added hastily, "but he says you'll teach us all we need to know, and that you'll soon set us to rights."

She frowned. "Did you not attend university, or have tutors?"

"Both," Arnprior tersely replied.

An uncomfortable silence ensued.

"Then, what happened?" Victoria prodded.

The twins exchanged a puzzled glance, as if they expected her to already know the details.

"We got kicked out of university," Graeme finally said.

Argh. "Officially, or were you just sent down for a term?"

"Kicked out and told never to return," Grant said morosely.

What had they done to deserve so severe a punishment? When she looked at the earl, he seemed oddly detached from the conversation, as if waiting for her to react. Dominic sometimes wore that look, and she didn't like it.

"My lord, are you asking me to take over the lessons your brothers would have received at university?" she asked. "Because if so, I do not feel qualified. They should have a male tutor in that case."

The earl gestured toward her chair, his broad shoulders shifting under the dark cloth of his jacket. "Why don't we have tea first, and then discuss the matter? Would you mind doing the honors, Miss Knight?"

Alec, who'd obviously been throttling back his irritation, finally spoke up. "Arnprior, this should not be a complicated discussion. Simply tell Miss Knight what you expect."

"Tea first," the earl said. "Then I'll explain."

Alec threw up a hand. "Confound it—"

Arnprior cut him off. "Everyone sit down. *Now.*"

The twins scrambled to comply, all but tripping over themselves to sit on a scroll-backed settee across from Victoria. They plunked down so vigorously that she feared the settee's delicate cabriolet legs would collapse under the strain. Alec remained standing, glaring at his host. Arnprior crossed his arms over his brawny chest and lifted an imperious eyebrow to calmly stare back at him.

Alec finally rolled his eyes and capitulated. Her cousin was a big, confident man who'd also had a distinguished career in the military, and was heir to an earldom. But Arnprior was something different, and that difference was impressive. Victoria judged him to be at least ten years older than Alec, and he evoked an authority that suggested he bent to no man, even one of higher station.

His commanding manner and intense gaze produced an odd effect in Victoria. It made her insides seem to quiver, something she did not appreciate.

The earl handed her to the elegant walnut armchair. Victoria's skin prickled as his hand wrapped around hers, the feel of his callused fingers a bit unnerving. Ever since Fletcher's attack, she'd been skittish at the touch of a man. Chloe had assured her that those worrying feelings would eventually pass, and Victoria could only hope such would be the case. She hated having to suffer a fearful response whenever a stranger, or even an acquaintance, so much as brushed against her.

Arnprior pulled over a wingback chair and sat at one end of the tea table. Though the chair was massive and heavy looking, the earl picked it up as if it had been constructed of mere twigs.

"Ooh, seedcakes," said Graeme, reaching for the cake plate as Victoria began to pour. "Taffy's are the best, Miss Knight. Cook's aren't nearly as good."

"Actually, Cook's are rather dreadful," said Grant. "And Taffy only makes hers for special occasions. Hand me one, will you, Graeme?"

Victoria clutched the Chinese porcelain teapot and stared at the twins. Not only were their hands in a distressing state of grubbiness, they were wolfing down the cakes like . . . well, ravenous wolves. To say their manners were appalling understated the case.

"Good God," muttered Alec when Graeme wiped his mouth on his sleeve. It was a sentiment Victoria shared. The earl had claimed that his brothers were gentlemen, yet so far she'd seen no evidence to back up that assertion.

She peeked at Arnprior to gauge his reaction to his brothers' disgraceful behavior and almost dropped the teapot. He was, once again, singularly focused on her. Was he waiting to see if she would reveal her distaste or faint dead away at the twins' boorish behavior? If so, he was in for a surprise.

Still, she had to close her eyes for a few seconds to clamp down on a surge of frustration. She was tired and crabby from the long days on the road, and she had yet to even wash her face or brush the travel dirt from her clothes.

Alec touched her arm. "Victoria, are you quite well?"

She forced a smile. If the earl was testing her ability to maintain her poise—which seemed the only reasonable explanation—then she was more than ready to show her mettle.

"I'm quite well, thank you," she said as she prepared Alec a cup. After handing it over, she regarded her host. "And what do you take in your tea, my lord?"

"I take it plain." Arnprior nodded his thanks when she served him, and then began chatting with Alec while she prepared cups for the twins.

Graeme gave her a pointed wink when she handed one to him, which she just as pointedly ignored. Victoria already had his measure. He was basically harmless, and best dealt with by refusing to respond to provocations he cast in her path.

When Grant bobbed his head and shyly thanked her, she rewarded him with a smile that prompted a scowl from his twin. Clearly, Graeme was the mischief-maker, while Grant simply followed his brother's lead. If left to his own devices, Grant would probably be much less disposed to get into trouble. It was a vulnerability she intended to exploit—if she decided to stay in this madhouse past the next twenty-four hours.

She glanced at Mr. MacDonald, sitting apart by the fireplace. She didn't know if he was chilly, or making a point by being standoffish. Probably the latter. "Mr. MacDonald, what do you take in your tea?"

"Milk and two lumps," he barked.

She prepared the cup and held it out. The old man sneered, crossing his arms over his chest. Victoria refused to budge from her chair. She had to draw a firm line or be forever bullied by him and everyone else who might be inclined to follow his lead. Having been a governess for several years, she'd come to expect a certain disregard from those she served. But she would no longer tolerate bullies or any sort of brutish behavior, even from someone holding a favored position in the household.

Especially if he had a favored position, given the disaster of her last situation.

The room had fallen silent again.

"Is there a problem, Miss Knight?" the earl finally asked.

"Not at all, my lord." She continued to hold the cup

steady, resisting the urge to stalk over and dump it on the old man's head. Or Lord Arnprior's, for that matter, if he didn't stop scowling at her.

Out of the corner of her eye, she saw Alec struggling not to grin, and that gave her a boost of courage. Her arm was beginning to tire, though, so she hoped the impasse wouldn't last much longer.

"For pity's sake, Angus," the earl said, "just fetch your blasted cup."

The old man jerked up his chin. "If ye think I'll be panderin' to some—"

Grant jumped to his feet. "I'll bring it to you, Grandda."

The young man snatched the cup from Victoria's hand, slopping tea into the saucer, and hurried over to his grandfather.

Mr. MacDonald smiled at his grandson. "Yer a good lad. Anyone who thinks ye need tutorin' on your manners is daft." Then he shot Victoria a triumphant sneer.

She forced herself to calmly pour her own cup, taking a sip while she composed her thoughts. Arnprior had gone back to observing her with that steady but rather grim regard. She apparently was *not* passing the test, even though she'd kept her poise under trying circumstances.

After setting her cup down on the table with a decided click, she met the earl's gaze. "I have a few questions, my lord, if you don't mind."

"About your tasks?" Arnprior nodded. "Yes, we'll get to that in a minute."

"I think we should get to it now," Alec said bluntly. "Miss Knight can then determine if she wishes to take up the position or return to Glasgow with me."

Mr. MacDonald *and* the twins perked up considerably. It seemed the twins were not looking forward to her tutelage, after all.

"I didn't realize Miss Knight was thinking of bolting already," the earl replied.

"Of course I'm not thinking of bolting," she snapped.

Well, actually she was. She managed to keep a straight face—but just barely—when the earl regarded her with an ironic gaze.

"I'm glad to hear it," he said. "Before I outline your duties, perhaps you'd care to give me some sense of your experience. Sir Dominic's letter was lacking in details, I'm afraid." His glance slid over her, head to toe. "You seem rather young to have done much teaching."

"I am five and twenty, my lord, and I've been teaching for seven years," she said stiffly.

"That long?"

Mentally consigning him to the devil, she folded her hands in her lap.

"Perhaps you can outline both your education and your previous teaching positions," he added.

"Certainly, sir. I attended school for several years at Miss Kirby's Seminary for Young Ladies in Lincoln, which has an excellent reputation for both academics and music. I teach all the usual subjects like history and geography, along with French and Italian, and I'm proficient in music, playing both the pianoforte and the harp."

"Kade will like that, won't he, Nick?" Grant piped up. "All he thinks about is music."

"Unfortunately," muttered Mr. MacDonald.

Victoria then gave the earl a thorough rundown on her past employment. Arnprior listened with a skeptical air.

"You clearly have a great deal experience teaching girls of all ages," he said when she was finished. "But you said little about boys. How many have you taught over the years?"

"Not many, as I'm sure you'd already deduced."

"That leads me to wonder why you think you can take on the teaching of older boys, or even young men."

"Arnprior, you do realize that Sir Dominic would never have recommended Miss Knight for the position if he didn't think she could do it," Alec said in an irritated voice.

The earl flashed a humorless smile. "One would think so. Miss Knight, I understand you do not have a reference from your last employer. Why is that?"

Fortunately, Dominic had coached her on how to respond to this predictable but still nerve-wracking question. "Because I decided to leave the position. I felt it did not suit my skills."

His expressive eyebrows lifted once more. "Really?"

"Yes, really," she said firmly. "My pupils were too young to benefit from my experience and level of skills."

"And are you always so particular about what positions you take?"

"Indeed I am, my lord. Which is why I'd like to—"

The door opened and a man strode into the room. Garbed in a kilt and leather vest like Mr. MacDonald and the twins—although a good deal cleaner, thank God—he was clearly a Kendrick. He was a few years older than the twins and his hair was burnished chestnut rather than flaming red. Unlike his brothers, his handsome features lacked any trace of good humor.

He stalked over, his long stride marked by a limp. As he stopped directly in front of Victoria, his striking green gaze swept over her, eyeing her with disdain.

"So you're the new tutor," he growled as she stared up at him. "I'll warn you right now, lassie. You can stay the hell away from me."

Chapter Five

Nick's brothers were obviously colluding with Angus to make things as difficult as possible for the new governess. At this rate, they might even succeed in driving her away.

"I was not expecting you until dinnertime," Nick said to Royal. He'd hoped to introduce his siblings in small batches.

His brother shot him an angry look. The lad was always angry these days, unfortunately.

"I'm well aware you wanted to keep me away for the day," Royal said. "But since your benighted plans will have an impact on me as well, I have a right to be here when you interview our new teacher."

Miss Knight peered up at him as he loomed over her. Then her gaze flew to Nick. "My lord, what is going on here?"

"This is my brother Royal," Nick said through clenched teeth. "I apologize on his behalf, since he has clearly forgotten his manners." His brother's behavior was why he needed her help, which should be screamingly obvious to her by now.

"I'm disappointed in you, Royal," Alec said, shaking his head. "Never knew you to be rude to the ladies before."

Royal threw Alec a startled glance. The two had become

friends during the war, and Royal had a great deal of respect for the future Earl of Riddick.

There was a long moment of uncomfortable silence before Royal gave the governess a terse nod. "Forgive me, ma'am. It would seem that my manners have gone begging. Of course, that's why you're here, isn't it? To turn us into the daintiest set of gentlemen ever to hit the marriage mart."

Miss Knight's big blue eyes went wide with surprise and, Nick fancied, horror. "I am?"

Royal shrugged. "That's the plan, although I have no intention of going along with it."

"Of course not," snapped Angus. "There's nothin' wrong with the lot of ye, as any right-thinkin' Highlander would know."

"Tell that to Nick," Graeme piped up.

"I have, ye booby," his grandfather shot back.

"Repeatedly," Nick said.

Miss Knight sucked in a deep breath. Nick had to admit he was impressed with her self-discipline and her ability to defend herself. Both were qualities she would need in abundance in his household.

As embarrassing as it was to watch his family behave so boorishly in front of a genteel young woman, he'd allowed it up to a point. He needed to know if she could manage the Kendrick men and the nonsense they would throw at her.

Unfortunately, they were throwing a bit more at her than Nick had anticipated.

"I would be grateful if you would step away," Miss Knight said to Royal. "You are exceedingly tall, an affliction apparently common in your family. I do hope you won't all be looming over me on a regular basis. Otherwise, I will be forced to wear a neck brace."

That brought a snort out of Royal. "God forbid. We

already have one cripple in this household. We don't need another."

The governess studied him for a few seconds, and then simply nodded.

Royal limped over to settle in a wingback chair on the opposite side of the fireplace, grimacing slightly as he stretched out his leg. There were days when the old wound still troubled him, days when he pushed himself too hard. But that was Royal—he never gave an inch or acknowledged weakness, and never asked for help.

The qualities that had made him an outstanding soldier and officer were now pulling him ever deeper into quiet despair.

Miss Knight's voice broke into Nick's gloomy thoughts.

"My lord, it's time to be frank with each other." She was regarding him with severity, as if about to box his ears or send him to stand in a corner.

For some bizarre reason, it made Nick want to laugh. The girl was so out of place in a roomful of brawny, bad-tempered men that she resembled a kitten facing down a pack of half-tamed wolfhounds.

"What exactly would you like to know, Miss Knight?" He couldn't resist the temptation to tease her, just to see how she would react.

"I would like to know *exactly* what my duties would be in regard to your older brothers." She carefully enunciated every word, as if talking to a half-wit.

"Oh, that's easy," Graeme broke in. "You're supposed to teach us how to be proper gentlemen, just like Royal said."

"*And* help you find wives?" she asked, disbelief coloring her tone.

Grant nodded eagerly. "You're to help us find *suitable* wives. Nick says that no suitable woman would have any of us as we are now."

Graeme jabbed his brother in the shoulder. "But what about the unsuitable ones, eh?"

The twins burst into raucous laughter. When Nick shot them an evil glare, they clamped their mouths shut in mid-guffaw. In the sudden silence, he could practically hear Miss Knight's churning thoughts.

From the look on her face, those thoughts weren't good. "My lord, I am a governess, not a matchmaker."

"That is exactly why I hired you, Miss—"

"Not yet, you haven't," she interjected.

"Why I hope to hire you," Nick finished. The girl had an imperious streak, an unusual quality in a servant. For his needs, however, it would be a useful trait. "I wish to hire you to tutor my youngest brother, especially in music. That will comprise the majority of your duties."

"But clearly not all of them," she said.

"As a governess of your standing, I assume you are an expert in decorum and appropriate social standards."

"Of course."

"And I also assume you've taught those standards to the girls under your care?"

"I have."

"And no doubt those standards apply to young men as well as young ladies?"

She pressed her lips together, obviously searching for an argument to counter him.

"Miss Knight?" he gently prompted.

She shot him a look of pure hostility. "Yes, my lord. Of course the same standards apply."

"Good. Then what I wish you to do is remind my brothers what those standards are. They *were* raised as gentlemen, but certain events have caused them to forget themselves. A refresher course is required."

"And what would such a course entail?" She cast a disapproving glance at his brothers. "Beyond the obvious."

Nick shrugged. "The usual one—how to engage in polite conversation with young ladies, how to conduct oneself appropriately at a dinner party, how to dance—"

"They already know how to dance," barked Angus.

"Just reels, Grandda," Grant said. "Oh, and the sword dance. But I don't think many girls know that one."

Alec choked, trying not to laugh. When Nick shot him a glare, his friend simply gave him a bland smile.

"And it would be fun to learn how to waltz," Graeme said, suggestively waggling his eyebrows at Miss Knight.

"Ye wish to be caperin' about like dandies?" Angus growled.

Miss Knight seemed to shake herself free of some sort of mental paralysis. "I am not a dancing teacher, my lord. I'm an educator."

"For God's sake, Arnprior," Alec said. "Why don't you simply hire a dancing master? Surely he could help the lads with those other"—he waved a vague hand—"social things."

"I tried that. It didn't work." The horrific experiment of a few months ago remained vivid in his memory. The dancing master had barely survived the week.

"Bloody caper merchant," Angus muttered.

"Let me see if I understand you correctly, my lord," Miss Knight said. "You wish me to tutor your youngest brother. As well, I am to train your older brothers to be accomplished, well-mannered gentlemen for the purpose of putting them out on the marriage mart. And I am to do that without the help of other instructors who specialize in such matters."

Nick met her irate gaze with an approving smile. "That sums it up nicely, I think."

"Would you also like me to teach them fencing and boxing?" she asked sarcastically.

"Oh, we already know how to do those," Grant piped up.

"Good Christ," Royal said, shaking his head. "This is a complete joke."

"I am forced to agree with your brother, Lord Arnprior," Miss Knight said. "This must surely be a joke."

"It surely is not," Nick said. "And I never joke."

"That's actually true," Graeme said.

Miss Knight momentarily pressed a hand to her forehead. "Please forgive *my* lack of manners, my lord, but you are not paying me enough to take on such an insane task."

"Actually, we've yet to discuss your wages, Miss Knight," Nick said.

"Whatever it is, it won't be enough."

Nick tamped down the frustration stirring in his gut. If she refused the position, God only knew what he would do. He'd envisioned a scenario that would have allowed him to judge the governess in a calm and reasonable fashion. His family, as usual, had blown his plans to smithereens.

As had Miss Knight. Because she'd not been what he was expecting, she'd initially thrown him off his game. Now, though, he was convinced she was the perfect person for the job.

"I'm sorry to hear that," he said. "Sir Dominic assured me that you were more than capable of taking on these additional duties and would be happy to do so."

"He did?" she asked with disbelief.

Nick nodded. "Indeed, and I assured Sir Dominic that I would pay you handsomely for your efforts. I'm disappointed you do not feel up to the task."

She jerked as if someone had jabbed her with a pin.

"Arnprior," Alec said, "she's entirely capable of whatever you ask."

"Apparently not."

"Sheer nonsense," Alec growled. "She's worked in some of the best houses in England."

When Miss Knight shot Alec a glare, he looked perplexed

before wincing on the realization he'd undercut her. She did not, however, contradict his assertion.

"My lord, while I am flattered by Sir Dominic's confidence in me . . ." she said.

"You should be flattered," Nick interrupted with a smile. "He is not a man who gives his approval lightly, as we both know."

"Yes, but—"

"In addition to paying you exceedingly well, I will give you a sterling recommendation when you wish to leave my employ."

From the way her eyes narrowed thoughtfully, it was clear that a good recommendation was even more important than money. He would be happy to exploit that bit of knowledge, too.

But then she shook her head. "You are generous, my lord, but I am doubtful this plan will succeed."

Royal hauled himself up from his chair. "Stop badgering the girl. She doesn't want to be here, and we don't want her, either."

Nick also rose. "Sit down, Royal."

Every line of his brother's body spoke of mutiny, but Nick stared him down. He'd led a regiment for five years, and had been Royal's commanding officer. His brother had never defied him during the war. Now, though, defiance was a regular event for Royal and for everyone else in the blasted household. The fact that Nick was willing to employ a slip of a girl to help him impose order at Kinglas was a measure of how desperate he'd become.

Royal muttered an oath and plunked back down in his chair.

"Coward," Angus muttered at Royal, who ignored him.

When Nick resumed his seat, he was surprised to see Miss Knight regarding him with a wariness that was quite at variance with her previous pert demeanor. Had she expected him and his brother to start pummeling each other?

"There's no cause for concern, Miss Knight," he said. "My brothers do have enough sense to refrain from brawling in the presence of a lady."

One of her eyebrows went up in a haughty arch. "It was not your brother I was worried about."

"Touché, lass," Alec murmured.

Nick forced an apologetic smile. "Forgive me if I frightened you, Miss Knight."

Angus leaned forward in his chair. "If the lass is too dainty to put up with a little brawlin' and argumentation, then she should leave. We have no need of her fancy English ways here at Kinglas."

She threw daggers at the old man but kept her lips firmly shut.

Nick hung on to his last bit of patience, because he needed to make this work. He needed *her*. "Miss Knight, I realize this might be considered something of a challenging assignment . . ."

When she let out a ladylike snort, he ignored it.

"All I ask is that you defer making a decision for another few days," he continued. "Kade has been under the care of our family physician in Glasgow, but he will be arriving home tomorrow. I hope you will meet him before deciding to stay or go."

Her full, pink lips pursed sideways in a girlish gesture he found unexpectedly charming. Then she shook her head. "I truly don't think—"

"Is it not the least you could do for Sir Dominic?" he gently interrupted.

When she flinched, Nick knew he'd scored a hit. He calmly regarded her troubled expression, letting her sense of guilt do the work for him.

"You've come all this way, lass," Alec said, resting a hand on her arm. "What's the harm in meeting the boy and then making your decision?"

For several long seconds, Alec and Miss Knight seemed to hold a silent conversation, during which Nick had to repress the urge to knock his friend's hand from her arm. He didn't like that Alec was so possessive with her and he surely didn't like that he was so bothered by it.

Finally, the girl gave a tight nod. "Very well, my lord. But I must tell you that I'm not inclined to give a favorable answer unless I'm convinced your family is prepared to welcome both my presence and my guidance. I will not take up a position that is destined from the outset to fail."

"Duly noted," Nick said dryly.

When Angus let out a triumphant little snicker, he wanted to dump the teapot on the old codger's head.

Victoria was braiding her hair when a soft knock sounded on the door.

"Enter." She rose from her chair in front of the scrolled walnut dressing table. The carved and gilded pier mirror mounted above it was lovely, but so old that the glass was cloudy. In the soft light of the candles, the mirror made her look fuzzy and rather worn. Or perhaps that was simply the way she truly appeared after the long, gruesome day.

Mrs. Taffy—who Victoria had decided was the only sane member of the household—bustled in, carrying an armful of fluffy white towels. "I came to see that ye had everything ye needed," she said in her soft, pleasant brogue, putting the bundle down on the washstand by the hearth.

By the critical look the housekeeper cast about the room, Victoria suspected she'd come up to make sure the room was up to her exacting standards. Mrs. Taffy had snowy-white hair, neatly confined under a lace cap, and a wrinkled face that suggested she was approaching her seventies. But she was sturdy and moved with a briskness that would put a woman half her age to shame. When she ran a finger across the mantel, Victoria bit back a smile.

Kinglas might be rather worn around the edges, with furnishings and carpets years out of date, but it was a well-maintained house. She suspected that the servants knew their duties and carried them out with a minimum of fuss. The redoubtable housekeeper was clearly responsible for that, since there was no butler or house steward.

"Yes, thank you," Victoria said. "This room is lovely. I imagine it's one of the nicest bedrooms in the castle."

She'd been surprised by how lovely. From what she could tell, most of the rooms in the tower house—the true *castle* part of the castle—were compact rather than spacious. Like narrow, stacked blocks, each floor held only three or four rooms. The drawing room, where they'd had tea this afternoon, was in the newer, more elegant wing of the manor, as were the dining room, the library, and a number of other public rooms.

Compared to the newer wing, the tower house was positively medieval, with thick walls of stone, low-timbered ceilings, and wooden floors and wall panels mellowed by age to a dark smoky brown. She could almost wish to remain at Kinglas simply for the opportunity to explore such a noble castle.

Almost.

Living with the Kendrick men was a daunting prospect. The idea of spending the winter with them, in the remote Scottish Highlands, was gruesome to contemplate.

Except for the earl. You wouldn't mind spending time with him, would you?

She squashed the temptation to dwell on Arnprior's handsome face and compelling gaze.

Mrs. Taffy gave her a warm smile. "This was her ladyship's room. It's one of the coziest in the castle."

Victoria blinked. "This was the bedroom of the Countess of Arnprior?"

"Aye, of the previous laird's second wife, that is. There's a suite of formal rooms in the east wing, but her ladyship wanted to be closer to her husband. The laird's bedroom is directly below this room. His lordship used to just nip up the stairs and be with her ladyship in a trice."

Victoria felt her face heat at the notion of the formidable Laird of Arnprior sleeping so close by.

"Thank you for putting me in so comfortable a room, Mrs. Taffy. It's much too grand for a governess, but I do appreciate your consideration."

"Och, it's the least I could do. I'd prepared one of the more modern rooms in the west wing, but that blocked chimney caused quite a mess. The only other bedrooms in a fit state are in the old barracks wing, near Mr. Royal and his brothers. That wouldna be proper for a young lady at all."

"Thank you," Victoria said with a grateful smile. The notion of sleeping anywhere near a boisterous group of males—even relatively harmless ones—made her chest tighten. Oddly, sleeping a short staircase away from the earl failed to evoke a similar anxiety.

"About that chimney," she added, "I suspect it wasn't a bird's nest that caused it to smoke, was it?"

The housekeeper scoffed. "As if I'd let my chimneys get in such a state."

"One of the twins, I suppose," Victoria said dryly. When Grant commented on the state of the chimney at dinner, with a small smirk on his face, she'd guessed that trying to smoke her out of her room had been part of the scheme to drive her away.

"They don't mean any harm. Not really. They were left to run without a strong hand to guide them, when the laird was off to the war. I'm sorry to say they went a bit wild."

Despite her firm intention not to get sucked into the affairs of Arnprior's family, Victoria couldn't entirely suppress her curiosity. "What of their grandfather? I understood he had the management of the estate and his grandsons during that time."

"Och, that Mr. MacDonald. He encourages the lads in their bad behavior. He'll have no truck with English ways, as if being civilized and good-mannered is only fit for foreigners."

"We're all subjects of the Crown and members of one union, are we not?"

"Many a Highlander would disagree. Especially one whose clan fought on the wrong side at Culloden."

"But that was decades ago," Victoria said.

The housekeeper sighed. "Some of the older generation willna get over the loss. They cling to the old ways, when men were warriors and not afraid to live rough."

"Lord Arnprior is both a warrior *and* a civilized man. Surely Mr. MacDonald sees that." No one in his right mind would accuse the earl of being soft. One only had to look at his brawny physique and his stern features to know the idea was laughable.

"Aye, but Mr. MacDonald thinks the laird is too modern. That he's turning his back on the past. To some of the older folk, that's nothing short of betrayal to the clan and to Scotland. That's why Mr. MacDonald encourages the lads. He's afraid they'll forget who they are."

"I'm sure the earl simply wants his brothers to behave in a more gentlemanly fashion."

From what she'd seen at dinner, it seemed a hopeless task. Although the earl had done his best to manage the situation, the twins had been especially ridiculous. They'd done their grandfather proud, speaking out of turn and wolfing their food like barbarians. Royal, on the other hand, had barely said a word, eating like an automaton, then throwing down his napkin and stalking from the table before the dessert course was served. Alec and Lord Arnprior had manfully tried to carry on a normal conversation, but by the end of the evening his lordship had looked ready to murder everyone at the table.

He'd taken to scowling at Victoria halfway through the evening, which she thought unfair. She'd tried her best to be polite, but after being repeatedly rebuffed by Royal or ridiculed by Angus for her "Sassenach ways," she'd descended into silence, which had obviously displeased the earl. Could anyone blame her from excusing herself from tea in the drawing room and fleeing upstairs to bed?

Mrs. Taffy fixed her with an earnest gaze. "The laird is doing his best, but he's at his wit's end. He needs a fine, ladylike teacher such as yerself to assist him."

"He may even need an Act of Parliament." Victoria winced as soon as the caustic words passed her lips. "I'm sorry, that was very rude of me. I can only suppose I'm more fatigued than I thought."

The housekeeper rearranged a porcelain shepherdess on the mantel. "No one could blame ye, miss, and that's a fact. Yer a saint to take on the job."

A bubble of laughter welled up in Victoria's chest at the idea of anyone calling her a saint. After all, she'd killed a man only a few short weeks ago, which was a most unholy, if unintended, act.

Mrs. Taffy turned down the bedclothes, then fetched the bed warmer from the hearth and began passing it between the sheets. "And never ye fear. The lads will eventually do what the laird tells them to do."

When Mrs. Taffy noticed Victoria's silence, she glanced

up from her task. "Yer thinking of not giving us a chance then, miss?"

Victoria was startled by the accusatory tone in the housekeeper's voice. "I . . . probably not. I don't think I'd be able to do much good here," she said.

She mentally winced at the crestfallen expression on Mrs. Taffy's face. While feeling guilty was silly, since she'd been all but lured here under false pretenses, she hated letting people down. Even as a child, Victoria had done her best to please her aunts and uncles, working hard to make up for the fact that her very presence was a stain on the Knight family's reputation.

But if disappointing a few strangers—or even Dominic— was the price of avoiding a hopeless situation, then so be it. Her position in Lord Welgate's household had certainly taught her the devastating outcomes that could result from ignoring one's instincts.

But under the older woman's frowning gaze, Victoria found herself wanting to shuffle her feet. She almost felt like a naughty child caught with her hand in the cookie jar.

"I don't agree with ye, miss," said the housekeeper. "Lord knows the earl could use help from a lass such as yourself. He needs someone with yer bonny face and kind nature."

Victoria felt her cheeks flush. "I'm not sure what you mean."

"The laird has seen a lot of trouble and heartache over the years," Mrs. Taffy said in a somber tone. "It takes a toll on a man. Turns him grim. Hard, even."

Although Victoria nodded sympathetically, the observation wasn't exactly an incentive to accept a position in the earl's household. "I'm sure that most men who've been to war have seen terrible things. I have no doubt it's a burden."

Mrs. Taffy flashed a humorless smile. "Aye, war takes its toll on a man, but I wasn't referring to that."

"Then what, may I ask?"

The housekeeper seemed to consider for a few moments, then simply shrugged. Victoria got the sense that Mrs. Taffy had been about to reveal something personal about Lord Arnprior, but had changed her mind.

That seemed for the best, she told herself, squashing an unseemly curiosity. The earl was a compelling man, but after tomorrow she would probably never see him again.

"What I meant to say was that the laird could use an intelligent, genteel woman about the house," Mrs. Taffy said. "His stepmother was one such a lady. She was the kindest woman one could hope to meet, and there wasn't a thing her sons and stepsons wouldn't do for her. Her ladyship was a wonderful influence."

"But she was their mother," Victoria said. "Surely that accounted for a good measure of their respect."

"I'm sure yer right, miss," Mrs. Taffy said briskly, carrying the bed warmer back to the hearth. "Now, just listen to me babbling when ye must be anxious to crawl into that nice bed. I don't know what's gotten into me."

Victoria smiled politely. By tomorrow afternoon she would be back on her way to Glasgow and then on to London a few days later. Meeting Lord Arnprior and his colorful family would be no more than an odd, brief detour in her life. No good could come from her remaining at Castle Kinglas, no matter what Dominic, Alec, or anyone else believed.

But as exhaustion pulled Victoria into sleep, a stern, handsome face drifted through her dreams—one whose piercing blue gaze chastised her for running away from those who needed her most.

Chapter Six

Victoria bolted upright. She'd been dreaming of climbing a staircase that stretched endlessly upward inside a tower. Below, in the shadowy depths, something had pursued her. As she struggled on leaden legs to climb, the stairs had dissolved into a craggy, steep hillside. Lost in the mists below, her pursuer had screamed out a horrible, high-pitched sound.

The sound she heard right now.

Bagpipes.

She'd heard them for the first time in Glasgow, when a pipe and drum band had marched past the church where she and Alec attended Sunday services. Victoria had enjoyed the spirited rendition of "Amazing Grace," so soulful and moving that she'd had to choke back a few tears.

But there was nothing moving or beautiful about what was happening in the courtyard below her window now. In fact, it was quite possibly the most hideous noise she'd ever heard, and she had little doubt the display of musical desecration was intended for her benefit. If she weren't so exhausted, she'd storm over to the window and shout that the Kendrick men needn't bother trying to drive her away. There wasn't enough money in the world to convince her to remain at Castle Bedlam.

But since she was exhausted, and because ladies didn't generally make a habit of screaming out windows at near strangers, she flopped down and stuffed one of the pillows over her head. It deadened the sound a bit, but certainly not enough to allow her to go back to sleep. Hopefully, some-one would get sick of the racket and put an end to it—if not the earl then Mrs. Taffy. The redoubtable housekeeper was clearly dismayed by the antics and bad behavior of "the lads."

Within minutes, the horrific wail cut off with a final screech. Through the muffling of the pillow, Victoria heard raised voices arguing. Not long after, though, a blessed silence once more fell over the castle.

She eased the pillow away from her head and snuggled under the wool blanket and velvet coverlet, taking comfort in the fact that by this time tomorrow she would be sleep-ing in one of the lovely bedrooms in Alec's Glasgow manor house. Closing her eyes, she began to drift once more toward sleep.

Another blast of sound—one distressingly similar to an unmentionable bodily function—split the night. Victoria yelped and almost pitched out of bed. She sucked in sev-eral deep breaths to still the wild beating of her heart.

Muttering imprecations about deranged Highlanders, she rolled out of bed and grabbed her wrapper and felt around for her slippers. Despite the banked fire in the hearth, the room was freezing and wreathed in thick shadows.

Her foot connected smartly with one of the thick wooden bedposts.

"Confound it!" She hopped around for a few seconds before getting down on her hands and knees to search for her slippers. She mentally cursed every last Kendrick man, the earl included.

She found her blasted footwear and marched to the door, determined to put an end to the madness down in the courtyard.

As she came out to the hall, another door flew open and Alec stormed out of the room next to hers. Clad only in breeches and a shirt and holding a candle, he looked as murderous as she felt.

"Obviously, that hideous racket woke you, too," she said.

"There was no sleeping through that charming rendition of 'Queen Mary's Escape from Loch Leven.'"

"Good God, how can you even tell the song? More importantly, which madman is abusing those pipes?"

"Whom do you think?" he growled.

"Mr. MacDonald?"

"Spot on. I'm on my way down to throttle him—if Arnprior doesn't get there first. He's the one who got Angus to stop the first time."

"Not you?"

"No. I roared down to the courtyard, but Arnprior was already tearing a strip off Angus like you wouldn't believe. I almost felt sorry for the old codger. But since the yelling obviously didn't take, my sympathy has died a quick death."

She wrinkled her nose. "They must not like me very much if they're willing to go through all this trouble to be rid of me."

He shook his head. "No, I think the twins like you rather a lot. They're just afraid showing it will bring their grandfather's wrath down on them."

"Perhaps, but Royal most certainly doesn't approve of me."

"He doesn't like anyone right now, and I have a feeling

that Arnprior's at a loss as to how to deal with him. Royal obviously can't make his peace with his discharge from the army, and he can't figure out what he's going to do with his life."

Sympathy stirred in Victoria's chest. "Is he in pain? His limp is quite marked."

"I'm sure he is. He was badly injured at Waterloo. Almost died, from what I understand. Arnprior told me he was lucky to keep the leg."

"Poor man. I'm more than willing to excuse his bad behavior, if that's the case. But the others . . . even the earl doesn't seem all that keen on trying to convince me to stay."

Alec frowned. "Trust me—he wants you to stay. It's just that . . ."

She touched his arm. "It's all right. You can tell me."

"He senses that you're holding something back—that *we're* holding something back."

Her heart jammed against her ribs. "Did he tell you that?"

"Not in so many words, but after dinner he all but interrogated me about why you left Welgate's employ so precipitously."

She grimaced. "Oh, that's not good."

"He also wished to know why Dominic took such an interest in you."

"What did you tell him?"

"I simply explained that Dominic has known the Knight family for years and has been of assistance in helping you to secure employment."

"Did he accept that answer?" Her mentor had worked hard to obscure the fact that she was the Prince Regent's illegitimate daughter. Her first employer—a wealthy merchant—had known her family history and had not taken exception, but most in the *ton* would hardly see it as anything but scandalous.

Alec waggled a hand. "He seemed to, but it doesn't help that you don't have a reference from Welgate."

She sighed. "It would appear his lordship doesn't like me any more than the rest of his family." Then again, why did she care what Arnprior thought of her? After all, it wasn't as if she wanted the job.

"I'm sure he thinks you're just what he needs."

"If you say so." She cast a scowl back at the window as another blast of pipes rent the air. "If that wretched noise doesn't stop, I swear I'm going to find a pistol and murder that man. Or beat him to death with his blasted bagpipes."

Alec laughed. "Spoken like a true Sassenach. I'll go down and . . . ah, finally." The wailing had abruptly cut off.

Victoria sagged against the door frame, letting the tension drain from her body.

"Arnprior must have gone down to roust him again," Alec said. "It should be fine now."

"Captain Gilbride, allow me to say that you hold an excessively optimistic view of life."

He flashed a rueful smile. "I know. Go back to bed, Victoria. I'll deal with any more problems that might arise tonight. I promise."

"Thank you." She cast him a hesitant glance. "Alec, I hate to disappoint Dominic, and I know it will cause complications, but I don't think I can accept this position."

His gaze warmed with sympathy. "Why don't we talk to Arnprior in the morning and see how things stand? I'm sure the situation won't appear as dire after a good night's sleep."

She rolled her eyes. "As I said, you're excessively optimistic."

"True, but rest assured that I will support whatever

decision you finally make. Now, see if you can get some sleep."

"I'll do my best." Victoria closed the door and trudged back to bed, so weary she was convinced she might sleep through anything, even hideous bagpipe serenades.

Unfortunately, she was mistaken about that. A short time later, the twins decided to hold a carouse just below her window. After suffering through no fewer than three ribald drinking songs, she leapt out of bed and stormed over to the window. As she struggled to open the old casement, Arnprior erupted from a shadowy doorway and stalked across the courtyard toward his brothers.

The earl was wearing nothing but a kilt, and was in the process of securing it around his waist. With an almost full moon shining down, she got more than an eyeful of broad, muscular shoulders and an exceedingly brawny chest. In the moonlight, he seemed nothing like the civilized aristocrat who'd pulled out her chair at dinner. This man looked like a wild Highlander, ready to go on a rampage.

With a lamentable lack of feminine sensibility, she stared down at him, unable to avert her gaze.

Graeme and Grant quickly took to their heels in self-preservation. Given the ferocity of the earl's demeanor, she had little doubt the twins would have emerged worse for wear from an encounter with their much-put-upon brother.

Arnprior came to a halt beneath Victoria's window, staring after his younger half-siblings with obvious frustration. He propped his hands on his hips and glanced up at her window, appearing to meet her gaze.

She was transfixed. Moonlight gleamed over his half-nude body, lovingly highlighting his tall, muscular form and his imposing presence. In the shimmering light, out there in the cold and unforgiving night air, he didn't seem quite real. Victoria was not a woman prone to excessive imaginings, but she could see Arnprior as a creature from a more primitive time—perhaps a fierce Celtic warrior, or even a pagan god come to claim a virgin sacrifice.

And here you are, gaping down at him like a henwit.

She glanced down at herself, suddenly aware that her nightdress had slipped off her shoulder and her cap had fallen from her head, exposing her tumbled-down hair.

Scrambling backward, she sank down to the chilly floorboards. Victoria pressed a hand to her heart, trying to catch her breath and think rationally. The earl couldn't have seen her, since it was all-but pitch black in her room and she'd never managed to get the window open. And even in her nightdress she was covered from head to toe, which was a great deal more than she could say for him. Yes, it was his castle and his brothers were acting outrageous, but that was hardly a good excuse for a gentleman to run about half-naked.

No matter how handsome and well built that gentleman might happen to be.

She edged up and peered out the window to see that Alec had finally made his way to the courtyard, having taken the time to get properly dressed first. As he and Arnprior quietly conferred, she couldn't help noticing that the frigid night air didn't seem to bother the earl in the least, despite his unclothed state.

When they went back inside, Victoria stumbled back to bed, praying that the antics were over for the night. The morning was bound to be a tense affair, since she would have to inform the earl that she would not be accepting the position.

The final indignity of the night occurred a few hours later, when a rooster started crowing below her window. There was, of course, nothing unusual about roosters crowing at daybreak. Victoria refused to believe, however, that the Earl of Arnprior made a habit of housing barnyard animals right below the family bedrooms.

By the time the maid arrived an hour later to light the fire and bring a pot of tea, Victoria was up packing her bags. She'd spent that hour mentally rehearsing a speech in which she would tell the earl exactly what she thought of his deranged family. And once she finished, she would leave Castle Kinglas behind her forever.

Nick was bolting down his second cup of coffee, hoping to clear the mental cobwebs. Various irate persons would start showing up any minute, and he wanted to be prepared.

A rap sounded smartly on the library door.

Not even a minute.

"Enter."

Alec stalked into the room, looking as tired and frustrated as Nick felt. His friend, however, would have the good fortune to escape this madhouse in just a few hours, whereas Nick would be an inmate for life.

"Before you take my head, sit down and have some coffee," Nick said, waving to one of the leather club chairs.

Alec came to a halt in front of the large walnut desk and glared at him. "Hell, no. We're going to have this out right now. Why the devil can't you control your bloody household? In your regiment, no soldier in his right mind would have dared to defy you."

"I believe the phrase 'right mind' captures the essence of the problem," Nick said.

"Not good enough," Alec snapped.

"The last time I looked, *Captain* Gilbride, this was my castle, not yours, so please refrain from issuing orders. Just sit the hell down and have a cup of coffee." His emphasis of Alec's rank was a reminder that he'd once been a junior officer under Nick's command.

His friend fumed for a few more seconds before a reluctant smile cracked the edges of his mouth, then he sank into a chair with a half-hearted grumble. "You always were more imperious than a royal duke, Arnprior."

"You would know, I suppose."

Alec eyed the large coffee service on the desk. "Expecting a crowd, are we?"

"I expect at least three more to join me before breakfast, each anxious to give me a piece of his—or her—mind."

"I'll wager Miss Knight will be down next," Alec said as he poured himself a cup. "If I were you, I'd find some cotton batting to stuff in your ears."

"That bad, eh?" Nick said.

Of course it was that bad. Only the dead could have slept through last night's mayhem.

"She's not happy," Alec said.

Nick rubbed his temples where a headache was forming. "I'll apologize to her, naturally. And make what amends I can in the hopes of convincing her to stay."

"Good luck with that, old son," Alec said with a bland smile.

Nick stared at him from between his hands. "As much as I hate to admit it, *old son*, I need the girl's help. And I'd be much obliged if you would do what you can to assist me."

Alec shook his head. "My only concern at this point is what's best for Victoria."

"I didn't realize you and Miss Knight were on a first-name basis," Nick said. "How . . . unusual."

Alec's genial gaze faded. "What the hell are you suggesting, Arnprior?"

"I'm just curious as to why you're so protective of her."

After a moment of staring at him, Alec let out a guffaw.

"You are utterly daft. You do remember meeting my wife, don't you? Would you cheat on Edie?"

"Mrs. Gilbride is, of course, entirely charming." Nick's taste, however, did not run to buxom, vivacious blondes. Skinny, tart-tongued blondes were apparently more to his liking, which was a rather unwelcome revelation, under the circumstances.

"You know I would never betray my wife," Alec said, "and Victoria Knight would never engage in scandalous behavior, in any case. If you think she might, then rest assured she will be returning to Glasgow with me."

"I'm happy to hear I was wrong," Nick said. "Nor was it Miss Knight's behavior that led me to make what was clearly an unfortunate assumption."

"Was that an apology?" Alec asked suspiciously.

"Feel free to take it that way, if you wish."

Alec shook his head. "You can be a right bastard sometimes, Arnprior."

"I'm sure my family would agree with your assessment. But surely you don't believe Miss Knight could come to any harm under my roof. My grandfather and brothers may be idiots, but they would never lay a finger on the girl."

"I know," Alec replied.

"Then what's the problem? Sir Dominic assured me that Miss Knight was both qualified and eager for a good position."

Alec seemed to wrestle with himself. "She certainly *needs* the damn job, I can tell you that."

Again, Nick felt a stirring of unease. A qualified governess with good recommendations was invariably in high demand. Miss Knight, however, seemed to be having some difficulties in that respect, despite her sterling qualifications. But since he needed the confounded girl, he simply had to trust that Dominic and Alec wouldn't steer him wrong.

After putting his coffee cup on the desk, Alec pinned him with a warning gaze. "All right, I'll do what I can to persuade her to take the position. But know that Miss Knight is under Dominic's protection, and mine as well. I trust you understand what that means."

Before he could reply to the thinly veiled threat, Royal limped into the room.

Nick flashed his brother a brief smile but kept his attention on Alec. "We will treat Miss Knight like royalty, I promise."

Alec snorted. "See that you do."

Royal sank into the other club chair. "After last night's performances, I'm amazed the lass didn't steal a horse and ride pell-mell back to Glasgow."

Nick caught his brother's slight grimace as he rubbed his thigh. "Your leg is bothering you again?"

"It's nothing." Royal's voice was tight, and his eyes looked weary and shadowed.

"I can send for the surgeon, if you like."

"That old sawbones is useless."

"Very well. But don't overdo it today. You'll destroy that leg if you're not careful." Nick ignored Royal's scowl and returned his attention to Alec. "Then we'll present a united front to Miss Knight when she comes down?"

"For God's sake," Royal said, "isn't it time to give up this mad scheme to turn us into a pack of bloody debutants?"

"Not to stir up the pot, Arnprior," Alec said, "but why *are* you so determined to pretty up your brothers? They come from one of the most distinguished families in Scotland, so I'm sure they're capable of making respectable marriages."

"What if some of us don't want to get married?" Royal said sharply.

Alec shrugged. "Then I expect you could all take up

a profession. Make yourself useful instead of twitting governesses and pretending to be witless boors."

"The twins were just acting up to prove a point," Royal said. "And you're correct. If Nick would leave us alone, we'd figure something out."

Nick knew that wasn't the case. "Royal, I know you don't want to hear this, but your military career is over. You need to accept that."

"I was a good soldier, one of the best in our regiment," he snapped. "It wasn't my fault I was wounded."

"Of course it wasn't. And what happened to you was incredibly unfair," Nick said quietly. "As it was for many men."

"There is life after the military, Royal," Alec said. "A good life, if you put some effort into finding it."

"That's easy for you to say, Gilbride. You're heir to a bloody rich earldom. I'm a younger son—just one of several. I don't know how to do a damn thing except be a soldier, and my brothers know even less. That's why Nick's so keen to marry us off to wealthy wives. We're not good for anything else."

Alec threw Nick a troubled glance. "Surely some of the lads could take up a profession. Make something of themselves."

"It seems not," Nick said. "With the exception of Braden, who wants to be a physician, none of my brothers has shown any interest in the law, business, or even estate management. And God knows the Church is out." He shook his head. "Could you imagine either of the twins as a minister? They'd probably ruin half the girls in the congregation."

It was only by some miracle that Graeme had yet to impregnate one of the village girls and get murdered by an irate father. Nick had been forced to put the fear of God into the twins, threatening to permanently run them off Arnprior lands if they so much as thought of taking advantage of one of the local girls.

As for the local gentry, they already viewed his brothers as unacceptable mates for their daughters.

"I see the problem," Alec said.

"Especially for poor Nick," Royal said. "And he's stuck with us for the foreseeable future since none of us can support ourselves." He gave Nick a rueful smile. "I truly am sorry about that."

"No, *I'm* sorry. I've failed all of you." He'd failed his entire bloody family, including his wife and little boy.

Even Logan, the brother he'd once been closest to, had run away after Nick all but killed him. Overcome with self-hatred and guilt, Nick had then fled too, joining the army. He'd abandoned his family when they needed him most.

"You did your best for us," Royal said. "None of us ever blamed you. Never that."

In fact, they'd all worried about him, instead. Royal had even followed him into the army, largely to keep an eye on him. If not for that, Royal would have stayed at Kinglas, safe from the war that would rob him of his innocence, his health, and perhaps his future.

Nick shook off the despair that was his daily companion. "Nonsense. As the head of this family, I *am* responsible for all of you. That means you and your brothers will do exactly as I say. You will submit to Miss Knight's direction and hopefully become respectable gentlemen who give honor to the Kendrick name instead of pulling it into the damn gutter."

His brother rolled his eyes. "Bloody hell, you never give up."

"I'll never give up on you, you idiot," Nick said with a wry smile.

"May I suggest we defer further argumentation until

Miss Knight gives us her answer?" Alec said. "That should be momentarily, if I'm not mistaken."

Because Royal had left the door open, Nick could hear the murmur of voices in the hall before a determined set of feminine footsteps approached the library. A moment later Miss Knight sailed into the room, looking ready to fire all guns. It would be a broadside, from the scowl on her pretty face, a cannonade aimed right at him.

Chapter Seven

Victoria almost stumbled when she confronted three sets of intent male gazes. Once again, she'd been caught flat-footed.

It was the right decision to leave Castle Kinglas, but it was never a pleasant thing to admit defeat, especially when doing so would disappoint those trying to help her. Victoria hated disappointing people, and she hated giving up. She had no desire to engage in what was sure to be a humiliating discussion in front of witnesses, even if one was Alec.

The gentlemen rose from their seats, and Alec gave her a warm smile.

"Good morning," he said. "Why don't you join us for a cup of coffee?" He glanced at the large coffee service. "As you can see, his lordship has been expecting us."

The earl stood quietly behind his desk, regarding her with an unnerving, calculating gaze.

Blast.

He wasn't going to make it easy on her, even though she had a stack of objections that, if written down, would be a foot high. Enumerating all those objections—and her reluctance to deal with them—would be embarrassing enough in private.

"I beg your pardon for the interruption, Lord Arnprior," she said, edging backward toward the door. "I can return later after your business with Captain Gilbride and Mr. Kendrick is concluded."

"Miss Knight, you *are* the business under discussion," the earl said, a growly note coloring his voice. "Please join us."

The shadows under his eyes and his unshaven jaw gave him an unexpectedly rakish and arrogantly masculine appearance. That she found it a dangerously appealing look was a disturbing discovery.

It's just your nerves, you nitwit.

Lord Arnprior was *not* the sort of man she normally found attractive. "Thank God," she muttered.

"What was that, Miss Knight?" the earl said.

"Only that I'm sorry I interrupted you, my lord. Again, I'll be happy to return later."

"Nonsense. We need to have this discussion immediately, and it makes perfect sense for Captain Gilbride to remain."

He flicked a covert glance at Alec, who continued to regard her with a deceptively innocent expression, as if they were all at a jolly little tea party. Victoria had the distinct impression that the men were conspiring to manipulate her. Well, except for Royal, who simply looked bored.

"Arnprior thought you'd be more comfortable with me here," Alec said. "We're just going to have a little chat about the situation and see how we can improve things."

Oh, dear. Her cousin had clearly gone over to the other side.

"Situation?" she inquired politely. "Would that be the circus troupe that performed underneath my window last night?"

Alec winced and Arnprior looked even more annoyed.

Royal, however, chuckled. "I heard there was something of a ruckus in the courtyard. So sad that Taffy had to move you to a bedroom in the tower. It's always much quieter in the east wing of the house."

The earl slowly turned, his gaze narrowing to ice blue slits as he stared at his brother. Royal shrugged, but a flush crept up the young man's cheeks.

Arnprior's attention came back to her. "That is one of the topics I'd like to discuss with you, Miss Knight." His mouth edged up in a rueful smile. "And apologize for. It seems I've had to do that quite frequently over the last twenty-four hours."

"I assure you, sir, I am not keeping count," she replied graciously. So far, he'd apologized at least four times, and she might have missed one or two.

His skeptical look suggested he realized that she *was*, in fact, keeping count. That was rather embarrassing.

"That is most kind of you," he finally said. "Now, do sit and join us for a cup of coffee. I'm sure you can use it."

That was true.

Alec came to escort her to one of the leather club chairs. Arnprior's library, while not large, was well organized with inset, glass-fronted bookshelves that carried an impressive number of volumes. The walls were painted a deep burgundy, and the fireplace boasted a beautiful and elaborately carved granite surround topped with a handsome timepiece in dark polished wood.

The centerpiece of the room was the earl's desk, an impressive piece of cabinetry with medieval-looking carvings on the legs and across the front. Ledgers and papers were stacked in neat piles on its leather-bound surface, hinting of the earl's active role in estate business. The room seemed a reflection of its occupant—a serious man who kept close watch over everyone and everything in his domain.

The rather somber atmosphere was lightened by the

view of the loch out bay-fronted windows. That view was compelling, with white-crested waters, and craggy hillsides covered in bright autumn foliage rising up on all sides. Sunlight streamed into the room, making the dark red walls and polished floorboards glow with warmth. If she were alone, Victoria would be tempted to sink down on the comfortable-looking chaise in front of the window and allow herself to be lost in the beauty of water, hills, and sky.

Then again, within a matter of weeks the winds would howl and snow would pile up around the high castle walls. Then she'd be trapped for months with demented strangers. Not that she would call Lord Arnprior demented, but spending the winter in close quarters with him was not a comfortable prospect for reasons she had no intention of admitting to anyone.

"All right, lass?" Alec murmured.

She nodded.

"Good," he said. "And you're not to worry. We'll figure it all out."

Victoria eyed her cousin with suspicion as she sat down in the club chair in front of the desk, but he refused to meet her eye.

She took the cup of coffee the earl offered her. When their hands touched, her insides skittered and her cup rattled. The earl, blast him, raised an ironic eyebrow, which she did her best to ignore—even though she was tempted to scowl at his arrogance.

The coffee, blessedly hot and strong, gave her a needed jolt. Arnprior and Royal resumed their seats, while Alec propped a shoulder against a bookshelf. She couldn't help feeling a bit abandoned, although she knew that was silly. Alec might try to persuade her to take the position, but he would never attempt to force her.

The earl lounged back in his chair, lacing his hands across

his flat stomach. "I take it you've reached a decision, Miss Knight."

She set down her cup on the corner of his desk. "I have, my lord. As much as I regret doing so, I find I must turn down your kind offer."

Royal let out a snort. "Regret escaping from our circus, as you called it? I highly doubt it. You'd be an idiot for staying, and I don't think you're an idiot, are you?"

Victoria almost gaped at his appalling display of honesty. If she did stay—which she wouldn't—she'd certainly have her work cut out teaching him proper manners.

Arnprior simply gave her a shrug and a polite smile.

Well. Two could play at that game.

"You are correct, sir," she said to Royal with a polite nod. "But I did not wish to give offense by stating how I truly felt about his lordship's offer of employment."

"Your feelings on the matter are already quite clear, Miss Knight," the earl said. "After all, you did label my family a circus."

She'd walked right into that one.

"I beg your pardon, my lord," she said as heat crawled up her neck. "I am not myself this morning. Last night obviously unsettled me more than I realized."

His eyes gleamed with sudden amusement. They really were the most extraordinary shade of blue, deep and yet clear, like ice on a mountain lake. He had the eyes of a Viking, perhaps a Nordic ancestor who had crossed the frigid seas of the north centuries ago, bent on plunder and conquest.

"I think we can also agree that 'unsettled' is an understatement," he said. "And 'circus' fits quite handily as a description."

"Perhaps next time you could sell tickets," Alec suggested.

"There won't be a next time," Arnprior said. "Miss Knight,

if last night's unfortunate events caused you to decline my offer, I would ask you to reconsider."

"Forgive me, my lord," she said, "but I don't think you can guarantee that a similar commotion will not occur again."

"Trust me," the earl said in a cool voice. "My brothers will do as I tell them, or suffer the consequences."

She stiffened. "I don't want them to suffer any consequences. Not on my behalf."

Royal snorted. "He's not going to beat us or throw us in the dungeon, Miss Knight."

"Actually, I considered the dungeon," the earl said.

Royal ignored him. "No, my sainted brother will simply scowl and lecture, and convey a great sense of disappointment until he has us begging for mercy. Or else he'll scold us until my brothers and I throw ourselves off the castle battlements. Problem solved."

"Thank you for that charming depiction of my character," Arnprior said. "I'm sure you've done much to convince Miss Knight to stay."

Royal smiled. "You're welcome."

A muscle ticked in Arnprior's jaw as he quite evidently ground his molars. Victoria couldn't help feeling sorry for the poor man. He was trying to do his best for his family, and they were fighting him every step of the way.

Still, that was not her problem.

"Forgive me for speaking bluntly, my lord," she said. "But I believe Mr. MacDonald will do everything he can to undermine me, and at least some of your brothers appear greatly influenced by him."

"She's got you there, Arnprior," Alec said from his corner. "Old Angus will drive you all crazy if she stays."

The earl shot him a nasty look. "You're supposed to be helping me, remember?"

"He is, is he?" Victoria wasn't surprised but couldn't help feeling annoyed.

Arnprior nodded. "Captain Gilbride feels it would be in everyone's best interests—including yours—if you were to take up the position."

She glanced over her shoulder to glare at Alec, who was looking sheepish. "I didn't put it quite like that," he said.

"I should hope not, since it's not your decision to make," Victoria said.

"No, but his advice is worth noting," Arnprior said. "And following."

"My lord, it is not up to you or my cou—" She caught herself just in time. "It's not up to you, Captain Gilbride, or anyone else to decide what is best for me."

The earl's gaze narrowed thoughtfully. When he finally lifted a hand in a dismissive gesture, she could breathe again.

"Of course," he said. "But we don't always know what is truly in our best interests, do we?"

She stared at him, amazed by his casual assumption that *he* would know what was best for *her*. Arnprior's response to her stare was a slight but infuriatingly arrogant smile.

"Best give it up, lass," Royal said, looking sympathetic. "When Nick decides on something, you might as well surrender. He generally takes the field no matter the odds."

"I am hardly a battlefield, Mr. Kendrick," she snapped. "Nor do I have any intention of surrendering anything."

"Well, since you are neither a battlefield nor an opposing army," the earl said, "there is no need for surrender. I think we can, however, have a reasonable conversation about the advantages of taking up a position in my household, can we not?"

Argh. The blasted man would not give up.

Victoria rose to her feet. "No, my lord, we cannot. Please

accept my apologies, but I must definitively state that I cannot—"

When a knock on the door interrupted her, she was tempted to pick up her cup and throw its contents at Arnprior—or Alec, or Royal, or any other stubborn, arrogant man who came within throwing distance.

Mrs. Taffy bobbed a curtsy. "Begging your pardon, but Mr. Braden and Master Kade are here. The footmen are helping the wee master into the entrance hall."

The earl was already striding around his desk.

"What the hell are they doing here so early?" Royal said, hauling himself up. "Surely to God they didn't travel through the night. Not with Kade still so weak."

"We'll soon find out," Arnprior said. He paused at the door. "Forgive me, Miss Knight. We'll have to finish this discussion later."

"My lord, I believe you already know . . . oh, blast," she muttered as he disappeared. To her mind, the discussion was over but Arnprior was clearly not ready to concede. She would probably have to sneak out to the stables and pole up the horses herself in order to make good her escape.

Royal limped to the door. "Come along, Miss Knight. You might as well meet the pupil you're going to abandon."

She stared at him in disbelief. "Excuse me, but I thought you wanted me gone."

Royal shrugged. "I'm fine with you teaching Kade. I simply don't want you teaching me." Then he followed his brother out of the room.

Victoria pressed a hand to her forehead. "The Kendricks are all quite mad, if you ask me."

"No more than the average Highlander," Alec said, coming to join her.

She glowered at him. "I thought you were going to support me, no matter what I decided."

"And I will. But if we can manage to sort Angus MacDonald out, I do think there are advantages to you remaining at Kinglas."

"Name one," she retorted.

"It's the perfect place to fade back into obscurity," he said. "Out of sight, out of mind, remember? Dominic was quite clear as to the necessity of that, and it doesn't get much more obscure than an old castle in a remote Highland glen. Besides, Arnprior is bound to give you a good reference if you stay. It can only help to have the support of a well-regarded earl when you set up your own establishment, don't you think?"

She sighed. "Must you be so rational?"

He grinned and took her arm. "Unnerving, isn't it? Why don't we go out and meet young Kade? At least you'll have a better idea of what you're in for if you decide to stay."

"Oh, very well." She allowed him to pull her out to the corridor. "But don't expect any miracles." Kade would certainly have to be a very talented musician *and* a nice boy to convince her to take on the rest of the lunatics in his family.

"I won't."

They made their way to the great hall, a hive of activity as footmen dashed about, hauling in bags and trunks under Mrs. Taffy's careful direction. Despite the commotion, the servants performed their duties swiftly and silently, casting worried glances at the small family group clustered around a chair in the center of the hall.

Huddled in the chair sat a boy, swaddled in a heavy coat and a blanket. The earl crouched in front of him, speaking in a low tone. Royal hovered close by, regarding the pair with a somber expression. Next to him stood a serious-looking young man in spectacles, also dressed for travel. His hand rested protectively on the back of the boy's chair.

Victoria and Alec halted several feet away, not wishing to intrude. The earl glanced up and smiled, waving them over. She thought the smile looked forced, and there was no mistaking the tense set to the broad shoulders under his dark green coat.

The earl rose as they approached. "Miss Knight, I'd like you to meet my youngest brothers, Braden and Kade. Braden is currently at the University of Glasgow, while Kade, as you know, has returned home to study. Alec, I believe you met the lads last summer while you and your wife were in Glasgow."

Braden Kendrick was tall but still boyish-looking, not yet having attained the brawny masculinity of his older brothers. He wore spectacles and had a thoughtful, diffident air that set him apart from the rest of the Kendrick men.

As he began to bow, Alec forestalled him by extending a friendly hand. "Well met, Braden. How go your studies? Arnprior tells me that you're a splendid scholar, and that you wish to study medicine."

The young man gave Alec a shy smile that lit up the deep green gaze he shared with Royal and the twins. "My studies are going well, sir. Thank you for asking. With any luck, I'll be attending medical school at the University of Edinburgh in a year or so." He cast a quick look at the earl. "If Nick approves, of course."

Arnprior clapped him on the shoulder. "Lad, why wouldn't I approve? I know you'll do us all proud."

"God knows someone has to," Royal said sarcastically.

When Braden shot him a disapproving glance, Royal shrugged a half-hearted apology. After shaking his head at his older brother, Braden turned his solemn and surprisingly astute gaze on Victoria.

"Miss Knight, it's a pleasure to meet you," he said with a bow.

"And I can't tell you how happy I am to meet you, Miss Knight," Kade broke in eagerly, gazing up at her with a wide smile. "Because I could hardly wait, I made Braden leave a day early, I was that eager to get home to Kinglas and my studies."

Oh, dear. Victoria mustered a smile and gave the new arrivals a shallow curtsy. "It's a pleasure to meet you both. I hope your travels were not too taxing."

Kade shook his head. "It was worth it, knowing I would soon be home and beginning my lessons with you."

"Don't worry, Nick," Braden said, obviously reading Arnprior's troubled expression. "We spent the night at the coaching inn at Arrochar. The innkeeper and his wife took splendid care of us."

Kade huffed out an exasperated breath. "You're all fussing too much. I'm quite well. No need to worry about my stamina, Miss Knight."

The boy smiled up at her from the depths of his woolen cocoon, his gaze eager. His eyes were a vivid blue, the color of a loch on a sunny day. He more closely resembled the earl than his other brothers, with his dark hair, high, intelligent brow, and the beginnings of rugged features that promised he would someday grow into a handsome man.

But even under the coat and blanket, and with a flannel scarf around his neck, Victoria could tell he was much too thin. And his coloring was dreadful. He was as white as milk though with a hectic flush splashed across his narrow cheekbones. But he was obviously thrilled to be home—and to start working with her.

It made her heart sink that she would have to disappoint the boy. He seemed utterly sweet and charming, and apparently, he had considerable musical talent. Under other circumstances, she would have leapt at the chance to have him as her pupil.

But although Kade was clearly happy to be taught by her, the other Kendrick men were not. That presented odds decidedly not in her favor.

She glanced up to find the earl watching her with an

ironic eye. He knew what she was thinking, and it made her flush.

Fortunately, Arnprior returned his attention to his brothers. "We'll be having a little chat about this mad rush to get back to Kinglas. I won't have you pushing yourself, Kade. We can't risk a relapse."

His little brother scoffed as he threw aside his blanket and began to unwind the scarf around his neck. "I'm perfectly well now, Nick. And Braden fusses over me like he's already a doctor—or my old nursemaid. He's practically locked me in my room."

Braden snorted. "As if anyone can control you when you set your mind on something."

"I'm not a baby anymore," Kade said, "and it's time you all stop treating me like one." He smiled at Braden, as if to take any sting out of his words. Then he glanced around the great hall. "Where are Grandda and the twins?"

"Your grandfather left early to visit some of the tenants," Arnprior said. "And Graeme and Grant are—"

"Still sleeping," Royal interrupted sardonically.

Victoria didn't wonder, since they'd been up most of the night tormenting the household.

"Oh, I thought they'd want to see me," Kade said, sounding crestfallen. "It's been months since they were in Glasgow."

The earl smoothed the thick, tumbled locks back from the boy's forehead with such care that it made Victoria's throat go tight. Though he was a rugged, hard man, he treated his young brother with incredible gentleness.

"We thought you were arriving later in the day, remember?" Arnprior said.

Kade brightened. "Oh, yes, that explains it."

"I can go wake them up, if you like," Royal said.

"No, Kade needs a rest," Braden said. "He should go straight up to bed."

Victoria had to repress a smile at the boy's decisive manner. He might be young, but he showed a maturity that stood in stark contrast to the behavior of the twins and even Royal.

"Agreed," the earl said. "You can see your grandfather and the twins at dinner."

Kade wrinkled his nose. "You're all beasts, but I suppose I could rest for a bit." Then his eyes widened and he flapped a hand at one of the footmen. "Please be careful with that, Andrew, and bring it straight up to my room."

"Aye, Master Kade," the footman said as he gingerly carried a small wooden case through the hall. "I'll not let anythin' happen to it."

"It's my violin," Kade said to Victoria. "Nick brought it back from France when he came home from the war."

"It must be a very fine instrument," she said.

He nodded enthusiastically. "It's splendid, as you'll hear. You play the pianoforte, do you not? I play that instrument, too. I've been studying some duets I thought we could try out together."

This time, Victoria's heart went straight down to her heels. "Oh, how . . . how lovely," she stammered.

"Then we can—"

"Enough, lad," Arnprior gently broke in. "You can speak with Miss Knight later." He cast her a look that threatened doom and destruction if she contradicted him.

She mentally swore, but gave Kade a smile. "That would be fine."

"Good," said the earl. "Now, up with you, young fellow."

He helped his brother stand. When Kade stumbled and grimaced, Arnprior hoisted him into his arms, cradling the boy against his chest.

That sight brought a sting of tears to Victoria's eyes.

Idiot. Stop being sentimental.

"Confound it, Nick. I told you I'm not a baby," Kade said, half laughing, half protesting.

"Of course not. But we don't want you falling and knocking yourself out on your first day home." The earl glanced at Victoria. "Miss Knight could hardly teach you if you had a cracked skull, could she?"

"And score one for Arnprior," Alec murmured in Victoria's ear.

She shot her cousin an irate glance. Still, she couldn't help but admire his lordship's ruthless tactics.

"I suppose you're right," Kade said. "Having my brains splattered all over the hall could be a problem. And Taffy certainly wouldn't approve of the mess."

"Good Lord, how appalling," the earl said as he headed toward the stone staircase. "I really don't understand why I agreed to let you come home."

"Because you missed me?" Kade asked.

"That must be it." Arnprior paused at the bottom of the steps and glanced at Braden. "Coming, lad? You probably need a rest too."

Braden shook his head. "I'd like to have a quick chat with you and Royal first. Just to catch you up on the report from Kade's physician." He glanced at Victoria. "You as well, Miss Knight."

Why would Braden wish to speak to her? And she certainly had no desire to further insert herself into the affairs of the family. "I don't think——" she started.

"If you don't mind," Braden said.

She frowned, but then was caught short by the distraught look that momentarily flashed across the young man's intelligent features.

"I think you'd better do it, lass," Alec murmured.

Surprised, she glanced up at him. Alec had clearly picked up on the change in Braden's demeanor. Royal also looked disturbed, directing a sharp, questioning look at Arnprior.

The earl, however, simply gave a nod and started up the stairs. "Very well. I'll get Kade stowed away and then meet you in the library."

"You don't need to stow me away like a piece of old luggage," Kade said in a suddenly sharp tone. "And Braden's making a big fuss about nothing. I'm perfectly fine, no matter what the doctor said."

"Lad, if I can't fuss over you, then who can?" the earl said in a reasonable tone of voice.

The boy looked mutinous for a few seconds, but then he sighed. "No one, I suppose." He rested his head on Arn- prior's broad shoulder, as if suddenly overcome with weariness.

As Victoria watched the earl carry his brother up the stairs, she had a sinking feeling that something was wrong, very wrong. It just might not be so easy for her to escape Kinglas, after all.

Chapter Eight

"I'm fine," Kade insisted as Nick helped him climb into the high, four-poster bed. "Now that I'm here at Kinglas, I'll be right as a trivet in no time." He glanced around the warm, cozy bedroom, blinking hard as he took in his books, old toys, and musical instruments.

Kade's erratic emotions had convinced Nick that something was wrong—something worse than his little brother's recent illness. There had been tears as well as relief on the lad's face when Nick bent down to greet him. That had startled him, since Kade was a child who rarely cried. He also had the distinct sense that Kade was hiding something from him, which was entirely out of character. Nick had always been more of a father than a brother to his younger siblings, and the lad especially confided in him.

"I'm supposed to worry about you, remember?" Nick said as he tucked him in. "And you were quite ill, brat. What the devil were you about scaring us all like that?"

His brother wrinkled his nose. "I didn't much like it, either."

During the worst of the fever, Nick had feared for Kade's life. It was now all too evident that his brother was not up to the rigors of attending school, so he would need private tutoring until he recovered his health and was ready to go to university.

"And I *hate* not being able to play my music," the boy added. "Bad enough I couldn't practice my violin at school, but then the physician gave Braden strict instructions that I was not to play until I was recovered. He said it was too exhausting, which is a lot of old rubbish."

Nick frowned. "Why couldn't you practice at school? That's why I sent you there in the first place—for the musical instruction."

Kade's gaze dropped to his lap as he fidgeted with the bedcovers. "Oh, I meant I couldn't play as much as I wanted to. But of course the music teachers were very good." He looked up, again giving Nick that wobbly, heartbreaking smile. "As they should be, since I know you paid them an awful lot."

Nick forced a lighter tone, even though tension gripped his insides. "That's why I hired a governess, since it's bound to be cheaper than school. You and your brothers will drive me to the poorhouse one of these days."

"Poor Nick, we're an awful burden, aren't we?" Kade said with a little grimace.

He smoothed the hair back from the lad's pale face. "You're never a burden, my boy. Don't ever think that."

Tears shimmered in Kade's gaze for a moment before he blinked them away. "I'm so happy you hired Miss Knight. She seems awfully nice." He grinned. "And very pretty, don't you think?"

"And much too old for the likes of you," Nick said with mock severity.

Kade laughed. "I'm just teasing. But when do you think we can begin my lessons?"

"Soon enough. There's no rush." The only rush was on the part of his erstwhile governess, who was champing at the bit to escape Kinglas.

His brother snaked a hand out from under the covers and grabbed his fingers in a convulsive grip. "I need to get back to work, Nick. I *need* my music."

Music had always been Kade's comfort and refuge. Clearly, he needed that comfort now more than ever. "I understand," Nick said gently.

"Then you'll speak to Miss Knight about getting started as soon as possible?" Kade's eyes pleaded with such eagerness it broke Nick's heart.

"I'll take care of it," he replied, leaving it vague.

"That'll be better for my health than anything, I just know it," Kade said in a pious tone.

"Now you're just trying to manipulate me."

"Is it working?"

Nick patted his brother's hand and then placed it back under the covers. "Yes. I'll talk to Miss Knight about when you can begin your studies."

Perhaps after you manage to convince her to stay?

And that, of course, meant he had to convince his family to stop acting like blockheads.

Kade sighed with relief as he slumped down on the thick pile of pillows. "Thank you. And thank you for bringing me home."

He heard the catch in the boy's voice. "Lad, you know you can always talk to me, don't you? About anything that troubles or concerns you."

When Kade's gaze darted off to the side, Nick had to tamp down his frustration.

"Of course. But don't worry, Nick. Nothing's wrong now that I'm home," he finally said, peering at the heavy velvet bed curtains as if he'd never seen them before.

Nick was debating whether to push him a bit more when the door opened and Taffy came in, followed by a footman carrying a tray of covered dishes.

"Now, Master Kade," she said. "You'll be having some breakfast and then a nice little nap, won't you?"

"I don't think I have a choice," Kade said, glancing up at Nick.

"No, you don't," Nick said. "And I expect to hear from Taffy that you ate all of your breakfast."

The housekeeper uncovered dishes of coddled eggs, toast, and scones with jam, but Kade eyed it all with distaste. "I'm not very hungry these days. Sometimes it seems like too much trouble to eat."

Jesus. "You just need some good, Highland food," Nick said, keeping his voice level.

"That's right," Taffy said, casting Nick a quick, worried look as she began preparing a plate. "Now, Laird, I've had breakfast brought to your library. The others are waiting for you there."

Nick knew a dismissal when he heard one. "Yes, Taffy." He ruffled his brother's hair. "I'll come up and see you later, brat."

When he reached the door, he glanced back. His brother looked so small and frail, swallowed up by a heap of bed linens and blankets. Fear wrapped an icy hand around his heart, and he grabbed the door frame, feeling slightly dizzy.

Get a grip, man. He could not afford to panic, especially when Kade's health was at stake.

His brother glanced up from the tray on his lap and gave him a cheery little wave. "See you later."

Nick managed a smile and got himself out of there before he did something stupid—like show his brother how frightened he was. He would *not* lose Kade, not like he'd lost his own wife and son. No matter what it took, he would provide everything the boy needed to get well again. And if that meant he had to tie Victoria Knight to a chair to get her to stay at Kinglas, he would bloody well do it.

Alec walked into the entrance hall as Nick came down the stairs.

"They're waiting for you in the library," his friend said.

"You're not joining us?"

"No, I'm going upstairs to pack up my gear. I'll be heading out before lunch."

That gave Nick a jolt. "And will Miss Knight be joining you?"

Alec cocked his head to study him. "If you play your cards right, I think you can convince her to stay."

"Any suggestions?" Nick asked sarcastically. "I've been spectacularly unsuccessful so far."

"Just tell her how much you need her," Alec said. "And mean it this time."

"Christ, man, I do need her. Kade needs her."

Alec clapped him on the shoulder. "Just say that." He started up the stairs, but then turned back. "Arnprior, if you fail to treat Miss Knight with the respect she deserves, I'll come back and murder you."

"As I said earlier, I will treat her like a royal princess."

Alec let out a guffaw. "Well then, see that you do."

Shaking his head at the man's odd sense of humor, Nick strode to the library.

His brothers and the woman he hoped would be his new governess were gathered around the low table at the window, which held a generous cold collation. Miss Knight was rigidly perched on the edge of the chaise, another cup of coffee and an untouched scone before her. No wonder she was as slender as a reed—the woman apparently never ate. She and Kade should be perfect for each other.

Perhaps Braden was making her nervous, since he was pacing and looking ready to jump out of his skin. Only Royal was availing himself of a hearty breakfast, plowing his way through a mountain of ham, cheese, and pastries. His enthusiasm might also account for Miss Knight's lack of appetite, since she was regarding Royal with a vaguely horrified expression.

If he weren't so tense himself, Nick would have laughed. Royal could always be counted on to eat, even in the middle of a crisis or a raging battle. During the war, Nick had encountered him more than once crouched behind a hedge or in a ditch and calmly eating whatever meager victuals he'd scrounged up.

"Never know when it's going to be your last meal, old boy," Royal had said one time as cannon shot whizzed over their heads. "Might as well make the most of it."

If nothing else, Nick admired his brother's intestinal fortitude.

"Finally," Braden burst out. "What took you so long? Is Kade all right?"

"He's fine," Nick said as he settled into one of the armchairs flanking the chaise. "He'll have breakfast and then a nap."

"Poor lad looked done in," Royal said, putting down his plate.

"You have no idea," Braden said.

"Then please stop beating about the bush and tell us," Royal growled.

"You needn't be so nasty," Braden said with a huffy sort of dignity. "I simply thought Nick should hear it first. He *is* Kade's guardian."

"I'm here now," Nick said, "so there's no need to argue." He glanced at Miss Knight. "Would you be so kind as to pour me a cup of coffee?"

"Oh, of course," she said, starting a bit. She carefully prepared him a cup, as if afraid of spilling. The girl was clearly rattled. Despite Alec's assurances, Nick sensed she'd love nothing better than to bolt.

"Lord Arnprior, I feel it's not appropriate for me to be

here," she said, confirming his suspicions. "Surely this is a private family matter."

"No, you need to stay," Braden said firmly. "Since you'll be teaching Kade, you should understand what happened to him. He's going to need quite a bit of support from you to recover."

Her gaze shifted to Nick, her big blue eyes pleading for him to explain.

He sighed. "Unfortunately, Miss Knight is having some reservations about taking up the position."

Braden slowly turned to Royal with a scowl. "You're all causing trouble, aren't you? What did you do to scare off Miss Knight?"

"I didn't do anything," Royal protested.

"Ha," the governess muttered under her breath.

"Royal is mostly correct," Nick said. "The lion's share of the blame rests with your grandfather and the twins."

"Then forget about them," Braden said impatiently. "It's Kade who needs help."

"I'd say *all* your brothers need help, Mr. Kendrick," the governess replied. "Not that it's any of my business," she added hastily.

"Perhaps, but not like Kade does," Braden countered. "The others are just being stupid and stubborn, but they're harmless. It's different for Kade. He's just a boy, and he's had an awful time of it."

"I'm truly sorry to hear that," she said quietly.

The sympathetic warmth on her pretty features was in sharp contrast to her rigid posture. It told Nick she wasn't entirely immune to Braden's plea.

Solve the biggest problem first, then tackle the rest once you've got her committed.

"Perhaps Braden is correct—we needn't worry about my other brothers," Nick said, rubbing his chin in a thoughtful fashion.

"Really?" she asked, clearly skeptical.

"Kade is my immediate concern. He would be the main focus of your energies, regardless of any other duties you agree to take on."

When she opened her mouth, likely to raise an objection, Nick forestalled her. "The choice of what duties to assume is yours."

Royal rolled his eyes, but he held his fire. He knew Nick *would* throw him off the battlements if he kept interfering. Besides, he was now as worried about Kade as Nick was. For all of them, that took precedence over everything.

Miss Knight regarded him with a troubled expression. Nick calmly waited her out.

Finally, she let out a sigh. "Very well, my lord. I'm willing to defer my decision, pending the results of this discussion."

"Thank you, Miss Knight," Nick said, giving her a warm smile.

She blushed and gave him a tentative smile in return.

Braden whooshed out a relieved breath. "Yes, thank you, ma'am. I don't know how much you know about Kade . . ."

"I know he's an accomplished musician," she said. "But that he suffers from uncertain health."

"That's one of the reasons I wish to become a physician," Braden said.

"Then he's a very lucky boy," she said with an approving nod.

Braden threw his brother an anguished grimace. "We never should have let him go away to school, Nick. We should have kept him safe at home."

"Kade has always been rather sickly," Nick explained to the governess. "He studied here, with tutors, until last year. That's when I placed him at Eskbank Academy in Glasgow."

"It was because of Kade's blasted music," Royal said

grimly. "We couldn't get good teachers daft enough to move to a remote castle in the Highlands."

Her eyebrows went up, but she refrained from pointing out the obvious.

"Kade pestered Nick for months about going to school," Braden said. "He pestered all of us, actually, and eventually wore us down."

"I chose Eskbank," Nick said, "because it has an excellent reputation for academics and music, as well as a headmaster who believes in progressive teaching methods." He'd had no intention of handing his brother to anyone who would mistreat him or neglect his health. "It's also in Glasgow, where Braden attends university."

"That way, I could keep an eye on Kade, or so I thought," Braden said in a bitter tone. "He was having trouble, but I didn't even realize it."

"But he seemed to be doing well," Royal said. "At least that was my impression when he was home on his summer holidays."

"He was doing well," Nick said. "I'm sure of it."

In fact, Kade had been eager to return to school and to his music tutors.

"What changed?" Miss Knight asked.

"He got a new head of house this term," Braden said. "And a new head boy."

Like other schools, Eskbank was divided into several houses, each supervised by a teacher who served as head. Head boy was usually the most senior pupil in the house.

"And?" Nick prompted.

"The new head teacher, a man named Corbin, took a sharp dislike to him," Braden said. "He began to single out Kade for all sorts of silly infractions, some of them invented."

"Good God," Royal growled. "How could anyone dislike that sweet lad?"

Braden shrugged. "The man's a bully, and bullies pick on those whom they perceive are weak. Corbin made it his mission to punish Kade whenever he had the chance. Those punishments included forbidding him to practice his violin."

"Christ," Nick muttered. Now it was beginning to make sense.

"The poor boy," Miss Knight said, shaking her head.

"When did he finally tell you about this?" Nick asked, forcing himself to remain calm.

"Not until he fell ill, and I brought him to Kendrick House. That's our residence in Glasgow," Braden explained to Miss Knight.

Nick frowned. "But I came down to Glasgow as soon as you wrote to me. Kade never said a word about any of this."

He'd driven like a demon to get to Kade's bedside and had stayed there for over a week. That vigil had been agony, all the old sorrows and guilt surfacing to torment him while he struggled with fear of losing Kade. The morning the lad's fever had finally broken and he smiled up at him with clear eyes was the morning Nick had started to believe in God again.

He'd only returned to Kinglas when he was certain Kade wouldn't relapse. He trusted that Braden and the residence staff—along with the best physicians in Glasgow—would properly care for the boy until he could finally come home.

"Kade didn't want to tell you," Braden said quietly. "He knows you worry about all of us, and he didn't wish to burden you."

"Oh, God," Royal said, pressing his hands to his eyes.

Frustration and guilt made Nick want to drive a fist into a wall. But for now, he shoved aside those emotions. This was about his little brother, not him. "Did Corbin physically abuse Kade?"

Miss Knight made a distressed sound as she covered her mouth, clearly understanding what he was asking.

Most boys who'd gone away to school knew what could happen even in the best establishments—beatings and degrading assaults that could scar a boy, physically and mentally. Nick had never experienced such humiliations, nor had his older siblings. Even as children, they'd been more than capable of defending themselves in the occasionally rough environment of boarding school.

Not Braden, though, nor Kade. That was why Nick had been especially careful when selecting their schools.

"Mr. Corbin never physically hurt Kade," Braden said. "He knew you would never put up with that."

"Did someone else hurt him?" Royal asked. He looked as sick as Nick felt.

"Yes. Lord Kincannon's oldest son, Richard," Braden replied. "He was appointed head boy for Kade's house this term. That's when circumstances took a bad turn."

Nick had gone to school with Kincannon. He'd been a mean-spirited weasel, and it sounded like the son had followed in his footsteps. "What happened?"

"Another student was a particular target for Richard and his cronies. That little boy also suffered a severe caning at the hands of Mr. Corbin for a very minor infraction. Kade was outraged by the mistreatment and complained to the headmaster."

"Damn," Royal said with a grimace. "He should have written to us, instead."

Miss Knight looked startled. "Why was it wrong to go to the headmaster? Surely he would wish to know if any of his pupils were mistreated."

"Unfortunately, that is rarely the case," Nick said. "There's no greater sin a boy can commit than telling tales on another student, especially a head boy or someone else senior."

She went rigid with disapproval. "That's ridiculous."

"Any sane person would agree with you," he said.

"The headmaster wasn't the problem," Braden said. "In fact, he reprimanded both Mr. Corbin and Kincannon's son. *That* was the problem. Richard was furious Kade had complained. He and some other senior boys waited until the headmaster was away overnight and then pulled Kade out of bed and dragged him out to the privy. They shoved his head inside the . . ." He glanced at Miss Knight. "Well, you know. Then . . . then they urinated on him."

Braden hastily turned away to peer out the window, obviously struggling to hold back tears. Nick no longer wanted to put his hand through a wall—he wanted to murder someone.

"Goddammit," Royal spat out. "I'm going down there right now, and I'm going to murder those little bastards." He pushed himself out of his chair. "And then I'm going to murder that bloody teacher, too."

Nick shared his thirst for vengeance, but the last thing he needed was a Kendrick brother committing mayhem and making the situation even more complicated.

"No, you're not. Sit down, Royal," he said.

His brother glared at him. "Sod off. If you're not going to handle this, I will."

"Sit. Down," Nick said again through clenched teeth. He had no wish to fight with his hardheaded brother, who was so angry he just *might* murder someone.

Miss Knight's calm voice cut through the tension. "Mr. Kendrick, I don't think Braden is finished," she said to Royal. "Surely it makes sense to hear all the facts before making any decisions on future actions."

Royal turned his fiery gaze on her. "Why do you even care? You're leaving, aren't you?"

She flinched, but then rose to her feet, holding Royal's gaze. "I care enough to know that you won't do your little brother any good by committing an act of violence, no matter how great the provocation."

Royal loomed large over her, seething with fury. Yet, the girl didn't back down. For such a frail-looking lass, she showed courage that was both surprising and impressive.

Braden turned around, now in control of himself. "She's right. You need to know the rest."

"Royal, please sit," Nick said. "Once we know everything, we'll figure out how to respond."

His brother glanced at Miss Knight, who nodded and gently patted his forearm. He muttered something under his breath and then thumped back down into his chair.

Holy hell. The girl had gotten his stubborn, hotheaded brother to cool down. It was a bloody miracle. Nick stared, transfixed by her calm, lovely features. She met his gaze with a quizzical little smile, and then resumed her seat.

He tore his gaze away and focused on Braden. "Go on, lad."

Braden gave a tight nod. "Kade said that was the worst part. After that, they dragged him to the courtyard and threw buckets of cold water on him—to clean him off, they said. But they wouldn't let him dry himself or go back to bed. They locked him outside, soaking wet and dressed only in his nightshirt. He spent the night huddled in a doorway. The porter found him the next morning, all but frozen."

"Jesus," Nick whispered. The image of his frail little brother, abused, alone and shivering with cold, tore at his soul. He'd experienced a great deal of tragedy in his personal life, and had survived the horrors of war. But this vile and senseless act . . . well, it might tip him over the edge. That Kade had suffered through such an ordeal without a shred of support was almost more than Nick could bear.

"Why the hell didn't he wake someone up?" Royal asked in an anguished voice.

Braden grimaced. "He was embarrassed, and he didn't want to make things worse for himself or the other boy."

"You mean they would have done even more to him?" Miss Knight asked in an outraged tone. "That's insane."

"Notions of male honor frequently are," Nick said.

"Because men are idiots," Royal said bitterly.

Her troubled expression made it clear she agreed with him.

"By the next day, Kade had developed a high fever," Braden said. "When the headmaster returned from his trip that afternoon, he sent word to me at Kendrick House. I brought Kade home immediately, and the rest you know."

Nick pressed a hand to his head, feeling as if his brain was about to erupt from his skull. He needed to think, and to do what was best for Kade. Too often in the past, he'd reacted *without* thinking, letting anger drive his actions. That had only led to more heartache, and his family had already suffered enough of that to last ten lifetimes.

"Well, what are we going to do?" Royal said.

"First, I'm going to talk to Kade, and then I'm going to Glasgow to take it up with the headmaster," Nick said. He would also both deal with Corbin and speak to Lord Kincannon about his disgusting whelp of a son.

"No, you won't," Braden said, settling his spectacles firmly on his nose.

Royal scoffed. "Why not?"

"Because I've already taken care of it," Braden replied. "As soon as Kade told me, I went to speak to the headmaster. I insisted that Kincannon's son be punished, and that Corbin be removed from his position."

"I'm sure he jumped right on that, didn't he?" Royal asked with heavy sarcasm.

"He did, actually. Richard was sent down and Mr. Corbin was let go without a recommendation."

Nick let out a disbelieving laugh. "How did you manage that?" While it was true that Braden had more brains than the rest of them put together and was mature for his age, he was still young and fairly unworldly.

"I threatened him with you, Nick," he said. "I told him that you would make it your mission to shut the school down and ruin the reputation of everyone who worked there."

"And he believed you?"

Braden gave him a puzzled smile. "Of course. In fact, I thought the poor man was going to have a nervous collapse on the spot."

Royal let out a short, harsh laugh. "Clearly, he's heard of Lord Arnprior's fearsome reputation."

"Yes, and it terrified him," Braden said with a satisfied little smile.

Nick winced as he shot a look at Miss Knight. The last thing he wanted to do was scare the girl off with exaggerated stories of his stern nature. She, however, didn't seem the least bit perturbed by Braden's characterization. In fact, her smile suggested she approved of his brother's tactics.

"Well done, lad," Royal said. "We'll turn you into a Highland warrior yet."

Braden's shoulders came down from around his ears, and he gave a tentative smile. "Lord, I hope not."

"Royal is correct," Nick said. "You did well. But I will be calling on the headmaster the next time I'm in Glasgow. I will also be paying a visit to Lord Kincannon and speak to him about his son." He paused, grimacing. "And I must talk to Kade about this incident as well. He shouldn't be hiding things from me."

He hated that the lad had kept such a terrible secret from him.

"You can't," Braden said decisively.

"But—"

"No. You'll humiliate him even more. You know how much he looks up to you. He's afraid you'll think less of him."

"I never would," Nick protested.

"Of course you wouldn't," Braden said. "But he doesn't want to talk about it now. It's best to let it be until he's ready to raise it with you himself."

"When did you become so smart?" Royal said with a wry snort.

Braden rolled his eyes. "I've always been smart. Smarter than the rest of you, certainly."

"I think you will make a very fine doctor," Miss Knight said warmly.

At least there was one member of the family she approved of.

Nick sighed. "All right, I'll be guided by you for now. But we've got to do something to help Kade. We can't act like this didn't happen."

"But we are doing something," Braden said in a patient voice, as if Nick was a bit slow. "We're hiring Miss Knight to be his tutor."

The governess blinked, her expression going from thoughtful to wary. "But I'm not a tutor. Wouldn't Kade be better served by a man with the appropriate experience in this sort of situation?"

Braden shook his head. "Not after that traumatic experience at Eskbank. Frankly, I think Kade will be more comfortable with a woman teaching him. I told Nick that last month."

She darted a questioning look at Nick.

He nodded. "It was Braden's idea to acquire a female teacher for Kade, and I now understand why he was so insistent. But it was my idea to have you also teach deportment to my other brothers."

When she began to scowl, he held up a hand. "We will defer that subject for now."

"Or forever," she muttered.

The knot inside his chest began to unravel. It seemed like she might be willing to take the job, after all.

Royal sighed. "It seems like we do need a woman's influence around this blasted place after all."

Nick raised his eyebrows. "Well, Miss Knight, what do you think? Are you up to the challenge?"

She frowned, clearly debating with herself. "Subject to Kade's needs and wishes, I will have full control over course material and teaching methods?"

He nodded, knowing he could trust her to treat Kade gently.

"And you will see to it that Mr. MacDonald will cease his campaign against me?"

"He will, but if he doesn't, I will," Braden said sternly.

His brothers seemed to join Nick in holding their collective breath, waiting for her decision. When she finally met Nick's gaze, her expression was both wry and resigned.

"Then, yes, Lord Arnprior," she said. "I will accept the position."

Chapter Nine

Victoria corrected Kade's fingering on the keys of the Broadwood grand piano. "Try that. And perhaps it might help to slow down while you're starting out, since it's such a challenging piece."

The boy gave her a comical grimace. "My music teacher in Glasgow used to tell me that I always pushed too hard when starting a new piece of music. He said I needed to learn patience if I truly wished to excel."

She smiled. "Don't tell anyone, but I've always thought patience is overrated. I don't think there's anything wrong in tackling something head-on and with enthusiasm."

Victoria invariably approached a new composition, especially something as technically complex as Beethoven's Sonata Twenty-one, with a sense of excitement that made her forget everything but mastering the challenge.

"I won't tell Nick you said that," Kade said with a chuckle. "He'd be shocked to hear my governess encouraging me to rebel against one of the cardinal virtues."

She leaned closer on the padded piano bench, as if sharing a confidence. "We'll make it our little secret, shall we? We can be rebels together."

The shy pleasure in his smile warmed her more than the roaring fire in the hearth.

"I'm so glad you came all this way to teach me," he said, returning his attention to the music stacked on top of the piano. "I hate that Nick worries about me. But he seems to feel better knowing I've got you to look after me. Not that I truly need anyone to look after me," he hastily added. "I'm not a baby."

"Indeed no," she said gravely. "In fact, I believe I spot a few gray hairs sprouting on the top of your head."

Kade snickered.

In truth, he was little more than a boy, and a very sensitive one at that. Every time she thought about the trauma he'd suffered she wanted to cry or rage at the heavens. She could hardly imagine that anyone could inflict so much harm on a child, though that was a foolishly naïve view of the world. Her own experience had taught her that cruelty lurked everywhere, even among the highest ranks of society. Victoria could almost believe that wealthy, powerful men like Thomas Fletcher were the worst, because they often used their privilege to abuse others.

As Kade began again, his fingers dancing over the keys, she fetched an Argand lamp from the sideboard and carefully placed it on the piano.

They were in the private family drawing room, waiting for the others to come upstairs after dinner. Since dusk came so early to the Highlands at this time of year, the Kendricks kept sensible—if unfashionable—country hours. She and Kade had already gotten into the habit of excusing themselves before the sweets course, going upstairs to spend time at the piano before the tea tray arrived and the brothers joined them.

She'd taken up the position of tutor with a sort of grim determination, unable to turn her back on Kade after listening to Braden's horrific tale. She would have done it for the boy's sake, of course, but there was another element that had caught her by surprise—her inability to say no to Arnprior. He'd clearly been devastated by Kade's plight, his grief and fury all but shimmering around him like a dark halo. He'd controlled his reaction with admirable discipline, but Victoria wasn't fooled. That he blamed himself for what happened to Kade was obvious. That he felt rather helpless in managing the situation was apparent, too.

So, when he'd quietly asked her to stay, she'd said yes. She wouldn't have been able to live with herself if she'd turned her back on the Kendrick family when there was even a remote chance she could help. Not even if it meant spending the winter holed up in a drafty, remote castle with what must be the most stubborn group of men in Scotland.

True to his word, however, the earl had somehow managed to bring his brothers under a semblance of control. It had been almost two weeks since she'd accepted the position, and Alec had departed for Glasgow with Braden. In that time, the twins had stopped bedeviling her, Royal had ceased being entirely surly, and even Mr. MacDonald had mostly pulled in his horns.

It helped that everyone at Kinglas was devoted to Kade, so when the earl decreed that Victoria was vital to achieving the mission of restoring the boy's health—even if she was a woman *and* a Sassenach—the family was forced, however reluctantly, to fall into line.

Kade's fingers stumbled when he launched into the final bars of the rondo.

"Pianissimo," she murmured. "This section is more delicate, almost like dance music." She reached in front of him and played a few notes with her left hand to illustrate.

"Oh, I see. Then I build to a rush at the end, is that right?"

She smiled. "Exactly. Try it again."

This time, he got it. Victoria watched in admiration as

his fingers flew over the keyboard, easily managing the rapid scales of the left hand, offset by the trills of the right. It was a composition that defeated performers with more experience, yet Kade dashed through the notes, throwing his soul into the performance.

When he ended with a triumphant flourish, she enthusiastically applauded. "That was splendid, Kade. You'll have the entire piece down in no time."

He swiveled to face her, joy shining in blue eyes that were almost a mirror image of the earl's. Whenever Kade sat down to the piano or practiced his violin, he seemed to forget his troubles. He was beginning to heal from his trauma, making steady progress every day.

Teaching Kade, knowing that she was truly helping him, had brought Victoria a peace of mind and a sense of purpose that had been missing since that awful night at Welgate Manor.

"Thank you," he said. "I love Beethoven, and this piece is particularly wonderful. Wouldn't it be grand to be able to write something so beautiful? I wish I could."

"Have you ever tried composing?"

A little crease appeared between his eyebrows. "I suppose I never really thought to do so. Besides, I'm not that talented."

"You never know until you try."

"Have you ever written music?"

She wrinkled her nose. "Yes, and I am definitely *not* talented in that regard. The results were appalling." One of her music teachers at school had delivered that message, although Victoria's ears had already told her the same. "My destiny is to be a teacher."

"But you're an awfully good musician."

"Not as good as you." She thought for a moment about what she wanted to tell him. It had to be in a way that didn't embarrass him or indicate that she knew his deepest secrets.

"The greatest composers are more than just technically proficient. They also feel great emotion, and see the world with a sensitivity and perception most of us lack. They can draw on the experiences of their lives—good or bad—and translate their feelings into music in a way that truly touches their listeners. You already bring that sort of emotion to your playing. It's something similar with composing, if that makes sense to you."

"I think I understand," he said softly. "It's almost like explaining without having to talk about it."

"Exactly. Some of the best composers did not lead easy lives. But they used their pain, sorrows, and joys to bring their music to life . . . to make it sing." She patted his shoulder. "I believe you have that kind of sensitivity, Kade. I'd bet you a bob you could write something lovely if you put your mind to it."

"You really think so?" he asked with a touching eagerness.

"I do, but only if you wish to. There's no need to push." She had the sense, though, that immersing himself even more deeply in his music would help.

"It might be fun," he said. "If you don't mind that I spend a little more time on that instead of practicing."

"Not at all. And I am happy to assist in any way I can."

He surprised her by throwing his arms around her neck. When he pulled back from the hug, his eyes were shining with boyish happiness. "Thank you, Miss Knight. Have I told you lately how splendid you are?"

It took her a moment to be able to control her voice. "I believe you have, sir, and I am most grateful for your approval."

"It's jolly to have a lady around the house again," he said as he turned back to the keyboard and began practicing trills. "Although Taffy is wonderful, of course. It's not that

I don't appreciate my brothers and my grandfather, but they can be a bit . . ."

"Rambunctious and argumentative?" she finished in a droll tone.

"Yes, and they're not really interested in my music. Nick tries, of course, but he's usually too busy to listen. I'm so happy he's home, though. I missed him terribly during the war."

"I'm sure you did."

His hands stilled. "He raised me, you know. My mother died when I was born, and I barely remember my father, since he died when I was three. Nick had to pick up the slack." He flashed her an uncertain smile. "What a burden we are for him."

"I doubt he feels that way," she said. "But I am sorry you never knew your mother."

"Thank you. Janet was very kind to me, though. She was also musical, and played the harp for me whenever she stayed at Kinglas. I liked that a lot."

Victoria had never heard anyone at the castle mention that name. "Who is Janet?"

He shot her a startled glance. "She was Nick's wife. Didn't you know he'd been married?"

Her brain seemed to trip over itself. "Ah, no, actually."

Kade suddenly looked uncomfortable. "It *was* quite a long time ago. I was only about seven when she died. Nick doesn't like to talk about it, so we generally don't mention her."

That was an understatement, since she'd heard not one reference to Arnprior's wife or his widowed state. In fact, she'd seen no evidence of the lady's existence at all.

Kade plunked one of the minor keys, playing a sad little note. "I still miss her."

"I'm sorry," she said softly. "It's sad when someone we love passes away."

"She fell ill very suddenly. Nick was quite broken up about it."

Losing his wife at such a young age? No wonder the earl was so somber a man. "I can imagine."

"Still, it wasn't as bad as what happened to—" Kade broke off, rolling his lips into a tight line.

"Happened to?" she prompted.

He flashed her a smile that was more like a grimace. "Never mind. I really shouldn't be airing the family's dirty clouts, as Grandda says. Nick wouldn't like me gossiping, either."

Victoria had to squelch an unseemly curiosity. The Kendrick family past was none of her business. "Quite right too, young man. Gossiping with your governess—how shocking. Everyone would think we're *terribly* vulgar."

His brow cleared. "Gosh, that sounds rather fun. Perhaps we—"

He broke off when the door to the drawing room opened. When Arnprior entered, Victoria felt her cheeks grow hot.

"You two appear to be up to some sort of mischief," the earl said, strolling over to join them. "What are you talking about?"

She and Kade exchanged sheepish glances. "Nothing," they chorused.

"From your guilty expressions, I suspect such is not the case," he replied in a sardonic tone.

"We've been discussing music, my lord," Victoria said. The last thing she'd want him to know was that they'd been talking about his wife. Her employer was a reserved, private man, and if he didn't wish to discuss his late wife—or even acknowledge her existence—then it behooved her to respect that.

Kade gave his brother a beatific smile. "That's right. We've been discussing Beethoven."

Arnprior propped his hands on his kilted hips—his tall,

lean form looked wonderful in the traditional garb—and blew out an exaggerated sigh. "I'm going to have to keep an eye on the pair of you. I have the distinct impression you are not to be trusted."

Kade let out a gleeful chuckle. "Yes, it's fun to finally have a partner in crime."

"You're as bad as the twins," Arnprior said.

"Worse," Kade said.

The earl laughed, his handsome face lighting with rare amusement. Heavens, the man was devastating when he smiled like that, especially when that smile was directed at her. Victoria was all but ready to melt into a puddle at his booted feet.

It was a ridiculous thought. She was not the sort of woman to melt at any man's feet.

Arnprior was about to reply when the rest of the Kendricks strolled in, followed by a footman and Mrs. Taffy with the tea service. The earl gave Victoria a nod and headed to the mahogany writing desk in the corner. He spent most evenings at that desk, attending to his correspondence while she and Kade practiced the piano or chatted with the twins over tea. Royal occasionally joined them, although he wasn't much of a conversationalist.

Tonight, however, Angus had also stomped in behind his grandsons, two of his beloved Skye terriers trotting in his wake. The old man gave Victoria a scowl before flopping into one of the armchairs in front of the fireplace, making his continued low opinion of her abundantly clear.

She swallowed a sigh. Although the old fellow had ceased his campaign of outright hostilities, he was still unhappy with her presence. Why remained something of a mystery, since Victoria was not, as he'd put it, trying to turn his grandsons into spoiled dandies. She'd finally decided he had a general dislike of English persons, and that it was best to ignore him whenever possible.

"Hullo, Grandda," Kade said, waving to him. The lad revered the old curmudgeon, and went out of his way to please him. Some days, she couldn't imagine how such a nice boy like Kade had survived in the tough world of the Kendrick men.

"Laddie, ye just had dinner with me," his grandfather said.

"I know, but you rarely join us for tea, so I'm happy to see you."

One corner of Angus's mouth twitched. She supposed even he couldn't resist Kade's artless charm. "Maybe I fancy a bit of music tonight," he said.

"Miss Knight and I have been practicing a Beethoven sonata," Kade said. "Would you like to hear that?"

The old man scoffed. "Now, why would I want to hear some frippery music by a foreigner? A good reel is what I have a mind for."

Taffy, who'd been arranging the tea things on the low table in front of the chaise, slowly straightened up and turned a gimlet eye on Angus. When he flushed a dull red, Victoria wasn't surprised. If there was one person with the ability to shame Angus MacDonald, it was Mrs. Taffy. They had what could only be called an interesting relationship, although Victoria had no desire to know the particulars.

"Angus, let the boy play what he wants," the earl said over his shoulder. "Beethoven sounds like a prime choice, Kade. I'd like to hear it."

"I must say, I rather agree with Grandda," Graeme said, reaching for a macaroon from the tiered plate of pastries. When Taffy slapped his hand, he yanked it back as if he'd been burned.

"Ye'll want to be waiting now for a moment," she said in

a reproving tone. "*After* the earl and yer grandfather have been served their cups."

"And you will listen to whatever Kade plays," the earl said, pinning Graeme with a stern look.

"But—"

Grant elbowed his twin in the ribs. "Shut it, Graeme." Then he smiled at Kade. "Play whatever you want, laddie. We'll enjoy it either way."

Kade gave his brother a rueful grin. "It's all right. I like the old reels, too."

"Right. I'll fetch my bagpipes to play with ye," Angus said, hauling himself from his chair.

"No!" the twins yelled. In fact, all the men appeared disconcerted.

The old man regarded his grandsons reproachfully. "But ye all love the pipes."

"Not the way you play them," Royal said ruthlessly.

"You heard him the first night you stayed here," Grant said to Victoria, as if she could possibly forget.

"Oh," she said. "I thought he was trying to be . . ."

Grant morosely shook his head.

"I see." She couldn't help giving the old man a sympathetic glance, since he looked so disappointed. "It wasn't that bad. In fact, it was quite . . . stirring."

Everyone stared at her like she'd gone mad.

Angus eyed her suspiciously, but then affected a casual shrug. "Well, get on with it, then," he said brusquely, waving at Kade.

"Why don't you play 'Shean Truibhais,'" Royal suggested, his brogue curling around the Gaelic name. He'd wandered over to the window that overlooked the back lawn, where he'd recommenced his brooding. As far as Victoria could tell, that was mostly what Royal did with his time when he wasn't picking a fight with the earl.

"That's Gaelic for Torn Trousers," Kade explained to her. "The reel is about how the kilt was outlawed after Culloden. The Highlanders were forced to wear trousers, so they wanted to tear them or kick them off."

"Bloody bastard Englishmen," Angus muttered.

"My, that sounds like an exciting dance," Victoria said. She rose from the piano bench. "I'll bring you a cup of tea and a scone when you're finished."

Kade nodded absently, shuffling through his sheet music. She would have to make him stop to eat, since the boy rarely thought about food unless someone reminded him.

As Kade played the lively reel, she poured out the tea, handing the cups to Grant to distribute. Grant was a very nice young man, she'd been pleased to discover, when Graeme wasn't leading him astray. Mrs. Taffy heaped up plates of biscuits and scones for the men, and then excused herself.

When Kade finished with a flourish, everyone clapped— except for Angus, who at least did nod his approval. Even the dogs barked enthusiastically, which necessitated a tart reprimand from their master.

The Kendrick family drawing room wasn't the most genteel of environments, and the men—and the dogs— could certainly be a handful. But the fact that no one was assaulting her or accusing her of murder was a distinct advantage. She was beginning to think that, with a little luck, she might make it through the winter unscathed. According to the most recent letter from Dominic, neither Lady Welgate nor her father had yet to take any action against her, and he didn't expect them to. If all remained quiet, she should be able to return to London sometime in the summer and begin to plan the opening of her girls' seminary.

She simply had to survive a winter and spring in Scotland with Lord Arnprior and his brothers first.

Graeme shoveled in another scone. "I do think . . ." he began around the enormous mouthful.

When Victoria pointedly raised her eyebrows, he grimaced, but chewed and swallowed before speaking again. She was not formally giving the twins lessons in deportment, but she couldn't refrain from the occasional quiet correction. Fortunately, looking aghast usually did the trick.

"As I was saying," Graeme said after he'd swallowed, "I still think it would be splendid if we could learn how to waltz, instead of just doing reels and country dances."

"If only we could learn how to waltz in time for Sir Duncan MacLeish's holiday ball," Grant said. He gazed dolefully at Victoria, as if he were a puppy who'd been kicked. Graeme adopted a similar expression, even going so far as to push out his lower lip.

Victoria was hard-pressed not to laugh, or to scold them for thinking she was foolish enough to fall for their blatant machinations. Yes, she might be willing to give them a little guidance now and then, but she was *not* a dancing teacher.

"Och, ye don't need to be swirlin' about like acrobats to catch the eyes of the lassies," Angus said. "There's nothing more manly and athletic than a good reel to attract a girl's notice. Even better, a sword dance."

"I doubt there will be any sword dances at Sir Duncan's affair," Royal said. He'd finally eased into a chair by the window, favoring his bad leg.

"I'd love to see a sword dance someday," Victoria said brightly, hoping to divert attention away from Graeme's unwelcome request.

Grant perked up. "We'd be happy to show you."

"And then *you* can show us how to waltz," Graeme added triumphantly.

Argh. She'd walked right into that one.

Grant jumped from his chair. "I'll just fetch some swords off the wall in the entrance hall."

Arnprior glanced up from his correspondence. "There will be absolutely *no* sword dancing in the house. I've told you that a hundred times."

"But, Nick—" Graeme started.

"No," the earl said firmly. He looked at Victoria. "It never ends well, and we have the broken furniture to prove it."

She tried not to look too relieved, although she was tempted to laugh at the mental image of the twins demolishing the sitting room. "I completely understand. Perhaps they can show me out in the courtyard, when the weather is more amenable."

When the twins groaned their dissatisfaction, their brother was unmoved. "You'll just have to be satisfied with the standard country dances, which I'm sure you can manage. Besides, Sir Duncan is an old-fashioned sort, and I doubt he will allow the waltz at any of his gatherings."

"Too scandalous for the Highlands, my lord?" Victoria asked with a smile as she carried over the pot to replenish his teacup. She could almost kiss him for coming to her rescue.

Almost?

"We're a little backwards up here, if you haven't noticed," he said, giving her a wry smile as he held up his cup.

She affected shock to cover for the fact that she was feeling flustered by the notion of kissing him. "Truly? Why, I hadn't noticed that at all."

A derisive snort from Angus told her what he thought of their playful exchange. Perhaps he thought she was flirting with his grandson, which she most decidedly was not. She was simply being . . . pleasant.

"Actually, the joke's on you, Nick," Graeme said. "They *are* going to be playing the waltz. Lady MacLeish is bringing in an orchestra from Glasgow to play all the latest music."

The earl set his cup down on the desk and gave the twins his full attention. "Really?"

Grant nodded enthusiastically. "Yes, really. We have it on good authority."

Arnprior stood and followed Victoria back to the tea table. Somehow, he managed to make the little stroll appear intimidating, or at least the twins seemed to think so. By the time he was looming over them, they looked nervous.

"And who is this good authority?" the earl asked. "Not someone you ran into *off* the estate, I hope."

Graeme flushed a bright red, while Grant went in the opposite direction, going rather pale.

On their brother's order, the twins had been confined to the estate for the last several days as a result of some incident that was apparently too shocking to discuss in front of a lady. Whatever it was, Victoria had the sense that those sorts of events happened on a regular basis.

"It was Mr. Allen who told the lads," Angus said from his corner by the fire. "They rode with me on my rounds of the tenant farms yesterday, and we stopped to have a wee dram with him. His wife heard it from Lady MacLeish herself."

The earl stared hard at his grandfather, who puffed away at his short-stemmed pipe with the easy assurance of either a man with a clear conscience or a born liar.

"That's right," Graeme said. "It was Mr. Allen who told us." He elbowed his twin. "Right?"

Grant bobbed his head like a nervous pigeon. "That's it exactly."

Arnprior studied them with disfavor. "I suppose I should be happy you're taking an interest in the workings of the estate," he finally said.

Angus removed his pipe from his mouth. "Of course ye should. It's what ye want, isn't it?"

"If it were true, I'd be delirious with joy," Arnprior replied.

"It's absolutely true," Graeme said, gazing earnestly at his big brother.

Arnprior stared down at him for a moment longer and then shrugged. "Good for you, lads. I'm sure your grandfather appreciates the help."

When he bent down to retrieve a biscuit, Victoria found herself admiring his lean hips and well-shaped backside, lovingly outlined by the draped fabric of the kilt. Not that she could *help* admiring those attributes, as impolite as that might seem, since he was standing right in front of her—at eye level, too. And although she'd never been a particular fan of the Highland costume, after seeing the earl in a kilt more than once this week, she'd decided the style was growing on her.

He straightened up. "Well, what's it to be, Miss Knight? Are you agreeable?"

She jerked her gaze upward to take in his amused expression. Good God. When had he noticed she was furtively inspecting his backside? Even worse, he obviously found it amusing to catch her in the act.

She, however, did not.

"Am I agreeable to what, my lord?" she asked, trying to adopt her most dignified manner. It was a challenge, since her face seemed to be going up in flames.

His eyebrows arched. "Why, teaching my brothers to waltz, of course. And since I already know the steps of that particular dance, I will be more than happy to lend you assistance."

"Do say yes, Miss Knight," Graeme said. "It would be the greatest thing, ever."

"Ever," Grant echoed with enthusiastic emphasis.

"Miss Knight, I beg you to do it," Royal added. "Or else these two idiots will pester us until we lose our minds."

She met the earl's sardonic gaze, resisting the unholy

desire to stick her tongue out at him—or kick him in the shins—for manipulating her so adroitly.

He'd backed her right into the position he'd chosen for her all along—and done it in front of his entire family, no less. Now he was daring her to refuse.

Chapter Ten

"Well, Miss Knight?" Nick asked again. "Shall we teach my brothers to waltz?"

She blinked several times, as if her pretty blue eyes were trying to focus. He'd caught her off guard—after catching her inspecting his arse. Her fiery blush was evidence that she wasn't the sort of woman who ogled men's backsides. Even her chest had gone pink above the narrow lace trim of her bodice. Standing over her, he could just see inside her gown where the gentle swell of her breast caused the fabric to gape. If he leaned over slightly—

Stop. It.

His reckless offer to help her teach the twins to dance was only partly explained by his desire for her to tutor his brothers. And now he was thinking of peering down the front of her gown. It mattered not a whit that she was both pretty and kind, and already making remarkable strides with Kade. Victoria Knight was still his servant, and he didn't dally with servants.

Nick didn't dally in general. In fact, he hadn't taken a woman to bed since he'd returned home from the war. He thanked God that Victoria was an exceedingly proper governess and a perfect lady, since he was finding her more enticing than he cared to admit. But he suspected she would no more flirt with her employer than she would run away and join a troupe of acrobats.

"Do you mean it, Nick?" Grant asked, looking boyishly hopeful. "You'll really help us?"

"Of course," he said. If he could persuade Victoria to help, at least something good would come out of his foolish impulse.

Sometimes, Nick could hardly believe the twins were old enough to start their own families—old enough to do something meaningful with their lives instead of acting like callow youths, tumbling from one mishap to the next. It had been a mistake to leave them without guidance for so long, with only Angus to ride herd.

Only last Sunday, they'd been caught breaking into the kirk with the intention of stealing the weekly collection. They'd done it on a lark, without a thought for the consequences. Nick had been forced to make a large donation to the kirk's building fund to make up for their bad behavior, *and* promise the vicar that his entire family would start regularly attending services.

As for the twins spending so much time helping Angus with estate business? Nick had serious doubts about that.

"Pah," scoffed his grandfather, puffing on his clay pipe. "As if the laird doesn't have better things to do than teach ye how to prance about like a pair of ninnies. It's bloody ridiculous."

"I quite agree, Mr. MacDonald," Victoria said, finally finding her voice.

Clearly, things had come to a sorry pass when the poor girl had to rely on her mortal enemy for support.

"Will wonders never cease," marveled Angus, his bushy white eyebrows reaching up to his hairline. "The Sassenach agrees with me. Well, that's it, lads. Miss Knight will *not* be teaching ye to dance, so ye'd best get over this nonsense of acting like bloody Englishmen."

Graeme and Grant looked so crestfallen that Nick had to swallow a laugh.

"You misunderstand me, Mr. MacDonald," Victoria said. "I meant that it wasn't necessary for the earl to inconvenience himself. I'm perfectly capable of teaching the twins how to waltz without his help."

"You mean you'll do it?" Grant asked with comical hope.

"It would seem I don't have a choice." Her little scowl and disapproving sniff when she glanced at Nick were adorably grumpy.

"Huzzah," said Graeme, jumping up. He grabbed his brother by the arm and pulled him to his feet. "What do you want us to do first?"

She pointed to the space between the chaise and the window. "You should pull some of the chairs out of the way and roll up the carpet. That way you won't trip and kill yourselves."

"Never fear, Miss Knight," Graeme said, "we're as light on our feet as anything. Best sword dancers in the county, in fact."

Royal snorted as he got out of their way. "Lumbering on your feet, more like it."

The twins protested, but they did lumber about, dragging furniture and talking over each other as they wrestled with the carpet. Victoria peered at them with concern, as if she'd just realized what she'd gotten herself into. The twins were tall, braw lads, although still a bit gangly. Only Logan was bigger and stronger than them. He was a veritable mountain of a man, able to toss the caber with awe-inspiring ease.

Not strong enough to save Cameron, was he?

Nick slammed the door on that flood of ugly memories.

No good ever came of thinking about the brother who'd fled from Kinglas years ago.

He flinched at the gentle touch on his forearm.

"My lord, is something wrong?" Victoria asked in an undertone.

"Not at all," he said brusquely. He glanced at the twins, who waited impatiently for their lesson. "I'm just afraid the lads will crush those wee feet of yours."

Her luminous smile seared away some of the ice around his heart. "My feet aren't little at all. And I'll be fine."

"I'd be more than happy to demonstrate the steps." He could think of few things more likely to dispel his ugly old ghosts than taking a pretty girl into his arms. It was a foolish temptation, but right now he wouldn't mind playing the fool.

Her gaze darted away for a moment. But soon she looked back, her governess expression firmly restored. "Thank you, my lord, but I'm sure you wish to return to your correspondence."

That she found his offer was neither welcome nor appropriate was clear. She was correct, of course, and he should feel relieved.

He didn't.

"Later," he said. "I have a feeling that watching my brothers learning to waltz will be more entertaining than writing a letter to my banker."

She gave him a wry smile by way of reply before joining the twins.

"Do you want me to play a waltz, Miss Knight?" Kade asked. "I'm sure I could stumble along all right if you had one in your music."

"No, that's all right, Kade. I'm going to show your brothers the basic steps, and then I'm going to play a waltz for them."

Grant peered down at her. "But who are we going to dance with if you're playing the piano?"

"You're going to dance with each other," she said calmly.

The twins stared at her and then at each other, clearly appalled.

"But . . . but I can't do that with another man," spluttered Graeme, "even if he is my brother. *Especially* if he's my brother."

His tone suggested she'd all but asked them to perform an unnatural act.

She tilted her head. "But you dance with other men when you perform reels and the sword dance, do you not?"

"Aye, but we're not hugging each other," Grant said in a disgusted tone.

"Muttonheads," Angus muttered. Still, the old fellow was starting to look amused.

"Young ladies dance with each other all the time when they're taking lessons," Victoria said.

"That's different," protested Graeme.

"Hmm." She tapped her chin. "Why is it different?"

"Because it just is," said Grant, awkwardly waving his arms.

Royal, who'd settled onto the chaise, flashed an evil grin. "Such impeccable logic."

Graeme shot him a scowl. "Bugger you."

"Watch your language," Nick said sharply. "You're in the presence of a lady."

The twins pulled almost identical grimaces. "Sorry, Miss Knight," said Graeme.

"Sorry, Miss Knight," Grant echoed.

"Apologies accepted," she said. "And if you don't wish to learn how to waltz, I will completely understand." She nodded and started to turn away.

Their loud protests brought her back around. "Ah, do I take it that you're now willing to partner each other?"

The boys looked at each other. "I suppose so," said Graeme. "If it means we eventually get to dance with *real* girls."

"That is the point of this exercise, isn't it?" she said with an approving smile.

By now, Royal was gasping with laughter, and Kade had clapped both hands over his mouth to contain his giggles. Even Angus seemed reluctantly impressed with the masterful way she'd managed the twins.

Watching his dainty, ladylike governess ruthlessly manipulate his brothers was the most entertaining thing Nick had seen in a long time.

Victoria shot Royal a stern look that had little effect on the rampant hilarity that Nick was glad to see. His brother never laughed anymore, and it was wonderful to see Royal's eyes once more light up with genuine amusement.

"Just ignore him," she said to the twins, who were glaring at Royal. She glanced down at their boots. "Now, those aren't exactly dancing shoes, are they?"

"We don't have any of those," Grant said.

"We'll have to order some if you're serious about learning dances for balls and parties," she said. "For now, you'd best just take off your boots. It'll be easier to do the turns in your stocking feet."

Once they'd obediently pulled off their boots, with Victoria looking rather horrified by the state of their socks, she showed them how to hold each other.

"You're the male partner, Grant, so hold your lady just so," she said, taking Graeme's hand and placing it on his brother's shoulder.

"Why does he get to be the man?" Graeme protested.

"Because he's nicer than you are," Victoria replied. "And for the purpose of this exercise, you are a frivolous young lady with a reputation for breaking hearts. All the mothers are talking about you, and not with approval."

"They are not," he said indignantly.

"That's not what I heard," she said, neatly making her point.

Graeme *was* developing a reputation among the local families, and not one that pleased Nick.

The lad grumbled a bit longer, which Victoria ignored. With light touches on their arms and precise instructions, she began to steer them through the steps. Unfortunately, the twins, who were normally athletic and quite graceful, kept stumbling over each other's feet.

"Ouch," Grant yelped when Graeme trod heavily on his toes.

"Let me show you, Grant," she said in a patient tone. "And you watch carefully, Graeme."

When she partnered with Grant, the lad flashed his twin a taunting grin. Nick couldn't blame him. Any man in his right mind would be happy to hold the graceful Victoria Knight in his arms.

She jabbed Grant in the shoulder. "Pay attention," she said sternly.

"Yes, miss," Grant replied in a meek voice.

Slowly and carefully, she moved him through the steps, explaining and counting out as she went along.

"Do you see now?" she asked, bringing him to a halt.

He nodded.

"All right," she said. "I'm going to add in the music, and I want you and Graeme to try it on your own. Just take it slowly and focus on the tempo."

She hurried to the piano bench, where Kade slid over to make room. She flashed the twins an encouraging smile. "Ready?"

The lads, holding on to each other tightly, looked as serious as if they were about to charge into battle. "Yes, miss," said Grant.

She began to play a familiar waltz, one Nick had heard

countless times. The lads began to shuffle through the steps with Victoria coaching them over the music. After a few minutes watching them cautiously twirl about the cleared space, she increased the tempo.

"That's it," she called out. "Keep up the pace."

Grim-faced, the lads stomped through the dance.

"Good God," Angus muttered. "That's bloody awful."

"They are rather butchering it," Kade said, wincing when Graeme almost tripped through a turn. It was a miracle they both hadn't ended up on their arses.

"Ignore the critics," Victoria called to the twins. "You're doing fine. Just keep counting your steps."

By this time, Royal was all but apoplectic with laughter, and Nick had to work to keep a straight face.

"I think I've got it," Grant crowed as he flung his brother through a wide turn.

Too wide, as it turned out. They clipped one of the armchairs and Graeme's stocking feet slipped on the polished floor. As he fell, Grant made a valiant attempt to grab him, but one of the terriers dashed forward, dove between Grant's legs, and tripped him. Both twins went down with a crash so thundering that the teacups rattled and the floor shook.

Everyone froze, including the dogs. Then the twins started yelling.

"Get off me, you clod," Graeme shouted, pushing at his brother.

"I'm trying," Grant yelped. "My bloody shirt is caught in your belt."

"Stop struggling," Nick ordered, striding over. He managed to untangle them with a minimum of damage and hauled them to their feet.

"You're not hurt, are you?" Victoria asked. She'd rushed over, fluttering around them like an agitated butterfly.

Graeme winced and rubbed his arse. "I think I broke my—"

"Careful," Nick growled.

"They're fine," said Royal, who'd limped over to inspect them. "It takes more than a little fall to damage their thick skulls."

Grant gave Victoria a mortified grimace. "I thought we had the hang of it, but I guess not."

"We were doing fine until those confounded mutts charged over," Graeme said with a glare at his grandfather.

The dogs, obviously aware they'd disgraced themselves, slunk back to take refuge under Angus's chair.

"Sorry, lads," their grandfather said. "But even the wee doggies could have made a better job of the dance than ye did."

The twins cast an imploring look at their teacher. "Was it so very awful?" Graeme asked.

"Ah . . ." Victoria left it at that, clearly not wanting to hurt their feelings.

"Perhaps they need to see it done correctly," Nick said. "By dancers who know the steps."

She frowned. "I don't think—"

"That's the ticket," Grant enthused. "Miss Knight, if we could see you and Nick do it properly, I'm sure we could figure it out in no time."

"Nick's quite the accomplished dancer, as I recall," Royal drawled. "Lord Arnprior in his dress kilt has caused many a female to flutter and swoon at the regimental balls."

"Really?" Graeme peered at Nick as if he saw him in a new light. "Women used to swoon over you?"

"Of course not," Nick said, glaring at Royal.

His brother shrugged. "But you do like to dance."

Nick couldn't deny it. He found few things more enjoyable than taking a pretty woman into his arms for a waltz, or even an old-fashioned country dance. Besides, it was all in a good cause, wasn't it? It was about helping the lads

to polish their manners, not about indulging in the desire to
hold his pretty governess in his arms.

"What say you, Miss Knight? Shall we give it a whirl?"
He extended his hand.

She rolled her lips into a prim line. It gave Nick the distinct impression she would like to dance with him but
didn't think it was proper.

Proper? It's bloody dangerous.

Still, how much trouble could he get into with a roomful of brothers, and a disapproving grandfather, standing
watch?

Oddly enough, Angus didn't look all that disapproving.
In fact, he was studying Nick with an expression that
seemed more perplexed than anything else.

"But I'm the only one who can play the waltz," Victoria
said, taking another stab at refusing.

"I can do it," Kade said. "I recognized the Sussex Waltz,
and I just found the music in your folder. It looks easy as
anything."

Nick almost laughed when she muttered under her
breath.

"Oh, very well," she finally said. "But I'm only doing
it to help the twins."

"Of course," he said, adopting a puzzled expression.
"What other possible reason could there be?"

When she blushed, he rubbed a hand over his mouth to
conceal his amusement. She was a sweet lass and he truly
couldn't remember the last time he'd enjoyed himself as
much. Of course, that was a sad reflection on life at Kinglas
these days. If teasing a wee Sassenach governess had
become the highlight of his week—perhaps his year—he'd
come to a sorry pass, indeed.

After Kade struck the first bars of the waltz and she
finally placed her hand in his, Nick felt an odd sense of

triumph, as if he'd won some sort of skirmish. He heard the sharp intake of her breath and saw the color in her cheeks deepen to a lovely rose.

Skirmish? Hell, he suddenly found himself in a full-out battle not to sweep the bloody girl up and carry her away to his bed. Thank God his family was in the room; otherwise, he'd be tempted to do something incredibly stupid. Victoria Knight was a gently bred woman *and* one of his servants, thus entirely out of bounds.

Besides, the last thing he needed was a woman—any woman—on a permanent basis. Shagging was now a simple, basic need and nothing more. Janet had certainly taught him that lesson.

Victoria finally looked up at him with a shy smile. Nick forced himself to smile back and then bowed as she dipped into a curtsy. Slipping his arms about her, he gently swept her into the first revolution of the dance.

She was graceful and elegant in his embrace—slender, fine-boned, and a small slip of a thing compared to him. But she danced with energy and grace, matching his movements with smooth self-assurance. She might give the impression of fragility, but she had a lithe body and pleasing feminine curves, evidenced by the swell of breasts that brushed against his chest when he swung her through a turn.

After a minute or so, during which she kept her gaze steadfastly pinned to his shoulder, she glanced up with a startled expression.

"You might be holding me too close, my lord," she said in a breathy voice.

His first clue should have been the fact that he could feel her breasts as they pressed against him, along with other lovely bits as their bodies rubbed intimately together.

"My lord, your brothers are watching us," she added tersely.

"Sorry," he said, loosening his embrace. "I suppose that's not the example we wish to set."

Her lush lips curved up with reluctant humor. "Probably not."

He glanced over at his family. The twins were watching with fierce concentration, as if taking mental notes. Royal had gone back to the chaise and resumed brooding. Kade was smiling at the keyboard, lost in the music.

Angus, though, was stroking his bristled chin and regarding them with a canny, oddly intent expression. Nick could all but see the wheels and gears turning in his head.

In response to his questioning frown, the old man gave Nick a bland smile and waggled a hand, as if to say *have at it*.

"Your brother was right," she said. "You're a very good dancer."

He glanced down. She was smiling, and her cheeks were flushed with pleasure. When she let down her governess guard, Victoria was more than simply pretty. She was like a princess from a fairy tale, with golden hair like Snow White and ruby lips like Rose Red.

And like a fairy-tale princess, she was casting a spell on him.

"I'm a little rusty," he said. "It's been quite a while since my last foray onto the dance floor."

"One would never know. How long ago was it?"

"The eve of Waterloo. It was at the Duchess of Richmond's ball," he said softly. Almost every moment of that night and the horrific days that followed were etched on his memory with painful clarity.

"Oh." Her blue gaze went misty.

"That's the last time Royal danced too," he added. His brother would likely never dance again.

"I'm so sorry."

He swept her through a few more turns, taking comfort in her warmth and enjoying the swish of her soft skirts as they brushed his legs.

"You needn't be sorry," he finally said. "He survived. *We* survived, while many didn't."

She slipped her hand a little higher, closer to his neck. "I can still be sorry, for both of you."

When Nick involuntarily tightened his grip, her breath seemed to fracture. He didn't want her pity. He wanted—

Kade concluded the piece with a flourishing trill. Momentum carried them through another revolution before Nick brought them to an awkward halt. In the sudden silence, he and Victoria stared at each other. Her gaze was wide and her pupils looked dilated, standing in stark contrast to the surrounding cornflower blue. When the tip of her tongue slipped out to wet her lips, it took a mighty effort to refrain from dipping down and capturing her luscious mouth in a devouring kiss.

She wriggled, silently asking for release. The delicious little movement had the opposite effect, but Nick forced himself to let go and take a step back.

When the twins began to applaud, Victoria smiled and dipped a curtsy, looking composed despite the blush coloring her cheeks.

"That last little bit seemed rather clumsy," Grant said. "But the rest of it was bang up to the mark, as far as I could tell."

"You *are* quite good, Nick," Graeme said with reluctant admiration. "No wonder all the ladies love you."

When Victoria shot him a startled glance, Nick wanted

to curse. "That is entirely ridiculous," he said in a stern tone.

"Not according to Royal," Grant said with his usual artless naïveté.

When Nick directed a glower at Royal, his brother gave him a taunting grin. "I may have exaggerated your social prowess while on the Continent by a wee bit," his brother said.

"There was no prowess," he replied sharply.

It wasn't his fault that more than one lady had pursued him from time to time. But he'd never chased after *them*, although he hadn't necessarily turned them down when they'd offered, either. After all, he was a widower, not a monk.

And, like any man far from home and family, he had occasionally suffered from pangs of loneliness—not that he would ever admit as much.

"Sorry," Royal said, not looking sorry at all.

Victoria was now regarding Nick with a wary frown. Leave it to his idiot brothers to ruin the one pleasant evening he'd had in months.

"Thank you for the dance, Miss Knight," he said, giving her a smile and a little bow. "It was delightful, and instructive for my brothers, I'm sure."

She gave him a dignified nod. "I'm happy to be of assistance, my lord."

The starched-up governess had returned. That was probably a good thing.

"Would you mind doing that twirly thing again?" Grant said, spinning his hand. "I want to watch your feet when you do that."

"Aye, Nick. Ye and the lassie should do it again," Angus piped up. "Show the lads how to do it proper."

Nick peered at his grandfather's suspiciously cheerful countenance. Only minutes ago he'd been objecting to the very notion of teaching the twins how to dance. What the hell was going on?

"Oh, I think I'm quite worn out with all that spinning around," Miss Knight said, edging away from him. "Perhaps we could resume the lessons another night."

Holy hell. She was now staring at him with something close to dismay. Was the girl actually afraid of him? Given how she'd reacted while they were dancing, that didn't make any sense.

Of course, Royal's inane prattling had probably given her the impression that he was a rake. Everything inside him rebelled at the false image, but he forced himself not to protest.

"I quite agree, Miss Knight," he said. "I'll be in my library if anyone needs me."

He took in the flare of relief in her eyes, then turned and stalked from the room.

Chapter Eleven

Victoria trotted the mare along the castle's curtain wall, returning from a glorious hour's ride across Arnprior lands. Kade wasn't yet up to strenuous physical activity, but she'd missed spending time outdoors and in the saddle, so she'd finally taken her courage in her hands and asked the earl for access to his stables.

Working in his library, Arnprior had put down his pen and studied her with the intensity that always unnerved her. Fortunately, she was now well aware of the impact he had upon her, and she'd mastered the outward signs of her disturbance.

For all that she bothered. These days, the earl seemed not to notice her, unless she asked him a question. She supposed she should be grateful for that, since she did not need the attentions of another rakish aristocrat. Not that Arnprior acted much like a rake, despite Royal's assertions. Given the earl's scowling reaction, it seemed that likely Royal had simply been teasing.

"I have no objection to you riding my animals," he'd said, "if you're proficient enough and strong enough to handle them. I have no slugs in my stables, Miss Knight."

She'd been annoyed by his obvious skepticism.

"I'm an accomplished horsewoman," she'd replied. "In fact, several of my previous employers asked me to provide riding lessons for my young ladies."

His clear amusement with her pronouncement had brought heat rushing to her face.

"You are indeed a woman of many accomplishments," he'd said. "Very well, I'll speak to my head groom. But don't leave the estate or stray far from the roads. You're not familiar with the area and the ground can be rough. I don't want you getting lost or taking a tumble."

She hadn't been able to repress a scowl. "I'm not a ninny, my lord. I will do neither."

"I would never call you a ninny, Miss Knight," he'd responded gently.

Victoria had mumbled an apology and fled the room, feeling nothing less than a *complete* ninny.

She slowed the mare to a walk as they rounded the last corner and entered a spacious courtyard, enclosed on three sides by a handsome set of red brick stables and several outbuildings. The main tower house at Kinglas might be ancient, but successive generations of Kendricks had modernized their holdings over the years by adding two spacious wings that jutted out from the original castle.

While the current earl was also keen on modernizing, his estate manager was not. Victoria had witnessed more than one terse disagreement between Arnprior and his grandfather, and she'd even heard a few shouting matches from behind the closed doors of the library. The old man had seemed to do most of the shouting, usually along the theme of the superior utility of traditional ways.

Since it was none of her business, however, Victoria usually pretended not to hear—no matter how much she might sympathize with her much put-upon employer.

As she guided her horse toward the mounting block, the earl strode out from the wide double-doors of the stable building in boots and breeches, wearing a leather jerkin over his shirt. In such an outfit, he might have been a groom—although she'd never met a groom as devastatingly handsome as Arnprior.

When her hands involuntarily tightened on the reins, the mare pranced a bit.

"Hush," she murmured, bringing the dainty lady under control.

The earl hurried over to take the bridle. "Problem, Miss Knight?"

"Not in the least, sir. In fact, we had a lovely ride."

His gaze ran swiftly over both her and her mount. Apparently satisfied, he nodded. "I'm happy you took advantage of the fine weather. I'm afraid it won't last much longer."

"You *would* have to say that," she said with a dramatic sigh. "I was just convincing myself that we were in for a mild winter."

He snorted. "Yes, we can pretend if it makes you feel better. Now, let me help you dismount, so the groom can take this lassie in and get her settled in her stall."

When she hesitated, his eyebrows went up in a faint, incredulous lift.

"Thank you, my lord," she said, forcing a polite smile.

She placed her hands on his broad shoulders and let herself slide into his arms. As he guided her to the ground, supporting her easily, she could feel the impressive strength in his body.

Victoria could feel quite a few other things too, like her breasts tingling when they brushed against his chest, and her legs quivering when they momentarily pressed against his thighs.

He kept his hands on her waist when she wobbled a bit. "All right?" he murmured. His breath whispered across her ear and neck, making her shiver.

"Are you catching a chill?" Arnprior asked when she didn't respond.

She shook her head and stepped back from his loose embrace. "I never get chills, sir."

He still looked worried, so she gave him a reassuring smile. "I may be rather slight, my lord, but I'm perfectly fit. Skinny but strong as an ox, my grandfather used to say when I was a child."

He laughed. "I take it your grandfather was a blunt-speaking man."

"That, sir, is an understatement."

"Then I suspect we would have gotten on very well."

She paused, arrested by the thought. "Yes, I think that's true."

"You must tell me about him someday."

"I'm sure you have better things to do than hear stories about my relations."

The earl nodded to the stable boy, who was patiently waiting to take the mare. "Not true. I'm very interested, especially since my coachman said you were able to diagnose a problem he was having with the old traveling carriage."

"Oh, that. It was simply a small issue with the roller bolt."

He braced his long legs in an easy stance and crossed his arms over his chest. The pose did lovely things to his broad shoulders and muscular arms, something she should not be taking note of.

"You are an exceedingly capable woman, Miss Knight," he said. "A talented governess *and* an expert on carriage repair."

She wrinkled her nose. "I'm rather good with horses, too."

"Apparently, although I'm still not comfortable with the notion of you going out without a groom or one of my brothers to escort you."

She adopted a horrified expression. "My lord, if your concern is my safety, then riding out with the twins might have the opposite effect."

"True enough. They can barely get out of bed in the morning without creating mayhem. I still don't like you riding alone, however. If anything happened to you . . . well, Sir Dominic would murder me."

He'd gone back to looking worried, which she hated.

"Sir, my grandfather placed me on my first pony when I was two years old," she said with a reassuring smile. "It's not an exaggeration to say that I grew up around horses. In fact, they were my first friends."

Her only friends, really, since she was the oldest of the grandchildren by several years. The stablemen and yard hands had always been kind to her, in their gruff way, but Victoria's aunts had frowned on forming friendships with the help.

"You must have had quite an unusual upbringing," he said.

"I suppose," she hedged. She usually avoided talking about her childhood. In addition to the embarrassment of her parentage, growing up in a coaching inn wasn't the sort of background one usually looked for in a governess.

"I won't hold it against you," he said matter-of-factly. "One should never look down on honest work, no matter how humble it might be."

In her experience, noblemen rarely took such a high-minded position, but Arnprior certainly looked and sounded sincere. She supposed there was no real harm in providing some limited detail.

"I grew up in a coaching inn," she said. "My grandfather owned two of them, just outside Brighton. My uncles and aunts helped to run them."

His expressive eyebrows went up again. "No wonder you're so good with horses."

"If you're ever short-handed in the stables, I'd be happy to help out," she joked.

Victoria couldn't help feeling awkward. Her family was prosperous, but their background was humble. Schoolmates at Miss Kirby's Seminary for Young Ladies had often teased her, suggesting a career as a groom rather than a governess. One particularly nasty girl, whose father was a successful haberdasher, used to sniff loudly and claim that their dormitory room smelled like a stable.

But growing up with a mother whose conduct had invited all manner of ribald remarks had taught Victoria—rather painfully—not to react to such insults, or even slights about her parentage. She'd earned a great deal of respect from her teachers for her restraint, though she'd raged inside, often dampening her pillow with silent tears at night. It had all seemed so unfair. Her father would one day be king of England, but the blue blood that ran through her veins meant nothing. All that had mattered was the sin her mother had committed in bringing Victoria into the world.

"I'll keep that in mind," Arnprior said with a mocking little bow.

She felt her shoulders inch up around her ears. "Well, if that's all, my lord, I must—"

He put a hand out. "Do you think your background bothers me? Because it doesn't. I was only jesting."

"Oh, I . . . thank you." She gave him a tentative smile.

"I'm a soldier, Miss Knight," he said. "And a glorified farmer, truth be told. I would be a fool to look down on anyone who makes a living through hard work or the use of her hands. In fact, I'd like to know more about your life. How did you go from coaching inn to governess, for instance."

She hesitated. "It's all rather boring, actually."

He took her by the elbow and steered her in the direction of the kitchen gardens. "You're not the least bit boring,

Miss Knight. Besides, I like to know as much as I can about the people who work for me."

While that made perfect sense, it was awkward, given several rather pertinent secrets in her past.

As if sensing her reluctance, he glanced down at her with a reassuring smile. "It's not an interrogation, I promise. I'm more than satisfied with your performance. In fact, I'd also like to speak with you about Kade. About how you think he's progressing."

"Of course, sir. I should be happy to update you."

As she snuck a sideways peek at his rugged profile, it occurred to her that she wouldn't mind spending some time with him. In truth, she was a little lonely. Most of her day was spent with Kade, which was lovely, but she longed for adult conversation. At dinner, she usually found herself seated between the twins—who while good-natured could hardly be deemed intellectual—or next to Royal, who barely spoke a word. As for Angus, the less said, the better.

She was now fairly certain that Arnprior had been avoiding her since that night they waltzed. She shouldn't be bothered by that fact, but honesty compelled her to admit she was.

Because you're a nincompoop.

"I thought we could stroll in the garden while we chat," the earl said, "since it's such a nice day. I like to spend as much time as I can outdoors before the snows and storms come."

"Please don't remind me about our impending doom. I'm convinced my flannel petticoats and woolens will not be nearly sturdy enough to get me through the winter."

When he made a slight choking noise, she wished for a sudden earthquake to swallow her up. Had she lost her mind, talking about undergarments in front of a man—her employer, no less? That was a page stolen right from her mother's disreputable book. Although God knows her mother would never have worn flannel.

"Ah, I didn't mean . . . that is . . ." she stammered.

"Come along, Miss Knight, before we get ourselves into trouble," he said in a dry tone.

He guided her between rows of neatly planted cabbages and boxes of herbs that were mostly empty by now. Victoria was so mortified she barely noticed her surroundings. Normally, she was the most composed of women, but something about Lord Arnprior unsettled her, although not in an unpleasant way.

Quite the opposite.

"You were about to tell me how you became a governess," he prompted as they passed under the trellis that separated the kitchen and ornamental gardens.

They strolled along a stone and gravel path set between large, rectangular flowerbeds, bright with late fall mums.

"As I mentioned, sir," she said, trying to order her thoughts, "my aunts and uncles helped manage my grandfather's inns. Everyone lived on the premises or close by, so a number of children were always underfoot. Since I was the oldest grandchild by several years, it fell to me to look after the little ones. It seemed natural that I begin teaching them their letters and numbers."

She smiled, remembering the simple but cozy schoolroom she'd convinced her grandfather to set up. "Because I had a surprising aptitude for teaching little children, my cousins were turned over to me when they were old enough to be away from their mothers."

"Surprising? Why?" he asked.

"Oh, I suppose it was because my mother wasn't particularly nurturing in that respect," she said vaguely. "Although I do get my musical talents from her."

Mamma's talents had found their expression in singing ribald songs for the men who frequented the taproom.

Victoria had hated her mother's willingness to put herself on display, as had her aunts. But Grandpapa hadn't minded. Men came from all around to hear Rose Knight sing, which meant more money spent on ale and spirits.

"Did your father also work at the inn?" the earl asked.

It was the question she hated more than any other. "No. I . . . I never knew my father."

"Ah, I'm sorry. He must have passed when you were very young."

The Prince Regent had certainly passed out of her life, so she supposed that was true. "Yes."

Arnprior moved closer, his shoulder brushing hers. "I was only seven when my mother died."

She glanced up, taking in his somber expression. "That is much too young for a boy to lose his mother."

He'd experienced a great deal of sorrow, first losing his mother at such an early age and then his wife.

"Fortunately, my father recovered from the loss and happily remarried a truly estimable woman," he said.

She couldn't help wondering if the man walking beside her had recovered from the loss of his wife. It didn't seem so, since he'd never remarried.

"And your mother never married again?" Arnprior asked.

"Er, no, but I was fortunate to have a wonderful grandfather and several fine uncles. Not to mention Sir Dominic, who has always been kindness itself. I have never lacked family to care for me."

Just a mother who truly loved her. And a real father.

"I understand Sir Dominic assisted with your education."

She smiled. "Yes, he sponsored my placement at Miss Kirby's Seminary. It's an excellent establishment. I was very lucky."

The earl's glance could only be described as enigmatic.

Inwardly, she groaned, realizing too late that any mention of Sir Dominic was bound to be fraught. After all, there was no way to describe their relationship without telling outright fibs.

"Sir Dominic was friendly with your grandfather, I believe," he said.

"That is correct."

He flashed her a wry smile. "He seems acquainted with half the population of the kingdom, does he not?"

"Indeed."

"And how old were you when you met Sir Dominic?"

"Nine, sir," she said tersely. Victoria held her breath as he gently nudged her in the direction of the lawn leading down to the loch.

"And how many years did you spend away at school?" he finally asked.

She breathed a mental sigh of relief that they were leaving the potentially fraught topic of Dominic behind. "Six, the last as a teacher's assistant. I would have been happy to stay longer, but there wasn't a placement for me. I took my first position as a governess when I was nineteen and have been teaching ever since."

He stopped by a stone bench that looked out over the water and was partially sheltered by a tall hedge. She'd discovered this spot on her first foray into the gardens, and it had become a favored retreat when the weather was mild. The bench retained the warmth of the sun, was out of the wind, and was perfectly situated to take in the magnificent vista of loch, mountains, and sky.

Arnprior waved a hand to invite her to sit. He remained standing, propping a booted foot onto the other end of the bench.

"And so here you find yourself," he said in a lighter tone. "Far from civilization and all but buried alive with a group of scapegrace Highlanders. I wonder what could have brought you to this sorry pass?"

"I believe it's the excellent salary you're paying me, sir." That, at least, was the truth.

He looked politely incredulous. "Surely a governess of your caliber is in great demand, is she not?"

The man was as persistent as a dog with a bone. "My lord, is there a specific question you wish to ask, or a particular concern you'd like me to address? I feel we are beginning to retread old ground."

His sudden grin was so charming that her heart skipped a beat.

"And here I thought I was being so clever," he said.

She took a moment to gather her wits around her like some sort of armor. "Since I cannot reasonably respond to that comment without causing offense, I will simply encourage you again to ask your question." She gave him an apologetic smile. "My lord."

His laugh was low, warm, and seductive. She curled her hands into fists, fighting a silly, girlish response.

"Very well," he said. "In all seriousness, I cannot fathom why a woman of your obvious skills, one who has excellent references *and* the sponsorship of Dominic Hunter, would choose to accept a position that most would run screaming from."

"I almost did run, as you recall, particularly after meeting your grandfather."

"Ah, yes. Angus is one of the reasons we've had difficulty keeping tutors in the first place. He all but ran off the dancing tutor I managed to hire from Glasgow—at the end of a dirk. And I wish I was joking about that."

She contemplated that alarming image for a few moments.

Then Arnprior leaned down and rested a forearm on his thigh, bringing them to eye level. "You seem to have declawed the old fellow, though," he said with a faint smile.

"Really? Why, just yesterday he reprimanded me for bothering the twins with a lot of frippery and nonsense."

"What were you doing?"

"Suggesting they refrain from slurping their soup."

He laughed. "Poor Miss Knight. Well, that example certainly makes my point. Why *are* you putting up with my sorry family, and with such patience? And don't say it's the salary, because I know that's not the only reason."

Clearly, he was not going to give up. "Well, if you want to know the truth—"

"I do."

His smile took some of the sting out of his words, but she heard the warning. Arnprior still had doubts about her, and she knew it stemmed from the glaring lack of references from Lord and Lady Welgate. Although the twins and Royal would be as likely to commend her for killing her attacker as not, the earl was something of a high stickler. He would *not* approve, she suspected, so she needed to continue to tread carefully.

"After my last position, I needed a change," she said.

"You felt your pupils were not a match for your skills, I recall."

"They were a bit young, but there were also other difficulties."

"Go on," he prompted.

"There was a family member who was quite f-forward." She winced at her stammer. "He made my situation difficult, so I decided to leave."

When Arnprior straightened up, Victoria breathed a sigh of relief. The earl never frightened her, but he was a big man and he'd been all but looming over her. And although she trusted him implicitly, recalling those ugly memories made her feel skittish.

"Did this man injure you, Miss Knight?"

His manner was calm, but his gaze glittered with barely

contained anger. Oddly enough, that quick blaze of fury warmed the cold bits inside her, remnants of shame and fear that still lingered as a result of the attack.

She shook her head. "Not in any lasting way, but I couldn't stay there."

His mouth flattened into a hard line, and he stared at the loch for several long moments. When he looked back at her, his gaze remained deeply troubled. "I regret you were subjected to such ugliness. But you now find yourself in a rough and tumble bachelor household, one certainly lacking in decorum." He grimaced. "This cannot be a pleasant situation for you, given your recent experience."

"I assure you, sir, my last position was in a very good household, and that still wasn't enough to protect me."

When he started to protest, she held up her hands. "You misunderstand, my lord. I have no concerns for my personal safety at Kinglas. Your brothers, despite their rough edges, are kind men. Anyone can see they would never willingly hurt a woman or a child. And while your grandfather can be vexing, I believe he's harmless. Mostly," she added with a smile, hoping to reassure him.

His mouth twisted sideways in a smile that looked more bitter than rueful. "It's the *mostly* part that worries me. And I'm sure we're not what you're used to." He took his foot off the bench and half turned toward the view of water and sky. "And this place is not exactly Brighton or London. It's going to get bloody challenging here in the winter, I assure you."

She stood and joined him, gazing out at the craggy hills and the narrow, steep-sided glens that rose up to majestic peaks. The bright autumn foliage of a few weeks ago had faded, creating a dappled landscape of browns and grays, broken only by an occasional stand of pines. The breeze off the rippling waters of the loch was crisp, carrying a whisper of the storms that would surely come. She knew there would be days when she longed to escape the cold and the isolation, fleeing back to the civilized bustle of London, or even lovely old Brighton.

But the Highlands were also incredibly beautiful and different. So different that she could believe this place was helping her to make a fresh start in life. Everything about Kinglas was completely disconnected from her past, and far removed from the ugliness her life had become.

"Actually, I think it's splendid here," she confessed.

He glanced down at her, surprised. "You do?"

"Yes. The Highlands sweep away all the dusty, unnecessary bits, don't you think? And Kinglas is truly a fascinating and noble old place."

He exhaled a deep breath, as if something inside him had unexpectedly settled. "I always thought the same. When I was away for all those years on the Continent, it surprised me how much I missed the Highlands."

"My lord, if you're concerned that I'll abandon my post and flee back to England, you need not worry. I intend to stick it out." Then she cast him a droll glance. "Still, ask me again in January. My views may have changed by then."

"I will." His smile was approving and warm. So warm it made her blush.

"And then there's Kade," she said, ignoring her fluttering insides. "He's wonderful. Even if I had to eat haggis every day and sleep in the stables, he would be worth it. He truly is the sweetest boy, and so talented."

Arnprior's austere features softened into an expression that set her heart tripping over itself. He reached up and brushed away a lock of hair the wind had plastered across her cheek. "He's certainly taken to you, lassie. And no one could blame him for that."

"Oh, ah, thank you," she stammered. She stood frozen, entirely flustered by that simple touch.

He shoved a hand in the pocket of his leather vest and

looked away with a slight grimace, as if suddenly realizing he'd embarrassed her.

"Yes, Kade has made excellent progress." He looked back at her, cool and collected, once more the stern-faced earl.

"I believe he has," she said, matching his brisk tone. "I have to prod him to spend time on his other studies, though, because he'd spend every moment practicing his instruments if I let him."

"He's always been that way. Miss Knight, I also wanted to ask if the lad has confided anything about the trauma he suffered at school?"

"No, my lord. It's clear he's still reluctant to talk about it."

He frowned. "I got the sense when I came into the sitting room the other night that you were having a private conversation about that very issue."

Drat.

Victoria didn't see the point in dancing around this subject, either. She could respect anyone's wish to keep secrets, but it was a little hard to continue ignoring the fact that her employer had once been married. "Actually, we were speaking of your family. Kade missed you very much when you were away."

"I was gone for too long. It was a mistake," he said grimly.

"And he also mentioned how much he missed the countess."

He went from brooding to puzzled. "Kade's mother died in childbirth. He would have no memories of her."

"He was speaking of your wife," she said gently.

The earl didn't move a muscle or vary his expression one iota, but she got the odd sensation that her words had just leveled him.

"I'm sorry if that causes you distress, sir," she said. "Such was not my intent."

He flicked a hand, startling her with the sudden, sharp movement.

"It's fine. I wish to know everything that troubles Kade," he said. "I didn't realize he even thought about my . . . wife. He was quite young when she died."

"He mentioned that they shared a love of music."

"Yes, the countess was an accomplished musician. When she actually stayed at Arnprior, she would play for the lad. She was quite fond of him."

Victoria found his choice of words and his tone somehow jarring. "Her ladyship did not spend much time at Arnprior?" she cautiously asked.

"She preferred our mansion in Glasgow."

Ah, she recognized *that* tone. It said: *Rough ground ahead. Keep off.*

Before he flicked his gaze out to the loch, Victoria saw bleakness in his expression.

"I'm truly sorry, sir," she said quietly. "You must miss her very much."

That brought his attention snapping back. "Must I? Yes, I suppose I must. After all, I loved her."

Her consternation must have showed in her face.

He blew out an exasperated breath. "Forgive me, it's just that—" The earl broke off, frowning as he gazed past her and toward the castle.

She spun around to see Mrs. Taffy hurrying toward them through the garden, her face crinkled with worry.

"That does not look good," Victoria murmured.

"You have a talent for understatement, Miss Knight."

When he strode to meet his housekeeper, Victoria picked up her skirts and rushed after him.

"Begging your pardon, Laird," Taffy said, bobbing a curtsy. "But we have visitors, asking for you."

He frowned. "We're not expecting anyone, are we?"

"They're customs men," she said tersely.

He put up his hands in silent question.

"They want to ask you about a whisky distillery on Arnprior lands," she said.

"We don't have a—" His mouth clamped shut for a few seconds. "The twins," he said through clenched teeth.

"So it would seem," Taffy replied.

"And Angus. Is he involved?"

The housekeeper's gaze went as flinty as the earl's. "I'm not sure of that, but I will be by the end of the day."

"Goddammit," Arnprior said. "I will bloody well kill them all."

He stalked toward the kitchen garden, little pieces of dirt and dried grass spraying up in the wake of his pounding, booted footsteps.

"Oh, Lord," Taffy sighed. "Just when things were starting to calm down."

"I thought it was legal to distill whisky in Scotland," Victoria said.

"Not without a license, miss, which the Kendricks do not hold. Now, if you'll excuse me, I'd best go see that the laird doesn't carry through on his promise."

"I'll go with you," Victoria said, hurrying to follow.

After all, one murderer in the household was certainly more than anyone needed.

Chapter Twelve

Victoria glanced up from her lesson plan when Kade hit another discordant note. The lad stared gloomily at the keyboard as he picked his way through the Haydn sonata she'd given him this morning. Even the new music had failed to lift his spirits.

After their ripping argument yesterday, Angus had stormed out of Kinglas in a fury while the earl had stormed off and locked himself in his library. Their very public shouting match had all but shaken the ancient timbers of the entrance hall to the ground. Neither man had shown up for dinner, leaving Victoria to make strained conversation with Royal while Kade and the disgraced twins morosely picked at their food.

When Kade heaved a dramatic sigh and slid her a sideways glance, Victoria put aside her work. She'd always tried to distance herself from the personal lives of her various employers, but her pupil was clearly suffering and needed her support.

"Why don't you take a little break and have some tea?" Victoria said, patting the seat next to her on the chaise.

"Taffy made some of your favorite seedcakes. It would be a shame to let them go to waste."

The boy came to join her. "It *is* awfully hard to concentrate, what with Nick and Grandda on the outs. They brangle quite a lot, but this is different."

"You can tell me all about it, but first you must eat. You barely touched your breakfast or luncheon."

"It's hard to have an appetite when your brother and grandfather wish to murder each other."

"It's just a lot of noise, I'm sure," she said gently. "And I hardly think starving yourself is going to help matters, now is it?"

What might help matters would be to line up the Kendrick men and box their ears for being so pigheaded and stubborn.

Kade accepted a cup of tea. "At least when I'm sick, they usually stop fighting."

"Dearest, it's not your responsibility to solve your family's problems. It's their job to take care of you, not the other way around."

The boy saw himself as the peacemaker in the family. Generally, that meant just being his cheerful self, since the earl was fiercely protective of his baby brother. But yesterday's blowup had destroyed the delicate equilibrium of the household. From the shadows under Kade's eyes, it was clear he'd slept poorly. He'd also lost the appetite he'd started to regain over the last few weeks.

That was unacceptable, and Victoria intended to tell the earl just that once she worked up the nerve to beard the angry lion in his den.

"Nick hardly ever loses his temper," Kade said, echoing her thoughts, "but I thought he was going to bash Grandda over the head."

"I thought it was more likely he was going to bash the twins," she said wryly.

Kade wrinkled his nose. "It was bad of Grant and Graeme to set up a still, despite what my grandfather thinks."

According to the customs officers, the twins had set up a small but thoroughly illegal whisky distillery in a secluded glen on Arnprior lands. While it was a fairly common practice in the Highlands, it could provoke serious legal consequences. Fortunately, the officers had agreed not to press charges after the earl promised to dismantle the operation and punish the twins himself.

"Well, it *is* against the law," she said, "and it was very embarrassing for the earl to be caught so unawares." Arnprior had clearly been mortified that the twins had been brewing moonshine under his very nose. Even worse, Angus had known about it.

Kade put down his teacup, looking worried. "The officers aren't going to come back and arrest them, are they?"

She gave him a reassuring smile. "No, they're going to allow the earl to manage the situation as he sees fit, as long as the still is dismantled."

"Thank goodness. It would be awful if the twins ended up in the clink."

"Indeed," she said dryly, refilling his teacup. From what she'd seen yesterday, the earl had been sorely tempted to consign the twins and their grandfather to a long stay in the local gaol.

"And maybe Grandda has a point," he said thoughtfully. "What right do the English have to tell the Scots what to do and what not to do?"

"I suggest you disregard your grandfather on that point, dear." Angus had tried to make that argument after the customs officers had departed.

"Besides," Angus had said, scowling at Arnprior, "what

else do ye expect of them? The puir lads have to support themselves somehow."

The earl had regarded his grandfather with disbelief. "I expect them not to get tossed out of university, and I expect them to learn a bloody profession. Also, I expect their grandfather to encourage them in those laudable and legal goals."

"But the lads *are* learning a profession, dinna ye ken?"

"Moonshining? Are you insane?"

"I don't see ye coming up with anything better," Angus had retorted before glaring at Victoria. "Oh, aye, except to have herself turn them into a pair of twiddle-poops so they can find some silly twits to marry. No wonder the lads don't listen to a bloody thing ye say. Who can blame them, running off to war like ye did? As if *ye* were the only one who grieved, and the rest of us felt nothing."

And just like that, the atmosphere in the entrance hall had gone from bad to explosive. After clearly trying to wrestle his anger under control, the earl had suddenly looked as if he were about to strangle his grandfather on the spot.

"That's enough," Royal had barked, limping forward to stand between the two men. "You're not to say another word about any of that, Grandda."

"Ye ken as well as I—" Angus had said hotly.

"No," Royal had interrupted. He'd stood nose to nose, giving the old man a threatening glare. Then he'd turned back to his brother with a reassuring smile.

But the earl's gaze had transformed into one so bleak and angry that it had chilled Victoria to the bone.

"Nick, he doesn't know what he's saying," Royal said. "Don't listen to him."

Arnprior had nodded to his brother, then turned on his booted heel and stalked off. Royal had followed him and

Angus had slunk away, while Mrs. Taffy had shooed the staff back to their duties.

Victoria had retreated upstairs to the schoolroom to find Kade immersed in his studies, thankfully unaware of the debacle below. She'd been tempted to ask Taffy for clarification on the obscure charges Angus had leveled at the earl, but had decided it was none of her business.

Since then, the entire household had held its collective breath, as if they were staring into a simmering volcano, waiting for the final eruption.

"I don't know what's going to happen if Nick doesn't forgive the twins," Kade said. "Or Grandda."

For the sake of Kade's peace of mind, it was time for Victoria to take drastic measures, even if it meant interfering in Kendrick family business. "Would you like me to speak to the earl about the twins?"

He glanced up with a hopeful expression. "Would you?"

"Yes, and I'll talk to Royal as well. Between the two of us, perhaps we might even restore civil relations."

He smiled at her little joke. "That would be splendid, because I'm worried about Nick. He hasn't been this upset since—" He suddenly clamped his lips shut.

"Since when?" she gently prompted.

He seemed about to answer when Grant charged into the drawing room.

Startled, Kade almost dropped his teacup.

Victoria scowled at Grant. "I would ask that you go back into the hall and reenter the room like a gentleman."

"Sorry, miss," Grant puffed with excitement. "But we have a visitor."

"Who?" Kade asked.

"Logan," he burst out. "Logan has finally come home."

Kade's face went slack. "Truly?"

Grant nodded. "He just arrived."

"Does Nick know?"

"Royal's gone to fetch him."

Before Victoria could say a word, Kade flew off the chaise and pelted for the door.

"Kade, don't run," she called after him.

When his older brother started to follow, she came to her feet. "Grant, please wait one moment."

He turned, vibrating with impatience.

"Tell me who Logan is," she said.

"My older brother."

"*Another* brother?"

"Half-brother, actually. Logan is second oldest, after Nick. His mother was my father's first countess."

Victoria realized she was gaping at him like a trout. "Why have I never heard about him before?"

Grant shifted uncomfortably. "Because Nick doesn't like to talk about him. They had . . . a falling out."

His lordship didn't like to talk about his wife, either. The man seemed to have a great many secrets.

Like you?

"If you don't mind, Miss Knight," Grant said, "I've got to go downstairs. I'm not sure what's going to happen when Nick finds out Logan's here."

She scurried to catch up with him. "I'll come with you."

"Maybe you'd better not," he said as she hurried beside him in the corridor. "There might be some fireworks. Nick told Logan never to come back to Kinglas. In fact, none of us have seen him in over six years. He's been in Canada."

"Why would the earl exile him?" she asked breathlessly, all but trotting to keep up with his long-legged stride.

As they reached the landing at the top of the main staircase, he came to a halt so sudden that her soft leather shoes slipped on the polished floors. He grabbed her by the arm.

"Don't fall, miss." Grant had a knack for stating the obvious.

Annoyed, Victoria pushed an errant lock of hair away from her face. But tart words died on her tongue when she took in Grant's worried expression. He was normally the cheeriest of young men, impervious to all but the most severe setdown from his big brother. Right now, though, he looked almost frightened.

She could hear voices below in the entrance hall. Ignoring them, she rested a gentle hand on Grant's forearm. "What is it, my dear?"

He glanced past her, as if making sure they weren't overhead. "You know that Nick was married."

"Yes. I'm aware that the earl doesn't like to speak of her loss."

"That's not the only loss he doesn't like to speak about."

"Go on."

He seemed to debate with himself for a few moments before capitulating. "You'll find out anyway, so I might as well tell you. Nick and his wife had a son—a little boy named Cameron."

She stared blankly at him. Her brain couldn't seem to catch up. "He died?"

"More than six years ago."

Now it became clear. "About the time your brothers became estranged?"

He nodded as he cast an impatient glance over her shoulder. The voices in the hall were growing in volume. "Miss, I've got to get down there."

"Very well, but just tell me . . . blast," she muttered as Grant brushed past and ran down the stairs. She didn't immediately follow, giving herself a moment to sort through all she'd just heard.

Despite the occasional flashes of genuine charm, Arnprior was a deeply somber man who carried a heavy weight of responsibility. Now she knew he carried a terrible weight of sorrow as well due to the death of both his wife and his son. Her heart ached for him, and for the rest of the family, who were all but drowning in painful secrets.

Victoria tucked a few stray hairs back into their pins and smoothed her lace cuffs, then took the stairs down to the entrance hall. Grant was probably correct—she should go back to her room and mind her own business. But she had no intention of abandoning Kade, or Lord Arnprior, for that matter.

In the center of the hall was a giant of a man dressed in breeches, boots, and a travel-stained greatcoat. Like all the Kendrick men, he was muscular and well built, but in this case exceptionally so. He topped the twins by at least two inches, and seemed even more brawny than the earl himself.

Kade had thrown himself into Logan's arms and was all but swallowed up in the big man's embrace. The twins and Angus hovered nearby, looking torn between excitement and apprehension. Several servants milled aimlessly and Taffy stood off to the side, dabbing a handkerchief to her eyes as she struggled to contain herself. The dogs added to the mayhem, tumbling about and adding to the din reverberating off the high rafters. With so much noise, it was all but impossible to hear voices.

The room was chilly, since the footmen, apparently as excited as the dogs, had forgotten to close the front door. Victoria hurried to shut the door, then sidled past the dogs and the servants to join the housekeeper.

Taffy gave her a watery smile. "Och, miss, we're at sixes and sevens, what with Mr. Logan's return home from Canada."

Victoria leaned in close. "I take it no one was expecting him?"

"No." The housekeeper gave her nose a quick wipe and

then stowed her handkerchief up a sleeve. "Ye'll be thinking I'm a silly nit for crying, but it's been years since we've seen the lad. He's been sorely missed, I can tell ye."

"But not by the earl, I take it."

Taffy shot her a wary glance. "What did Mr. Grant tell you?"

"Only that the earl and his brother are estranged. Oh, and that his lordship had a son," she added. "That came as a bit of a shock."

Taffy had the grace to look sheepish. "I'm right sorry for not telling you, lass. The laird doesn't like us talking about the poor wee boy."

"Or his wife or brother, apparently."

The housekeeper raised her hands in a helpless gesture. "You have to understand how things were for the laird. First Lady Arnprior died so suddenly, and then—"

"Miss Knight," Kade shouted over the noise. "Come meet Logan." He waved excitedly at her from his brother's embrace.

She smiled and waved back. "I'll be right there." She returned her attention to the housekeeper. "I take it that the earl is likely to be displeased about this development."

"That, miss, is an understatement," she said grimly. "Mr. Royal went to look for him and to try to prepare him."

"Then might I suggest we at least try to enforce a little decorum before the earl arrives. This sort of upset is not likely to improve his already unhappy mood."

"Right you are, miss. I'll have tea brought to the family drawing room when things settle down."

While the housekeeper set about restoring order among the servants and the dogs, Victoria made her way over to the family group.

Kade grabbed her hand. "Miss Knight, this is my brother Logan." His eyes shone with excitement. "He's been in

Canada for over six years. *And* he's apparently as rich as Croesus, which is rather fun."

She dipped into a curtsy. "It's a pleasure to meet you, Mr. Kendrick."

"And you as well, Miss Knight," he replied in a deep, resonant voice. He gave her a sweeping bow.

When he straightened, he towered over her, forcing her to peer up at him. She found herself looking into laughing blue eyes that were almost a match to the earl's. In fact, Logan strongly resembled his brother, having the same rugged, handsome features and hair so dark it appeared blue-black.

Unlike the earl, however, he had an easy smile and a charming manner that suggested he was entirely at ease with the awkward situation. If Logan was worried about his older brother's reaction to his sudden return to the ancestral home, he certainly didn't display it.

"Kade, you neglected to tell me how pretty your new governess is," he said. "No wonder you're enjoying your studies so much. I might even ask Miss Knight to give me a few lessons too."

Victoria blinked. Was he attempting to flirt with her in front of most of the family and half the servants?

The twins exchanged a disconcerted glance and even Angus looked nonplussed.

"Now, don't ye be teasin' the lassie," the old man hastily said. "Miss Knight takes her duties verra seriously."

"Yes, you mustn't tease," said Kade earnestly. "She's a splendid teacher *and* an accomplished pianist. I'm very lucky to have her as my tutor."

"Even better, since I love music. Will you play something special for me if I ask you very nicely?" he asked her.

When he punctuated that comment by giving Victoria a roguish wink, all she could do was gape at him. How could the man behave in so outrageous a fashion and under such fraught circumstances? She could only hope the earl wouldn't expect her to try teaching Logan Kendrick how to behave with propriety. She already had her hands full with the rest of the family, and this new addition seemed like a particularly hard case.

Then again, it was possible that the earl would shoot his errant brother rather than attempt to reform his manners.

Suddenly the dogs stopped barking. At the same moment, Logan glanced beyond her, the rakish, charming smile fading from his features. She spun around to see the earl standing at the back of the hall, with Royal standing at his shoulder.

Her heart sank as she absorbed the cold fury that shimmered in the atmosphere around Arnprior.

"Ah, Nick," Logan said in a quiet voice. "There you are."

The earl finally moved, prowling forward into the center of the hall with Royal a protective shadow behind him. Angus and the twins retreated a few steps, and even the dogs had the sense to slink away.

Victoria took Kade's hand in a comforting grip. His fingers wrapped around hers, his gaze steady on the earl.

"Look, Nick," the boy said in a bright voice, as if his good cheer could chase away the approaching tempest, "Logan's finally come home."

"So I see." The earl's voice was a soft but terrifying growl.

He and his brother sized each other up. The silence in the room was so fraught that the back of Victoria's neck started to prickle.

"My lord," Logan finally said, giving his brother a correct bow. His casual manner was now considerably more wary. "It's good to see you again."

Arnprior's flat gaze clearly indicated he felt the opposite. Though Logan was indeed the bigger man, the earl's imperious, almost menacing presence made everyone else in the room seem small by comparison.

"Is it?" the earl replied. "Because I find myself most displeased to see you again."

When Arnprior finally smiled, Victoria almost fainted. It was the sort of smile a cold-blooded killer might give a man just before he stuck a knife between his ribs.

"In fact," the earl added, "I suggest you leave my house while you still have the chance to do so in one piece."

Chapter Thirteen

Nick had spent years clawing his way out of a black hole of despair, a brutal climb through paths of heartache, bloodshed, and discipline. Now he could feel himself slipping back again.

Logan.

His brother's appearance was the final insult coming on the heels of the ugly scenes of yesterday. It felt like an awful, cosmic joke, one that said he had no control over his life.

Logan stared at him with a wary gaze. "Nick, just let me talk to you," he said gruffly. "Let me explain why I'm here."

"There's nothing to explain. My son is dead because of you. There is no forgiving that."

In the silence that gripped the hall, Nick heard Victoria gasp. He'd been so focused on Logan that he'd almost forgotten her presence. She stood beside Kade, holding his hand. She looked shocked, of course. Likely she hadn't even known about his son.

When their gazes met, she pointedly raised her eyebrows in a clear warning. He told himself he didn't care about her opinion, or anyone else's. Not with Logan inside Kinglas, where Nick had forbidden him ever to step foot again.

"I'd do anything to change what happened," Logan said. "You know I would."

"The only thing you can do is get the hell out of my house before I take my boot to your arse," Nick replied.

Kade wrenched free from Victoria and rushed forward. "That's not fair. You know it wasn't Logan's fault."

"He needs to go, Kade," he said, ignoring the pleading note in the boy's voice.

Anger flared in Logan's eyes. "How long are you going to punish me, Nick? For the rest of our bloody lives?"

Nick was vaguely surprised to hear a snarl emerge from his throat. "You won't have much longer to live if you don't leave right now."

"My lord, surely such threats are not necessary." Victoria's cool, clear voice cut through the haze in Nick's brain, like a bracing gust off the loch dispelled a winter mist.

He glanced at her, narrowing his eyes.

"And your little brother is present, in case you've forgotten," she added, not the least bit intimidated.

"Then I suggest you get him out of here," Nick snapped.

She stepped protectively in front of Kade. "I should be happy to do so, sir, once I'm convinced that neither you nor anyone else is going to commit murder."

Royal let out an exasperated sigh. "Don't worry about that."

"Maybe she should," Logan said with an ugly laugh. "Because it looks like I'll have to beat some sense into my brother's thick Scottish skull."

The servants let out a collective gasp. Logan had never known when to keep his mouth shut, or show a reasonable amount of deference. Years of exile had clearly not made a difference in that respect.

"Here, now. Ye'll be showing more respect to the laird," Angus said in a shocked voice.

Nick flashed him a smile that was all teeth. "Never mind, Grandda. I was always able to take him. He's clearly forgotten that."

His brother's gaze turned as flinty as slate. "I think you'll find things have changed, brother."

"Excellent," Nick drawled. "Shall we give it a go?"

He started to move but jerked to a halt when Victoria slipped in between them. She pressed a slim hand to his chest.

"My lord," she said quietly, "you are not thinking clearly."

"Nick, please listen to her," Kade said in an anguished tone.

Nick tore his focus from her calm face and glanced over at his little brother. Kade was now clutching Royal's arm, his mouth pressed into a quivering line. Royal grimaced and jerked his head toward the boy, clearly asking Nick to stand down.

When Nick glanced back down at Victoria, he saw understanding and compassion in the depths of her cornflower-blue gaze. He felt something give way, as if a physician had lanced a boil. But left behind was a weariness that dragged at his soul—and a pain he knew would never fade.

His little governess carefully patted his chest, as if trying to soothe a half-wild animal. He couldn't help but note the irony. On the battlefield, he'd always considered himself a civilized man, one who avoided wanton cruelty and brutality whenever possible. But now he still had to fight the urge to throttle his stupid brother.

"Are you all right, my lord?" Victoria asked.

"I'm fine," he said curtly.

When her hand fell away and she stepped back, he had the feeling he'd just lost something vital.

"I'm relieved to hear that, my lord," she said. "This sort of scene is not helpful to Kade's recovery." She flashed an imperious glare around the room, taking in his entire family. "The last few days have been exceedingly hard on him."

When Angus and the brothers—including Logan— exchanged sheepish glances, Nick felt a little more of the poison inside him drain away. Every inch the governess in her neat brown dress and prim white collar, Victoria was fearless in her defense of Kade. His brothers could easily hoist her in the air with one hand, and yet she'd reduced them to shuffling their feet like naughty schoolboys.

She was simply . . . wonderful.

"I quite agree with you, Miss Knight," Nick said. "And I apologize for my role in those unfortunate events. I suggest you take Kade upstairs so as to avoid any more upset."

Kade threw him a defiant scowl. "I'm old enough to be part of any family discussion, Nick. And I'm not leaving until you promise not to hurt Logan."

Logan's anger had abated as well, and he now stood watching Nick with a sort of relaxed wariness, an easy smile lifting the corners of his mouth. Before tragedy had pulled their family to pieces, his brother had always believed that the world was a wonderful place indeed, full of beautiful women, fine whisky, and good cheer. He wondered if Logan still believed that.

Kade reached out and tugged on his waistcoat. "Nick, promise me."

He forced a smile. "Lad, have you looked at Logan? He must outweigh me by more than two stone. He'd probably flatten me."

"Too right," Logan said, his smile stretching into a taunting grin.

"Stow it, you idiot," Royal growled. "This is no time for jesting."

"Why not?" Logan asked. "This is something of a farce, after all. We even have a pretty heroine to complete the scene."

When he winked at Victoria, Nick's desire to murder his brother flared hot again.

"I asked you not to tease Miss Knight," Kade said. "It's disrespectful, and she doesn't deserve it."

Logan winced. "Sorry, lad. I'm a bit off my feed, I suppose. It isn't every day that a fellow returns to the ancestral home."

"I understand, and I forgive you," Kade said with touching dignity. "Now, please apologize to Miss Knight, as well."

Nick didn't know whether to laugh or cry. His little brother was putting them all to shame.

Logan gave Victoria a short bow. "Please accept my apologies for my unfortunate behavior, ma'am." Then he flashed the rueful, charming smile that had been the downfall of many a Highland maid. "It's simply that—"

"Apology accepted, Mr. Kendrick," Victoria interrupted in a brisk tone. She clearly had Logan's measure.

Nick ruffled Kade's hair. "Go upstairs with Miss Knight, lad. I'll come up in a bit."

The boy flicked a worried gaze between Nick and Logan.

"Och, no need to worry," Logan said. "We'll just curse and shout and probably throw a few breakables, but that's it."

"You both promise?" Kade asked suspiciously.

"We promise, imp," Nick said. "Now off you go."

His little brother dashed over to give Logan a quick, fierce hug. "You'll come see me before you go?"

"I promise, Kade."

Logan's reassuring smile fell away as soon as Kade turned his back. With a somber expression, he watched his little brother climb the stairs with Victoria.

Nick was furious with Logan for returning to Kinglas, but he was well aware of what exile had cost his brother.

No matter his success in Canada, he'd lost the chance to see Kade and Braden growing up. He'd lost his family, the Highlands, and the home he loved above all else.

Nick ruthlessly snuffed out the flicker of sympathy. His brother didn't deserve forgiveness. Logan was a constant, wrenching reminder of everything Nick had suffered and lost. To have him back at Kinglas was unacceptable.

He glanced around the hall. Once again, they had a large audience for another epic family brawl. "Taffy, I do believe today's performance is concluded. The staff may return to their duties."

The housekeeper gave a quick curtsy. "Aye, Laird. Shall I have the tea tray brought up?"

"That won't be necessary. Mr. Kendrick will not be staying long."

Logan's face tightened. "Are you truly not going to hear me out?"

"I can tolerate a brief discussion, but I'll be damned if I'll sit about drinking tea with you, pinkies extended. What I need is a damn whisky."

"At last, we agree on something," Logan said sardonically.

After the last few days, Nick needed more than drink. He needed to climb into the bloody bottle and live there.

"What do you want us to do, Nick?" Grant asked in a doleful voice. He and Graeme had actually managed to keep their mouths shut during the unpleasant scene.

"Stay the hell out of trouble," he said. Nick turned on his heel and headed to the library. The twins were the least of his problems at the moment.

He glanced behind to see his brother prowling in his wake, his gaze roaming the walls of the west gallery, taking in the portraits of their ancestors and looking like a man who'd forgotten his past but just remembered it. Angus, walking beside Logan, gave Nick a defiant stare, as if daring him to exclude him from the family council. The old man and Logan had always been close. In fact, they had corresponded frequently, although Angus believed Nick wasn't aware of that.

Of course he was, just as he was aware that Logan wrote to Kade and Braden as well. He'd turned a blind eye to it as long as Logan had the good sense to stay away. But since his brother clearly lacked in sense, hostilities were about to resume.

Royal caught up to him. "What are you going to do, Nick?"

"Hear him out, then kick him out."

"Don't you think—"

"No."

Nick opened the library door and stalked over to the glass-fronted mahogany cabinet with its collection of decanters and glasses. As the others filed in, he poured out a healthy dram of whisky—hoping it wasn't some of the illegal brew his brothers had cooked up—and shot it down, barely feeling the burn. Then he filled the glass again and took it back to his desk.

"You can get your own," he said.

"Not me. Someone in this bloody family has to keep a clear head," Royal said as he eased himself into one of the club chairs.

Angus retreated to his usual station by the fireplace, on the edges of the conversation. Nick had no illusions, however, that he would stay out of it.

In fact, he mentally braced himself for opposition from the entire family. Everyone missed Logan, and clearly felt it was time for him to be allowed to return home. After all, as Royal and Angus had pointed out, Cam's death had been an accident. But it was an accident that wouldn't have happened if Logan had been watching out for the little boy instead of flirting with a woman.

Women had always been Logan's weak spot, and that weakness had killed Nick's son.

Despite what his family might think, he had no intention of forgiving his brother—now, or ever.

Logan glanced at Royal, who was absently rubbing his bad leg. "Does it bother you much these days?"

Royal's reply was a terse shake of the head.

"It bothers him a great deal," Nick said. "That, however, is not your business. This *family* is not your business. I thought you had the sense to realize that and stay away."

Logan slammed his crystal tumbler down on the desk, sloshing whisky onto the polished surface. Nick watched it leach into the blotter, turning it a dark, ugly brown.

"The hell they're not my business," Logan snapped. "They're my family too. You don't own them."

"No, but I am their laird, as well as clan head. As I told you seven years ago, you forfeited your right to be either a Kendrick or a member of the clan when you let Cameron die through your negligence. In doing so, you destroyed *my* family."

Logan's blue eyes glittered with resentment as he leaned forward. "That's a bit dramatic. Perhaps we can also talk about the way *you* destroyed Janet's life. I'm not the only guilty party in this jolly family of ours, Nick, and you know it."

Nick found himself on his feet and halfway across the desk at his brother before he realized he'd even moved. "Say something like that again and I *will* kill you, Logan, regardless of the promise I made to Kade."

Royal reached out and whacked Logan on the arm. "What the hell is the matter with you? You're supposed to be apologizing, not making baseless accusations."

Logan straightened and rubbed his hands over his face. "Christ," he said in a thick voice, "you're right. Sorry, Nick.

That was a filthy thing for me to say. Chalk it up in my growing column of apologies."

Nick dropped back into his chair, weariness freighting his bones like chains. "You can keep your goddamn apologies, because I will never forgive you for Cam."

Janet's death was another story. As much as Nick hated to admit it, his brother was right about that.

"*Merde*," Logan muttered as he took the other seat in front of the desk.

When Nick first became earl, Logan had spent hours sitting in that very chair, helping to sort through massive amounts of estate business. Despite his devil-may-care approach to life, Logan had a sharp mind and a canny way with numbers. He'd turned that talent to his advantage, establishing a successful trade in timber and furs in Quebec.

Whatever the reason for his brother's return, it wasn't for money.

"I can understand how you feel," Logan finally said. "It was an accident, but it was still my fault."

Royal stared at him in disbelief. "Jesus, man, you almost drowned trying to save Cam. No one could have tried harder."

That was true, but Logan had persuaded Nick to let Cam go fishing with his uncles. Nick had made Logan swear to never take his eyes off the lad. His brother had promised, of course, with the reassuring laugh that came too easily to him.

It was the last time Nick had seen his son alive.

"Well, at least ye were able to bring the bairn home," said Angus. "That was a comfort."

Nick scoffed. "Comfort? Yes, a small one." But the image of his vibrant, darling child, locked away forever in a tomb of cold marble, still tore his heart into shreds. "At least my boy had a proper burial."

"What should comfort you is the knowledge that I will never forgive myself," Logan said.

"And you expect *me* to forgive you when you can't even forgive yourself?"

"Yes, because you're a better man than I am."

Nick reached for his glass. "Not according to your grandfather," he said before tossing down the rest of his drink.

Angus flushed, his bright red cheeks serving as a dramatic contrast to his snowy white hair. "Now, laddie, ye ken I dinna mean that. I just lost my temper a wee bit."

Royal hooted. "A wee bit? That's a laugh."

"What's going on here?" Logan asked.

Royal craned around to look at his grandfather. "Would you care to explain, or shall I?"

Angus began to inspect his boots.

"Someone better explain, or I'm going to start bashing heads," Logan said.

"That'll be different for you," Nick said sarcastically.

Logan scowled at him but had the brains to keep his mouth shut. When they were young, his brother had often gotten into fisticuffs just for the fun of it. He'd taken as easily to fighting as he had to drinking and womanizing. Logan had always been larger than life—a lovable rogue, as their stepmother had called him.

"All right, I'll tell you," Royal said. "My idiot brothers—"

"The twins, obviously," Logan interjected.

"Naturally. It would seem the twins set up a moonshining operation. Nick only found out about it yesterday when the customs officers came to call."

"Bloody hell," Logan sighed. "And Grandda knew about it, I'm assuming."

"Correct," Royal said.

Logan turned in his chair to glare at the old man. "What the hell is the matter with you?"

"According to Angus, I'm the problem," Nick said. "I abandoned the family when I 'ran off' to fight for my country. The twins' wild ways are, therefore, my fault."

Logan shook his head. "You were grieving, Nick. No one could blame you for that."

"It doesn't matter," he said impatiently. "Angus is right in the sense that I stayed away too long. All the boys needed my help and guidance, and I wasn't there to provide it."

"You weren't exactly whoring in a brothel or drinking yourself under the table all those years," Royal said. "You were commanding troops in battle."

"What's done is done. All I can do now is try to fix the problem."

With Victoria's help, Nick thought he might be able to polish up the twins enough to help them find respectable wives, at least if he didn't have the problem of Logan distracting him. Just being in the same room with his brother was starting to make him twitch.

"I think I might have a solution to that particular problem," Logan said.

"The twins?" Royal asked.

Logan nodded. "I know exactly what to do with them."

"There's nothin' wrong with the laddies," Angus said. "They're just young and full of vinegar."

"They're idiots is what they are," Royal said. "And the next time they get into trouble, Nick might not be able to get them out of it."

"They can work for me," Logan said. "I'm setting up an office and warehouse in Glasgow, and I can use the help."

When they all stared at him, he shrugged. "I'm a roaring success, as you might have heard. I've more than enough funds to support the twins, and then some." Logan cast a quick glance around the library. "And help out the estate, too, if need be."

"So you're just going to waltz in and fix everything, are you?" Nick jabbed a finger at Logan. "I don't need your damn help. I'm perfectly capable of taking care of the family *and* Kinglas."

"That's not what I heard," Logan said in a mild tone.

When Nick directed a hard stare at Angus, the old man winced. "Ye ken we need the help, lad. We're not as flush with funds as we used to be."

"And the reason for that is because of certain decisions *you* made while I was away," Nick said. "Decisions I am now trying to correct to put the estate back on its formerly sound footing."

"You did leave him in charge, Nick," Logan said. "I'm sure Angus did the best he could."

It was an entirely reasonable point. Unfortunately, Nick felt far from reasonable at the moment.

"Aye, that I did," Angus said with wounded dignity.

"Is that why you came back?" Nick asked his brother. "To assuage your guilt by buying me off?"

Logan's gaze narrowed to irritated slits. "I came back to help my family. Believe it or not, I miss them, including you."

"I repeat, I don't need your help," Nick replied in a cold voice.

"I think you do." Logan paused for a second, as if gathering himself. "And *I* need your forgiveness, so I'm not leaving until I get it."

Royal leaned forward, his gaze earnest. "It's time, Nick. You need to let it go."

Nick snorted. "You're one to talk—the man who never lets anything go."

"Like Logan said, you're a better man than we are."

Nick had heard quite enough about what a good man he was. Shoving back from his desk, he stood and glared at Logan. "Apparently, I'm not, because you'll be waiting until hell freezes over before I forgive you."

Chapter Fourteen

Victoria hurried down the hall to find Royal slouched on the floor by the library door and Angus pacing back and forth, all but wearing a path in the carpet. She paused to draw in a calming breath. The dramatics of the last few days were proving exceedingly trying—as were all the Kendrick men, starting with the earl and moving down the line.

Spotting her, Angus extracted an ancient-looking timepiece from his vest pocket. "Is the lad asleep? It's well-nigh eleven o'clock."

"Yes, finally. The poor boy was clearly worn out." Her short tone had the two men exchanging a guilty glance.

"How is he?" Royal asked as he pushed against the wall and clambered to his feet. "When I tried to talk to him, he would only say that we were all fatheads, and that he intended to ignore us until we stopped fighting."

"He's embarrassed by his family's behavior."

Angus bristled. "Embarrassed by his own family? Ridiculous."

"Personally, I think it's a sad state of affairs when a fifteen-year-old boy has more sense than his elders," she said.

The old man propped his hands on his hips. "Now, see here, lassie—"

"Oh, give over, Grandda," Royal interrupted. "She's right. We are fatheads, and that includes Nick."

Victoria glanced at the library door. "I'm assuming his lordship has yet to respond to any requests for admittance?"

"He has yet to respond to anything," Royal said tartly. "We've banged and yelled but he's ignored us."

Angus slumped against the wall. "He's swallowed a hare."

Victoria frowned. "I beg your pardon?"

"He's drunk, Miss Knight," Royal said. "Royally drunk."

"But his lordship rarely has more than a glass or two of wine at dinner." She'd never once seen him even slightly tipsy.

"True," Royal said, "but he's been drinking ever since Logan showed up."

"That's bad," she said.

"Lassie, ye have no idea how *bad* it truly is," Angus said with a sigh.

After the scene this afternoon, she'd taken Kade up to the schoolroom. They'd spoken a bit about Logan, though the boy hadn't wanted to discuss the incident that had led to the death of Arnprior's son or the estrangement between the brothers. All she could do was focus Kade on his studies as the best way to pass the time until someone came to speak to him.

When several hours passed with no visit from the earl or anyone else, Victoria had grown almost as worried as her young pupil. They'd finally gone down to dinner only to learn that the earl had ordered everyone to leave him alone and then holed up in his library.

"Then perhaps ye'd better tell her how bad it is," came Mrs. Taffy's voice from behind.

Victoria spun around to see the housekeeper in her neat cap and snowy apron, calmly regarding them.

"Dammit, woman," yelped Angus, scowling at Taffy. "Ye all but gave me a heart attack, sneakin' up like that."

"Taffy never sneaks," Royal said. "She's just very, very quiet."

The housekeeper threw a glance at the library door. "He hasna come out yet?"

Angus gloomily shook his head.

"That *is* bad," she said fretfully. "I think you should let Miss Knight have a try."

"Try what?" Victoria asked, surprised.

"Try to talk to him. The laird is not listening to his own family, and who could blame the puir man for that?"

"He won't like it," Angus warned. "No talking family business to outsiders."

Victoria sighed. "All this secrecy is getting to be quite trying, I must say."

"You're not truly an outsider anymore," Royal said.

It certainly didn't feel that way, but it wasn't Victoria's place to comment.

"Hmm," Angus said, "I think yer right about that, lad. And the laird would agree, I reckon."

A faint warning bell sounded in Victoria's mind. "I'm not sure—"

Angus interrupted her. "Ye ken the earl had a little boy named Cameron?"

She nodded. "Yes, and that he died in some way that led to an estrangement between the earl and his brother."

"Cameron drowned when he was four years old," Royal said bluntly.

"I . . . I'm so sorry," Victoria stammered.

"After the laird's wife passed, that little boy was everything to him," Taffy said with a quiet sorrow. "Master Cameron had the sweetest disposition, much like his uncle Kade."

"The laird was never the same," Angus said. "Cam's death all but destroyed the family."

"Why does he blame Logan?" Victoria asked.

"It was Logan's suggestion to take the boy fishing," Royal said. "He'd got Cam a little rod and reel for his birthday, and the lad was excited to try it out with his uncles. Nick was busy that day and couldn't join us, but Logan promised he wouldn't let Cam step a foot away from him."

Victoria pressed a hand to her stomach, feeling sick as her mind conjured awful scenarios. She'd seen a drowning once, at Brighton, and the horrible event had stuck in her mind for months afterward.

"We took him to a favorite spot—a burn just north of here that runs into the loch," Royal continued. "It was spring, and the water was running fast. As was Cam," he added with a bittersweet smile. "He was so excited, the scamp. Logan was practically run off his feet keeping him out of trouble."

"But he did get in trouble," Victoria said gently. "What happened?"

Taffy sighed. "A lass happened. As usual, with Logan."

"One of the daughters of the local gentry happened by," added Royal. "She was out riding. Logan was not a man to be tied down, but he actually seemed serious about that girl."

Angus heaved a sigh. "Aye, the lad was always a dab hand with the lassies. But he was fair taken with that one. Pretty as a picture, she was."

"Naturally, she pulled his attention away from Cam. The twins and I were farther upstream, just far enough away to make a difference. When Cam slipped and fell into the water, only Kade was close enough to make a grab for him."

Victoria gasped. "Kade went in after him?"

"Without a second thought," Royal said, shaking his

head. "That boy has more heart than the rest of us put together. As soon as he saw what was happening, Logan went in and started swimming for Cam, while I went after Kade. I managed to reach the boy and pull him back to shore, but barely. It's a miracle we didn't both drown in that swift current."

"That was when Kade caught that terrible fever," said Taffy. "He's been delicate ever since."

"The earl blames Logan for that as well, I suspect," Victoria said. The others didn't deny it.

Royal continued the grim tale. "The current swept Cam downstream toward the loch. We knew that if Logan didn't reach him before then, there would be no hope of saving him."

"But he did reach him," she said softly.

Royal nodded. "I've never seen anything like it. Logan battled the cold and the current for what seemed like forever. He wouldn't give up, even when we all knew it was too late to save Cam." He rubbed his chest, as if it pained him. "But he got the lad, he did. At least he was able to bring his body home to Nick."

For a few seconds, Victoria couldn't speak. "What a horrific nightmare," she finally managed. She thought of her own childhood. For all its tensions and strains, it was idyllic compared to what this family had suffered.

Angus rubbed his eyes and sniffed, so sad that Victoria wanted to envelop him in a hug. "We thought puir Nick would lose his wits when he saw the wee laddie dead."

Royal seemed to shake free of his emotion, resuming the story in a flat voice. "Yes, it was an awful scene. Nick blamed Logan, and they . . . fought. I'll spare you the details. Eventually, we managed to calm Nick down, mostly because Kade needed our attention. After Cam's funeral, Nick barely left Kade's side."

"Except to toss Logan out on his arse," Angus said bitterly. "That was when Nick told him never to step foot on Kendrick lands again."

"Can you blame him?" Taffy said sharply.

"Nay, but it isna right for them to still be feudin'. They've both suffered the guilt for too long."

"If there's one thing Nick does well it's feel guilt," Royal said.

"It seems to run in the family," Victoria commented.

"Ah, nicely done, Miss Knight," Royal said with the ghost of a smile. "Are there any other trenchant observations you'd like to make about us?"

"Possibly, but time is pressing and I'm growing quite concerned about Lord Arnprior. As are you, or you wouldn't be lingering in the hall like Macbeth's witches."

"There's no need to be insulting, lassie," Angus said indignantly.

She scoffed. "I can think of much worse insults to level at your family right now, sir. But the question remains— what is the earl doing in there?"

"Drinking himself into a stupor," Royal said.

"If that's all it is, then he'll recover," Victoria said. "But *is* that all he's going to do?" She was beginning to get a *very* bad feeling about the earl's state of mind.

"Are you afraid he might hurt himself?" Royal asked. "I wouldn't have said it was possible, but I haven't seen Nick this low—or this drunk—in years."

"It's more likely he'll go after Logan and shoot him," Angus said in a tone that suggested she should be consoled by that notion.

"No one is shooting anyone." Victoria rapped loudly on the library door. "Lord Arnprior, it's Miss Knight. I'd like to speak with you."

A deafening silence met her effort. She placed her ear against the door, but either the oak was too thick or the earl had fallen into a stupor—or worse.

She banged louder. "Sir, it's Miss Knight. Open up, please."

Angus winced. "Och, lass, if he dinna hear that yelling, he's already gone to the other side."

"And if he isn't dead, I'm quite sure he knows it's you," Royal said with a glimmer of humor.

"I fail to see the humor in the situation," she snapped.

"Then you're not looking hard enough," Royal said.

Victoria forced herself to ignore his jibe. "Is there another key to this room?"

"Taffy had one, but Nick made her hand it over," Royal said.

"The laird was insistent," Taffy said unhappily. "I've been going through the old keys to see if I can find an extra, but no luck yet."

Victoria sighed. "Can you keep looking?"

With a brisk nod, the housekeeper retreated to the main part of the house.

"We need to get into that room now," Victoria said, fighting a growing sense of panic.

Angus shook his head. "The laird gave strict orders to be left alone."

"Not to me. Is there another way we can get in?"

Royal snapped his fingers. "Good God, yes. The library windows overlooking the loch. If one is open, I can climb in and—"

"No, I will climb in and speak to the earl," Victoria interrupted. "He clearly has no desire to talk to any of you. I cannot say I blame him, since you *are* all acting like fatheads."

She ignored spluttering protests from Angus and set off toward the rear entrance to the wing.

Royal caught up with her. "Miss Knight, if he is awake, my brother is bound to be in a very foul mood. God only knows what he could do."

"What he will not do is hurt me," she said, with more

confidence than she felt. She was unnerved by the notion of venturing into Arnprior's lair, but she couldn't bear the idea of him suffering alone and without comfort.

"She's right," said Angus, who stomped along behind them. "Best let the lassie try her hand first."

Victoria glanced over her shoulder. "You actually agree with me?"

The old man gave her a bland smile. "No harm in tryin'."

She couldn't shake the feeling that Angus was up to something, but she didn't have leisure to parse the bizarre turns of his mind.

"You're both crazy," Royal said as he picked up the night lamp from the small table by the door.

"That we are, laddie," Angus said with a suspiciously cheerful demeanor.

They carefully picked their way around the side of the west wing. It was a dark night, with only a waning crescent moon to cast a pale shimmer over the gardens. The old tower house loomed like a ghostly remnant from ancient times, a few of its casement windows glowing with soft light. A cold wind gusted off the loch, the waves pounding against the shore with a distant crash.

All around them, the mountains were massive, inky blots against the sky, craggy peaks outlined by faint moonlight. It was a primitive, forbidding landscape, and Victoria couldn't repress an apprehensive shiver. Nor could she rid herself of the sense that something monumental was about to happen. If the king of the fairies had risen up from the ground before them, she wouldn't have been surprised.

Of course, she did *not* believe in premonitions, apparitions, fairies, silkies, or any other such Scottish nonsense. She was simply cold.

Royal voiced her thought. "You're not dressed for this weather."

"How perceptive of you to notice."

His only reply was a chuckle.

Angus, who'd gone ahead of them, peered into one of the library windows. "I canna see a bloody thing."

Victoria went up on tiptoe to peer over his shoulder. The only light in the room came from the fire, which had burned low. It barely penetrated the Stygian gloom. She could make out the outlines of the big leather club chair in front of the grate, and the gleam from the polished leather of large booted feet.

"I believe his lordship is sitting near the fire," she said.

Royal elbowed Angus aside. "He's not moving, from the looks of it. Probably drunk as an emperor by now."

"Then we can only hope he's fallen asleep," Victoria said. "If so, I can open the door and let you both in. Then you or the footmen can carry him to his room."

"If you can find the key to the door," Royal said. "He might not have left it in the lock."

"Oh, blast. I hadn't thought of that."

"Ye can search his body," Angus said in a helpful tone. "I'm sure Nick wouldna mind."

"I will do no such thing, Mr. MacDonald." Victoria couldn't help blushing at the idea of running her hands over the earl's brawny form. Thank God it was too dark for anyone to see her color up.

Royal smothered a laugh. "If it's not in the door, it's probably in his waistcoat pocket. I'm sure there will be no need to violate my brother's dignity in any comprehensive way."

"Please just open the window," Victoria ordered.

She saw the gleam of Royal's teeth as he smiled. Then he wrestled with the sash for a moment before opening the window.

"Last chance," he said. "Are you sure you don't want me to go in?"

Her nerve failed for a moment, then she shook her head.

"No, the earl is probably asleep. And if he's not, he's less likely to fire up at me than he is at one of you."

"She's right, lad," Angus said.

"I don't like it, but I suspect that's true," Royal said. "Up with you, then."

He took her by the waist and boosted her up onto the sill. She perched for a moment, getting her bearings, then swung her legs over and dropped down to the floor. Treading as softly as she could, she made her way toward the fireplace.

The earl's lanky body was stretched out in the club chair, his boots propped against the firedogs and his hands laced over his stomach. His chin rested on his chest, his posture deeply relaxed. Even before hearing the slow, steady rhythm of his breath, she'd known he was asleep.

She spied an empty whisky decanter on the floor beside his chair, along with a crystal tumbler on its side. The earl had obviously drunk his way into blessed oblivion. Still, a frown marked his brow and worry lines bracketed his mouth, signs that restless dreams disturbed his slumber. She wished she could smooth them away with a gentle stroke of her fingertips.

Or her mouth . . .

Victoria almost jumped out of her shoes when Angus's stentorian whisper echoed through the silence. "What's happening, lassie?" he hissed.

She pressed a hand over her thudding heart. "He's . . . he's asleep."

"Check the door for the key," Royal said quietly.

"Right." She scolded herself for being a ninny as she hurried over to the door. Why was she fantasizing about kissing Arnprior? Even in her dreams, she had no business thinking of her employer in so scandalous a manner, no matter how handsome he might be.

And no matter how much she was convinced he needed her—needed her in some way she had yet to define.

There was no confounded key in the door. But just to make sure, she rattled the knob. The door remained firmly locked.

A freezing gust blew through the open window, causing the drapes to billow out like a giant's cloak. Shivering, she hurried back to the others.

"It's not there," she said.

"Naturally," Royal said.

Angus, now carrying the lamp, jerked it up to look at her. With the light flickering erratically over the men's faces, casting their eyes into deeply shadowed sockets, they looked rather like ghouls.

Victoria tried to repress a shiver, annoyed that she was letting her nerves get the best of her.

"Are ye all right, lassie?" Angus asked.

"Yes, but it's gotten very cold, hasn't it?" The wind off the loch had picked up.

"Aye, cold enough to freeze the brass—"

"Yes, quite," she hastily said. "I suggest you gentlemen go back inside and wait by the library door. I'll find the key and let you in."

"I think I should come in now," Royal said, preparing to hoist up.

"You'll do no such thing," she said. Royal had been favoring his leg all day and the last thing Victoria needed was an injured man on top of an inebriated one. "I'm perfectly capable of searching for the key and letting you in as soon as I find it."

"If my brother wakes up—"

She shoved him back and started to pull down the sash. "He'll only wake up if you keep arguing."

"But—"

She closed the window in their faces. When they scowled

at her through the glass, she made a shooing motion, then soft-footed her way back to the earl.

The fire had burned down to embers that cast a soft glow, highlighting the planes of the earl's rugged face. He hadn't stirred, even though they'd made an ungodly amount of noise.

Arnprior's hands were loosely clasped over his stomach, making it tricky to reach into his waistcoat pocket without waking him. If he came awake while she was in the midst of groping him, he could only think such behavior was highly inappropriate on the part of his employee.

Well, as her grandfather used to say, nothing tried, nothing gained.

Leaning over him—and trying to ignore the rise and fall of his exceedingly brawny chest—she carefully pushed aside the edges of his tailcoat. Thank God he'd unbuttoned that, at least. The thought of undressing him to any degree was having a rather marked effect on her pulse.

She'd just started to wriggle a hand into the pocket of his waistcoat when he moved so quickly that it was a blur. Between one breath and the next, he'd wrapped his long fingers around her wrist.

Startled, she let out a squeak and all but toppled into his lap. He clapped his other hand around her waist, holding her steady but awkwardly poised over him.

She jerked her head up to look at him. His amazing eyes gleamed at her like molten silver.

"Why, Victoria Knight," he purred in a low, seductive voice. "What in the world are you doing?"

Chapter Fifteen

"Ah . . . ah, my lord . . ." Victoria stammered like a schoolgirl, unable to voice a coherent thought. In fact, she seemed unable to do anything but stare into his riveting gaze.

"Well, Miss Knight? Are you picking my pockets or trying to grope me?" His brogue had deepened, lending a seductive tone to his voice.

"Of course I'm not trying to grope you." She tried to sound and look appropriately indignant, but she had a bad feeling her cheeks were glowing as red as the embers in the hearth. And her voice came out disappointingly weak.

When she tried to pull away, he held her wrist in a gentle but inexorable grip. "Ah, I was so hoping you were about to have your way with me."

"My lord, really," she huffed.

"And you didn't deny you were picking my pocket."

"No."

Victoria shifted, all too aware that she was still leaning over him, almost chest to chest. She was so close she could see the tiny lines around his eyes and the fine grain of his beard scruff where it darkened his jaw.

She was also starting to get a sore back from bending over.

"May I ask why?" he purred in that husky brogue.

"I was trying to find the key to the door. Sir, this is a rather awkward and painful posture," she said, giving another tug against his hold.

Humor gleamed in his eyes. Blast him, he was finding this entire humiliating situation amusing.

"Of course," he said. "Especially for a woman as starched-up and proper as you are."

"I am not—"

Suddenly he pulled her toward him, and in the blink of an eye she was sprawled inelegantly across his lap. While her brain scrambled to catch up, he arranged her neatly across his thighs.

He had *very* muscular thighs, ones that she felt quite easily through his tight-fitting breeches and the too-thin fabric of her gown and shift.

"My lord, what are you doing?" she finally managed to gasp.

"Correcting your awkward posture. Surely this position is much easier on your back."

She stared at him, taking in the wicked curve of his sensual mouth. She should be shrieking the house down around their ears, and yet all she wanted to do was snuggle closer.

Clearly, she had lost her mind.

Victoria tried once more to gather her wits as well as her morals, which had gone missing the moment he touched her. "My lord, I only came in here to check on you, not engage in . . ."

Well, she really didn't know quite how to classify the moment. The earl was not a man to dally with any woman, nor did this feel remotely like that frightening experience with Thomas Fletcher. She felt instinctively that if she tried to scramble off his lap, he would make no effort to prevent her.

Arnprior leaned forward and kissed the tip of her nose. "Engage in what, Miss Knight?" he murmured before brushing his warm lips across her cheek.

When she recovered from that shock, she tried to summon a stern look. "Sir, I believe you are not at all yourself tonight."

His eyebrows arched up in an offended lift. "If you think I'm trying to seduce you because I'm drunk, Miss Knight, you are very wrong. I may be a bit jug-bitten, but I have not clipped the King's English."

She frowned. "I have no idea what that means."

He leaned in, nose to nose. Her heart galloped around her chest.

"It means I am in perfect command of my faculties," he whispered.

"I cannot agree with you." She began to wriggle, trying to communicate her desire to get off his lap. It seemed to produce the opposite effect, though, since he let out a strangled groan and held on even tighter.

A moment later, she knew why. A quite formidable erection was now pressing into her backside. "Sir! I think you'd best let me go before something untoward occurs."

God, she sounded like a complete ninny.

He sucked in a deep breath, as if composing himself. "I disagree that it would be for the best, but very well."

Victoria let out a panicked squeak when he leaned over and reached for the footstool beside the chair.

"I'm not going to drop you, love," he said, holding her securely with his other arm.

Love? Despite his protests, he must be even more foxed than she thought.

With his easy strength, he placed her on the footstool, then smoothed down her skirts with exaggerated care.

"Better?" he murmured.

A good part of her did not think it was better, but of course she would die before admitting as much. "Yes, thank you, sir."

He settled back in an elegant masculine sprawl, looking much too comfortable given the upsets of the last few days. Victoria couldn't help noticing the continued evidence of his arousal, since it thrust aggressively against the fall of his breeches. While that should alarm her, she was sorry to say it seemed to be having the opposite effect.

"Now, my little governess," he said with a lazy smile, "tell me why you climbed through my library window."

She sighed. "You heard."

"The three of you were as loud as a cavalry regiment on a charge. No sleeping through that."

"Then why didn't you open the confounded door when we knocked?" she said with exasperation. "We were worried about you, so I came in to find the key to let the others in."

"Ah." His silvery gaze narrowed to irritated slits. "And I chose not to answer because I didn't want to. Obviously."

She pressed a finger to her lips, trying to quell her irritation. Unfortunately, that brought his focus down to her mouth and the seductive gleam back to his eyes.

He reached out to gently tug a lock of hair straggling down by her cheek. "In any case, both keys are on my desk. It wasn't necessary for you to grope me."

"Royal said the key would likely be in your pocket," she said defensively.

He flashed a sardonic smile. In all fairness, she *had* been groping him.

"I did it with good intentions," she said.

He nodded. "As you said, you were worried about me."

"Your *family* is worried about you. I volunteered to check on you."

"By stumbling around in the dark and then crawling through the window?"

Put like that, it did sound rather absurd.

He craned over the arm of his chair to stare down at the whisky decanter. "Dammit, it's empty. Miss Knight, would you be so good as to fetch me another decanter from the sideboard."

"I believe you have had enough drink for one evening," she said in her best governess voice.

His disgusted snort told her what he thought of that assertion.

"Sir, if you would—"

"Why did *you* crawl in here instead of Royal or Angus?"

She tried to think of a diplomatic way to phrase it. "Because it was fairly evident that you would not welcome an intervention from them."

He snorted. "You mean you were afraid I'd bash their heads in. As were they, no doubt."

She waggled a hand. "Royal was quite willing to take the risk. However, I didn't think a brawl would be helpful at the moment."

"So you were the noble sacrifice, sent into the lion's den?"

Victoria couldn't hold back a wry smile, since that was exactly what she'd been thinking just before she'd crawled through the window. "I was fairly certain you wouldn't bash my head in."

He leaned forward, his lips curling up in a rather menacing sneer. "So, you think me a tame lion, Miss Knight?"

She refused to be intimidated. "No, I think you a gentleman, sir. And a kind man, as well."

He slumped back with a sigh. "Not according to my brothers or Angus. To them, I'm a bastard for keeping Logan away."

He looked so grim and weary she instinctively rested a hand on his knee. "They know you're still grieving."

"They told you everything, I suppose," he said.

She was surprised to find herself leaning against his leg. Somehow, though, it felt entirely natural.

"I'm so very sorry about your little boy," she said.

For several long moments, all she heard was the ticking of the clock on the mantel and the hiss of the embers in the grate.

"I still miss him so much," he finally said.

The quiet sorrow in his voice all but broke her heart. "What was he like?"

He stared into the fire. "Cam was a bright light for all of us, lass. The sweetest boy. I know it sounds a cliché, but he was the best thing that ever happened to me."

Not his wife. Victoria tucked that bit of information away for later.

"Did he look like you?" she asked.

He chuckled. "He was a Kendrick, all right. He had black hair and blue eyes, and he was always happy. Cam was much like Kade in that respect, a good-natured child who loved everyone. He also had a knack for getting into trouble, just like the twins."

"Boys usually do."

The warmth faded from his expression. "My wife didn't know what to do with him. She'd wanted a girl, someone like her instead of a rambunctious Kendrick male."

Victoria hid her surprise. Most aristocratic women felt like a failure if they didn't produce a male heir within a few years of marriage.

As if sensing her surprise, Arnprior shrugged. "Janet was never truly comfortable with children, especially boys. She loved our son but did not see the need to involve herself in his care."

Victoria tapped his knee. "Which is why people like you hire people like me."

He flashed her a rueful smile. "True, but I loved spending

time with Cam. I was used to managing boys, because I had to raise my younger brothers."

"Surely you had Angus to help with that, too."

"Yes, he was a grand help," he said sardonically.

"I know he's a trial, but he cares for you and wishes to support you. As do your brothers."

"One would never know it, considering the way they've behaved lately."

"And we're working to change all that, are we not?"

He reached for her hand and laced his fingers with hers. The touch of his warm, rough skin, the way his hand all but swallowed hers up, made every nerve in her body skitter with anticipation.

"I failed them," he said gruffly.

"I don't follow."

"After Cam died, I lost myself. I did things I'm not proud of."

Victoria squeezed his hand. "You lost so much. First your wife, and then your little boy."

"No, Angus was right. The rest of them were grieving too, but I didn't care. I didn't care about anything other than Cam was dead and Logan was responsible."

From what she'd heard, Logan had taken the loss almost as hard as his brother, but now was not the time to make such an argument. "I'm sure you did the best you could for everyone."

He scoffed. "I abandoned my family when they needed me the most, using my military duty as an excuse. I was a coward."

"Now, that is just nonsense. And I might venture to add, my lord, that it is not productive to engage in self-recrimination when one is feeling, ah, under the weather."

"Spoken like a true governess," he said, gently taunting. "Do you have any other advice for me?"

She thought about it for a moment. "Perhaps you might stop blaming yourself for everything?"

Arnprior snorted. "You must admit I've done an appalling job with my brothers, especially the twins. I should have been here to ride herd over them, as well as attend to the rest of my responsibilities."

"Graeme and Grant are grown men. They are not entirely brainless and are certainly old enough to know better." She frowned. "Well, Graeme acts as if he is rather brainless, but I'm still hopeful we can work on that."

He softly chuckled, then let go of her hand only to capture her chin between his fingers. "Miss Knight, have I told you lately how happy I am that I hired you?"

She stared at him, once more transfixed by his amazing eyes. "I think you have, from time to time, communicated your appreciation."

When he chuckled again, she couldn't help wincing at how starched up she sounded.

A silence fell over the room, broken only by the occasional pop of the embers and the slow, steady rhythm of his breath. And perhaps he could hear the thrumming of her heart, which was beating so hard she wanted to press a hand to her chest. It seemed impossible to move, even though she should be scrambling to put distance between them.

His gaze slid down to her mouth, and then he tilted her chin up to bring her closer as he leaned in. He was going to kiss her, and she couldn't do a thing to stop him.

Correction. She didn't *wish* to do a thing to stop him, even though stern warnings were writing themselves across her brain in big, black letters.

His warm breath whispered over her face. "Och, lassie, I don't believe I've shown my appreciation quite enough."

It was the brogue that did it, by adding a rough, husky

note that seduced her as nothing else could have. Her eyelids fluttered shut, her entire being waiting for his kiss.

The soft sweep of his callused thumb brushed over her lips, then traced their outline. That simple touch weakened every muscle in her body. When his mouth descended on hers, it took every ounce of strength not to collapse into a heap at his feet—because *that* would have been an extraordinarily stupid waste of the moment.

Arnprior kissed her slowly but possessively, with soft, damp caresses that teased her mouth with delicious warmth. His tongue slipped gently along the seam of her lips, not pushing or rushing, but simply tasting. After several moments of soft teasing, he then kissed her again with a provocative pressure that made her want to cling to him.

By now, both of his big hands were cradling her head as he kissed her with leisurely expertise. Her fingers fluttered up to rest on his wrists as she absorbed the heady taste of whisky and a man who knew exactly what he wanted. She sensed the barely leashed passion in him and the danger that the slightest push would tip him over the edge. He would then take what she so tentatively offered, dragging them down a path from which there was no return.

Victoria wanted him as much as he wanted her. But the earl was drunk and weary of soul, no doubt simply seeking comfort in the first available warm body. It surely had nothing to do with her, and everything to do with the grief and worry that threatened to overwhelm him.

So stop him. Now.

His firm mouth moved over hers in a seductive slide that somehow obliterated any desire to retreat or deny him. When his tongue slipped out to gently press open her lips, she couldn't hold back a moan.

In an instant, everything changed. He growled low in his throat, his tongue surging into her mouth as he devoured her with a soul-searing passion she'd never imagined could exist. Victoria's entire body began to throb with desire, urging her to press herself against him without restraint or shame.

When he suddenly let her go, she gasped and clutched at his knees to keep from toppling over. For a moment, they stared at each other. His blue eyes were hungry and turbulent, his breath unsteady. Victoria knew she should take the chance to escape, but all she could do was stare at him, transfixed by the irresistible pull of his passionate gaze.

"Come here, you," he growled.

A moment later, he clamped his hands around her waist and swept her up into his lap. She sucked in a startled breath, amazed by his almost frightening strength. This time, however, when he tried to settle her across his lap for more devastating kisses, she resisted, slapping both hands on his chest to hold him off. For a moment, she was distracted by the feel of his hard muscles under the slippery silk of his waistcoat.

His gaze narrowed. "What's wrong?"

"You cannot possibly wish to kiss me." She'd hoped to sound more decisive, but her voice came out on a breathy squeak.

His lips curved up in a wicked grin. "I assure you, Miss Knight, I wish to kiss you very much."

When his head bent to hers, she pressed her fingers against his lips. "Stop, please."

He pulled back with an exasperated sigh. "Perhaps you'd like to enlighten me as to why you wish me to cease something that is clearly pleasing to both of us."

She had to give him credit. For a man thoroughly in his cups, he sounded remarkably articulate.

As she was reclining in his lap in a graceless, immodest sprawl, she struggled to sit up.

He sucked in a pained breath. "Careful, my dear."

"Sorry, sir." That impressive bit of masculinity was again

pressing against her bottom. Apparently, wriggling about too vigorously might damage it, which was—

Stop thinking about it.

But that was almost impossible when sitting on the aroused lap of the most virile man she'd ever met.

Victoria cautiously sat up and met his gaze. Rather than a passionate lion, he now looked more like a surly bear— one awakened from a long hibernation. She'd read that such bears could be very dangerous, since they were both grumpy and hungry.

Arnprior was definitely hungry.

Blowing an errant bit of hair from her face, she tried to adopt her most stern governess look. Unfortunately, his only response was a blink and then a slow smile curving up the corners of his mouth as he settled his hands around her waist.

"All right, Madam Governess, try to convince me that I don't wish to kiss you."

"You're simply trying to distract yourself, sir. You're feeling . . . a bit under the weather."

"Is that so?"

"Resorting to pleasurable activities is often what people do when they're feeling . . ."

"Under the weather?" he finished with a grin that resembled a smirk.

She sounded utterly ridiculous, but she had no choice but to stick it out. "Yes, exactly."

When he shifted underneath her, she had to bite back a gasp at the feel of his hard thighs and even harder erection.

"Miss Knight, let me reassure you that I am feeling quite a lot," he murmured. He punctuated his comment by kissing the tip of her nose. It was a sweet, funny gesture that almost made her giggle.

Giggling was not allowed, since it would only encourage

them both. He certainly needed no such encouragement, and she felt like she was hanging on by her fingertips.

He cupped her chin and once again rubbed his callused thumb gently over her lips, drawing forth tingles of pleasure. The man was a menace—a handsome, seductive sorcerer.

"Tell me what's wrong, my sweet?" he murmured.

"Aside from the fact that I'm sitting on my employer's lap?" she asked tartly.

"Yes, aside from that," he said, seeming to believe it was entirely reasonable for her to be perched on top of him.

At the moment she seemed to be having a problem in marshaling arguments for *not* sitting on his lap.

Think harder. "We've already verified that you're only kissing me as a way to distract yourself."

He frowned. "What's wrong with that?"

"Everything."

"I disagree. I'm entirely in possession of my wits, and I know exactly what I want to do."

"My lord—"

He tipped her back over his arm, taking her mouth in another deliciously passionate kiss that all but blasted her resistance into the next county. Helpless to do anything but clutch at his broad shoulders, Victoria held on and kissed him back with dazed enthusiasm.

But when one of his hands went to her knee and started inching up her skirts, she froze, her brain seeming to knock about in her skull. Then she hurtled into a memory, one that flashed vivid and horrible. Thomas Fletcher was holding her down as his sweaty hands tried to pull up her gown.

Panic squeezed her chest and rocketed through her veins. She reacted instinctively, jerking away and swatting at the brawny body that encircled her.

"Stop, stop," she gasped, struggling to get away. Blind fear ruled her body, making it clumsy and stiff.

Instantly, Arnprior retreated. "All right, love, all right. But stop struggling or you'll hurt yourself."

She was in the grip of something stronger than reason. Her intellect knew she was safe with him, but her body rebelled. "I . . . I . . . can't . . ." she stuttered.

A moment later, she found herself deposited back on the stool.

"Just breathe, Victoria," he said, gently stroking her hair. "You're safe with me. I won't hurt you."

She nodded, feeling utterly miserable and more stupid by the second. But Arnprior just continued to stroke her hair, murmuring comforting words in a low, soothing voice.

Soon, she felt herself again, but also embarrassed. She knew Arnprior would never hurt her. She'd even wanted that kiss as much as he had, and yet she'd been unable to control the fear that had swept through her like a raging storm off the loch.

"Do you want to talk about what just happened?" the earl asked.

She shook her head. She hated talking about Fletcher. Dominic had also made it abundantly clear that no one, not even Arnprior, should know that her attacker had died at her hand.

Besides, if she told the earl, he would probably view her with disapproval or even disgust. And the notion that he might then send her away was more distressing than she could ever have imagined.

"I'd rather not," she whispered.

Arnprior looked puzzled, but then slumped back in his chair. "God, what an idiot I am. I forgot that you'd been subjected to this sort of behavior in your previous position. I beg you to forgive me for acting in so disgusting a manner, Miss Knight. I can't imagine what you must think of me."

He closed his eyes, looking disheartened. He'd certainly

never meant to hurt her, and she couldn't bear to let him feel worse than he already did.

Victoria smoothed her skirts, composing herself. Then she rested a hand on his knee. His eyes lifted and his gaze fastened on her face.

"I think you are the most honorable man I've ever met," she said gently.

"Yes, as my behavior tonight has so clearly indicated." He shook his head. "You should go, my dear. I'll be fine."

She knew with total conviction that he would not be fine if she left him.

In fact, she never wanted to leave him again.

Victoria packed that astounding revelation away in the back of her mind, to be examined later when she was calm enough to be rational about it.

She slipped off the stool and onto her knees in front of him. "I'm not leaving you, sir." Cautiously, she rested a hand on his chest, right over his heart. It thumped hard and fast under her palm.

"What are you doing?" he asked gruffly.

She shrugged. "Honestly, I haven't a clue."

That startled a laugh out of him. "I suppose I don't have a clue, either. But I do know one thing."

"What's that?"

"I want to hold you," he said, gently stroking her cheek. "Just that and nothing more. Would that be all right?"

"I think I'd like that."

"Are you sure?"

She gave him a tremulous smile. "Yes."

As he came down to her, gently lowering her to the floor, she castigated herself for being ten times a fool.

But Arnprior needed her warmth and her comfort. And *she* needed to comfort him, with a desperation that almost stole her breath.

She found herself flat on her back on the carpet, the soft

woolen pile prickling the back of her neck and her calves. He wrapped his body around hers, his face resting on her chest. Her bodice had slipped a bit, and his bristly cheek nestled against her sensitive skin. He was incredibly big and muscled, and the size and strength of him should have scared her out of her wits.

Instead, it felt wonderful.

Arnprior tucked her close and let out a long, weary sigh that wrenched her heart. She rested a hand on the back of his head, stroking his thick, soft hair as their breaths settled into one steady rhythm. Peace stole over her, the kind she'd not felt in a long time. All her tensions and fears slid away, allowing her to feel warm, safe, and cherished.

She drifted into a dreamy state for a minute or two before realizing his breathing had changed. It was now slow and deep. His body had also relaxed to the point where he was slumped heavily on top of her.

"My lord?" she murmured.

No answer.

"Lord Arnprior," she said in a louder tone, nudging him in the shoulder.

A soft snore was his only reply.

She groaned and let her head fall back to the carpet. Perfect. Not only had he passed out on top of her, he was so heavy she would probably strain her back just trying to move him.

As she was trying to deduce the best way to wriggle free, she heard an alarming series of rattles, then approaching footsteps. Her startled gaze flew up to meet the equally startled gazes of Angus, Royal, and Mrs. Taffy. All three stared down at her, their mouths gaping in almost identical ovals.

"I see you found an extra key," Victoria finally said in a weak voice.

Royal recovered first. "And I see *you've* done quite a good job of calming Nick down," he said with a chuckle.

"Aye, that she has," Angus said in a thoughtful tone.

"This is not what it looks like," Victoria protested.

Taffy's perusal traveled slowly over their tangled bodies. "I'd venture it's exactly what it looks like, Miss Knight."

Victoria craned her head to look down at herself and had to repress a groan. Her skirts were hiked around her knees, exposing her garters, and her bodice was a disaster. The earl's head rested comfortably on her breast, his mouth only a fraction of an inch from where her nipple was barely concealed by her chemise.

"Would you like help getting up?" Royal asked politely. "Or would you prefer to spend the night on the floor with Nick."

She thunked her head back onto the floor. "I'd prefer you leave and pretend you never saw anything."

Angus grinned. "Sorry, lass, but there's no unseeing this."

Victoria sighed. "Then you'd best just shoot me and get it over with."

Chapter Sixteen

A bloody great headache awaited Nick on the other side of sleep. And was he lying on a block of wood? It was either that or his mattress urgently needed restuffing.

He cracked open his eyelids. Above him was the plaster-work medallion of his library ceiling, not the canopy of his bed.

"It's about time ye returned to the land of the livin'," barked a voice he had no trouble recognizing. "We were about to send for the surgeon."

Nick shot upright into a sitting position, then clutched his head as pain knifed through his skull. "Jesus." He squeezed his eyes shut. "Don't yell."

"He was practically whispering." Royal said. "At least as much as Grandda can whisper."

"I can whisper," Angus loudly protested. "I can be silent as the bloody grave, ye ken."

Nick opened his eyes to glare at them. "Would you both shut it? My head's going to explode."

He couldn't remember ever having felt this disgusting. He had any number of character flaws, but getting piss drunk wasn't one of them.

"Aye, yer stale drunk this morning, laddie," Angus said in a sympathetic voice.

The old man was sitting in one of the chairs in front of the fireplace. Royal stood behind him, leaning a casual elbow on the back of the club chair.

"Thank you for stating the obvious." Nick tried to rub out the ache at the base of his neck. "And could one of you explain what I'm doing down here?"

"You drank almost an entire decanter of whisky and passed out," Royal said. "And since you're too bloody heavy to move, we left you to sleep it off."

Nick tossed aside the blanket that someone had thoughtfully placed over his legs. "I do remember getting jug-bitten, which I will never do again, by the way. But how did I end up on the blasted floor?"

Angus shrugged. "We dinna ken. Ye'll have to ask the lassie."

A vague image started to coalesce in the back of Nick's mind. "The lassie?"

Royal nodded. "Miss Knight. She was the only person in the room when you, er, ended up on the floor."

"When ye both ended up on the floor," Angus corrected.

Nick braced his elbows on his bent knees and rested his throbbing head in his palms. Fractured memories of the previous evening started punching their way up through the fog, flooding his brain with vivid images—Victoria sitting on the footstool before him, Victoria sitting on his lap, and, finally, Victoria lying beneath him on the floor, with his cheek cushioned on the gentle swell of her breasts.

Bloody. Damn. Hell.

Most vivid of all, he remembered the glorious taste of her mouth as he took everything she'd sweetly and innocently offered. Even as wretched as he felt now, with wet wool for brains and a mouth like the inside of a cave, his body stirred at the memory.

"Och, ye were like an old married couple snug in yer bed," Angus said with an expansive wave. "It fair brought a tear to mine eye to see ye so content, lad. Like wrapt up in warm flannel, ye were."

Royal tried to smother a laugh at the stupid joke. *Wrapt up in flannel* was cant for blind drunk.

"Christ," Nick sighed. He flopped back to the floor and rubbed his aching temples. "Please tell me I didn't hurt or frighten the poor girl."

"Oh, not a bit," Royal said. "She seemed more than happy to offer you comfort in your time of need."

And he'd clearly been more than happy to receive it. It had all come back to him now. His wretchedly foul mood and how he'd tried to drown it in whisky, and then Victoria climbing through the damn window, doing her best to talk sense into him. Her gentle warmth had chased away the grim memories haunting him last night.

He sat up and tossed aside the plaid blanket, hauling himself to his feet. His head swam for a few moments, but he refused to give in to the urge to find the nearest bucket and empty his stomach. He wanted to know exactly what happened last night, and he needed to think about Victoria and how to do right by her.

Nick made his way over to the bellpull and yanked it. He desperately needed coffee. "You shouldn't have let her come in here," he growled as he stalked back to his desk.

"Couldn't stop her," Royal said, taking the chair in front of Nick's desk.

"You couldn't stop that wee slip of a girl from climbing in the bloody window?" Nick asked in disbelief.

"We tried," Angus said in a soulful tone. "But that lass was fair insistent."

"Cowards."

"Can you blame us?" Royal said.

Nick snorted. "Yes."

The door opened and Andrew cautiously peeked in. "Ye rang, Laird?"

"Tell Taffy to bring up a pot of coffee."

"Aye, sir."

"And don't slam the—" Nick winced when the footman, in his haste to escape, banged the door shut. It would appear he'd terrorized the entire household, with the exception of Victoria.

"Ye'll be feelin' as queer as Dick's hatband, I'm thinkin'," Angus said.

"Trenchantly put, as always," Nick replied. "But that hardly matters. What matters is what happened in here, and how it will affect Miss Knight's reputation. How did she seem about all"—he circled a hand—"this."

"She asked me to shoot her," Royal said.

"Good God," Nick said.

"Aye," Angus said happily. "No other choice but to marry the puir lass. The sooner, the better."

Nick was reaching the same inevitable conclusion. Surprisingly, he felt quite sanguine about the notion. But for Angus to approve? "Why are you so bloody pleased? You don't even like Victoria."

His grandfather shrugged. "She's not bad for a Sassenach, and she's a dab hand at managin' the lads."

Nick narrowed his gaze. The old man had been pushing him to remarry for years. Now it looked like he was finally going to get his way.

"I don't think you have much choice," Royal said. "You either have to marry the girl or send her quietly back to London and hope no one hears about last night's events."

"What are the odds Sir Dominic or Alec won't get wind of this little incident?" Nick asked. "If the girl's reputation comes under any sort of question, those two will murder me."

They probably would anyway, unless he did the right

thing and married her. There was, however, a large question yet unresolved.

"You're wondering if Miss Knight will agree to marry you, I'm guessing," Royal said with his usual perception.

"How could I not?" Nick asked.

His brother waggled a hand. "I'd say it could go either way. After we managed to get her out from under you, she flew out of here like hellhounds were baying at her heels."

Nick had to wince at the description, though it instantly conjured up the enticing image of Victoria under him, naked in bed.

"The lass made us promise not to say anything about what we saw," Angus said. "I told her it would be verra hard to unsee that particular sight."

The door opened and Taffy marched in with the coffee.

"And did you keep your mouths shut?" Nick asked.

Taffy glanced at Angus and made a scoffing noise as she placed the tray on the corner of the big desk.

"As if Grandda could keep his mouth shut about anything," Royal said.

Nick sighed as Taffy poured a small packet of headache powders into a glass of water. "So, what *do* the servants know?"

"They ken the laird was locked away with the governess for quite some time," she said tartly.

"And that you were drunk," Royal added in a helpful tone.

Nick shot down the headache powders in one gulp, ignoring their bitter taste—and his brother's amusement.

"Sir, Miss Knight may be a wee bit rattled by last night's events," Taffy said as she handed him a cup of coffee. "But she's no fool. She knows verra well what this means."

"And what needs to happen next," Royal said.

Nick took several gulps of the hot brew, waiting for the usual jolt to clear his head. While he was prepared to do the right thing, was Victoria prepared to accept him? She'd seemed more than happy to receive his kisses last night, though that might have been mostly motivated by pity.

That was a remarkably unappealing conjecture.

"It's time, laddie," Angus said. "Ye need to get on with yer life. Besides, yer the laird, and a laird needs a lady."

"Even if she's a Sassenach?"

"She won't be once she marries ye. Besides, ye must admit she's a lady to the tips of her wee toes."

"It would be grand to have a true lady around the house again," Taffy said wistfully.

Nick studied the faces of the three people who were his greatest supporters, even if they sometimes drove him mad. They were clearly united in purpose, an unusual event in his household.

"I sense a conspiracy," he said.

"One that is surely in your best interest," Royal said. "And Miss Knight's."

"She might not agree with that." Nick knew her history—at least some of it—and he had no wish to force her into an unpalatable relationship. But her reputation and her future were now at stake.

"There's only one way to find out," Royal said.

Nick shoved back from his desk. "Where is she?"

"In the schoolroom with Master Kade." Taffy eyed him. "But ye'll surely be wanting to have a change before speaking with her, sir."

"Later," he said as he strode to the door.

"Good luck," Royal said.

"Ye'll need it, lookin' like that," Angus yelled after him.

As Nick took the stairs two at a time, he considered taking their advice. But he couldn't wait to make sure she was truly all right. Besides, she'd already seen him at his worst. At least he was now sober.

He reached the second floor, where the schoolroom,

nursery, and bedrooms for nursemaids and tutors were. He rarely came up here, since those rooms carried too many painful memories of his little boy. But someday, perhaps, they would once again be filled with the sound of children's laughter.

Pausing outside the schoolroom door, he ran a quick hand through his hair and straightened his waistcoat. He had no idea where his coat was but supposed it didn't matter. As far as marriage proposals went, this one would be unconventional at best.

He eased open the door and quietly entered the spacious, low-ceilinged room with its tall windows looking east. Sunlight streamed in, burnishing the dark paneled walls and polished floorboards with warmth. All was tidy and cheerful, with books lining the sets of shelves, two large globes on stands next to a chalkboard, and a small spinet near the windows. The cushions and blankets piled neatly in front of the hearth suggested a comfortable reading retreat in front of the crackling fire. It was Victoria's addition, he suspected.

Nick had spent hours in this room as a boy, and he'd never imagined it could be so welcoming.

The reason for all that comfort and cheer sat with Kade at a large table in the center of the room. Dressed in a green, kerseymere gown buttoned at the throat and sleeves, Victoria looked remarkably prim for a woman who'd only last night melted into his kisses. Sunlight gilded her hair and made her skin glow like pearls. Seeing her again made Nick's head clear and his heart lift.

She and Kade had their heads bent over an atlas. As Nick strolled down the length of the room to their worktable, they glanced up to meet his gaze. Victoria's eyes popped wide, and her cheeks flushed rosy pink.

"Oh, ah, my lord, I thought you were the maid with

breakfast." She clambered up from her straight-backed chair without her usual grace. "I . . . I didn't expect to see you this morning."

"I'm not surprised, given my state last night," he said with a reassuring smile.

Kade wrinkled his nose. "You're looking rather grim this morning, Nick. Are you sure you're all right?"

"I'm fine, lad. I'm sorry I was such a bear, yesterday. I hope I didn't frighten you."

His brother scoffed. "No, although I was a wee bit worried you and Logan might kill each other."

Nick tapped him gently on the shoulder. "No fear of that, but we will not discuss Logan at the moment, if you please."

Kade nodded. "I'm sorry yesterday was so troubling for you. I hope we can talk about it at some point, though."

"We will. Soon."

Nick glanced at Victoria, who stood behind her chair, clasping her hands over her stomach. Her eyes were shadowed and her mouth was set in a tight, worried line. He had to repress the impulse to take her into his arms and kiss away her anxiety.

"Kade, why don't you go down and get some breakfast? I wish to speak to Miss Knight."

Her hand flew up, as if to ward him off. "The maid will be here soon with tea and biscuits, sir. And surely you'll want to change, given what . . . what . . ." She winced and clamped her lips shut.

Kade looked suspiciously at the two of them. "What's going on, Nick?"

He thought about it for a moment, and then decided to tell the truth. "I'm here to propose to Miss Knight."

Victoria made a choking noise.

Kade gaped at him. "Propose marriage?"

"Yes."

"Huh," his brother said. Then he smiled. "Good for you, Nick. Miss Knight's a wonderful person."

She stared at Kade, dumbstruck.

"Indeed, she is," Nick said. "But don't say anything to your brothers just yet. Miss Knight and I have to discuss the particulars first."

"Wait," she finally said. "Lord Arn—"

He held up a hand. "A moment, please, Miss Knight. Off with you, scamp."

Kade headed for the door and gave Victoria a cheery wave. "See you later, Miss Knight."

Victoria managed a weak wave in reply, but Nick could see she was also working her way up to a thunderous scowl. She looked so adorably fierce that he was tempted to laugh. Common sense, however, dictated caution. Madam Governess had her own ideas about how the world should be ordered, and those ideas might not include him. For one thing, she might be appalled by the notion of spending most of her life in a drafty old castle in the Highlands.

Janet had loathed it, after all, and she'd been born and raised in Scotland.

But Victoria was not Janet. Where his wife had been dramatic and sentimental, Victoria was clear-eyed and sensible. She would never succumb to girlish notions of wedded bliss, or expect Nick to act dashing and romantic. They would have a satisfying partnership based on mutual esteem, affection, and a sensible view of family and duties.

And we will have a great deal of splendid sex.

"My lord, are you well?" She'd stopped scowling and now studied him with vague alarm.

Imbecile. Letting his mind wander was no way to court a skittish lady. "I'm fine. Why do you ask?"

"You're not going to be sick, are you?" She ran a quick, practiced eye over him, not looking much impressed.

He probably should have taken the time to shave and change after all, but it was too late now. "No, I feel perfectly fine."

When her eyebrows shot up, he shrugged. "Very well. I do have a bit of a headache, but it's nothing to worry about."

"I'm not surprised," she muttered.

"Miss Knight. Victoria—"

"Won't you sit down?" she firmly interrupted. "I could ring for the maid and see what's taking so long with the tea."

He strolled around the table to her side. "I don't need tea. I just need you."

She narrowed her gaze. "I'm not sure what that means."

Taking her determined little chin in his hand, he tilted it up. "It means I'd like to kiss you."

Her lovely lips parted on a gasp, but she simply stared at him. Then, as he slowly lowered his head, she blinked a few times, and one of her hands came to rest on his chest.

"I don't think—" she started.

"Exactly, don't think."

He slid his arms around her back. She trembled but didn't resist the embrace. Instead, her other hand joined the first to rest on his waistcoat. Nick huffed out a small, triumphant chuckle just before their lips met.

"Oh, dear!" She flattened her hands and pushed back.

He loosened his grip. "What's wrong?"

Victoria crinkled her nose with evident distaste. "I don't like to criticize, my lord . . ."

"Yes?"

"It's your breath. It's quite . . . gruesome."

He sighed and let her go. "Sorry about that. I seem to have forgotten the basics when it comes to courting a lady."

She scooted around to the other side of the table. "Sir, there is absolutely no need to court me."

He smiled. "Good. Then we'll marry as soon as possible?"

Her eyes widened with shock. "Really, Lord Arnprior, this is entirely unnecessary, as I told your brother last night."

"And also Angus and Taffy," he helpfully supplied.

She winced. "Yes."

"That's three people who caught us in a compromising position. And despite my *best* efforts to quell any gossip—"

"You obviously just woke up," she said with disbelief.

"—I fear Angus has not exercised the same discretion we would," he finished, trying to sound regretful.

"But I made it very clear to Mr. MacDonald that I would depend upon his discretion."

"Angus, discreet?" Nick couldn't hold back a chuckle.

She glared at him. "Sir, I was *not* compromised. You were feeling . . . unwell, and I was simply trying to . . . to support you."

"By kissing me, and then rolling about on the floor with me?"

"We weren't rolling," she snapped.

"I stand corrected. But I *was* lying on top of you with my head cushioned on your, er, chest." He could still recall how delightful her breasts had felt under his cheek.

A fiery blush climbed up her neck. "That particular posture was an accident, as were the kisses."

"A very enjoyable accident, I must say."

"They were not meant to happen," she said hotly.

Something unpleasant congealed in the pit of his stomach. "Are you saying I forced myself on you?" He'd shoot himself if that were the case.

"No, of course not!" she exclaimed. "I know you would never take advantage of me, or any woman."

His gut unclenched. "Then you're saying that you willingly returned my caresses? That I did *not* force myself on you."

She looked like she was chewing on her words. "That is correct, sir."

He spread his hands wide. "Then, my dear, I see no other option but for us to marry. You are a lady, and gentlemen don't take advantage of ladies."

"Again, you did not take advantage of me," she said in a frustrated tone. "And I'm not a lady. I'm a governess, entirely able to support myself without you making such an unnecessary sacrifice."

"You won't be a governess for much longer if this gets out. And it *will* get out."

Nick was quite certain of that. He wouldn't be surprised if Angus was right this minute blabbing to the tenant farmers and anyone who would listen that the laird was to marry Kade's Sassenach governess.

She sucked in a slow breath. "Then I will leave my position today, Lord Arnprior, before there is opportunity for gossip to spread."

His heart jolted, but he forced himself not to overreact. "Such a sudden departure will have the opposite effect, my dear."

"Sir—"

"And what about Kade? You don't wish to leave him, do you?"

"Of course not," she said. "I'm exceedingly fond of him."

"And do you wish to leave me?" he asked casually.

She grimaced. "That . . . that is hardly the point, my lord. You cannot wish to marry someone like me." She seemed genuinely shocked by the notion, as if he should be revolted by the very idea of marriage to her.

"You're right—I don't wish to marry someone like you," he said quietly.

Hurt darkened her pretty blue eyes, and her mouth twitched a wee bit. Then she steadied herself and nodded. "Of course not."

"I wish to marry *you*. Specifically," he added, just to make it clear.

She looked so perplexed he could almost imagine he was speaking in tongues and that neither of them had received enlightenment.

Then her chin went up in a stubborn tilt. "As I said, that will not be necessary."

His headache was starting to worm its way back into his brain. Perhaps it was time to take a different tack. "It is entirely necessary if you don't wish to see me ruthlessly maimed and then murdered."

She crinkled her brow. "Sorry?"

"What do you think will happen when Sir Dominic and Alec hear what happened between us? And, trust me, they will." He would tell them himself, if he had to.

Victoria sank down into a chair. "Oh, God, this is a disaster." She flicked him a scowl. "One of *your* making, I might add."

He raised a skeptical eyebrow.

"All right," she huffed. "*Mostly* of your making. I did kiss you back."

"You did. But rather than a disaster, I see this as an opportunity—for all of us."

She crossed her arms. "Oh, really?"

"I get a wife, you get an earl, *and* we set a grand example for my brothers. If I marry such a kind, thoroughly good woman, it should encourage them to do the same."

"We should get married to encourage your brothers?"

He winced at her sharp tone. "The most important reason is that I refuse to see you harmed in any way by my actions."

She leaned forward and rested her forehead in her palms.

"Victoria, do I repulse you?" he asked gently.

"You know you don't," she said, looking up.

"Do I frighten you in any way?"

"I told you last night that you do not frighten me."

"Excellent. Then perhaps you might like me a little bit, after all?"

She sighed. "Again, not the point."

"Then what is the point?"

"I am neither gently bred nor a lady."

He frowned down at her. "Of course you are."

"Would you please sit? I'm getting a crick in my neck staring up at you."

He bit back a smile and took the seat opposite her. "Now, tell me why you don't think you're a lady."

"Because I was born illegitimate." The words came out in a rush.

He suddenly felt muddle-headed again. "I don't understand. You said you were raised by your parents in your grandfather's coaching inn."

"No, I was raised by my mother. Barely," she muttered.

"Yes, but you said you lost your father at an early age."

She waggled a hand. "He was never part of my life, but he didn't die."

He drummed his fingers on the table. "I don't like being lied to, Victoria."

"I'm sorry for doing so," she said. "But it's not a point one wishes to advertise, especially as a governess."

He noted her worried expression and the hands tightly clenched on the tabletop. "I can imagine how that would be an impediment. But you were raised in a respectable household, were you not?"

She nodded. "I can vouch for the good character of my aunts and uncles. They're very well regarded in Brighton, as was my grandfather."

After a moment's consideration, he shrugged. "Then unless your father is a murderer, a brigand, or a highwayman, I fail to see the problem."

When she blanched, his muscles seemed to tighten all at once. "Please tell me your father is none of those things."

"He's not."

Nick's patience started to run out. "Then what?"

She hesitated. "Must you insist?"

"Yes!"

Victoria scowled back at him. "There's no need to bark at me."

"Clearly there is, since your delicacy is making this conversation ridiculously convoluted."

"Oh, very well. If you must know, I'm the natural daughter of His Royal Highness, the Prince Regent."

He nearly fell out of his chair. "You're what?"

"You heard me. The Prince Regent had a brief affair with my mother when he was first staying in Brighton. I was the result," she finished sarcastically.

He stared at her, taking in her fiery blush and her defiant but touching glare. Something bubbled inside his chest, fizzy and hilarious. The poor lass thought that being the byblow of a prince—the next king, for God's sake—would put him off.

"Say something," she said tersely.

"I—" Nick pressed a hand to his lips.

She eyed him with distaste. "My lord, perhaps you now understand how unsuitable I am to be your wife, and why it's better that I leave your employ as soon as possible. I only ask that you not penalize me for something that was beyond my control, and hope you will be generous enough to write a recommendation based on my teaching skills and work, not my unfortunate background."

Her absurd little speech did it. Nick burst out laughing, doubling over to clutch his stomach. When he finally caught his breath, he looked up to meet Victoria's best governess glare. That, unfortunately, only sent him off again.

"Lord Arnprior, I don't know how you can find any of this amusing," she said in freezing tones.

Nick sucked in a breath and wiped his eyes. "Sir Dominic is aware of your parental history, I'm sure."

"Yes, and you're not to hold it against him for not telling you. He was only trying to protect me."

"I won't. And so you're also cousin to Alec Gilbride."

"Again, that is correct, although I didn't know that until just before I came to Kinglas."

"That cheeky bastard. How dare he not tell me?" Nick laughed again. The entire thing was so gloriously ridiculous. His prim, proper governess was the daughter of one of the biggest scoundrels in England's history.

Of course, that also meant she had the bluest of blood running through her veins.

"I truly don't know why you're laughing," she said grumpily.

"Because it's sweet but utterly silly that you believed I would hold such a thing against you. Love, you do realize that many royal by-blows marry exceedingly well, and often have titles conferred upon them."

She'd blushed, probably at his term of endearment. "Yes, but they're men, for one thing."

"Not all. There's the Duchess of Leverton. She's the Duke of Cumberland's daughter."

She pushed her lower lip out, as if thinking. Nick had to resist the urge to lean over and nip it.

"True, but the duchess comes from a very good family to begin with," she said. "I do not."

"Your family is entirely respectable, Victoria—hard-working and prosperous by your own account. They pose no impediment whatsoever, as far as I'm concerned."

He got up and moved around to her side of the table, settling into the seat next to her. When he took her hand, she swallowed nervously but didn't pull away.

"I know the circumstances are not ideal," he said gently. "But you would do me a great honor if you would consent to be my wife."

"Far from ideal," she protested, even as she tightly clung to his hand. "You're an earl, and I'm—"

"The daughter of the Prince Regent."

"The daughter of a barmaid. And I'm also an entirely ordinary governess."

"You're not ordinary in the least. And I can tell you unequivocally that I would be delighted to be your husband." Every moment that passed made him more certain of that simple fact.

She seemed to waver, but then pulled her hand away. "It's very kind of you, my lord, but you have done me no wrong. There is absolutely no need for you to feel obliged to marry me."

The woman was both exceedingly principled and insanely stubborn.

"I suspect your father would not agree." He scrubbed a hand thoughtfully over his chin. "Nor would Sir Dominic. Unless we marry, he'll shoot me when he finds out what we've done."

"I . . . I . . ." she stammered.

He snapped his fingers. "Hang on. I'll write to your father and ask his opinion in the matter."

She gaped at him. "The Regent?"

"It is commonly accepted to ask a father for permission to marry his daughter, is it not?"

She quickly realized he was twitting her. "Now, see here," she started, waving a finger at him.

He gently grasped her hand. "You know I'm just teasing, sweet lass. No need to fall into a tizzy."

Nick couldn't remember the last time he'd had so much fun. Considering his black state of mind only last night, she was a bloody miracle worker.

When he gently cupped her cheek, the remaining fight seemed to go out of her.

"I . . . I don't know what to say," she whispered.

"Say yes," he whispered back.

She swayed toward him, as if about to do just that, when the door flew open. Victoria jerked away as the twins charged into the room.

"Is it true?" Graeme asked. "Are you going to marry Miss Knight?"

Nick gritted his teeth. "Your grandfather told you?"

"Yes," said Grant, smiling at Victoria. "You should say yes, miss. Nick is a splendid chap, really. And if you marry him, then you'll be our sister, and you'll have even more time to teach us how to be gentlemen and find proper wives."

She gave the twins a horrified look before turning her gaze back on Nick. He was tempted to curse, but instead he spread his hands in a placating gesture.

"Really, how can you say no to such a tempting offer?" he asked.

She seemed to struggle with herself for a moment. "You're demented, all of you," she finally said.

Then she got up and stalked from the room.

Chapter Seventeen

"Accepting Lord Arnprior's proposal is certainly the most sensible thing to do," said Edie Gilbride as she plucked a lobster patty from the plate in front of her. "And if Sir Dominic believes it's for the best, you might as well get on with it."

Victoria put her teacup down with a decided click. "Perhaps, but it's not his decision to make, is it?"

She was still annoyed with Arnprior for writing to Dominic, asking permission to court her. Her mentor had agreed with alacrity, as had Victoria's brother, Aden. Why they thought it was any of their business was a mystery to her, and she'd made that clear to them in tartly worded letters. Her missives, however, had been met with deafening silence.

"Alec thinks it a splendid idea too," Edie said, "and he has a nose for matchmaking. He knew we were going to end up together even when I still believed he was a dolt."

Victoria shook her head. "Men. They always stick up for each other. By the way, where is your dear husband?"

Edie perused the elegant supper room, where they'd managed to secure one of the larger tables in a spot behind a few potted ferns. Graeme and Grant were intently engaged in conversation with two young dancing partners, while Victoria and Edie awaited the appearance of the rest of their party.

"I expect he's still at the Tontine Coffee Room, droning on with his business partners," Edie said. "He'd better get here soon, though, or we'll miss the dancing."

"He's a dimwit for talking about business when he could be dancing with you."

Edie laughed. "I agree, but I'm happy we've had the opportunity to have a quiet chat about your situation."

Alec and Edie, ensconced in Glasgow for much of December, were throwing a grand Hogmanay ball on New Year's Eve and had invited the Kendricks. That sudden invitation had apparently been the only excuse Arnprior needed to whisk them all to the city, two days after his stunning marriage proposal. They were now in their second week at Kendrick House, and Victoria felt like she was still catching her breath from the whirlwind of activity.

She also felt curiously vulnerable.

Kendrick House was a gracious mansion with every convenience, and the staff already displayed a tendency to treat her as the lady of the manor. But that only increased her sense that she was somehow tempting fate by taking up such public residence in Glasgow. For all the problems at Kinglas, she'd felt safe and happy in that drafty old castle in its quiet glen.

"Speaking of husbands, where is Arnprior, anyway?" Edie asked.

Victoria glanced at the twins, seated close enough to eavesdrop, and gave her friend a warning grimace.

Edie chuckled. "Dearest, everyone knows Arnprior is courting you, especially his family."

"Yes, but I don't want them to assume I'm going to say yes."

"Playing hard to get, are we?" Edie winked at her. "I did

that with Alec—unintentionally, I must admit—and it had a splendid effect on him."

"I'm not playing . . . oh, never mind."

For the last ten days, she and Arnprior had been at a stalemate. He was acting as if they were already betrothed, and she was steadfastly maintaining they weren't. So far, though, she was convincing no one. In fact, the entire family seemed thrilled, and their enthusiasm made it awfully hard to keep her distance. Of course, her foolish heart urged capitulation as well.

Despite her reluctance, she was falling more in love with her handsome, mysterious laird every day. And yet so many obstacles stood between them.

Edie briefly pressed Victoria's hand. "I'm teasing. I know how tricky these situations can be. But you shouldn't doubt that Arnprior is devoted to you. All of us see that."

Victoria ignored the leap of her heart and made a point of looking about her. "So devoted he has left me entirely in charge of his scapegrace brothers."

Edie grinned. "The bounder. But the twins are behaving themselves quite nicely. From what Alec had told me, I was expecting a pair of blue-faced, bare-chested Celts bent on terrorizing Glasgow."

"Yes, they've been doing very well so far. I'm rather proud of that."

The twins were still chatting with their dance partners. Miss Lainie MacBride was the daughter of a vicar, while Miss Anna Peyton was the only child of a wealthy Glasgow businessman. It was rather mind-boggling that Graeme seemed entranced by a vicar's daughter, but he'd latched onto the charming Miss MacBride from the moment they'd met. As for Grant, he and Miss Peyton had danced on three occasions in the last week alone.

"They've been inspired by their elder brother's example, no doubt," Edie said with a twinkle.

"Don't think his lordship hasn't pointed that out to me," Victoria said tartly. "Repeatedly."

"It's annoying when men are proven correct, isn't it?"

Victoria let out a reluctant laugh. "Yes, but I shouldn't be taking my frustrations out on you."

"Dearest, I understand how disconcerting your situation is. I was caught in a similar position with Alec, while he was betrothed to another woman, no less. You can imagine how embarrassing *that* was."

"Good Lord. What happened?"

"You mean, what were Alec and I doing when we were caught?"

"No," Victoria said. "How did you get out of it?"

"We didn't. And if you and Arnprior were similarly compromised, I'm afraid you must face the consequences of your actions, too."

"But I was merely comforting the earl when he was, er, distraught."

"Comforting? Is that what they're calling it up at Kinglas?" Edie asked politely.

"All right, it wasn't entirely innocent, but Arnprior is making too great a fuss."

Edie's good-humored gaze turned serious. "Victoria, if you truly don't wish to marry the earl, I'll support your decision. But you need to know there's already quite a bit of gossip about you and Arnprior."

"I know. Everyone seems to take it for granted that we're already betrothed," Victoria said gloomily.

Edie hesitated for a few moments. "My sense is that you have strong feelings for the earl. Am I correct about that?"

"I suppose it's rather obvious, isn't it?" she said with a sigh.

"Rather, since you look moony-eyed as soon as he walks into the room. It's also obvious how eager he is to make you his wife, so I'm not sure why you're holding out."

Victoria thought there was a distinct possibility Arnprior felt more obligated than eager, but there was an even greater impediment. "I am considering his proposal. It's just that—"

Distracted by movement to her left, she broke off. Graeme was whispering in Lainie's ear with alarming intensity, and it looked like one of his hands had disappeared under the table.

Leaning across the chair between them, she jabbed Graeme in the thigh with her fan. He jumped a good two inches, and his hand suddenly reappeared. He grimaced in reply to Victoria's warning scowl, but sat up straight and started talking to Grant.

"I wonder where Lainie's mother has gone," Victoria said, turning back to Edie. "She's supposed to be chaperoning those girls."

"She's in the card room. I'm sure Mrs. MacBride trusts that you'll keep an eye on things."

"Keeping an eye on the twins keeps me busy enough. I don't need two pert misses added to the mix."

"Oh, they're all fine. Now, let's get back to you and Arnprior. Why *are* you dragging your feet?"

Victoria leaned in close. "Do you truly imagine the earl would be keen to have a killer for a wife?"

"But you were simply defending yourself, dearest. Besides, Dominic and Aden have the situation well in hand, I'm sure. That matter shouldn't stand in your way."

Dominic had said as much in his last letter, although there were apparently still a few minor details to clear up with Lady Welgate and her father. In the meantime, her mentor had advised that it was best to maintain complete silence on the matter to prevent the spread of any injurious gossip. She could tell Arnprior the details once everything was resolved, although Dominic didn't seem to feel that was strictly necessary, either.

Victoria hadn't known whether to be more annoyed at his assumption that she would be marrying the earl, or that she would keep something so monumental from her future husband. "It simply doesn't seem right not to tell him, no matter what Dominic says."

"If you think it's best to tell him, then you should." Then Edie held up an admonishing finger. "But only after Dominic says you may. You need to trust him in this matter, Victoria. He knows what he's about."

"I know. It's just that . . ." She hesitated, knowing how silly it would sound.

"What?"

"Since we've been in Glasgow, I've had the sense that someone is watching me, and that it's somehow connected to Fletcher's death." She gave an uneasy laugh. "It seems ridiculous, but I swear it's true."

Edie frowned. "What are you talking about?"

"When I've been out running errands, I'm quite sure someone is following me." More than once, she'd caught glimpses of a man furtively watching her.

"I see. Believe it or not, the same thing happened to me before Alec and I got married. That fellow tried to kill both of us."

"Edie, that is hardly reassuring."

Her friend wrinkled her nose. "I'll mention it to Alec and see what he thinks." She glanced across the room. "And speaking of my errant husband, there he is."

Alec waved to them from the doorway but was promptly waylaid by an elderly gentleman.

"One male down, two to go," Edie said. "Arnprior and that handsome brother of his should be along anytime now, don't you think?"

"Lord Arnprior was stopping by his club for a bit. As for Royal . . ." Victoria shrugged. "Who knows?"

She'd all but ordered Royal to join them tonight, but no

one could tell the blasted man to do anything. He'd much rather lurk about the house and brood, like a hero from a romantic novel.

"Oh, rats," said Edie. "I wanted to introduce him to Ainsley. I'm quite determined they should be friends."

"Really?" Victoria asked dubiously. She suspected the combination of Royal Kendrick and Lady Ainsley Matthews could be combustible, and not in a positive way.

"Yes," Edie said firmly. "It'll be good for them both."

"If you say so."

The daughter of a wealthy earl, Lady Ainsley was staying with the Gilbrides before traveling north to visit Scottish relations. From what Victoria had seen of her, melancholy younger sons with no fortunes hardly seemed her type.

"Is Lady Ainsley enjoying her visit with you?" she asked politely.

"It's hard to say. She can be prickly but also quite fun. And there's a kind heart underneath her rather snobby manner. But something's changed since I last saw her in London, and I can't put my finger on it."

"She appears troubled by something, if you ask me."

"Yes, I think you're—"

"Look out," Victoria murmured. "Her ladyship just retrieved Alec and is heading our way."

"Finally," Edie said to her husband as he escorted Ainsley to the seat beside Victoria. "Was that Mr. Coltrane you were speaking with?"

Alec dropped a quick kiss on his wife's head before taking the seat next to her. "Aye. He's known Grandfather forever, so I could hardly snub the old fellow."

"I could," Ainsley said in her cool, well-bred tones.

"And did so quite well," Alec replied sardonically.

Edie threw her friend a displeased glance. "He's a totally harmless old man, Ainsley."

Ainsley's dramatic eyebrows went up in an elegant arch.

"That gentleman—and I use the term loosely—had the temerity to call me 'a pretty chit.'"

Ainsley was much more than simply pretty. Of average height, the girl had a lush figure showcased by expensive gowns perfectly cut to display her curves. Her coloring was equally striking, with pale, perfect skin, violet-blue eyes framed by thick lashes and slashing brows, along with silky black hair. With her elegant features and proud carriage, she commanded male attention the moment she walked into any room.

Women generally had a different reaction, since Ainsley possessed a rather haughty, unapproachable manner. She was far more likely to provoke jealousy than invite confidences from other girls on the marriage mart.

Oddly enough, she'd never been anything but polite to Victoria, who found it unusual. Most girls of Ainsley's standing were likely to treat a governess with disdain, if not outright contempt.

"That's a Scot for you," Edie said. "Plain speakers, as I well know."

"Och, that we are," said Alec, adopting his thick, comical brogue. "Although ye are an outspoken lassie yerself, dinna ye ken?"

Edie laughed, but Ainsley groaned. "That accent gives me the headache just listening to it."

"You'd better get used to it, pet," Edie said. "You'll be hearing a lot of it when you get to Inveraray."

"Don't remind me," she said gloomily.

"And don't forget the bagpipes," Alec teased. "They'll send you leaping for the closest loch by Easter."

That pulled a reluctant smile from the girl. "Thank you for adding insult to injury."

"Is that where you'll be staying, Lady Ainsley?" Victoria asked. "I understand that Inveraray Castle is the Duke of Argyll's ancestral home."

"I'll be close by," Ainsley replied. "I am related to the duke on my father's side, but I'll be staying at my great-aunt's manor outside Cairndow, a small village at the head of Loch Fyne."

"'Small' being the operative word," Alec said.

"And remote." The girl's frown seemed more thoughtful than gloomy.

"I've heard of Cairndow," Victoria said. "It's not all that far from Castle Kinglas."

Ainsley gave her a tentative smile. "Perhaps you might consider making me a visit at some point."

Victoria repressed her surprise. "I'd like that. Or perhaps you could visit Kinglas. I'm sure the earl would be pleased to see you."

Ainsley's friendly manner instantly shifted. "I doubt it. In any event, I'm sure I'll be too busy for visiting."

Everyone but Ainsley looked awkward, but then Edie brightened. "Look, there's Mr. Kendrick."

Graeme shot to his feet and began waving both arms like windmills. "Over here," he called to Royal.

"Sit down, Graeme," Victoria said. "You are not at a sporting event."

"Sorry." He subsided into his seat, giving Lainie a sheepish grin. The girl simply giggled. Though a vicar's daughter, she rather seemed to enjoy Graeme's brash behavior.

As Royal wended his way through the room, Victoria breathed a sigh of relief to see that he was correctly dressed for once. He looked handsome in a black tailcoat, his white cravat and pearl-gray vest softening his rather austere appearance. With hair that tumbled over his brow, a sardonic expression, and a pronounced limp, he was the very picture of the poetic type swooned over by impressionable young girls. In fact, many female gazes followed avidly in his wake.

But there was one female who appeared decidedly unimpressed, if Ainsley's expression was any indication.

If Royal treated Ainsley with the disdain he displayed for pampered society girls, they would be sure to see fireworks before the evening was out.

"High flyers and barmaids are more to my taste, Victoria," he'd bluntly informed her last week when she tried to persuade him to join the family at a fashionable musicale. "And if my sexual preferences shock you," he'd added, "then I suggest you bloody well stop trying to polish me up for the marriage mart. It's a hopeless cause."

Victoria had no intention of giving up. Royal needed her help as much as every other male in the Kendrick family.

"Hallo, old man. Good to see you," Alec said, standing up and extending a hand.

"Gilbride, it's—"

Whatever words had been about to emerge died on Royal's lips when he finally noticed Ainsley. Victoria watched in amazement as his eyes widened and a flush bronzed his sharp cheekbones. While her ladyship was a beautiful girl, he was hardly the sort to be instantly smitten by any female.

Edie shot Victoria a smug glance before smiling up at Royal. "Mr. Kendrick, I'd like to introduce you to my friend—"

"I know who he is," Ainsley interrupted. "Unfortunately."

Everyone at the table froze, although her remark seemed to jolt Royal out of his odd reverie. "Och, Lady Ainsley, how nice to see you again."

"You two know each other?" Alec asked.

Royal crossed his arms and stared at Ainsley with a sardonic expression.

After glaring back at him for a few moments, she finally answered. "I had the *vast* pleasure of meeting Mr. Kendrick at a troop review in London last winter."

"And then I had the *vast* pleasure of sitting next to her ladyship at a dinner party a few weeks later," Royal drawled back in bored imitation.

Victoria frowned. At the moment, Royal was acting like a hardened society rake.

"Again, unfortunately," Ainsley snapped.

Royal flashed her a smile that was mostly teeth.

"That must have been some dinner party," Edie said.

Ainsley's snort was delicate and dismissive. "You have no idea."

"Royal, I didn't know you were in London last winter," Victoria said brightly.

"Nick dragged me down to see a bloody sawbones," he said. "Best doctor in London, he said."

"Ah, splendid fellow, Arnprior. Always looking after his brothers," said Alec in an inanely hearty voice. "I hope the doctor was able to give you some relief."

"He suggested amputation for my leg."

"Oh, dear," Edie said faintly.

"Too bad he couldn't amputate your tongue," Ainsley said in an airy tone.

Again, a horrified silence fell over the table. Victoria mentally scrambled to stave off the impending disaster.

Fortunately, Royal guffawed. "Ah, Lady Ainsley, charming as always. How fortunate that you've decided to grace the peasants of Glasgow with your exalted presence."

"Not for long, thank God," she muttered.

Victoria patted the chair on her other side. "Royal, why don't you sit next to me and tell me about your day." She'd been hoping to save that seat for Arnprior, but preventing bloodshed now took priority.

He hooked an empty chair from the table next to them and dragged it over to face directly across from Ainsley.

"I'm fine right here," he said, settling in and thrusting his long legs out in a casual stretch. His posture was disgracefully informal, but Victoria suspected it had more to do with his bad leg than any desire to be rude. Knowing him, though, the rudeness would be a bonus.

He proceeded to let his gaze momentarily drift down to Ainsley's chest as his lips curled up in an astonishingly seductive smile. "You're looking well, my lady, but I think you've gained some weight since last winter. Still, I must say, you carry it splendidly."

Ainsley pressed her lips into a tight line as red spots of color sprung up on her cheeks.

"Royal Kendrick, behave yourself," Victoria hissed.

He kept his green-glass eyes fastened on his target.

"There's nothing wrong with having a little meat on one's bones, old man," Alec said in a warning tone. "After all, look at my dear wife. She's as pretty and plump as a partridge, and I wouldn't have it any other way."

When every woman at the table glared at him, Alec flushed. "What?"

"You are a dimwit, Alasdair Gilbride," Edie said in a terse voice.

"Oh, blast," he sighed. "Sorry, love, I was just trying to make the point that—"

"I know," his wife replied. "Trust me when I tell the point would be better left unsaid."

"Lady Ainsley, when do you leave for Cairndow?" Victoria asked, desperate to gain control of the conversation. Where was Arnprior, confound him? When Royal fell into one of his moods, only the earl had any ability to manage him.

Ainsley momentarily ceased shooting death glares at Royal. "Not for a few more weeks. Certainly not until after the Gilbrides' Hogmanay Ball."

"Why the devil are you going up to Cairndow?" Royal said abruptly. "There's not a bloody thing up there but mountains and water."

"My great-aunt is there," Ainsley snapped. "I'm going to spend the winter with her."

Royal frowned and—thank the merciful gods—fell silent.

For the next few minutes, they gamely tried to engage in normal conversation. Victoria pulled the twins and their companions into the discussion and the tension abated.

But it wasn't long before Ainsley glanced over at Royal, who was studying her with a reflective frown. "Mr. Kendrick, has no one ever told you it's rude to stare?" she hissed.

He shrugged. "Probably, but I suppose I forgot."

"Well, please stop it."

"Is my attention making you nervous, my lady?" he asked with exaggerated politeness. "Fear not. An impecunious younger son—a cripple, no less—would never be so bold as to importune you." That seductive smile again curled up the edges of his mouth. "Unless you want me to importune you."

Victoria, scowling madly at Royal, felt rather than saw Ainsley go stiff as a hitching post. She glanced over and saw all the color drain from the girl's face.

"Are you all right, Lady Ainsley?" she asked.

When the girl finally looked at her, Victoria got a jolt. The expression in Ainsley's eyes was one of desolation.

"Yes, I'm fine. If you'll excuse me for a moment." She rose clumsily to her feet.

"Ainsley, wait," Royal said, starting to drag himself up.

"Leave me alone," she snapped, then all but fled the table.

Because she'd been conversing with Alec and the twins, Edie hadn't heard the ugly exchange. She turned as Ainsley rushed off. "Where's she going?"

Victoria stood. "Just to the retiring room. I think I'll join her."

Edie gazed suspiciously at Royal, who stared after Ainsley with a perplexed expression.

"No need to worry," Victoria said. "I'll check on her ladyship."

As she passed Royal, she jabbed him in the arm. "Sit down and behave yourself," she said in an undertone.

Surprisingly, he complied without argument.

Victoria threaded her way through the crowded supper room, smiling blandly at anyone who looked curious. When she reached the relative quiet of the hall that ran the length of the classically designed building, she breathed a sigh of relief. Music filtered down from the upstairs ballroom, and a few couples and sets of girls strolled along the corridor, but the high-ceiling space was blessedly calm.

She hurried toward the back of the building and the ladies' retiring room. But when a man stepped out from a shadowed window alcove, she bit back an exclamation and pulled up short.

"Pardon me, miss," the man said. "I surely didn't mean to startle you."

His accent suggested London with a hint of the East End. Dressed neatly and with propriety, he was neither tall nor particularly handsome, although his features were pleasant enough. At first glance, he seemed entirely bland and inoffensive.

But as he continued to smile and block her way, Victoria felt the hairs prickle along the back of her neck. For a man who appeared harmless, one word bizarrely jumped into her mind.

Menacing.

She forced a smile. "No harm done, sir. Now, if you'll excuse me."

When she made to go around him, he smoothly slid into her path.

"Please forgive my forward behavior, ma'am. Believe me when I say I have no wish to offend."

She ignored the stirrings of fear in her belly. He couldn't do anything to harm her with so many people within calling distance. "Then I suggest you move aside, sir."

"You are Miss Victoria Knight, are you not?"

She hesitated to answer. Was this the man who'd been watching her?

It would be easy enough for him to discover her identity. Anyone in the other room could tell him. "I am. Why do you ask?"

"And you are the governess to Lord Arnprior's brother?"

She frowned. "May I know your name, sir, and why you would ask?"

"My name is Mr. Archibald Pence," he said, giving her a slight bow. "I am acquainted with one of your previous employers."

Victoria's stomach all but leapt into her throat. "Which one?"

"Mrs. Havergill. She spoke very highly of you."

"I see," she said, feeling relieved. "Are you interested in hiring me, sir? If so, I am afraid I will not be available for some time."

Or ever, if Arnprior had his way.

He held up his hands. "No, I simply wished to satisfy my curiosity. Forgive me if I alarmed you." He glanced toward the front of the building. "Ah, it appears the earl is coming to fetch you. Have a good evening, Miss Knight."

He stepped around her and quickly walked away.

Turning, she saw Arnprior striding toward her, a scowl marking his brow. When Pence came level with him, the earl slowed and gave the man a hard stare. The Londoner merely doffed his hat and proceeded on his way.

"Was that fellow bothering you?" Arnprior rested a gloved hand protectively on her shoulder, the leather cool and smooth on her bare skin. "I can follow and thrash him, if you like."

She smothered a laugh. "Your generous offer won't be necessary, sir. He wasn't truly bothering me." Still, she couldn't help moving closer to his reassuring warmth.

He tucked her against him. "He *did* make you nervous. Who was he?"

"No one, really."

"Victoria—"

"His name is Mr. Pence. He knew one of my previous employers, that's all."

"I'm not familiar with the name. I'll see what I can find out about him."

"Thank you, but I'm sure it's nothing." Though he could be ridiculously overprotective, she was secretly glad of it.

Arnprior tipped her chin up with a finger. "By the way, what are you doing wandering the halls by yourself, waiting to be accosted by strange men?"

Now he was just being silly. "The Glasgow Assembly Rooms are hardly the stews of London, sir."

"Still—"

"I believe she was looking for me, Lord Arnprior," said a clipped voice.

They turned to see Ainsley regarding them with her usual imperious manner.

Victoria went to her. "My lady, are you feeling better? You looked a bit unwell when you left the table."

She scoffed. "That's one way of putting it. But I'm perfectly fine now."

Victoria winced. "I'm sorry if—"

She held up a hand. "No need to apologize. If you don't mind, I'll rejoin the Gilbrides." She gave them a brusque nod and sailed off in the direction of the supper room.

"What was that all about?" Arnprior asked.

"I'm afraid Royal insulted her."

"Good God," he said, sounding disgusted.

"It wasn't entirely his fault. Lady Ainsley was just as rude. More so, actually." She studied his frown. "I didn't realize they knew each other."

He nodded. "They seemed to get along quite well when they first met, but then they had a falling out. Royal refused to talk about it."

She pressed a dramatic hand to her chest. "I'm deeply shocked to hear that."

When he laughed, she took his arm and started forward. "We'd best go back and try to prevent further hostilities from breaking out."

He gently reeled her back into his embrace.

"Lord Arnprior!" She glanced around the hall. Fortunately, no one was about at the moment. "This is most inappropriate."

He ignored her objection and feathered a kiss across her lips. "I think you've had enough of my family for one night."

She had to swallow before she could reply. "Sir, your family is my job."

His smile was infinitely arousing. "Not tonight, lass. Tonight, your job is to take care of me."

Chapter Eighteen

His seductive smile was all but impossible to resist. Still, Victoria felt compelled to make an effort. "Lord Arnprior, I do not believe that falls under the description of my duties."

"Then I suppose I should amend them," he said with a roguish twinkle. When she disengaged from his loose embrace, his smile faded. "Lass, I'm only teasing. You never have to do anything you don't wish to do."

"Thank you," she said, now feeling foolish.

He studied her for a long moment. "Tell me what troubles you."

She hesitated for a moment before answering. "I suppose I'm not sure of my standing in your household anymore."

"You are the woman I hope to marry. As far as I'm concerned, you're already a member of the Kendrick family."

She read only sincerity in his gaze. "It's more complicated than that."

"Not to me. And right now I wish to be alone with you, without my blasted family taking all your notice."

Victoria wavered, tempted more than she cared to admit.

Still, there was a great deal to consider before taking their relationship further, starting with the fact that she was keeping some exceedingly troubling secrets from him.

He flashed her a rueful smile. "You've been avoiding being alone with me since we came to Glasgow, lass."

"Not deliberately."

When he raised an eyebrow, she sighed. "It's just that it feels rather confusing at the moment. I've never been . . ."

"Compromised before?"

"That works."

"Then spending time alone might be the best way to clear up any confusion."

She'd been telling herself for days not to succumb to her feelings, but perhaps he was correct that the most sensible course of action was to spend time together like rational adults. What more harm could it do?

"Well, Miss Knight?"

She gave him a tremulous smile. "I admit I would like that."

When his mouth curved up in a satisfied grin, she couldn't resist teasing him. "At least spending time with you is bound to be more restful than running herd on the twins. Or keeping Royal and Lady Ainsley from murdering each other."

"That sounds like a challenge," he said, taking her arm and steering her toward the front of the building. "One I will be most happy to rise to."

When he comically waggled his eyebrows, Victoria tried to look shocked. Fortunately, she was spared the need to reply when Edie emerged from the tearoom.

"There you are, Victoria. I was beginning to worry." She nodded a greeting at Arnprior.

"Good evening, Mrs. Gilbride," Arnprior said. "Miss Knight is feeling rather fatigued, so I'll be taking her home."

"Will Royal and the twins be going with you?" Edie asked.

"No," Victoria and Arnprior said in unison.

Edie grinned. "Ah, I thought not. Very well, Alec and I will both chaperone the twins and make sure that Royal and Ainsley keep a safe distance."

Victoria winced. "Oh, dear. They're still fighting?"

"At the moment they're just glaring at each other, so perhaps we've reached a state of armed truce."

Victoria glanced at the earl. "Maybe we should go in."

"God, no," Arnprior said.

"Not to worry," Edie said. "We have everything in hand." She made a shooing motion. "You two go off and have fun."

Victoria blushed at the knowing look in her friend's eye before she allowed Arnprior to lead her to the cloakroom.

He eyed her feet. "I thought we'd walk home, but those dancing slippers will hardly do the trick."

"Actually, the twins and I came on foot." Kendrick House was only a short walk from the Assembly Rooms. "My half-boots are with my cloak."

"I thought you didn't like being out in the cold."

"It would appear I've gotten used to Scotland's climate."

Much to her astonishment, she'd found herself missing walks and rides in the bracing Highland air. She missed drafty Castle Kinglas, too.

After an attendant fetched their various outer garments, Victoria sat in a convenient alcove to change to her boots. When she struggled to stuff her slippers into an inside pocket of her cloak, Arnprior plucked them from her hand and stowed them inside his greatcoat.

He offered her an arm. "Ready?"

As she gazed into his handsome face, she realized she was more than ready for whatever was to follow. "Yes, my lord."

They went down the shallow stairs to the street, where he paused to carefully pull up her hood.

"Don't want you getting a chill," he murmured.

She appreciated his thoughtfulness. "It's impossible to catch a chill in this cloak. It's the best Christmas present I've ever received."

The Scots didn't fuss about Christmas, reserving most of their celebrations for Hogmanay. But Edie had insisted on having a special holiday dinner a few days ago, with the traditional foods and English customs. Afterward, she'd pulled Victoria aside and given her the sumptuous, fur-lined velvet cloak. Victoria had protested, claiming that no governess would ever wear such a garment. Edie had replied that she wouldn't be a governess much longer, and that she needed sturdy clothing to survive the gruesome Highland winters.

"Besides, you're family," Edie had added, hugging her. "And there's nothing wrong with family giving each other nice presents."

Victoria hadn't been able to resist such impeccable logic.

"I'm rather annoyed about that cloak," Arnprior said. In the light of the streetlamps, he did look a little disgruntled.

"Whatever for?"

"Because you wouldn't let *me* give you a Christmas present."

He'd tried to take her shopping last week, but Victoria had steadfastly refused to countenance a public display of Arnprior lavishing gifts upon her. Glasgow was already gossiping about them enough as it was.

"The Scots don't exchange presents on Christmas, remember?" she said.

"You made an exception with Edie and Alec."

"But they're family. It's different."

It was lovely to be able to acknowledge that Alec was her cousin, and Victoria had been astounded by the earl's easy acceptance of her scandalous parentage. She'd been sure he would be horrified by the discovery.

"And I will be family sooner rather than later, Miss Knight," he said with mock severity. "As such, I claim the right to give you a present whenever I wish."

"Perhaps you can give me something for Hogmanay. I do need some new supplies for the schoolroom."

"Saucy minx," he said as he guided her across the street.

Victoria smothered a grin and changed the conversation to the twins and their new friends.

Despite the chill, it was a lovely night with a clear sky and a crisp feel to the air. The streetlamps cast a soft glow over the cobblestones, and the chimes of a nearby church rang out the hour with solemn grace. As they strolled along, Victoria allowed herself to breathe in a quiet joy. It was the most common of things to walk down the street on the arm of a man, and yet it felt magical. Because, in defiance of all common sense and social convention, the wonderful man who walked by her side wished to marry her.

Her, Victoria Knight, a perfectly ordinary woman, despite her royal father. She'd always been content to be ordinary. Her greatest wish had been to spend the rest of her life in sensible obscurity as a schoolteacher, finding her happiness in meaningful work.

Now, though, an entirely different path had opened before her, one she'd never thought possible. The idea of spending her life with Arnprior was more exciting than anything she'd ever imagined.

It was more frightening, too, because she wanted it so much.

A few minutes later, they climbed the steps to Kendrick House, a spacious mansion built in the last century. Initially, Victoria had been struck by its stylish furnishings and modern conveniences, which posed a stark contrast to the antiquity of Kinglas. When she'd asked Arnprior if he spent much time there, he'd frowned and tersely replied in the negative, saying Braden was the only regular inhabitant of the house.

Victoria was certain young Braden was not responsible for the mansion's decorative flair.

"Tea in the study?" Arnprior asked once they'd handed their things to the footman.

"I'd rather a whisky." Although not one for strong spirits, she'd developed the taste for an occasional dram, especially on a chilly evening.

Humor gleamed in his eyes. "Spoken like a true Scots-woman."

"I know it's not very ladylike," she said sheepishly.

He paused, his hand on the doorknob. "Victoria, you can have anything you want. Anything I can give you."

His quiet sincerity warmed her more than any liquor could. Arnprior was not one for casual promises or flip remarks. His words were spare and always trustworthy.

"Thank you," she whispered.

She must have appeared like a lovestruck schoolgirl, though Arnprior didn't seem to mind. He moved close, as if to kiss her, but when the study door opened, he jerked away.

Angus almost barreled into them. "Why the devil are ye lurking about like a pair of rum coves?" he barked as he fumbled to hang on to the ledgers he carried.

Arnprior helped his grandfather restack the ledgers. "We were about to enter *my* study to have a drink, in point of fact."

The old man snorted. "After a bit of canoodling in the hall, I ken."

"I was hoping for a little more privacy before we engaged in the canoodling," Arnprior calmly replied.

"We were not . . . never mind." Victoria frowned at the earl. "And you're as bad as he is."

"Ye could only hope so, lass," Angus said, giving her a wink as he backed out the door.

"Good night, Angus." The earl firmly closed the door in his grandfather's face.

"What did he mean by that remark?" Victoria asked as he towed her to one of the needlepointed wing chairs by the fireplace. "Or do I even want to know?"

"I'm sure we'd be horrified to find out," he said. "Almost as horrified as I am to see him mucking about with the ledgers again."

"He just wants to help you." She settled into the chair and tugged off her boots, stretching her chilled feet toward the roaring fire. It was rather shocking behavior on her part, but she was feeling bold tonight.

"Angus is incredibly old-fashioned and controlling," Arnprior said as he fetched their glasses from the drinks trolley next to his desk. "Some days he treats me like I'm still in short pants."

Victoria smiled at the thought of the earl as a little boy. She imagined he was a little too solemn for his own good, but thoroughly adorable.

He handed over a glass and settled into the chair next to her, glancing at her feet with a smile. "Getting comfortable, are we?"

She wriggled her toes, luxuriating in the heat pouring from the fireplace. "I hope you don't mind."

"Not at all. In fact, I'm hoping to get you out of the rest of your garments by the end of the evening."

She slopped some whisky onto her hand.

He reached over to take her glass, putting it on the round table next to his chair.

"What are you doing?" she asked.

"Helping you to clean up."

When he drew the back of her hand to his mouth and licked away the drops of whisky, Victoria gasped. And when he turned it over and dragged his tongue across her palm, she went positively light-headed.

"Sir, what if someone walks in on us?" she protested in a weak voice.

Mischief glinted in his eyes. "They've already done that, remember?"

"Yes, and look what that led to."

"This."

He nuzzled the inside of her wrist, and she all but melted.

"I have no quarrel with the result of that episode," he added, keeping hold of her hand. "My only regret is that I was so drunk I fell asleep in the middle of it, which was ridiculous of me."

"Not as ridiculous as *my* position when Royal and the others walked in on us."

"Would that be lying on the floor underneath me?"

When she tried to yank her hand away, he laughed. "Sorry, love, but I'm sure it wasn't nearly as terrible as you think."

"Well, the parts before you fell asleep weren't," she admitted.

"So why don't we give it another go? I guarantee I won't fall asleep this time."

She studied his easy smile, wishing she could say yes to him—to them. She longed to be back in his arms, exchanging more than a few stolen kisses. But so many doubts and worries still cautioned her to maintain a careful distance.

A slight frown erased his smile. "Sweetheart, there's no shame in taking a little pleasure in each other. After all, we're to be married soon."

"Are you sure about that?"

He looked startled. "Of course. Why would you doubt it?"

She sucked in a deep breath. It was time to be honest with him—at least about some things. "I have to doubt it, because I don't know how you truly feel about me. Especially since I think . . ."

"Yes?"

She forced herself to say it. "Since I think you're still in love with your wife."

It was a humiliating admission to make, even though she certainly honored his feelings in that regard. But part of her couldn't shake the worry that Arnprior saw her as a convenient solution to managing his fractious family, a solution forced on him by circumstances and his own sense of duty—to her and to the Kendricks.

When he let go of her hand and reached for his drink, Victoria's heart sank. He took a healthy swallow before setting the glass aside.

"You're wrong," he said. "I'm not in love with her anymore."

"But you were."

"Yes, passionately." He threw her a veiled glance. "Do you really want to know more?"

Not truly, but how could she agree to marry him without knowing how he felt? "I do."

He grimaced slightly. "Very well. My wife, Janet Lockhart, came from a well-regarded family with a modest estate near the Borders. We met when we were quite young. Her family also kept a town house in Glasgow and my stepmother became acquainted with Janet's mother." His mouth curled up in a rueful, almost embarrassed smile. "It's not an exaggeration to say I fell in love with her almost instantly."

Victoria squashed an unseemly spurt of jealousy. "How young were you?"

"Very. I was fifteen and she was thirteen. I suppose you could say we were childhood sweethearts."

"She was also instantly smitten?"

"It took her a bit longer, but by the time she was out on the marriage mart, she was convinced I was the epitome of the romantic Highland laird—or laird-to-be, I should say."

Now she heard an edge of bitterness in his tone.

"If she saw you in a kilt, I can understand why," Victoria said matter-of-factly. "Highland garb seems expressly designed to lead impressionable young ladies astray."

A reluctant chuckle rumbled in his chest. "Since I thought her a veritable fairy princess, I suppose I was as foolish as she was."

"You were young."

"And foolish."

She poked him in the bicep. "Young people generally are so. I'm sure you were boringly ordinary in that respect."

His smile was wry. "Thank you for the reminder, Miss Knight."

"You're welcome. Now, I take it she was very pretty?"

"She was a grand beauty," he said softly. "Janet had hair like spun gold and eyes the color of sapphires. She was a dainty lass too, petite and delicate. But she had a vivacious, laughing manner. She . . . she positively sparkled. Janet could weave a spell around most anyone, even perfect strangers."

In other words, just the exact opposite of Victoria, as Arnprior had to know better than anyone. "She sounds utterly charming," she said, trying not to sound like an envious harpy.

"Everyone thought so, including other men." His tone was not approving.

"That's to be expected, given she was a great beauty."

He didn't answer, instead staring moodily at the fire.

"When did you marry?" she gently prodded.

"Hmm? Oh, we wished to be married as soon as she turned eighteen, but my father was determined I finish university. He did not approve of Janet. I know he was hoping she would throw me over for someone else."

"Why didn't he approve?"

He lifted a negligent hand. "He believed Janet was a flighty, irresponsible girl who didn't have the character to be a future Countess of Arnprior."

"That seems a harsh judgment of so young a lady."

"Our discussions on the matter were not pleasant, as you can imagine."

"I'm sorry," she said softly.

His shrug seemed anything but casual. "I wore him down, but then Father died in a riding accident, which led to another delay. Janet became so impatient that I thought she would break our betrothal."

"But you were clearly doing your best." Victoria would probably wait years if she knew Arnprior loved her that deeply.

"Yes, but when Janet was frustrated, she became . . ." He paused, searching for the right phrase. "Emotionally volatile. I convinced myself that her behavior was due to her eagerness to be with me." He threw her a sardonic look. "I was wrong."

"I'm sorry." What else could she say?

He nodded. "Eventually we married, much to the relief of Janet's family. They thought me capable of controlling her more erratic impulses."

She frowned, unsure if she should continue to press him. It was becoming obvious that his marriage was not the idyllic relationship she'd assumed it to be.

He glanced over at her and sighed. "My wife was unstable, Victoria."

"I see," she said cautiously. "That must have been difficult."

"Eventually that was the case. But for the first year of our marriage, we were happy. I took Janet to London, and we then spent several months in Glasgow. She redecorated Kendrick House and became the most popular hostess in town, cutting a swath through society and charming everyone." There was a fraught pause. "Especially the men."

Now she understood where his tale was going, and it made her heart ache for him.

"But I couldn't remain in Glasgow forever. My brothers needed me, as did the estate. We had to return to Kinglas. Unfortunately, she wound up hating everything about it."

For a young and clearly immature woman, the isolation must have been difficult. "I suppose she missed her family," Victoria said, trying to be tactful.

His laugh was harsh. "No, but she hated *my* family, especially Angus. They fought constantly."

"Well, he can be rather trying."

He threw her a veiled glance. "You seemed to manage him."

She shrugged. "I'm neither delicate nor overly sensitive, as you know."

"Thank God for that."

She tried not to wince, knowing he meant it as a compliment. "I take it she didn't do well with your brothers, either."

"To be fair, she was kind to Kade, sharing her love of music with him. She and Logan rubbed on well together too. He can charm any woman, and God knows my wife wasn't immune to charming men."

That sounded like another black mark against Logan Kendrick. "I'm sorry it was so difficult."

"Life is difficult, is it not?"

"Too much, sometimes," she replied softly.

He rubbed his forehead with the tips of his fingers, like she did when she had a headache. "Forgive me for sounding so mawkish, Victoria. Our life together wasn't always terrible. When Janet became pregnant with Cam, I brought her down to Glasgow. She was happy there, until our son was born. But then she fell into a profound melancholy. Though I had the best doctors treat her, they simply counseled patience and prescribed laudanum."

She grimaced. "Laudanum was probably not helpful in her situation."

He glanced at her in surprise. "You know women who suffered that condition?"

"In one of my positions, the lady of the house suffered a similar ailment after the birth of her third child. It took several months for her to recover. Alcohol and laudanum drops only seemed to worsen her condition."

He pondered that for a few moments before continuing. "Janet's spirits improved somewhat after I procured a wet nurse and took Cam back to Kinglas. Her doctors thought it best for her to remain in Glasgow, and she seemed genuinely happier for a while. She even began socializing again. After a time, I asked her to return to Kinglas, but she refused."

"And she didn't mind being separated from her husband and baby?"

He hesitated, as if searching for the right words again. "She loved Cam, but she believed it best that he remain with me at Kinglas. As for our relationship . . ."

She reached over and took his hand, sure about what would come next. His fingers wrapped around hers, holding tight.

"Eventually, rumors began to circulate that Janet was engaging in affairs. When I came down to Glasgow to confront her, she broke down and admitted they were true. She'd taken a lover." He stared intently at the fire, as if to avoid her eye. "More than one, actually."

Even though she'd been expecting infidelity, Victoria was still shocked. She could feel the intensity of Arnprior's pain and bewilderment. It seemed that all these years later his wife's betrayal remained a devastating mystery.

After a minute or so, she finally dared break the fraught silence. "What did you do?"

He glanced down at their hands, as if surprised he was still holding on to her. "Oh. I forgave her, or at least tried to. She was genuinely distraught that she'd hurt me and distressed by her reckless conduct. When she begged me to give her another chance, I couldn't say no." He flashed her a rueful smile. "I never could."

"Because you're a good man and you loved her."

"If I *had* said no earlier on, if I'd been more decisive with her, she might still be alive today. I might have been able to save her."

She frowned. "Your wife fell ill and died, did she not? How could that be your fault?"

He finally met her gaze. "Janet killed herself. And the fault for that rests with me."

Chapter Nineteen

When Arnprior released her hand, Victoria let it hang slack between them. All she could do was stare at him. He looked like he hated himself—and the world.

"I . . . I don't know what to say," she said, struggling with disbelief, "except that your wife must have lost her reason. Surely she had no cause to take her own life."

"She was desperately unhappy. Unfortunately, I didn't realize how unhappy. I thought she was simply angry with me because I insisted she move back to Kinglas if she wished to save our marriage. Staying in Glasgow was not an acceptable option."

"Indeed not," she said gently.

"Janet thought that I should trust her enough to let her remain at Kendrick House." He sighed. "I truly wish I had let her do so, regardless of what might have happened."

He didn't seem to realize he'd just contradicted his belief that he should have been more decisive with his wife. As far as Victoria was concerned, that confirmed he'd been dealing with an impossible situation.

"What happened after you brought her back to Kinglas?" she asked.

"Nothing, at first. She was happy to see Cam again, and

we both made an effort to try to recover what we once had. But my blasted family didn't make it easy. They were hurt by her betrayal of me and the Kendrick name."

"One can hardly blame them."

"No, but I should have realized the effect their disapproval would have on her sensitive nature. I should have done a better job of protecting her, especially from Angus."

Victoria knew how furious the old man would have been over the betrayal of his laird and grandson.

"They fought, I'm guessing."

"Yes. Janet had been chafing at what she'd begun to refer to as her incarceration. It had been a particularly cold and dreary winter, and she'd been pressing me to let her return to Glasgow. Angus told her that her duty was to remain at Kinglas with her husband and child, and she should stop acting like a spoiled brat. Naturally, that started a tremendous row."

She winced, well able to imagine the dreadful scene. "That does sound like Angus."

"Indeed. When I refused to take her immediately to Glasgow, Janet accused me of not trusting her." He grimaced. "At that point, I also lost my temper and told her that her past conduct made such trust all but impossible. That was when she claimed that if I'd loved her enough and been there for her, she wouldn't have sought comfort with other men."

It took Victoria a moment to tamp down her anger toward the unfortunate woman. "That, sir, is utter nonsense. Your wife's accusations point to the fact that her mind was sadly disordered. It was not a rational claim to make."

"In hindsight, I see that. At the time, I simply thought Janet was punishing me when she said she'd rather die than keep living at Kinglas." He shook his head. "Not for a minute did I think she was serious, but that night she took an overdose of laudanum. Her maid didn't realize she'd done so, and I . . . well, I wasn't with her, so none of us knew what happened until it was too late."

Victoria had to swallow a few times before she could speak. "It was hardly your fault that you weren't sharing her bedchamber, given the state of your relationship."

"I should have—"

"No," she said firmly. "You would never have left her if you thought she would do such a thing. Only a deeply troubled person would take so tragic a step, leaving behind a husband and a child who loved her." When he didn't say anything, she tugged on his hand. "You realize that, do you not?"

His reluctant smile was more of a grimace. "My poor wife was indeed a deeply troubled soul. I will also say that it wasn't even fully clear that she meant to kill herself. According to her maid, she'd grown reckless with her dosing. The physician was exceedingly sympathetic to our situation and recorded the death as an accidental overdose."

She breathed out a relieved sigh. "Thank God."

"It allowed us to give Janet a Christian burial. I was very grateful, especially for Cam's sake."

"Poor little boy," she said softly.

He lifted her hand to his mouth and pressed a brief kiss to it before letting it go. She got the oddest sense that he was withdrawing from her.

"Cam was upset, naturally, but he recovered quickly. Although she loved him, Janet never spent much time with him."

"That was a small blessing, I suppose."

"Yes, and with him to care for, I could not afford to wallow in grief. Until I lost him as well, of course, and then I wallowed and raged to my heart's content." He glanced at her, his mouth pulled into a bitter line. "I warned you that it wasn't a pretty tale, Victoria."

"You did, and I'm grateful you trusted me enough to tell me," she said quietly.

"Of course I trust you." He placed his hands on his thighs and frowned. "More than anyone I know, I'm beginning to think."

"Then please trust me when I say that you did all you could to help your wife. That is patently evident."

He let out a skeptical snort and reached over to retrieve his glass. When he saw it was empty, he started to rise from his chair.

"No," Victoria said, jumping up. She planted a hand on his chest and pushed him back down. "No more whisky."

He scowled at her. "I don't need your pity, lass. I need another drink."

"No," she said, plucking the glass from his hand and putting it on the table.

Before she could think better of it, she clambered awkwardly into his lap. When he shifted, clearly startled, she had to make a grab for his broad shoulders.

"What are you doing, daft girl?" he said, clamping his arms around her waist. Even though he didn't seem inclined to push her off, he scowled at her. "I already told you—I don't need your pity."

"This isn't pity."

"Then what is it?"

"I'm offering comfort, you thick-headed, stubborn Highlander."

He scoffed. "I'm not one of your pupils, Miss Knight. I don't need you to pet me or jolly me out of my doldrums."

"No, but I do think you stand in need of a lecture."

"And you will deliver one, whether I wish it or not," he said, one corner of his mouth lifting in a reluctant smile.

Still, sadness lurked in his gaze. She sensed how easy it would be for him to again retreat behind a somber façade.

Arnprior had seemed much happier these last few weeks, despite Logan's reappearance and the opening of old wounds. Victoria couldn't bear the idea that her handsome laird would again let grief and guilt darken his spirits.

She leaned in and kissed him on the tip of his nose, as he'd done to her a number of times over the last few weeks. When that gesture pulled up the other corner of his mouth in a full smile, it gave her the courage to proceed.

"Lord Arnprior, let me just note that you are the kindest, most principled, and most decent man I have ever met."

"That's not much of a lecture," he said, moving one hand to caress along her spine.

Victoria had to force herself to concentrate instead of lean into his strong hand. "That was just the introduction, sir. In addition to my prior comment, you are also stubborn, arrogant, and prone to an exaggerated sense of responsibility. I understand completely how difficult life has been for you and your family, and you have personally suffered more than any man should. But the tragedies that befell you were not your fault. You did the best you could to love and care for your entire family, and no rational person could ask more from you than that."

His hand came to rest between her shoulder blades. "*I* could have asked more of myself."

She poked him in the cravat. "What you must accept is that life can be messy, irrational, and horribly sad. Some things and people are simply out of our control, no matter how hard we try to manage them. It serves no purpose to waste energy in questioning every action you may or may not have taken. Such unending reassessment simply weighs you down and keeps you from appreciating the gifts that life has granted you, here and now."

Ironically, Victoria realized she needed to apply the same lesson to herself. For weeks, she'd partly blamed herself for the debacle with Thomas Fletcher, for not being smarter or more careful. But the fault lay entirely with her attacker, and to continue to blame herself stood in the way of her own peace of mind.

Arnprior adopted an expression of polite interest. "That was an excellent lecture, Miss Knight. No wonder you're a governess."

"I apologize if I overstepped my boundaries, sir."

"I'm teasing. You could never overstep with me. Your words are both kind and wise, and I will do my best to take them to heart." He gave her a wry smile. "And I confess that you're not the first person to make a similar point."

"Royal?"

"Indeed, although as a younger brother, I can ignore him in good conscience. You, however, I cannot. After all, you're going to be my wife."

When he leaned down to kiss her, she placed a hand on his chest.

"Now what?" he asked with an aggrieved sigh.

"I meant it when I said you were not obliged to marry me."

"Really? Sir Dominic and your brother would likely say otherwise."

Suddenly nervous and very aware of the burgeoning erection pressing into her bottom, she fidgeted with his cravat. "Yes, about that. I do think I should have a say in the decision too."

His hand dropped away from where it had been resting in the curve of her lower back. "I would never force you to do anything you don't wish to do, Victoria. But your choices are limited. You are a gently bred young woman who was found with a single gentleman in compromising circumstances."

"I know, but—"

He frowned. "Are you against marriage in general? If that's the case—"

She patted his chest. "No, it's not that, although I will miss teaching and spending time with children. It's probably odd of me to admit it, but I enjoy my work."

"You don't have to give that up, at least not entirely. Two of the villages attached to Kinglas are in dire need of proper grammar schools. That has been on my list of priorities, and I would be happy to turn my plans for that over to you."

"You would do that for me?" she asked. To be able to establish her school in some form after all . . . it seemed almost too good to be true.

"You've got it backwards, love. You would be doing it for me."

"That's . . . that's very kind of you," she stammered. To have both Arnprior and the work she loved was more than she could ever have asked for.

"I'm not being kind, Victoria, because I'm getting something out of this too."

Her heart sank. That, right there, was the heart of the matter.

"Why does that bother you?" he asked, reading her consternation. "Do you not think we will suit? If so, understand that I emphatically disagree."

Victoria carefully rested her hands on his shoulders. "Why do you think we suit?"

She should have just asked him directly what he *got out of it*, but her nerve had failed.

"You mean besides the fact that you're beautiful and desirable, and I will finally get you into my bed?" he murmured, sliding his hand up to curl possessively around her neck.

"Yes, aside from that," she said skeptically. There was nothing wrong with her looks, but she was no great beauty, either.

He laughed. "Love, you are a difficult woman to persuade. Very well. In what other ways do we suit? For one, you have taken to Kinglas and the Highlands. At least, you don't entirely hate the old pile."

"Of course I don't. It's a splendid old place, and it's your home. How could I not like it?"

"Excellent. Now, for another thing, you manage my family and household exceedingly well. Everyone adores you."

Including you?

"Not Angus," she said.

"Don't be so sure. Actually, I think the old fellow is quite smitten with you."

She had to smile. "That's silly."

"On my honor as a soldier. You've completely tamed him."

"If you say so. Now, what about you?" she made herself say.

He gave her a perplexed smile. "Have you tamed me? I didn't know I needed taming."

"That's not what I meant. I'm wondering if you're . . . smitten with me, too. Just a little bit, anyway," she added awkwardly.

When he gave her an incredulous stare, she wanted the floor to open up and swallow her. Of *course* he didn't love her. He desired her and he had practical need of her, but it was ridiculous to think that a man like him could ever love a woman like her.

"Just ignore me," she said, forcing a laugh. "I'm teasing."

When she tried to slide off his lap, his arms clamped around her.

"You're not going anywhere, madam," he said sternly. "To be honest, I cannot believe a woman of your intellect can be so utterly devoid of sense in this regard."

She bristled. "There's no need to be insulting, sir."

"Smitten with you, just a little bit," he echoed. "Good God, Victoria. You're all I bloody well think about, day and night—especially the nights. You would realize that if you stopped avoiding me."

She stopped trying to escape his grip. "Are you sure? I need you to be sure."

"Am I sure? Let me show you, just a little bit."

He took her mouth with a kiss that ignited fire in her veins. When she opened to him, he growled low in his throat, the sound raw and seductive as it reverberated through her.

Victoria slid her hands around his neck, lacing her fingers through the silky hair that curled over his collar. Then she wriggled, snuggling deeper into his embrace. He groaned and flexed his hips as he nudged his erection against her bottom.

It shocked her how much she wanted to feel him—all of him. She'd never wanted that before, but she did with Arnprior, and with a reckless desire that made her shift restlessly on his lap.

He kissed her until she lost all sense of time and place, endless, luscious kisses that had her trembling in his arms. Then he slowly pulled back, when all she wanted was more.

She opened her eyes to meet his molten gaze. "Why are you stopping?"

His smile looked more like a grimace. "Lass, if I don't slow down, I'm going to have you flat on your back with your feet in the air. That is not what I have planned for you tonight."

She blushed at the graphic description, mostly because it sounded so enticing. "I . . . I wouldn't mind."

"God, don't tempt me," he said, flexing his hips. "I don't want to frighten you, my sweet."

Her gown and chemise provided only a whisper of protection as his erection rubbed her most sensitive part. She was tempted too, wanting him to assuage the delicious ache building deep inside her body.

Victoria kissed him with a provocative pressure that was

new to her. When Arnprior responded by slipping his tongue between her lips, she boldly sucked him into her mouth. She could no longer doubt his feelings for her, or the shared intensity of their desire. Arnprior wanted her as a woman— *his* woman—not as a helpmate or useful convenience.

He'd shared his deepest sorrows and secrets. He'd shared his soul, making himself vulnerable to show the depth of his need for her. To say no to him now would make her a coward, pretending to be sensible when what really held her back was fear.

Victoria was tired of being afraid, and tired of denying what she truly wanted.

She retreated from the kiss but slid her hands around to cup his face. His blue eyes were stark with a passion that all but scorched her.

"I'm not afraid," she whispered. "I want this too."

One corner of his mouth tipped up in a wry smile. "You're not afraid of anything, are you? But your first time shouldn't be like this. We'll need more privacy. And we'll need the entire night, since I want us to sleep together."

Victoria blew out an aggrieved sigh. Now he was saying no to her?

He caressed her thigh. "Don't worry, lass. I'll take care of you."

"I do hope so," she said, before she could think better of it. She winced at his delighted chuckle.

"Very well, madam. Tell me what you want."

She wasn't sure how to put it into words, so she turned the question back on him. "What do *you* want?"

One of his dark brows went up at the challenge. "For starters, I'd like to see more of you." He traced a fingertip along the top of her bodice, leaving a trail of heat across her skin. "I've spent an inordinate amount of time fantasizing about your breasts."

"That's ridiculous," she said, trying to repress a smile.

"You asked."

"Help me sit up," she said.

He supported her as she squirmed fully upright. That was actually quite delightful, since it pressed his erection against her sex. When he nudged her, she couldn't help wriggling a bit more, gasping at the small spasm that pulsed deep between her thighs.

"We won't get very far if you keep that up," Arnprior said in a strained voice.

"I'm not doing anything," she said.

When he narrowed his eyes and gave her a mock growl, she couldn't hold back a giggle. She'd never imagined this could be fun, but teasing him was both amusing and exciting.

Victoria reached around to unbutton the top of her gown, then slipped the short sleeves off her arms, letting the bodice sag to her waist. The hitch in his breath bolstered her courage to keep going, so she pulled down the straps of her chemise, pushing that down to her waist too.

That left her covered only in stays, an exceedingly plain set that laced up the front. It certainly wasn't a garment designed for seduction.

He settled his warm hand on her chest, just above the stays. "God," he murmured, "you're so beautiful."

When he dipped a finger inside, the callused tip brushing over her nipple, Victoria had to bite her lip to hold back a moan. He teased her until the nipple fully beaded up, stiff and throbbing with pleasure.

"Would you like me to take off my stays?" she said breathlessly, wanting more.

His eyes lit up with a combination of lust and amusement. "Since I've been trying to peer discreetly down the front of your gowns for weeks, I'd say the answer is yes."

She huffed out a nervous laugh as she began unlacing. His gaze narrowed as he watched her.

Victoria drew the process out, covering for a sudden spurt of nerves. No one would ever call her buxom— skinny was more apt. Because men seemed to like ladies built along more generous lines, she couldn't help wondering if he would find her lacking.

Impatiently, Arnprior brushed aside her hands and tugged down the stays. Her breasts spilled out, soft and pale in the flickering light of the fire.

"Damn, Victoria," he murmured. "You're a bloody goddess."

He curled a hand around her breast, gently massaging it and playing with her nipple. Sensation sparked underneath his fingertips.

"Now you're just being silly," she managed in a breathless voice.

Arnprior's gaze came up to meet hers, and he leaned in, flicking his tongue along the seam of her mouth. When he nipped her lower lip, she groaned and grabbed for his shoulders. When he stroked her again, she felt heat and dampness build between her thighs.

"Look at your nipples," he murmured. "Stiff and pink, and perfect for my mouth."

When he gently pinched one between his fingertips, she whimpered. He bent her back over his arm, then came down to her, sucking the rigid tip into his mouth.

Victoria melted into his powerful embrace. When his firm mouth drew on her, the pleasure was so sharp it made her shudder. She wrapped a hand around the back of his head, holding him close to her breast and silently urging him on.

Arnprior pleasured her with a relentless passion, going from one breast to the other, lavishing attention on her sensitive nipples. She clung to him, her eyelids fluttering shut, her body adrift on a dark, languid sea. When he gently bit one of her nipples, she couldn't hold back a soft cry. Her insides clenched as small spasms rippled deep within.

When he pulled away, she opened her eyes and tried to focus through the pleasure fogging her brain.

His gaze devoured her, as hard and bright as diamonds, and his smile curved with a fierce satisfaction. He'd never looked more like an untamed Highlander than he did at this moment.

"Lass, I've never wanted anything the way I want you," he said, his brogue lacing his voice with a delicious, deep note. "Of that you can be sure."

She found that hard to believe, but it was a lovely sentiment anyway.

He swept a gentle hand down her body, lingering on her breast and belly before coming to rest on her thigh.

Her naked thigh.

Victoria glanced down and blinked in surprise. She'd been so distracted by his sensual attentions that she'd failed to notice how he'd inched her skirts up over her knees. Her stockings and garters were in full view, as were inches of skin above them.

When he grasped her crumpled skirts and pulled them up even higher, Victoria squeaked with shock. He'd exposed *everything*, including the nest of silky hair at the top of her thighs, which only partly hid her most intimate parts.

She jerked when he brushed his fingers through those curls.

"Easy, lass," he murmured. "I just want to play with you and make you feel good." He petted her, as if she were a kitten, and flashed her a roguish grin. "I'd been wondering if you were as blond down there."

Victoria's face was burning up—as was the rest of her.

He leaned down to cover her lips in a searing, demanding kiss that left her breathless and wanting more, so much more.

When he raised his head, his amusement had vanished. His gaze was once more intent, and his handsome features were pulled in hard, almost savage, lines. He pressed his fingers through her curls, slipping bluntly between her folds. Victoria all but lifted off his lap.

"You're so wet," he muttered as he stroked her. "What I wouldn't give to taste you."

She clung to his arms. "Um, what?"

"I'll show you next time. Just relax, love. Enjoy this."

When his fingers dipped even lower between her thighs, she moaned. Her muscles went weak as he teased the slick entrance to her channel before moving up to gently massage the tight little bud that ached for his touch.

To relax was impossible. Yes, she felt all but boneless under his passionate attentions, shivering in his arms. But as her arousal built, gathering in her core, Victoria grew ever more restless.

She was familiar with her own body, and she recognized the approaching climax. But never had her need been so intense. The feel of his big hands on her body, blunt-fingered and hard yet also tender and knowing, was like nothing she'd ever experienced. His every caress seemed to pour heat and magic through her veins.

When he slipped a finger into her, Victoria curled forward. Sensation rippled outward, sending her to the edge.

"Nicholas," she gasped, squeezing her eyes shut and digging her fingers into his waistcoat.

"Yes, love," he gritted out. "Almost there."

When his hand slid down to her inner thigh, her eyes popped open. He slowly pushed open her legs, spreading her wide. Victoria's breath fractured as she gazed down at herself, sprawled in his lap. She was all but naked, her body flushed with passion, her curls dewy and glistening from her arousal.

She should be ashamed at the wanton display, abandoning herself to passion in the arms of a man not yet her husband. And yet, she felt no shame. Vulnerable, yes, and even a little frightened at the onslaught of such powerful emotions. But in Arnprior's strong arms, she'd never felt safer or more cherished.

She raised a hand to his face, tenderly cupping his cheek as she stared into his eyes. Then his gaze once again swept over her body, focusing on her parted thighs. He slowly pushed two fingers inside her as he flicked his thumb over her slick bud. When Victoria started to moan, he bent and fastened his lips to hers, swallowing the sound. She shook in his arms as pleasure stormed through her body. When her climax reached its peak, she breathed a sob into his mouth and then curled into the shelter of his broad chest.

His hand gently cupped her sex, softly stroking as the ripples faded away. Victoria sucked in air, trying to slow her pounding heart. When her lungs—and her brain—started working again, she opened her eyes and stared dazedly up at him.

Arnprior's eyes gleamed with unappeased hunger. "I trust that answers your question as to whether we will suit, Miss Knight. *And* that it lays to rest any further objections to our marriage. As far as I'm concerned, there isn't a damn thing standing in the way of our getting married tomorrow. Not one."

But there still was, of course, one very troublesome, very large impediment to their future wedded bliss.

And his name was Thomas Fletcher.

Chapter Twenty

As Nick handed Victoria up the carriage step, she gave him a shy smile. After that intense, sensual night in his study, he'd thought all was settled between them, and marriage would shortly follow.

But Victoria had responded to their sexual interlude by bolting off his lap and stammering out an apology. After struggling to right her clothing—he'd had to do most of the work for her—she'd then all but fled the room. He'd put it down to maidenly nerves, but now was beginning to think some other concern held her back. He intended to solve the mystery—and tonight, if possible.

In the meantime, he'd worked hard to convey his commitment to her, both privately and publicly. He'd taken her on a few outings around town, and up to Mugdock Castle to take in the splendid view. Kade had usually been their escort. The lad worked too hard and needed a break from his studies, and Victoria clearly felt more at ease with the company. When she was more at ease, she was more amenable to Nick's courtship.

He was, however, impatient to settle the matter between them, and wasn't above using a bit of encouragement to achieve his ends.

After waving Royal into the carriage, Nick climbed in and sat next to Victoria. When he carefully tucked the lap blanket around her waist, she gave a little shake of her head.

"Thank you, sir. I'm quite capable of doing that for myself."

"I like taking care of you," he said, giving her a warm smile.

"Obviously," Royal said.

"Did you enjoy the ball tonight, Royal?" Victoria asked brightly.

"The Gilbrides know how to throw a party, I'll say that much."

Alec and Edie had hosted the Hogmanay Ball at their manor house near Glasgow. The entertaining affair had included what seemed like half the citizens of Glasgow. To say it was a mad crush was an understatement.

Victoria gave a discreet yawn behind her gloved hand. "I'm not surprised the twins decided to stay. They seemed to be having fun."

"They'll be there well past dawn, I imagine," Nick said.

He'd been reluctant to leave them on their own until Alec vowed to keep an eye on them. Fortunately, they'd mostly behaved themselves. Graeme seemed greatly smitten with Miss MacBride, the vicar's daughter. She was a surprising choice for his rapscallion brother, although Nick couldn't help but notice she wasn't exactly a pattern card of modest behavior. The lass had even dragged Graeme onto the dance floor for a second waltz. Because that had set more than a few tongues wagging, it was time to give his brother a warning. Nick didn't need a scandal on his hands, especially while he was courting Victoria.

"Perhaps we should have brought the twins home with us instead of foisting them on Edie and Alec," Victoria said in a worried tone.

"Many of the guests will remain until dawn," Nick said. "It's a Hogmanay tradition. The Gilbrides will no doubt be providing breakfast for dozens."

"Victoria, in case you didn't notice, we were among the first to leave," Royal said. "For some reason, Nick seemed eager to get out of there."

"I didn't hear you raise any objections to our early departure," Nick retorted.

"I'm not much a one for parties." Royal then flashed Nick a taunting smile. "But it's a shame you felt the need to drag Victoria away before midnight. You never let the poor lass have any fun."

"Have you forgotten we arrived early to dine with the Gilbrides? We didn't exactly cut and run, you imbecile." Nick gave Victoria an apologetic grimace. "But I'm sorry if you feel I dragged you away. I thought you'd like to spend part of the evening with Kade and Braden. They're waiting up for us." That was very true, and also a convenient excuse.

"I was quite content to leave, my lord. I'd rather ring in the New Year with your family than with a roomful of strangers. I'm not used to attending balls and soirees, as you know. Governesses are rarely invited to such events."

Nick pretended shock. "You mean you don't miss being trampled by a mob on the way to an overheated supper room, or having to fend off impertinent young men in their cups?"

"No one would dare be impertinent with you glowering at every male under the age of sixty who even glanced her way," Royal said.

"Don't be ridiculous. Victoria danced with a number of gentlemen tonight, as you well know." Nick knew exactly how many, because he'd counted every blasted nincompoop who'd come sniffing around her skirts.

"And you looked like you wanted to murder every one of them."

"You seemed to be enjoying yourself too, Royal," Victoria said. "You spent quite a bit of time chatting with Lady Ainsley."

"I was seated next to her at supper, so I could hardly ignore the poor girl. As much as I would have liked to," he added, inspecting a seam on his gloves. "But one cannot be rude."

Nick scoffed. "That's never stopped you before."

In fact, he'd been worried to see that Edie had placed Royal and Ainsley together. He'd spent the first course directing warning glares at his brother, half expecting he'd have to leap in to prevent a verbal altercation. Somehow, though, Royal and the snooty beauty had managed to make it through dinner without any fireworks.

"Perhaps I thought it might be more amusing not to cause a scene," Royal said in a dour tone.

"I'm sure our hosts were grateful for your forbearance," Victoria said with an encouraging smile. "You were sitting with her during the dancing, and the two of you seemed to be engaged in quite a good discussion."

While Nick had missed that conversation, Victoria had obviously kept a careful eye on all his brothers. In fact, she'd developed into something of a mother hen when it came to the lads, including Royal.

Royal scowled at her. "I don't need you spying on me, Victoria. I'm a grown man."

"Though you don't always act like one," Nick said.

His brother flushed. "I was just explaining the sword dance to Ain—Lady Ainsley. I thought she might like to know what the steps meant, that's all."

Perhaps it bothered Royal that he could no longer take part in the dances. Before his injury, no one in the family—

indeed the entire county—had performed the sword dance with more grace and athleticism than his brother.

Dammit.

Perhaps dragging his brother along to this sort of affair wasn't such a good idea. Of course it would be a painful reminder of everything he'd lost to the war.

Victoria nodded. "That was very kind of you. I enjoyed it as well. How clever of Edie to arrange for performers to entertain the guests with some of the old reels and dances."

For the rest of the ride home, she kept up a steady stream of good-natured commentary about the party. But Royal barely said a word, and Nick was more than ready to get out of the damn carriage by the time they rolled up to Kendrick House. By the tiny sigh Victoria expelled, it seemed she'd had enough of Royal for one night, too.

When the footman opened the carriage door, Royal bolted out as fast as his injured leg would allow.

"Sorry, lass," Nick said. "He shouldn't treat you like that."

"No, I embarrassed him. I wonder—"

He tipped her chin up and pressed a quick kiss to her lips. "No more wondering or worrying about my brothers for the rest of the evening. You're off duty, Miss Knight."

She dimpled up at him. "As you wish, my lord."

"By the way," he said as he helped her up, "have I told you how pretty you look? I was tempted to carry you off to a secluded alcove and have my way with you."

"Hush," she hissed. "The footman will hear you."

He grinned and stepped out, then handed her down to the pavement. Royal leaned against the railing in front of the house, a brooding expression on his face. He looked the very image of a romantic hero, a thought that would no doubt appall the poor fellow.

"He looks like a poet," Victoria murmured, echoing

Nick's thoughts. "No wonder Lady Ainsley is so entranced by him."

Nick threw her a startled glance. "She is?"

"Undoubtedly."

If true, it constituted a welcome development for Royal to secure the interest of such a well-bred, wealthy young woman—

"Bloody hell, you two," Royal said. "It's almost time. Best get a move on or we'll miss it."

"Miss what?" Victoria asked.

Nick pulled out his pocket watch. Only a minute or so until midnight.

"First Foot," he said, escorting her up the wide stone steps to the front door.

"I've heard of it," she said. "It's an old Scottish tradition."

"The first person to enter the home traditionally brings good luck for the rest of the year—if the appropriate conditions are met."

"Appropriate conditions?" she asked.

"That it be a dark-haired male," Royal said. "Nick usually does it, when he's home."

"And I'll be doing it from now on," Nick said. "You have the coal?"

Royal held up a small lump.

"Good heavens," Victoria said with a laugh.

"Another tradition," Royal said. "Angus would kill us if we didn't carry in a piece of coal."

When the bells of midnight began to chime all over the city, Nick pulled out the small purse of gold sovereigns he'd stowed in his greatcoat pocket before leaving the house. Then he rapped on the door. It swung open, revealing his family and most of the servants, lined up awaiting their arrival.

He stepped over the threshold. "A Happy New Year and Good Tidings to you and yours."

Representing the household, Angus bustled forward. "Happy New Year, lad," he said gruffly, giving him a quick hug.

"Happy New Year, Grandda." Nick handed over the purse. "Make sure all the servants get one."

Angus nodded. "And Good New Year to ye both," he said to Victoria and Royal. He took a glass of whisky from one of the footmen and handed it to Nick. Another footman distributed small glasses to everyone else crowded in the hall.

Nick held up his glass. "*Slainte*, and Happy New Year."

They cheered and toasted him back.

After the glasses were drained, they all began hugging and slapping one another on the back. When Kade tried to sneak an extra dram from the footman, Nick plucked the glass from his hand.

"That's enough for you, laddie boy," he said with mock severity.

"Spoilsport," Kade said, then he threw his arms around Nick's waist and gave him a fierce hug. "Happy New Year, Nick. I'm so glad we're all here together."

"Except for the twins," said Braden, also coming up to give Nick a hug. "I suppose they had better things to do."

"Such as flirt with pretty girls and enjoy themselves?" Victoria replied with a smile. "What shocking activities for young men."

Braden rolled his eyes. "I know you think I'm an old stick-in-the mud, but I truly would rather be with my family."

"I think you're splendid," Victoria said, giving him a hug. "But I also think you work too hard."

Since coming to Glasgow, she'd been on a campaign to get the lad to ease up on his studies. But Braden was determined to gain admittance to medical school as soon as possible. He was the most disciplined, serious person Nick had ever known.

"Someone in this household has to earn his keep," Royal said. "God knows the rest of us spend our days lazing about."

"Speak for yourself," Kade said, poking him in the arm. "I work very hard, as does Miss Knight."

"True," Royal said, ruffling his little brother's hair.

Nick didn't miss the bitter twist to his brother's smile. Royal still hadn't a clue what to do with his life.

"How about another wee dram in the drawing room?" Angus said.

"Yes, please," said Kade. "I want to hear all about the party."

Nick frowned. "It's getting late, and you must be tired."

When Kade started to protest, Victoria smoothly intervened. "I think we can make an exception. After all, it's New Year's."

"So there." Kade stuck his tongue out at Nick.

They all laughed and the family followed Angus into the drawing room. Nick held Victoria back. "Are you sure the boy's not wearing himself out? He's looking a little peaked to me."

"He's looking no such thing," she said firmly. "The doctor said just yesterday how pleased he is with Kade's progress. Stop worrying so much. I'm sure it's not good for you."

"Do you fear for my health, Madam Governess? If I fall ill and take to my bed, you'll have to join me there. To personally attend to all my needs, of course."

"Sir, I cannot imagine what you're talking about."

"Lass, you know *exactly* what I'm talking about," he murmured, leaning in close. She smelled delicious, like peppermints and sweet tea.

Her lips twitched. "You are incorrigible," she said before marching past him.

Nick followed, not bothering to hide his grin.

Kade, sitting on the sofa by the fireplace, waved as they came in. "Miss Knight, come sit by me."

As she went to join him, Nick propped his shoulder against the edge of the mantel and accepted another dram from Angus.

"So, ye all had a grand time prancing about with the nobs, did ye?" Angus asked.

"We did," Victoria said. "It was a lovely party, and not everyone was a nob. For one thing, I was there."

"Aye, but ye are rather snooty," Angus said with a wink. "Even if ye are a governess."

Victoria simply rolled her eyes.

None of the others but Nick knew she was the natural daughter of the Prince Regent, since she'd sworn him to silence on that point. To his family, Victoria *was* only a governess, and yet they clearly respected her, including his grandfather, who would be more likely to hold her royal blood against her rather than see it as advantageous. And Nick's brothers would probably think it a great joke, something to tease her about.

"She's not snooty at all, Grandda," Kade said in stout defense. "And I'll bet Miss Knight was the prettiest lady there. Right, Nick?"

Nick smiled at her. "Without a doubt."

She scoffed. "There were far prettier girls. I know, because I watched them trail about after the twins. Graeme and Grant cut very dashing figures in their clan dress."

"As do you, Nick," Braden said. "I don't remember the last time I saw you kitted out in the full regalia of the Black Watch."

Since both Royal and the twins had worn the family colors, Nick had decided to honor both his old regiment and his host by hauling out his dress uniform. "It seemed fitting, given that Alec was also a member of the Watch."

"What about you, Royal? Did you meet any pretty girls?" Kade asked.

"No," Royal said, staring down at his glass.

Braden eyed his brother. "Did you sit in the corner all night and ignore everyone, as usual?"

"Of course not," Victoria said when Royal started to bristle. "He chatted with many people, including a guest who is visiting with the Gilbrides. That person was feeling a bit lonely, and it was very nice of Royal to spend time with her."

"Probably an old biddy no one else wanted to talk to," Angus said.

"Exactly," Royal dryly replied.

"Tell us what else happened." Kade pulled his legs up and leaned against Victoria's shoulder. "What did they serve for dinner? Was there any entertainment?"

"It was entirely splendid, as you can imagine," Victoria replied.

She snagged the wool lap blanket off the arm of the sofa and tucked it around Kade's legs. For years, the boy had longed for a mother's affection, and he'd finally found it in Victoria's warm, sensible nature. In fact, Nick believed that her presence was quietly repairing the holes that time and tragedy had punched in the fabric of his family's lives.

He'd reached the point where he was finding it difficult to imagine life without her.

Eventually, talk moved to plans for the next few months and the family's impending return to Kinglas. By the time the longcase clock in the hall struck the hour, Kade was dozing on Victoria's shoulder.

"Och, the wee lad's asleep," Angus said in his ridiculously loud version of a whisper.

"I'm just resting my eyes," Kade said sleepily.

Victoria nudged the boy. "It's late, and time we were all abed."

"Indeed," Nick said. When she glanced up at him, he winked.

She blushed and averted her gaze as she urged Kade to his feet. "Come along, young man."

"Anyone up for another dram?" Angus asked hopefully.

"No," Victoria said firmly.

Like the mother hen she was, she ushered them all out to the hall, ignoring Angus's protest. They wandered up the stairs in ones and twos, Braden guiding a protesting but sleepy Kade to his bedroom.

"Thank you for a delightful evening, Lord Arnprior," Victoria said as she paused outside Nick's door on the way to her room. "And Happy New Year."

"What, no New Year's kiss?" he teased.

She cast a quick glance down the hall. Royal and Angus were still at the head of the stairs, talking.

"Under the circumstances, I think not," she said, sounding regretful.

"Ah, perhaps later then," he said, waggling his eyebrows.

She gave him a wry smile. "As I said earlier, incorrigible."

"I do hope so."

"Good night." She marched off down the hall, the short train of her gown fanning out behind her in a ripple of silk. Conveniently for his plans, her room was at the back of the house and a good distance from the other bedrooms.

Nick dismissed the footman who served as his valet in town, and leisurely began to undress. He thought about putting on his dressing gown, but remembering what she'd once said about men in Highland dress, he decided to leave on his kilt.

After waiting a few minutes, he went to the door and cocked an ear. The house was silent, so he snagged a small box off the top of the tallboy dresser and tucked it into the back of his waistband, then headed down the darkened hall to the back of the house. Light flickering from under Victoria's door signaled she was not yet in bed.

He softly tapped on the oak panel. After a few moments, he heard a soft rustling, and then the door swung open. Victoria blinked up at him, obviously startled.

"Lord Arnprior, my goodness," she said in a breathless tone.

He let his gaze drift slowly down, desire starting a hard drumbeat through his veins. Her unpinned hair streamed like a waterfall of pale moonlight thick and straight over her shoulders. Thankfully, she was still dressed in her shimmering blue gown, a glorious confection of silk and lace that he'd been dreaming of peeling off since the moment he'd laid eyes on her in it.

Bracing a hand on the door frame, he smiled down at her. "Hello, lass. I've come to get that New Year's Eve kiss you promised me."

Chapter Twenty-One

Victoria blinked, stunned by the sight of the earl's muscular and very naked chest six inches from her nose. She could barely assemble a coherent thought.

Then she made the mistake of glancing down. He was wearing only his kilt, and it did a splendid job of showcasing his long legs, lean hips, and flat stomach, down which a trail of black hair disappeared under his waistband toward his—

Stop it.

With one brawny arm braced against the door frame, his shoulders filled up nearly the entire space. Victoria was now used to living in a house full of tall, broad-shouldered men, but the earl was something entirely different. He always carried himself with a quiet power and dignity, but at the moment he looked almost raw, as if he were a wild Celtic warrior come down from the hills in search of plunder.

The fact that he barely looked civilized was considerably more exciting than she cared to admit.

"Um, what?" Then she winced at her silly response. Instead of gaping up at him like a henwit, she should be slamming the door in his face.

A rogue's smile lifted the corners of his mouth. Placing his hands around her waist, he walked her backward into the room, then kicked the door shut with his heel.

"A New Year's Eve kiss, remember?" he said. "You're supposed to give me one."

She made a concerted effort to stop acting like a silly girl. "I don't believe I ever promised to do such a thing, my lord."

He adopted a thoughtful frown as his hands drifted up her rib cage to come to rest under her breasts. "Are you sure?"

"Quite."

His eyes smoldered like molten silver. "I think you should give me one anyway. It's tradition, for good luck."

Victoria felt her willpower crumbling like the ancient wall at the bottom of the castle garden. "Well, I suppose if it's tradition . . ."

Besides, she could certainly use a little good luck.

As he started to lower his head, she braced her hands on his chest and unconsciously went up on her toes to meet him. His big hands slid back down to her hips, gently tucking her into the shelter of his body. When they connected, she gasped at the feel of his erection pressing against her belly.

Her shock was swept away as his lips took hers with a passion that robbed her of strength. When she swayed against him, he curled his fingers into her hips, crumpling the fabric of her gown.

His kiss was like a storm roaring down from the craggy heights overlooking Kinglas. Victoria desperately clutched at his shoulders as he ravished her mouth with an intensity she'd never experienced—not even during their sensual interlude in his study, when he'd brought her to a shivering climax in his arms.

When Nicholas nipped her lower lip, she moaned and parted for him. The kiss turned hot and wet, his mouth demanding and greedy as he seduced with dominant, expert kisses. He'd clearly been holding back when he kissed her before. Even that first time, when he was drunk, he'd been gentle, protecting her in spite of his need. Now his kisses said *you are mine*. This was the laird, the Highland chief, and he was claiming what rightfully belonged to him.

God help her, Victoria wanted to be claimed. For once, she wanted to belong to somebody, to come before all others, body and soul.

And she wanted to claim him, too.

She wrapped her arms around his neck, pressing close to his chest as she whimpered into his mouth. He growled in response, low in his throat like a wolf. Everything inside her quivered at the delicious sound, and she wriggled against him, trying to assuage the ache that had tightened her nipples to hard points.

And assuage the building ache between her legs. Without thinking, she rocked into him, pressing the softest part of her against that incredibly hard part of him.

When Nicholas stilled, Victoria's eyes flew open and she met his wide gaze. His pupils were dilated, as if he'd been drugged, and there was a flush high on his cheekbones.

They stared at each other, both panting for breath.

"What . . . what's wrong?" she stammered.

When he didn't answer, a realization doused her ardor like a cold bucket of water. It was one thing to respond to your presumed fiancé's kisses with pleasure and approval. It was another thing entirely to lose control and crawl all over him like a tart.

Like my mother would have.

"I'm sorry, my lord," she gritted out, trying to struggle free. "I cannot imagine what you must think of me."

While he was also behaving very badly, a respectable woman had no business throwing her principles to the wind. Not even if she was madly in love with the man trying to seduce her. She should have given him a peck on the cheek and sent him on his way.

The earl's amazing blue gaze warmed with understanding, then he picked her up, turning in an effortless motion to press her against the door. When he crowded close, she didn't know what was harder—the door at her back or his brawny physique at her front.

He gently cupped her chin. "You are the sweetest, kindest, bonniest lass that ever walked the earth. And nothing you do with me would be wrong or sinful, so get that out of your mind." His smile was dark and seductive. "Your enthusiasm simply surprised me for a moment—in the best kind of way."

Embarrassed, she squeezed her eyelids shut. "But we shouldn't be doing this. We're not even married."

"And whose fault is that, may I ask?"

She sighed and opened her eyes. "Mine. But I can't help feeling that . . ."

He nuzzled her cheek with a soft kiss. Even more than his strength, his tenderness completely undid her.

"Feeling what?" he whispered.

"That I'm not right for you."

"I do believe I'm the one who's best able to decide that question."

She thought of the secrets she carried. "I'm not so sure of that."

"I am, and I'm happy to show you exactly why."

When he took her mouth again, she didn't have the heart to push him away.

His lips wandered across her cheek, then nibbled along her jaw and down her neck. Victoria tilted her head sideways, helpless to do anything but give him what he wanted—what they both wanted. When he clamped his hands around her waist and lifted her up, holding her against the door as he rocked into her, she gasped and clung tight.

"God, lass," he rasped. "You'll make me spend before I even get inside you."

She swallowed, both shocked and excited by his blunt words.

With easy strength, he held her against the door, flexing his hips and nudging his erection against her throbbing sex. Desire rolled over her, making her light-headed. Victoria clamped her hands around his head, kissing him with a fierce intensity. Her emotional *and* physical need for him was almost visceral, as if she would die if she couldn't have him.

Vulnerable and frightened almost out of her wits, she hoped Nicholas *never* stopped kissing her.

A moment later, he froze again.

She opened her eyes. He was frowning, his head tilted away from her.

"Now what?" After finally letting down her guard, she just might murder him if he stopped now.

"Hush, love," he whispered.

Now she understood. Someone treaded at a stately pace down the hall. It was undoubtedly the butler, making his final rounds.

Nicholas held her securely but her position was less than comfortable, with her shoulder blades wedged against the hard-oak panels and her toes just skimming the floor.

And she was rather precariously perched on the broad head of his erection, which had somehow found its way out from under the folds of his kilt and was now rubbing into the thin silk of her gown. It was an awkward—if stimulating—position that made her feel more than slightly ridiculous. Propped against a door and all but riding on a gentleman's manly appendage was certainly not where any proper woman should hope to find herself.

Why not?

Victoria firmly brushed aside the question.

The earl's head was still turned away as he listened to the fading footsteps. She tapped him on the shoulder, and he cocked an eyebrow at her.

"Could you please put me down?" she asked politely.

"Must I?" He nudged her a bit, making her squeak. "I'm quite enjoying this particular position."

"I'm not," she said tartly. Well, not entirely, anyway.

"Spoilsport." He eased her down in a stimulating slide. It took a moment for her to catch her breath.

"I suppose we'd better keep away from the door," he said in a casual tone. "It was bound to get a bit noisy if we continued along as we were. That would be entirely inappropriate for your first time, anyway."

Victoria's mouth sagged open. "You can do *that* against a door?"

"Love, you can do it against a door, in a chair, in a carriage, or just about anyplace else you can think of." He grinned. "You can even do it from behind, on your hands and knees. I'll be happy to demonstrate some of the more adventurous positions once we've mastered the basics."

She of course wondered if he'd done those things with other women. "With my luck, I'd probably get a splinter from the door," she blurted out.

His eyes gleamed. "Och, lass, I'll be happy to doctor your pretty arse if that happens."

She blushed. The conversation had become entirely mortifying.

"I'm sure there will never be the opportunity to do so." She pushed her tangled hair back over her shoulders. "And now that we've fulfilled the demands of tradition and exchanged a New Year's kiss, thus ensuring good luck, I think we should bid each other good night."

She did her best to dignify her ridiculous little speech with a quick curtsy.

Nicholas choked out a laugh. "Victoria, that's just cruel. Especially considering this." He glanced down at the erection that was tenting his kilt, something she'd been doing her best to ignore.

"Sir, it's almost two in the morning. The entire house is abed."

"I'd be happy to put you to bed too, Miss Knight," he said with a comical wiggle of his eyebrows.

She didn't know whether to laugh or scold him—or run into his arms and kiss him. She'd rarely felt more confused, poised between pure joy and the fear she was making an awful mistake.

Though Nicholas seemed entirely at ease, his gaze turned serious. "Love, why are you fighting this so hard?"

"I . . . I told you. I want to be sure you're not making a mistake."

Sympathy flickered across his handsome face. Or, perhaps it was pity.

She turned and made her way to the fireplace, taking the iron and clumsily poking the logs.

"Give me that, you daft girl," he said as he came up behind and plucked the tool from her hand. "You're making a mess."

Victoria let out an aggrieved sigh. "We can both agree on that."

He leaned the tool against the marble fireplace surround and then steered her to the high back chair in front of the hearth. Going down in a crouch before her, he clasped her hands.

"Is it your parentage you're worried about?" he asked. "Because I believe we've addressed that."

"But—"

"It's not an impediment, and you know it. Now, tell me the real reason you're feeling so hen-hearted."

There was a simple, stark reason for his apt description of her worries, and his name was Thomas Fletcher. Nicholas would never blame her for defending herself, but no sensible man would wish to marry a woman with a potential murder charge hanging over her head, especially not a man whose marriage had ended in tragedy and scandal. Although Fletcher's death wasn't Victoria's fault, in the eyes of the *ton* she would still be considered suspect—if not outright guilty.

Nicholas had already suffered too much for her to make his life more difficult.

But more than anything, she feared losing his respect. She feared seeing the warmth in his gaze fade away, replaced by shock and dismay. He would surely recall all the reasons why she was so unsuited to be his bride.

Then she would lose him forever.

"Victoria?" he prompted gently.

"I . . . I'm no saint, my lord," she said. "I've done things I'm not proud of, and I'm nobody's idea of the perfect woman."

"That's good, because I'm far from perfect myself." He smiled. "I have no interest in marrying a paragon, because I cannot imagine anything more boring."

"But—"

"Sweetheart, you're aware that I've done things I'm not proud of too. And you've not held that against me, have you?"

"Of course not. You were simply trying to survive terrible situations."

"And when you did those things you weren't proud of, what were *you* doing?"

She sighed. "Trying to survive."

"Exactly. Now, tell me, have you ever intentionally hurt anyone or acted contrarily to your principles?"

"No," she said, trying to be fair to herself. "Not intentionally."

"I didn't think so. Victoria, clearly there are things in your past that trouble you, and I hope someday you'll tell me about them. But I respect your privacy, and I respect your secrets. How could I not? I've kept secrets from you until my blasted family forced them into the open." He leaned forward and briefly kissed the tip of her nose. "I will not force anything from you, love. I will wait until you're ready to share them of your own free will."

His generosity made her feel like an absolute worm, but she couldn't deny a sneaking feeling of relief.

"Thank you, my lord. I'm . . . I'm very grateful."

A slight smile lifted the corners of his mouth. "You don't seem grateful. In fact, as Angus would say, you look as queer as Dick's hatband."

She wrinkled her nose. "I do?"

"Yes, but I know just the thing to jolly you out of your bad mood."

"I'm not . . . never mind." At the moment her emotions were such a mess that there was no point in trying to explain herself.

With a quiet laugh, he reached behind and extracted something from the waistband of his kilt. When she saw the small jeweler's box, her heart began to thud.

"Another present, sir?" She forced a smile. "Indeed, it's not necessary. You've already given me so much, including this lovely dress."

"Which I had to compel you to accept, as I recall," he said dryly.

"It's not appropriate for you to purchase my clothing."

They'd had more than one fraught discussion about it, since the earl had insisted on garments appropriate to her status as his future countess. She'd finally agreed to allow him to purchase a few things for her, including the gown for tonight, partly because Edie and Alec had taken his side.

"Then I'll be happy to divest you of all your clothing, after I give you this," he said.

When he flipped open the box, she gasped. Nestled in dark red velvet was a flawless pink pearl surrounded by small but perfect diamonds and set on a plain gold band. Simple and elegant, it was the most beautiful ring she'd ever seen.

"Good God, I cannot possibly wear that, my lord."

"I don't see why not." He took her limp hand and slipped it onto her finger.

"Because everyone will think we're betrothed," she said in a tight voice, feeling like bursting into tears.

"They already do. Might as well make it official."

She wavered a moment, and then shook her head. "Lord Arnprior—"

"Nicholas," he murmured, taking her hand and placing it on his chest. His muscles felt hot and hard under her fingertips, and the pearl shone with an almost mystical gleam. "Or Nick, if you prefer."

She stared up into his handsome, wonderful face, and her willpower slipped completely away as she tumbled into helpless, hopeless love. She wanted him so much it made her chest ache.

"Wear it for me, at least just for tonight." He feathered a soft kiss across her lips.

Victoria slid her hands around his neck and went nose to nose with him. "All right, Nicholas."

His eyes flared bright with triumph, and he rose, pulling

her up with him. Sweeping her into his arms, he strode toward the canopied bed.

Tomorrow. I'll write to Dominic tomorrow. She would tell her mentor in no uncertain terms that she refused to keep secrets any longer.

And then thoughts of anything but Nicholas scattered like flotsam as he plopped her on the bed and braced his fists on either side of her thighs.

"I'm going to make love to you now, Victoria," he said gruffly. "Is that all right?"

She had to swallow twice before she could answer. "Yes, please. Sir."

A husky laugh was his only reply as he began to undress her, starting first with her shoes and stockings. In no time at all, he'd stripped them from her body, reaching up under her skirts to quickly work her garters down her legs. She shivered at the feel of his big hands brushing over her skin, sending waves of delicious anticipation rocketing through her body.

Nicholas tossed her stockings and garters in the general direction of the chair.

"My lord, those stockings were very expensive," she said, shocked by his cavalier attitude.

"I know exactly how much this ensemble cost, lass," he said wryly. "I paid for it."

She tentatively stroked his broad shoulders. His hard muscles twitched beneath her fingertips. "And it was very nice of you to do so."

He tipped up her chin, studying her expression. "Victoria, I want you so much I can barely see straight, but there's no need to rush this."

"I am a little nervous," she confessed.

"Just tell me if there's anything I do that makes you uncomfortable. All right?"

He looked so serious that she couldn't help smiling. "That sounds perfect."

"Good. Now are you ready to get out of that dress?"

She heaved a dramatic sigh. "Yes, although it's so beautiful that I hate to take it off."

"I can work around that," he said with a gleam in his eyes. "Although it might get wrinkled by the time I'm finished."

"Goodness, that would be dreadful," she said, pretending to be shocked.

When she reached behind to unfasten her buttons, he brushed her hands away and swiftly undid the buttons before whisking both her chemise and gown over her head.

He certainly wasn't wasting any time.

When he looked like he was about to fling the garments over his shoulder, she scowled. "Don't even dare."

He snorted, then swiped up the stockings from the floor and casually tossed the bundle of clothing onto a chair.

"Happy, now?" he asked.

She had to stifle a smile. "Your courtesy is much appreciated, my lord."

"What I appreciate is the way you look right now," he said as his gaze roamed over her body.

She blushed, feeling awkward to be perched on the edge of the bed wearing nothing but her new stays. Unlike her usual undergarments, the front-lacing set was frivolous in the extreme. Embroidered with pink and red flowers, it was trimmed with red silk bows on the straps. Because it was cut so low and close to the body, it did a spectacular job of pushing up her breasts to form plump mounds. Although Victoria had initially been reluctant to wear them, the modiste had claimed the new ball gown wouldn't fit properly without them.

"I'm glad you approve," she joked, "because they were ridiculously expensive."

"And worth every damn shilling. No, don't take it off. Not yet, anyway."

She dropped her hands from the laces.

When he tugged on the stays, her breasts popped out even more, exposing her flushed, tight nipples. "Now, *that* is what I call perfect," he murmured.

He gently tugged on the sensitive points. Victoria whimpered and grabbed his biceps as sensation streaked through her. Between her legs, she felt a trickle of warmth.

"Does that feel good, darling?" He thumbed her nipples, then rubbed his palms across them, making them throb with a delicious ache. "Do you want more?"

She answered by grabbing his head and pulling him down for a frantic kiss. He huffed out a startled laugh but he obliged her, surging into her mouth with deep, hot glides. Victoria poured all her passion into the torrid kiss.

For so long she'd held back, trying to keep her emotions in check. But now her barriers had crumbled. Nicholas knew she had secrets and knew she had a troubled past. His trust was a strong, bracing wind that swept aside the dusty doubts that had resided in her soul.

For delicious minutes, he seduced her with his mouth while caressing her breasts, teasing her and making her squirm. He'd promised not to rush her, but at this point she was ready to leap out of her skin.

When he gently pinched one of her nipples, she pulled back with a fractured breath. "You are driving me mad."

"That's the point, sweetheart."

He clamped his hands around her waist, tossing her back onto the fluffy pile of pillows at the head of the bed. This was probably the most important moment of her life, but she wanted to laugh out loud or jump to her feet and spin in silly, happy circles until she grew dizzy with joy.

Her desire to laugh faded when Nicholas unwrapped his

kilt, exposing his formidable and very naked masculinity to her gaze. To say he was imposing was a massive understatement.

With the emphasis on massive.

Slowly, Victoria came up on her elbows to watch him, her heart banging against her ribs. He was huge and hard, an intimidating sight that should trigger a swoon in any innocent, proper young lady. She *was* feeling a little light-headed, but certainly not from fright. And she was obviously neither sufficiently innocent nor proper because a naked, aroused Nicholas was the most exciting thing she'd ever seen in her life.

As he moved to the edge of the bed, Victoria fell back against the pillows, her hair tumbling around her breasts and shoulders. His smile was both arrogant and seductive as he climbed up on the mattress.

Nicholas pushed her legs wide, kneeling between her thighs. When he slipped a hand between her thighs, dragging a finger across the tight bud hidden within her curls, she all but rocketed off the bed. In response, he clamped a hand on her hip, gently but ruthlessly holding her down while he massaged her aching sex. Victoria moaned, trying to arch up into his hand as fire poured through her veins. Tiny spasms began to ripple out from her core, and she closed her eyes, falling into the dark, velvety pleasure.

"Open your eyes, Victoria," he ordered in a husky voice as his hand stilled.

She dragged open her eyelids. "Why did you stop?"

"Because I want you looking at me while I play with you."

The words gave her a delicious jolt. When he slicked a finger over her bud, as if to reward her, she whimpered.

"That's it, my darling," he murmured. "Now, unlace your stays."

With trembling fingers, she complied. It was a task she'd done thousands of times, but she was clumsy now that he was drowning her in pleasure. He spread her wide as he rubbed and played, even pushing his fingers into the slick entrance of her body. But every time her hands slowed on the laces or her eyes started to close, he paused.

"Now you're just being mean," she protested when he brought her right to the edge and then stopped once more.

His only answer was a deep laugh replete with male self-satisfaction.

When she scowled at him, he deftly finished unlacing her, uncovering her completely. She lay before him, restless and wanton. Her breasts were flushed and hard-tipped, aching so much she was tempted to stroke them herself. Firelight burnished her nude body, and the fluffy triangle at the top of her thighs was glistening with her arousal. She could have been a pagan offering laid out for him to devour.

And, at the moment, with his muscled body and his erection long and broad-headed, he looked rather primitive too. Victoria felt weak with longing, trembling for his touch.

"This is how I want you," he said. "With nothing between us."

There were still secrets between them, but right now they didn't matter much at all.

"Please don't stop," she whispered.

He loomed over her, taking her mouth in a kiss full of power and possession. She wound her arms around his neck as she sucked his tongue into her mouth. Wriggling down, she pressed her sex against his hard thigh, gasping as sensation arced through her in a delicious pulse that went straight to her womb.

Nicholas groaned. "God, lass, I need to taste you."

Then he was nibbling and kissing his way down her body. She writhed beneath him as he lingered over her breasts, drawing strongly on her nipples. When she cried out, he moved lower, shifting down to lie between her spread thighs.

When he clamped his hands under her bottom and lifted her to his mouth, Victoria stiffened. Before she could register an objection, he began kissing the most intimate part of her body. Stunned, she went up on her elbows to stare at him.

Nicholas glanced up. His expression was hard but his gaze was diamond-bright. "What?"

She had to clear her throat before she could answer. "You cannot possibly be enjoying that."

When he slowly and deliberately licked his lips, her jaw dropped.

"I beg to differ, my love. You taste delicious." His avaricious expression seemed to indicate he was telling the truth.

"Well, then, carry on," she said inanely.

He laughed before planting a hand on her chest and gently pressing her down to the mattress. Then he returned to his task, lavishing pleasure on her with his mouth and tongue. He held her relentlessly wide as she bucked against the sensations that stormed through her.

When he flicked his tongue over her tight bud then sucked her into his mouth, Victoria cried out. Her back arched off the mattress as she clutched the coverlet in a desperate grip.

After a few moments, she opened her dazed eyes to find Nicholas sitting back on his heels, watching her. His gaze shimmered with unappeased lust.

"Are you ready for me, lass?" he asked in a guttural tone.

All she could do was nod.

He reached down and slipped his hands under her shoulders. Lifting her with easy strength, he positioned her so that she was straddling his thighs.

When he went to guide himself into her, she brushed his hands away. "Let me," she said.

His gaze flared, and he gave her a tight nod.

Cautiously, Victoria wrapped a hand around his erection. She swallowed, both nervous and excited at the prospect of its intrusion into her body. When she clumsily stroked it, Nicholas hissed out a breath.

"Aye, that's it, lass," he growled. He began to massage her bottom. "Now rub yourself against me."

Tentatively, she shifted closer. When she rubbed the broad head of his erection against her sex, she quietly moaned as sensation again sparked to life in her body.

"You feel amazing, Victoria," he said through clenched teeth. "Yes, keep doing that."

She leaned against him, her eyes drifting closed. Nicholas groaned and began kneading her bottom with hard, erotic pressure.

When he suddenly brushed her hands aside and shifted to press into her, Victoria was more than ready. Still, she gasped as the broad head forged past her tight entrance.

"Hold on, love," he gritted out.

When he flexed his hips, she felt a sharp pinch and a brief, lancing pain. Then he was fully inside her, so deep she could barely catch her breath.

Her eyes popped open. "Good heavens."

Nicholas tipped up her chin and pressed a soft kiss to her lips. "Sorry," he said in a rueful tone. "That's the worst of it, I promise."

She nodded, clinging to his arms. He rubbed her back in soothing circles as he gently rocked her against him.

Soon the pain began to fade, replaced by a pleasurable sense of fullness. It seemed almost impossible to fathom that he was actually inside of her.

And it was beginning to feel rather amazing, too.

"All right?" he murmured in her ear.

She kissed his shoulder. "Better than all right."

His lips parted in a seductive smile. "Excellent. Now, how about this?"

When he flexed his hips, she moaned. "That's . . . that's very nice too."

When he did it again, she clung to his shoulders. The angle of his body, his slow, controlled rhythm, rubbed her both inside and out. She pressed close, relishing the feel of his muscled chest against her aroused nipples, as his strong thighs spread her wide.

With soft, erotic words, he tutored her movements, guiding her up and down his thick length. Victoria let her eyes drift shut and her head drop back, her hair falling like a curtain down her back.

But then he increased the pace, and soon they were moving in a sharp, almost frantic rhythm as passion built between them. Nicholas tipped her chin up, pressing a hot, openmouthed kiss to her lips. And when he clamped a possessive hand on her breast, rubbing her sensitized nipple, Victoria felt herself teetering on the verge of climax.

Suddenly, he reached down and stroked a finger over her aroused bud. Victoria wrenched her mouth from his and cried out. Shudders wracked her body as her inner muscles clenched around his length. Luxurious spasms rippled out from her womb as he surged into her, high and hard. He cursed, then ground into her again, holding her hips tight against him.

Nicholas shook with his release, so deeply inside her that she felt like he'd touched her heart.

When he stopped shaking, he curled his big body protectively around hers. Victoria turned her cheek into his neck, squeezing her eyes shut to hold back tears. His pulse beat hard and steady under her ear as his hands stroked in a soothing rhythm along her spine.

Then he carefully lifted her up. She winced a little as he withdrew, muscles both inside and out and smarting from their passionate encounter. With a soothing murmur, he laid her down on the bed and tucked her close, her cheek to his chest, sheltering her within his brawny embrace.

Victoria drowsed for a bit, feeling entirely warm and contented.

"One last question before you fall asleep, lass," he murmured after a few minutes.

Since they were nose to nose and she was so tired, it was a struggle to focus on his face. He looked very serious.

"What is it?" she asked.

"Victoria Knight, will you marry me?"

She managed a sleepy smile. "Yes, my lord. I'll marry you."

Snuggling closer, she let herself drift into a sublime oblivion.

Chapter Twenty-Two

"How lovely to have a quiet family dinner before you return to Kinglas," Edie said, giving Nick a warm smile. "Thank you for inviting us tonight."

Nick lifted his glass to her. "And since we *are* shortly to become family, please call me Nicholas—or Nick."

"Family," Edie said. "That sounds lovely, doesn't it?"

He glanced at Victoria, who was halfway down the table between Kade and Braden. Since she wasn't yet his wife, she had yet to take her proper place opposite him. To his credit, Angus, who sat there now, had tried to persuade her to sit in that place of honor, but she'd blushingly refused.

Soon, though, she'd be mistress of both Kendrick House and Kinglas, and Nick could hardly wait. Underneath that neat, sensible exterior lurked a very sensual woman. Victoria had thrown herself into lovemaking with an enthusiasm that surprised even him.

In fact, she'd all but made the eyeballs roll back in his head. Although inexperienced in bed, she was a mature, intelligent woman. His lass had responded with a passion suggesting she would always be his equal, both inside and outside the bedroom.

She also possessed a quiet beauty that set his heart on fire.

"'Lovely' is the word for it," he said.

Victoria glanced up and met his gaze, then gave a tiny shake of the head as if reprimanding him for staring. But when she turned back to Kade, a happy smile edged the corners of her mouth.

"You're a lucky man," Edie said. "Victoria is a truly wonderful person. Both Alec and I adore her, as you can imagine."

"I am well aware of my good fortune." Since they were eating informally, he reached for the wine bottle to replenish her glass. "I sense a warning in your tone, however."

She laughed. "A wee friendly one. Alec feels very protective of her, as you know. He would protect any person in need, of course, but Victoria is now one of our own."

"I understand. But Victoria is also—or will shortly be— a Kendrick, and one of *our* own. Every one of my brothers would give his life for her."

Including Logan.

He mentally frowned at that jarring thought before turning his attention back to Edie.

"I'm happy to hear it, because if you ever injured Victoria in any way, our family—including me—would tear you limb from limb, Nicholas. Literally," she finished.

He almost laughed at the contrast between her cheery delivery and the bloodthirsty vow. "That would hardly be the action of a loving family member."

"You haven't spent much time with my extended family—although yours is quite lively too. My servants are still repairing the mess your brother made at my Hogmanay party."

Nick winced. Grant had overindulged a wee bit on New Year's Eve, and Edie's morning room had taken the brunt of the damage.

"Sorry about that," he said. "And you can be sure the lad is paying for the damages."

"He's already paid Alec five guineas and promised to perform any errands or tasks my husband thinks appropriate."

Alec, who'd been talking to Royal, switched his attention to their conversation. "Please don't remind me about that blasted party. The memory still gives me nightmares."

"Don't be ridiculous," Edie scoffed. "Nothing gives you nightmares."

"The resulting bills did."

"I understand entirely," Nick said dryly.

Alec laughed. "Actually, old man, it wasn't that bad. And Grant has been a great help to me these last few days. I've been shorthanded at the Glasgow manor house since my old steward retired a few weeks ago. Your brother has been quite helpful in lending a hand with some estate business."

"Er, I'm happy to hear that." Nick glanced at his brother, deep in conversation with Angus. Both twins had seemed more mature of late, perhaps finally growing up.

"Your brothers are all fine men," Edie said. "They simply needed a little guidance."

"Beyond my own," Nick said ruefully.

"Victoria has made tremendous strides with you lot, I must say." Alec forked up a piece of beef and thoughtfully chewed it. "Best make sure you take care of her, Arnprior," he added after he swallowed.

"Not to worry, Gilbride. Your wife has already leveled the appropriate threats."

"That's my girl," Alec said, holding his glass up for a refill.

"You outdid yourself with that ring, Nicholas," Edie said. "I'm pea green with envy."

Alec heaved a sigh. "Sweetheart, if you wanted a pearl ring, all you had to do was ask."

Edie's eyebrows arched up over the gold frames of her spectacles. "The point is to *surprise* me with something that shows how much you adore me, you silly man. Haven't you learned that yet?"

"Better come up with something good, old fellow," Nick said. "Or else."

"Edie won't have long at all to wait before I come *up* with something very good." Alec gave his wife a comic leer.

She tried to look stern. "Good God. Behave yourself, Alasdair Gilbride."

Nick leaned back in his chair, enjoying their banter. Soon, he'd share that same sort of pleasing intimacy with Victoria. He would always feel sadness over Janet's unhappy life and death and would never fully recover from the loss of Cam. But, for the first time in years, he'd regained something he'd thought lost to him forever.

He'd regained a sense of hope.

"So, Arnprior," Alec said. "When do you and Victoria tie the knot?"

"We haven't really had a chance to discuss our plans."

Victoria had been like a whirlwind the last few days. When she hadn't been writing a stream of letters, she'd been getting the family organized for the move back to Kinglas. Nick had barely gotten ten minutes alone with her, and when he had, he hadn't wasted those precious moments on wedding plans.

"I'm sure Victoria would like some of her family to attend," he added. "So it will take a little planning."

"Which family?" Alec jested. "She has several of them."

"That's an excellent, if rather alarming, point. We'll have to—" He broke off when his butler entered the room. Henderson had an excellent game face, but Nick had known the fellow for a long time. Something was wrong.

Henderson bent over his chair. "My lord, you have a visitor."

"At this time of night? Who is it?"

"He didn't wish to give his name, sir, but said it was a matter of urgency."

Nick snorted. "If he won't give his name, I have no intention of abandoning my guests. Tell him to return tomorrow."

A slight spasm crossed his butler's face. "I suggested that, my lord. He said to tell you that if you wouldn't see him tonight, he would return tomorrow with a constable."

"Really," Nick muttered.

"One of your brothers?" Alec asked.

"Probably." Nick threw down his serviette. "Please bring him to my study, Henderson."

The butler bowed and retreated.

"What's up, Nick?" Grant asked.

"I don't know. But if one of you lads got into trouble again, there will be hell—"

Victoria raised her eyebrows.

"There will be consequences," Nick amended. When the twins and Royal exchanged furtive glances, he wanted to curse. He just hoped that whatever transgression it was, it wouldn't poke holes in his purse.

"Do you want me to go with you?" Alec asked.

Nick stood. "Not necessary, but thank you. Stay here and finish your dinner. And try to keep my blasted brothers from sneaking off." He managed a brief smile for Victoria, who wrinkled her nose in sympathy.

Henderson waited outside Nick's study, looking grim. The butler had excellent instincts, so his demeanor didn't bode well.

A tall, slightly stoop-shouldered man waited inside the room, huddled against the fireplace seeking warmth. He looked to be in his late sixties, with a complexion that spoke of the pox or a life spent in harsh climes. Although not in evening kit, his tailoring was excellent and his proud manner suggested a man of consequence. He was certainly not an aggrieved farmer or publican seeking restitution for a foolish lark committed by one of his brothers.

"Are you Lord Arnprior?" the man barked, stepping forward. His flat vowels and the sharp edge to his voice suggested a self-made man.

His attitude radiated hostility.

"I am," Nick replied in a cold tone. "Perhaps you can finally identify yourself and say why you felt the need to interrupt my dinner."

"I am Mr. Richard Fletcher. My daughter is Lady Welgate."

When Nick frowned, the man's tight mouth parted in a smile that looked more like a sneer.

"Since you recognize my daughter's name," he said, "you might now guess why I am here. Whether intentionally or not, my lord, you are sheltering a murderess in your household. And I demand that you immediately turn Miss Knight over to me—and to the proper authorities."

After the whirlwind of the last few days, Victoria should have been exhausted. Instead, she felt like champagne was fizzing through her veins. Every time she snuck a glance at her ring—approximately every minute—she could barely sit still. Her happiness was so effervescent, it seemed almost impossible to contain within her own body.

A body, she might add, that now craved her lover's touch. She'd never imagined that sexual relations could be so stimulating or so intensely emotional. If she'd imagined herself in love with the Laird of Arnprior before, it couldn't compare to what she felt for him now that she'd finally said yes.

He'd taken her with a sensuality she would never forget, and cherished her with a tenderness that lit up her soul.

"Lassie, yer lookin' flushed," Angus said. "Are ye feeling poorly?"

How embarrassing to be caught dreaming of Nicholas while sitting at dinner. "I'm simply a bit concerned about what called his lordship away," she said. "I do hope nothing's wrong."

"Och, dinna fash yourself. I'm sure everything's fine."

Victoria studied the old man's suspiciously angelic expression. That was normally a sign of trouble.

"I hope we get away in good time tomorrow," Kade said. "I miss Kinglas."

"Oh, I'm sure we'll get away *very* early," Graeme said.

When Grant smothered a laugh, Victoria narrowed her gaze on the twins.

"Stow it, Graeme," Royal said with a warning glower.

She mentally sighed. They were definitely hatching some scheme. Maybe that was why Nicholas was called away.

"Ye miss Kinglas, laddie? Well, that's grand to hear," Angus said brightly. "We'll make a Highlander of ye yet."

Kade rolled his eyes. "Grandda, I *am* a Highlander, born and raised."

"Aye, that ye are," Angus said, bobbing his head like a partridge.

"What is going on here?" Victoria asked the old man in a low voice.

Angus widened his eyes in a dreadful imitation of innocence. "Why, nothin', lass. Yer a tad jumpy tonight, I ken."

"I am not—"

She broke off when the butler came into the room. "His lordship wishes to see you in his study, Miss Knight. And Captain Gilbride, as well."

That gave her a slight jolt.

"Did he say why?" Alec asked.

"No, sir. He just asked that you join him in the study without delay."

Victoria's nerves tightened another notch. If this were about the twins or Royal, why would Nicholas wish to see Alec?

She shivered, chilly for the first time all day. The first stirrings of fear attached to her, as if someone had hooked a narrow chain around her ankle.

Kade touched her arm. "Victoria, is something wrong?"

She mustered a smile. "I'm sure it's nothing."

"It doesn't sound like nothing," Royal said.

"Then I suggest we find out what it's all about." Alec stood and gave Victoria a reassuring smile. "Come along, lass."

Feeling the chain tighten, Victoria forced herself to her feet.

"I'm coming as well," Edie said.

Victoria waved her off. "No, please stay here and keep an eye on things. We'll be back soon."

Edie grimaced. "Are you sure?"

"Yes." If Nicholas had wanted anyone else present, he would have specified.

"Any clue what this is about?" Alec murmured as he escorted her downstairs.

"I thought one of the boys, but . . ."

He stopped her at the bottom and braced his hands on her shoulders. "Whatever it is, you're not to worry. I'll protect you, and so will Nick."

"Thank you."

She prayed he was correct. If this was about Fletcher, she had no idea how Nicholas would react. She wanted to kick herself for not telling him everything days ago.

Henderson opened the door to announce them. "Miss Knight and Captain Gilbride, sir."

Victoria preceded Alec across the threshold but almost

immediately stumbled to a halt when she saw who stood by the fireplace. Though Alec bumped into her, she hardly felt it.

Fletcher gazed at her with so much fury and loathing it was a wonder she didn't immolate on the spot. "You thought you could hide from me, Miss Knight. And hide your heinous crimes from the rest of the world."

"Please refrain from such dramatic pronouncements, Mr. Fletcher," Nicholas said in a cold tone. "Come in, Miss Knight."

Shaking away the sensation that a viper's gaze had paralyzed her, she looked at her fiancé, and her heart promptly took a dive. Nicholas looked very much like the remote, unwelcoming man she'd met that first day at Kinglas. Of course, he'd be angry. She'd lied to him, to the man she loved, the man who had shared all his dark secrets with her.

She knew that to him, such a betrayal was the worst of sins.

"Come along, lass," Alec murmured. "Don't be worried. I'm right here."

She cast him a lopsided smile over her shoulder, then headed for the chair in front of Nicholas's desk. She sank down on the cool leather seat and smoothed shaking hands over her skirts.

"What's going on here, Arnprior?" Alec asked, taking up position behind her.

Nick sank heavily into the desk chair, as if a terrible weariness dragged on his bones. "I suspect you already know something of why Mr. Fletcher is here."

"Perhaps, but I'd like to hear it firsthand from your visitor." Alec put up a warning hand as Fletcher opened his mouth to speak. "But let me be clear that Miss Knight is under my protection. Nothing will happen to her that does not meet with my approval."

"She's under *my* protection too, Gilbride. And if you'd

bloody well told me about this, I could have done a better job of managing it." Nicholas threw a disgusted glance at Fletcher. "Instead of having this man issuing threats."

"I'm simply demanding justice for my murdered son," Fletcher said. "You've all done your best to hide the jade away, so no one could find her."

Nicholas leaned forward, his gaze menacing. "I've warned you, Mr. Fletcher. If you continue to address anyone in my household in such terms, I will throw you out to the street."

Fletcher clamped his lips shut and fumed. Obviously, he'd already said a great deal about her character. This was exactly what she'd feared—when she'd finally have the chance to defend herself, it would be too late. In the eyes of the world, only a guilty person didn't stay and fight. Only a guilty person ran away and hid.

"I'm so sorry," she said to the earl. "I wish I'd told you."

"She was under strict instructions from Sir Dominic and her brother to remain silent on the matter until it was completely resolved," said Alec before Nicholas could respond. "I also counseled her to do the same."

Fletcher sneered. "You were all trying to hide her away, but I hired an inquiry agent to track her down. It wasn't all that hard to find her."

"Because we weren't *hiding her away*," Alec growled. "We wanted her out of town to allow the gossip to die down. Such gossip, by the way, would do nothing for your son's reputation or the reputation of your family if the truth got out."

Nick fastened a hard stare on Alec. "It would appear that plan was rather flawed."

Alec shook his head, exasperated. "Obviously, but Dominic had the matter in hand when Victoria left London."

"Even the great Sir Dominic cannot shove a murder under the rug," Fletcher said contemptuously.

"She did *not* murder your son," Alec said. "Your son assaulted her, and she defended herself."

"That's a lie," Fletcher shouted. "She's a whore who tried to seduce my poor boy. When he wouldn't marry her, she murdered him in cold blood. I have the evidence to prove it."

When bile rose in her throat, Victoria pressed a hand to her mouth. Lady Welgate had flung out the same accusations the night her brother died, but she'd put them down to grief and shock, thinking no sane person could believe that was what happened.

It would appear she'd been wrong.

"Fletcher, if you say another word without my permission, you will live to regret it." Nicholas pointed to the settee by the bow window. "Sit down over there and get control over yourself. If you cannot, Captain Gilbride will escort you out to the street."

"I'll happily do it this moment," Alec said.

Fletcher's face mottled with anger, but he gave a stiff nod.

"Thank you." Nicholas transferred his cool regard to Victoria. "I do not wish to unduly distress you, Victoria, but I need you to explain why Mr. Fletcher would make such a serious allegation. He's been exceedingly vague about the circumstances of his son's death."

She swallowed, her throat so dry she could barely speak. "Very well."

"Just tell me the basics of what happened that night," he said.

"First, let me say how sorry I am that you've been troubled by this awful situation," she said. "And, again, how sorry I am that I didn't tell you."

"That decision was not your fault, Victoria," Alec said sharply.

She held Arnprior's gaze. It seemed difficult to believe

this was the same man who'd held her in his arms only a few nights ago, kissing her into ecstasy.

"I should have told him," she said to Alec. "And I regret that secrecy more than I can say."

When Fletcher loudly snorted, Nicholas sent another warning glance his way, then looked back at her. "Thank you. I appreciate that."

His polite reply killed her last bit of hope. Nicholas would never forgive her, nor could he truly protect her, since she would never be his wife. All her hopes now rested with Dominic, Alec, and her brother.

"I told you about some of the problems I experienced in my previous position." She related the details of that dreadful night, trying to distance herself from the memories as much as possible. When she described Thomas Fletcher's attack on her, Nicholas looked stunned. Then his gaze heated with stark fury as it fastened on Mr. Fletcher.

"That's not what happened," the man protested. "She's lying."

"Shut it, man," Alec growled at him, "or I'll shut it for you."

"Victoria, I am exceedingly sorry that you were forced to endure such violence," Nicholas said quietly as he returned his focus to her. "It's appalling."

Her chest was so tight she could barely draw in a breath. "Thank . . . thank you, sir. Shall I continue?"

"If you feel able to."

As sparingly as she could, she explained the horrible aftermath of Fletcher's fall down the stairs. Alec then took up the narrative, describing Dominic's actions and the magistrate's decision not to open an inquiry or press charges.

"He declared the death accidental," Alec said. "To spare both Victoria and the man's family."

"The magistrate no longer believes that," Fletcher said

hotly. "There's a witness willing to testify that Miss Knight was trying to seduce my son with the intention of forcing him into marriage."

Victoria knew it had to be the nursery maid, the one who disliked her from the beginning.

"Bollocks," Alec said.

"I agree," Nicholas said. "Miss Knight's conduct has always been above reproach."

Fletcher sneered. "Forgive me for saying so, but she appears to have duped you. You are betrothed to the woman, are you not?"

Something that flickered in the earl's gaze made Victoria's heart crumble to ash.

"The situation is not at all similar," Nicholas finally said. "In any event, I do not believe that she murdered anyone."

"I doubt the magistrate in London will agree with you," Fletcher said. "I will also add that I have been in touch with the Glasgow Justiciary. It would be best if Miss Knight comes with me now and turns herself over to the authorities."

Victoria had to grab the arms of her chair as the room swam before her eyes.

"Forget it," Alec said. "That will never happen."

"Miss Knight will not be setting foot outside Kendrick House, I assure you," Nicholas said, after glancing at Victoria with concern.

"You're just delaying the inevitable," Fletcher retorted.

"That may be, but while she is under my roof, she is under my protection."

"She's under *my* protection whether she's under your roof or not," Alec said, flinging it at Nicholas like a challenge. Then he glared at Fletcher. "Do you have any idea what you're stirring up, man? Do you have any idea who Victoria Knight actually is?"

Victoria gasped. "Alec, no." That was the last thing she needed—giving ammunition to the enemy.

"He needs to know who he's dealing with," Alec said.

"Gilbride, don't do it," Nicholas said in a warning voice.

"I don't care who she is," Fletcher snapped. "She'll be swinging from the gallows when I'm through with her."

Alec swarmed to his feet and took a menacing stance. Fletcher also stood, looking not the least bit intimidated. Victoria supposed that his rage and his need for vengeance supplied its own kind of courage.

"She's the natural daughter of the bloody Prince Regent, you fool. She will never hang," Alec growled.

"Christ." Nicholas scrubbed a weary hand back through his hair. "That was not a helpful intervention, Alasdair."

"Someone's got to defend the poor girl, since you're doing such a piss-poor job of it," Alec retorted.

Victoria jumped up and grabbed her cousin's arm, shaking it. "Alec, please stop."

"Listen, Victoria—"

"No," she said firmly.

When Alec rolled his eyes and grumbled his reluctant agreement, she turned to Fletcher, whose pale gaze was filled with astonishment and dismay. Not for a moment, however, did she believe the news would knock him off course for long.

"Sir, I am truly sorry for your loss," she said. "More than you can know. But I did not kill . . ."

The man's face turned an alarming shade of red.

"I did not *murder* your son," she corrected. "I defended myself from his assault, and I'm more than ready to testify to that fact when appropriate."

When Fletcher replied, his voice was low and harsh.

"You think to escape me just because you are the by-blow of that wastrel? By the time I'm through, everyone in England and Scotland will know who you are and what you've done. You might escape the noose, but I will destroy your good name and I will *ruin* your life. I will not rest until I do."

"That's enough, Fletcher," Nicholas said, coming around from his desk. "Gilbride, get this idiot out of my house."

"I'll hand him over to your butler, but I'm not leaving you alone with Victoria."

"Oh, for God's sake, Alec," Victoria said. "Be sensible." Nicholas would never hurt her—except perhaps demolish her heart, but he'd already done that.

Alec threw her a skeptical glance.

"Please," she said. "The earl and I need to talk."

"Very well, but, I'll be right outside the door."

"Do I need to throw you out in the bloody street too, Gilbride?" the earl snapped.

"All right, I'm going." Alec stalked over to Fletcher and clapped a hand on his shoulder.

The man shook it off. "I can see my own way out." Then he turned a hate-filled gaze on Victoria. "I will see you again, Miss Knight. Very soon."

"Do not set foot on my property again unless you have a proper warrant and a constable," Nicholas said in an arctic tone. "If you do not, I will have you placed under arrest myself."

Fletcher's laugh was disdainful. "Pretty words, my lord, but we shall see."

He flung open the door and strode out. Alec followed, pausing to give Nicholas a warning stare. "Remember what I said at dinner about hurting Victoria."

The earl's gaze narrowed to icy slits. "Don't threaten me, Gilbride."

"Alec, please just go," Victoria said.

Her cousin gave her an abrupt nod and stalked out, slamming the door behind him.

"Imbecile," Nicholas muttered.

Victoria nervously clasped her hands at her waist. "My lord, I deeply regret—"

"Christ, Victoria," he interrupted. "Why didn't you tell me? Have I not earned your trust a hundred times over?" He stalked back to his desk.

"Of course you have," she said miserably. "I was wrong not to tell you. But I was . . ." The words caught in her throat.

"What?"

"I was afraid you'd make me leave."

He stared at her for a few moments. "So you *were* just hiding out at Kinglas. Was the rest of what Fletcher said true as well? That you were just using me?"

She gaped at him. "No! How can you even think that?"

"Because you killed a man and neglected to tell me?"

Frustration began to push through her guilt. "I wanted to tell you, Nicholas. But Dominic was insistent that I not."

He crossed his arms over his chest. "Ah, yes. Sir Dominic. You can be sure I will be having words with him. He had no business withholding secrets of this magnitude, and asking you to do the same. Do you have any idea how this will affect Kade and the rest of my family?"

Victoria squeezed her eyes shut. Shock at seeing Fletcher had pushed all those considerations aside, but now guilt swamped her. She'd brought scandal and trouble down on the family she'd come to love, a family that had already suffered too much.

"Yes, and I'm sorrier than you can ever know," she said, opening her eyes only to blink back tears.

"Not sorry enough to be honest." He sank into his chair, looked grim. "Victoria, I told you every bloody, shameful thing about myself. I opened my damn soul to you. I asked you to marry me, for God's sake."

"It wasn't my idea to get married," she blurted out, wounded by his devastatingly accurate words. "You practically forced it on me."

He flinched.

Victoria held up her hands. "I'm sorry. I didn't mean that. It's . . . it's just that I tried to tell you it wouldn't work, but you wouldn't listen."

"Because you didn't tell me *why*." He rested his forehead on his palm. "Victoria, I already had one wife who lied to me about everything important. I don't think I can live with that again."

It felt like he'd jabbed a rusty blade into her chest, twisting its jagged edges in her heart. Victoria was nothing like his first wife, but if he couldn't see that . . .

But you did lie to him.

She'd known what her lies would mean to him and yet had still been too afraid to tell him the truth. To trust him. Because of that, he would never be able to trust her.

"No, of course you can't." As she walked to the desk, she struggled to pull the ring from her finger. "Thank you for your incredible kindness, my lord. I will never forget it."

When she placed the ring on his blotter, his head jerked up. His eyes were filled with so many ghosts she couldn't bear to look at him.

Turning quickly, she all but ran for the door. When she glanced over her shoulder, he'd picked up the ring and was frowning at it like he'd never seen it before.

"Good-bye, my lord."

"Victoria, wait—"

She closed the door and leaned against it, trying to hold back sobs. And she did wait, but no footsteps sounded from inside the library.

There's your answer.

He was done with her. His past, the losses he'd suffered and the kind of man that he was—all those things made it impossible for him to forgive her.

But Victoria had to admit that under her grief and fear and guilt, she was angry with him too. Why couldn't he understand?

She heard a quick footstep on the stairs and pushed away from the door, trying to compose herself.

"Dearest, I heard what happened," Edie said as she rushed up to her. "How perfectly awful."

Victoria fell into her friend's hug as she choked out a few strangled sobs. Edie patted her back, making soothing noises. After a minute or so, she pulled away and blotted her wet eyes on the backs of her hands.

"I'd like to kill that man," Edie said, looking fierce enough to do so.

"Which one?" Victoria replied. As jokes went, it was fairly awful.

Edie glanced at the door. "What did Arnprior say to you? Never mind. Alec said he was being difficult. I'll go in and set him straight."

Victoria shot an arm out to stop her. "Please, don't. He's very upset and rightfully so. I . . . I shouldn't have lied to him."

Edie glanced down at Victoria's bare finger. "Please don't tell me that he asked for that gorgeous ring back. I'll have to push him out the window if he did."

"No, it was my decision. He would never go back on his promise, but it couldn't possibly work." His feelings of pain and betrayal would soon turn to bitterness, and perhaps even hate.

Edie grimaced. "No one needs to make any decisions

tonight. Why don't you try to get some sleep? We'll talk it over in the morning."

"I'll be packing in the morning to go back to London." The sooner she got away from Fletcher and back to Dominic and Chloe, the better.

"That's probably not a good idea, pet. Legally, Alec thinks it's safer for you to remain in Scotland."

"Well, I can't stay here."

"Then you stay with us until we sort everything out." Edie smiled. "As you know, we also have a castle, and it's very roomy."

At the mention of castles, Victoria felt her eyes well up again. But she firmly blinked away the tears and forced a smile. "Thank you. That would be wonderful."

"I'm sure it will only be temporary. In a day or two, the earl will come to his senses, and Alec will get everything sorted out with this dreadful Mr. Fletcher. He's going to send an express letter to Dominic tonight, asking for his advice. We'll get our lawyers working on it as well."

"Thank you. I don't know what I would do without you."

Edie gave her another hug. "You're family, silly, and we take care of one another."

Victoria tried not to think of the family she'd just lost. But she had another family—one united both by blood and their odd history, ready to stand by her through the worst. For that, she was profoundly grateful.

"Alec is waiting for me," Edie said. "Try to get some sleep and we'll talk in the morning." She hurried away to the front hall.

Victoria went in the opposite direction, toward the servants' staircase. She couldn't bear the idea of running into any of the Kendricks, not tonight. Tomorrow she would face Kade, at the very least, and make her good-byes.

That thought was enough to incinerate what little heart she had left.

She trudged up the stairs. After locking the door to her bedroom, she sank down on the bed and finally indulged in a thorough cry. But it did nothing to relieve her emotions and only gave her a ripping headache.

After giving her nose a firm blow, she went down on her hands and knees and pulled her traveling bag out from under the bed. Then she began extracting the garments she'd brought with her from England or ones that Edie had given her. Though she was exhausted, sleep would elude her, so she might as well pack and be ready to leave at first light.

After organizing her clothes, she sat down at the writing desk to begin composing a letter to Dominic. Unfortunately, persistent tears obscured her vision. When a soft knock sounded on her door, she breathed a sigh of relief and put down the pen.

"Coming." While she desperately hoped it was Nicholas, she knew he had too much wounded pride to seek her out.

She was surprised to see Angus when she opened the door.

He grimaced. "Aye, ye look blue-deviled, and that's a fact. Ye and Nick had a fight, I ken."

She sighed.

"Over a Sassenach ye killed, I take it."

She narrowed her gaze. "Were you eavesdropping?"

He shrugged. "Couldna hear everything, but enough."

"Then you can understand why his lordship is so upset."

"Och, he may be my laird and my grandson, but he's a daft fool."

She stared at him. "Mr. MacDonald, I killed someone."

"Aye, but just a Sassenach."

"That is *not* a good enough reason to kill someone," she said, exasperated.

When he grinned at her, she couldn't hold back a disbelieving laugh.

His smile faded. "Lass, did he deserve it?"

"Well, I certainly deserved to defend myself."

"And the brute would have hurt ye if ye hadna acted so?"

"Yes, he would have."

"Then ye did the right and just thing," Angus said. "And I'll be settin' the laird straight on that first thing in the mornin'."

She was touched and rather astonished by his support. Then again, killing an Englishman had obviously raised her standing in his eyes.

"Thank you, but that won't be necessary," she said, forcing a smile.

"Yer not leavin' us, lass. The laird needs ye. We all need ye."

She blinked, trying not to cry again.

"Nay, no waterworks," he said. "Now, have a wee sleep and we'll sort it out later. I'd speak to Nick tonight, but I dinna have time right now."

She frowned. "Why not?"

He grinned and tapped the side of his nose. "Things to do, lass. Now get ye some rest."

Her suspicions during dinner reasserted themselves. "What are you up to, Mr. MacDonald?"

"Ta," he said with a wave and a smile. He strode away down the darkened hall, his kilt swirling around his skinny legs. A few seconds later, his rapid footsteps pattered downstairs.

For a moment, she wavered in the doorway, thinking she should follow him or go tell Nicholas about the old man's suspicious behavior. But the thought of seeing the earl again, or trying to deal with another problem, simply overwhelmed her.

Besides, the Kendricks were no longer her business. She had enough problems to worry about—ones that could even find her dangling from the end of a rope.

Chapter Twenty-Three

Victoria opened her bleary eyes. Why was someone knocking on her door in the middle of the night?

She forced herself upright. More like early morning, since the light of dawn was just starting to filter through the shutters.

Another tap on the door. "Victoria, please wake up." That was Braden's voice.

She grabbed her wrapper and fumbled for her slippers. When she opened the door, Braden stood there, dressed in a nightshirt over breeches.

"Nick needs to see you in his study right away," he said.

Her stomach clenched. Had Fletcher already got a warrant for her arrest? "Do you know why?"

He put out a quick, reassuring hand. "It's got nothing to do with what happened between you and Nick last night."

"Angus told you?" she asked, wincing.

"I don't know all the details and I don't need to. But I do know *you*." He smiled. "We all trust and respect you, Victoria. Please never doubt that."

"Thank you, Braden. That means the world to me."

"And Nick will get over it. He's just upset right now."

She sighed. "I can't blame him for that."

"Maybe, but right now he has other problems." He snorted with disgust. "My stupid brothers."

Her conversation with Angus resurfaced. "And their grandfather?"

"Nick will explain." He thrust his candle into her hand, then turned and all but ran for the stairs.

"Don't trip," she called out.

"Hurry up," he called back.

She went into her room and stared at her neatly packed bags. There was clearly another Kendrick Family Crisis to be dealt with and, for a moment, she was tempted to crawl back under the bedcovers and pretend the world didn't exist.

Really, what did she owe Lord Arnprior and his family at this point?

Your help.

They'd all given her a large measure of love and respect, so how could she turn her back on them now? Despite everything, Nicholas obviously still needed her too.

She snuffed the candle and went to her dressing table to find a nightcap, since she had no intention of going downstairs with wild, unbraided hair.

After cramming the tangled mess under her cap, she grabbed a shawl on the way to the door. As she hurried downstairs, she tried to calm her racing heartbeat. The prospect of seeing Nicholas again was decidedly unnerving.

Pausing for breath, she placed her palm flat on the study door and counted to ten before knocking.

"Enter," rumbled the earl's deep voice.

He was behind his desk, frowning at a note in his hand, while Braden stood nearby, nervously chewing a fingernail.

Nicholas gave her a swift glance, tracking over her from head to toe. "Thank you for joining us, Victoria." A faint smile lifted the corners of his mouth. "So quickly."

She must look ridiculous in her rumpled ensemble.

Nicholas was dressed—but for his tailcoat—in last night's evening kit. Apparently, he'd not gone to bed. She cast a furtive glance at the whisky decanter on the edge of his desk, breathing a tiny sigh of relief to see that it was mostly untouched.

"Don't worry, I'm not drunk," he said dryly. "And you could have gotten dressed. The house isn't on fire."

"Braden gave me cause to understand it was an emergency."

The young man grimaced an apology, and continued to chew on his nail. Victoria reached across and gently pulled his hand down. It was startling to see the normally calm and mature Braden so discomposed.

"It is an emergency," Nicholas said.

"How can I help?"

"Please sit and read this," he said, handing her the letter.

She took it from him and sank into the club chair. By the time she'd reached the second paragraph, her brain felt woolly.

"The twins and Royal have eloped," Braden burst out. "With girls."

"Yes, with girls, thank God for small mercies," Nicholas said. "Given all the jokes about Highlanders and sheep."

Victoria should scold him for making such an inappropriate jest, but she was too stunned by what she was reading. In the note, Angus set out his plan to help the brothers abscond with prospective brides. The twins had indeed eloped, with Miss MacBride and Miss Peyton. She was surprised to realize their relationships had grown so serious.

Her brain stumbled over the next paragraph.

"Royal eloped with Lady Ainsley?" she asked. "How is that possible? He doesn't even much like her."

"I will be sure to ask him when I run them all to ground," Nicholas said grimly.

She squinted down at the letter. "I don't understand. Why did they have to elope? This is Scotland. All they had to do was find a vicar."

"Keep reading," Braden said.

After a minute, she gave up trying to decipher the heavily blotted scrawl. "There's something in here about handfasting and then a kirk up in Kinglas, but I can't make out the rest."

"Angus has convinced them to do things the old-fashioned way," Nicholas said. "The Highlander way."

"Which is?"

"You seize the girls you want to marry and carry them off, hopefully to the nearest kirk," Braden said in an unhappy tone.

Victoria almost fell out of her chair. "Are you saying these girls were taken against their will?"

"That's what we need to find out." Nicholas glanced at the clock. "And I've got to get after them as soon as possible. If I take my curricle, I should be able to catch them. With a minimum of six people traveling—"

"Seven, with Angus," Braden added.

"Right, seven people and probably some luggage. I should be able to track them down before long."

"Do you know when they left?" Victoria asked.

"Sometime between one and four o'clock, as far as I can tell," he replied. "If we can get the girls back to Glasgow before tonight, we may just be able to avoid total disaster."

When he pulled his coat from the back of his chair and started to drag it on, Victoria held up a hand to stop him. "Wait. We must think. What will happen if you don't catch up with them?"

"Then I will be facing down two irate fathers—not to mention Alec—who are primed to shoot me and my brothers."

She shook her head. "Perhaps not. Those two girls are

smitten with the twins. In fact, I wouldn't be surprised if they went along willingly."

"But you're not sure."

She waggled a hand. "I'm not, especially in Miss Peyton's case." The girl certainly liked Grant, but she was also shy, and didn't appear the sort to run off in a scandalous fashion.

"We can also be fairly certain Lady Ainsley did *not* go along willingly," Nicholas said. "I cannot believe Royal did something this demented."

"Why would any of them?" Victoria asked.

"Because Nick wants them to get married," piped Kade from the doorway.

Nicholas groaned. "Christ Almighty, please don't tell me you were involved in this."

"Don't bark at him." Victoria stood up and smiled. "Dearest, please come in."

The boy trudged over, casting a guilt-ridden glance at his big brother.

"No one is upset with you," she said, hugging Kade. "Just tell us what you know."

"Well, I didn't know they were going to do *this*," he said. "I thought it was more of a joke than anything else."

"Lad, it would be very helpful if you could tell us everything you do know," Nicholas said.

"Of course. A few days ago, I heard Grandda talking to the twins about how you were right. He said they'd all been causing trouble for too long, and that it was time to settle down and start good Highland families."

"You mean you eavesdropped," Braden said disapprovingly.

Kade shrugged.

"Thank God you did," Nicholas said. "What else?"

"The twins agreed and said they weren't sure if Lainie and Anna would marry them, because they might not want penniless younger brothers. That's when Grandda said they should elope."

"They're not penniless," Nicholas said with an exasperated sigh. "They're just not rich. And Miss MacBride is a vicar's daughter. I don't imagine her father is that plump in the purse."

"No, but her mother's family is," Victoria said. "She's the daughter of a baron. He has a large estate outside of Edinburgh."

"I didn't know that," Nicholas said.

"You did hire me to help them court respectable girls, sir. Part of that means finding out everything I can about suitable prospects, especially if the twins already like them."

"Graeme and Grant are worried the fathers might not approve," Kade said. "But Grandda said that once they were all married, everyone would be happy to be related to the Earl of Arnprior."

"Possibly," Victoria said. "But we don't know if the girls truly wanted to marry your brothers."

Kade winced. "I'm sorry, Nick. I truly thought it was mostly joking about, at least in that respect. And Grandda swore me to silence. He said he didn't want to worry you with stuff and nonsense."

"He talked to you?" Nicholas said in surprise.

"Well . . . he caught me listening."

"Kade, this is very bad," Braden said. "You should have told us."

The boy looked stricken.

"Never mind, lad," Nick said gently. "I understand you wanted to help. Did Grandda say anything about Royal and Lady Ainsley?"

"No. I'm sorry I didn't tell you, Nick, but you already have so much to worry about, what with my illness and Royal's bad leg. And everything else."

The earl sank into his chair, propping his forehead in his palms. "I'm a bloody idiot. What a mess I've made of it all."

"It's not your fault," Braden said. "You're just trying to take care of us."

Kade nodded. "It's Grandda's fault."

"And our brothers," Braden added. "They're idiots."

"Actually, I agree with Lord Arnprior," Victoria said. "This *is* partly his fault for putting so much pressure on himself and for taking responsibility for other people's actions." She thought about their fight last night. "And also for acting like an idiot."

His head came up, eyes narrowing on her. "Are you quite finished insulting me?"

"Are you quite finished feeling sorry for yourself?"

Braden and Kade exchanged wide-eyed looks.

Nicholas let out a reluctant laugh. "I suppose I deserved that."

She shrugged.

He eyed her for a few seconds and then stood. "This is what's going to happen. Victoria, you're going to stay here and fend off the irate fathers. You must try to reassure them that their daughters will be returned before nightfall. Send Alec a note asking him to come here and back you up. With any luck, I'll have my lunatic family back in Glasgow with everyone's reputation intact."

"That is a ridiculous plan," she said. "I'm going with you."

He scowled. "You will do no such thing."

"Yes, I will. Because if anything goes wrong, sir, you're going to need a chaperone for those girls," she said firmly. "And I'm the only one you've got."

* * *

"This is a very bad idea," the earl said as they turned north onto the road for Arrochar. "I have no idea how I allowed you to talk me into this."

"I imagine it was my threat to procure another carriage and follow you," Victoria replied tartly.

They were almost the first words they'd exchanged in the hour since leaving Kendrick House in a fast carriage and accompanied by one groom—after a short but loud argument had awakened the rest of the household.

"For all your pigheaded ways, you are a sensible man," she added. "If we don't catch up to them before nightfall, you will need a respectable older woman on hand."

"You are *not* an older woman."

"Old enough, and I certainly hope I'm respectable." Of course, if Fletcher made good on his threats, her reputation would soon be a smoldering ruin. "I'm a governess, after all. Keeping young ladies out of trouble is generally part of our job description."

He threw her an irritated glance. "You're no longer a governess. You're betrothed to me."

Her heart stuttered, but she managed to keep a straight face. "That certainly wasn't my impression last night."

"*You* tossed the bloody ring at me, remember?"

"I did no such thing. After you made it clear that you couldn't marry another untrustworthy woman, what else was I to do but give it back?"

"I was simply surprised, and with good cause. So you'll have to forgive me if I wasn't entirely myself," he said sarcastically.

"If that was an apology, it was an exceedingly bad one." She was not ready to forgive him. She might never be ready to forgive him.

Then again, he might not even be apologizing.

He let out an exasperated sigh. "Victoria—"

"I don't wish to talk about it." She was holding on by a thread as it was.

"We *need* to talk about it," he said.

"Not today. Today we need to find your stupid brothers and get them back to Glasgow." She glanced over her shoulder. "And I don't wish to discuss this topic in front of your groom."

"Heckie can't hear anything. And even if he could, he knows better than to gossip about the family."

"*Everyone* in your household gossips, which is how we ended up betrothed in the first place."

He muttered something quite shocking under his breath.

For the next several minutes, he kept his attention on the horses before he finally glanced at her. "Are you warm enough?"

"I'm fine."

"Do you want another lap blanket? We can stop so Heckie can fetch the extra from the boot."

"That won't be necessary, sir."

Victoria had dressed as warmly as possible, wearing two sets of woolen stockings, a pair of walking boots, her sturdiest bonnet, and a long woolen muffler that Kade had insisted on wrapping around her shoulders and neck. Nicholas had then swaddled her in a heavy blanket after procuring a hot brick for her feet.

"Actually, I'm roasting," she added. "It's much warmer today, don't you think?"

The last day or so had been so mild it felt like a spring thaw.

"Too warm. It's playing havoc with the roads. I hope it doesn't start to rain or we'll find ourselves ankle-deep in mud."

"At least that would slow the others down. If we had to struggle with mud, so would they."

His only reply was a grunt as he eased their carriage

around a cart stuck off the side of the road. When the poor farmer gave them an imploring look, Victoria elbowed the earl. He scowled but pulled off to the side and handed her the reins.

"Apparently, you expect me to rescue everyone today."

"It's your job as laird, isn't it?" she said in a sugary voice.

He snorted, climbing down after Heckie. While it only took a few minutes to get the cart back on the road, both men ended up splattered with mud to their knees.

They drove off with effusive thanks from the farmer.

"Happy now?" Nicholas asked her.

"Deliriously so."

"I hope we don't encounter any more unfortunate souls, or we'll never catch up with my brothers."

Victoria pretended not to hear.

They made fairly good time after that as they headed north. So, unfortunately, did Royal and the twins, according to information provided by the innkeeper at their first stop. The lads were at least a few hours ahead of them, traveling in two coaches. Despite the size of the party, they'd lingered only long enough to change horses.

"They're better organized than I anticipated," Nicholas said.

"Did the young ladies in the party seem well?" Victoria asked the innkeeper.

Distracted by the bustle in the taproom, the publican barely glanced at her as he gathered up dirty glasses from the bar. "What do ye mean, miss?"

"Well, did any of the young ladies seem upset or annoyed?"

The man paused to scratch his nose. "One of the young ladies seemed fairly fashed. She was like to bite the nose off the young fellow with the limp."

Victoria and the earl exchanged a worried glance.

"Were those two fighting?" she asked.

"Nay. The lady was orderin' everyone aboot. She had them all leapin' to her tune." Then he hurried off to attend to a new set of customers.

"At least it doesn't sound like anyone was being coerced," Victoria said.

"Lady Ainsley would not suffer quietly if she were," Nicholas said as he led her back to the carriage.

"I simply cannot understand it. Why would Ainsley do something like this?"

He climbed in next to her. "She and Royal seem to have reached some kind of rapprochement, as you pointed out a few days ago."

"Yes, but marriage?"

"There's little point in speculating, Victoria."

"You needn't snap my nose off, my lord," she huffed. "None of this is my fault."

His gaze narrowed, but he wisely refrained from answering.

They took refuge in a grim silence and stopped only to change horses and for Victoria to dash to the necessary. The earl practically vibrated with impatience. More than once she even got the distinct impression he wanted to leave her behind. Still, whenever she climbed back into the carriage, she found another heated brick for her feet and Nicholas carefully tucked the lap blanket around her before starting off.

Fortunately, they were finally gaining ground. By the time they left Arrochar and approached Kendrick lands, they were less than an hour behind.

Victoria shivered as they drove out of the slanting afternoon sunlight into the shade of the large elm trees that lined the road. The densely wooded valley was the entrance to Arnprior's domain from the west. Once they cleared the forest, the glen would open up into the fields and tenant farms that surrounded the castle.

Arnprior glanced down at her. "Not much longer now. Once we clear the pass ahead, it's only a half hour to Kinglas."

"Do you think we'll catch them before they reach the castle?"

"Yes, but there's obviously no chance of getting them back to Glasgow today. I only hope Braden and Alec are able to lay down covering fire and keep MacBride and Peyton from coming after us."

"I'm fairly certain Alec will be coming after us," Victoria said. And he'd be breathing fire since she had the distinct impression her cousin had come to the end of his patience with the Kendrick men.

"He bloody well better not. I was very clear in my note that he was to remain in Glasgow and support Braden."

"Edie will help Braden, I'm sure," Victoria said. "But she and Alec are already worried about Ainsley and will wish to know that all is well."

He pondered that for a few moments. "Something is clearly wrong with her ladyship. Haven't a clue what it is, though."

"Royal no doubt does. Maybe this entire escapade has something to do with it."

The horses picked up speed as they hit a better patch of road. It was colder in the woods, and the roadbed less of a swamp.

"What I haven't been able to figure out," she went on, "is what they thought could be gained by this. Angus left us a detailed note, for heaven's sake. Did he not know we would pursue them?"

Nicholas smiled. "Finally thought of that, did you, lass?"

She flashed him an irritated glance. "I had a few other

things on my mind, like a possible murder charge. Perhaps that distracted me."

"Victoria, I don't want you to worry about Fletcher. I won't let him hurt you." He paused for a few seconds. "Regardless of what happens between us."

She tried to ignore the stab of pain at the implications of "regardless." "I appreciate the sentiment, sir, but you cannot guarantee that."

"I can and I do."

Unfortunately, even he didn't have the power to protect her unless they were married, a highly unlikely occurrence at this point.

"We'll have to wait and see what happens," she said.

"Victoria—"

"My lord," she said, determined to change the subject, "how could Angus think he could get away with this? It makes no sense."

He grumbled, but then answered. "The very fact that my brothers eloped with—or kidnapped—these young ladies could be enough to accomplish the deed. Whether they make it to Kinglas or not, the scandal will force our hands unless we return them to Glasgow before nightfall."

"Not if you and I are with them as chaperones at Kinglas. Everyone believes we're betrothed, so that should be enough to do it."

"MacBride and Peyton may not agree with your assessment."

"No, but might we please try to take the optimistic view for once?"

His sardonic laugh told her how ridiculous she sounded, particularly given her own fraught life.

"What I meant—" she started.

"Be quiet," he said.

She bristled. "I beg your pardon?"

He halted the carriage as they cleared the woods. "Victoria, please hush."

Something was clearly wrong.

Nicholas twisted to look at Heckie. "What do you think?"

Victoria wriggled around too. The young groom had risen from his perch at the back of the carriage. His brow was wrinkled as he gazed at the snow-shrouded hills that surrounded the pass through to Kinglas.

"Hard to tell, m'lord," Heckie finally said. He pointed to a high ridgeline that overhung the narrow gap. "That there looks a bit nasty."

Victoria glanced at Nicholas. "What's he talking about?"

"The snowpack on the ridge doesn't look as stable as I'd like," he said.

"You mean it could come down on us?"

"Probably not. The others got through all right, but I thought I just heard it shift."

"You can hear snow shift?"

"Aye, miss," said Heckie. "It cracks or whomps when it's startin' to move."

"It can happen when there's been a lot of snow and then a rise in temperature," Nicholas added.

Just like they'd experienced over the last few days.

Victoria gazed up at the ridge, which now seemed entirely menacing. "But the others did get through."

"Yes, but they probably shouldn't have taken the chance." The earl shook his head in disgust. "Royal knows better. Noise can trigger a slide, especially in a narrow valley where it echoes."

She swallowed, growing more nervous by the second. "Is there another way through?"

"Aye," Heckie said. "There's a good path—"

An unearthly din blared from up ahead, reverberating through the pass. They froze with shock.

It was the sound of bagpipes, magnified a hundredfold by the craggy hillsides framing the tiny glen.

Angus.

"Goddammit to hell," Nicholas growled. "I will kill that old fool."

"Is he doing what I think he's doing?" Victoria gasped.

Her question was answered when a loud *crack* and then a *whomp* thundered through the air.

"Heckie, get to the head," Nicholas snapped as he held fast to the reins. "Victoria, get down."

The groom tumbled off his perch and raced to secure the bridle of the lead animal. By the time Victoria managed to gather her appalled wits, the horses were already shifting uneasily.

"All right, just hold on," the earl said grimly.

She grabbed the side rail and watched the ridgeline in horror as cracks splintered the snowpack. A large slab detached and rumbled down the hillside with a roar, a growing cloud of icy mist and debris rising before it. The horses bridled and bucked, but the strong hands of Nicholas and the groom kept them from bolting.

Victoria could do nothing but pray as tons of snow headed straight for the valley floor.

It seemed like forever, but the entire event transpired in only a few minutes. Snow billowed up in a cloud a couple of hundred feet ahead of them, shrouding the pass in mist. Eventually, it subsided, and a strange quiet settled over the glen, broken only by the stamping of hooves and the jangling of bridles. Even the birds were silent.

Victoria peered ahead. "Is the road entirely blocked?"

Heckie glanced back. "Do ye have 'em, sir?"

"Yes, go," Nicholas barked.

The groom jogged up the road, while she and the earl waited in tense silence.

Soon enough, Heckie trudged back. "It was a small one, but it did the trick. The road's fair blocked, it is."

If that was a small one, Victoria had no desire to ever see a large one.

"Any chance of digging through?" Nicholas asked.

"Aye, if we can get enough men and shovels. But it'll take better part of a day." Heckie glanced up at the sky. "If this thaw holds, it should melt through in three or four days."

"Does this happen often?" Victoria asked.

"Usually once or twice a winter," Nicholas said.

She sighed. "Then it would appear your grandfather really did plan for this. And now no one can get to them in time." If she wasn't so furious, she might even admire the old codger's creative ploy.

Anger poured off Nicholas in waves. "I could throttle him for putting you and Heckie in danger."

"And you," she said. "But I suspect he knew exactly where we were when he set it off."

"She's right, sir," Heckie said. "I saw the old fellow up on the path on the other side of the valley. He kenned we were safe back here."

Suddenly, she wanted to laugh. "You have to give him full marks. It was quite a plan, if entirely mad."

Nicholas reluctantly smiled. "I would have preferred not to be dragged all the way up here only to be stuck at the end of a valley. He should have left us in blissful ignorance."

"I suppose that letter was to give us fair warning before the families of the young ladies descended on us."

"I have no idea what Angus really wants, and at this point I don't care." His brief flash of humor was gone. "Heckie, do you think the path is in decent enough shape to walk in?"

"Aye, m'lord. Might be a bit snowy, but the villagers use

it when they're afeared of the snowpack comin' down. The moonshiners, too."

"Moonshiners are still on my lands?" Nicholas asked in disbelief.

Heckie shuffled his booted feet. "Sorry, m'lord."

"If I find out that my blasted brothers are involved—"

Victoria grabbed his arm. "One problem at a time, sir."

He heaved in a breath. "Sorry. You're right."

He looked so frustrated she wanted to throw her arms around him and kiss away all his troubles. Unfortunately, she was also the source of one of those troubles.

"All right, Heckie. Take Miss Knight back to the inn at Arrochar. You can both return to Glasgow tomorrow."

Victoria wasn't having it. "I'm not returning to Glasgow."

"You cannot walk over the pass," Nicholas said in a tone that suggested she was an idiot.

"I don't see why not. I'm a very good walker, and I'm wearing boots as sturdy as yours."

"You are not used to walking in the Highlands in the winter."

"It's not that cold, and you know it. Heckie, how long will it take?" she asked.

Nicholas glowered. "You are not—"

"How long, Heckie?"

When the groom cast an uncertain look at his employer, she couldn't blame him. Thankfully, Nicholas simply fumed in silence.

"With a little luck, mayhap about forty-five minutes," Heckie finally said. "Most of the track is in full sun, so ice shouldna be a problem."

"Oh, splendid. Just a nice little stroll," the earl said.

She glared at him. "If I do not come with you to Kinglas, then all this has been for naught. You'd better reconcile yourself to the fact that I'm going."

"You are the most stubborn woman I have ever met," he said.

"And you are the most pigheaded man I have ever met. Now, might I suggest we set off? Dusk will come soon enough, and we can't leave these horses standing any longer."

Nicholas yanked his hat off, scrubbed his head, then slapped his hat back on. "Fine. Heckie, wait at the inn in Arrochar. Captain Gilbride and some angry fathers might be showing up there before too long. I will have to depend upon you to apprise them of our situation."

"Aye, sir," the groom said with only a slight wince.

Nicholas helped Victoria descend, then Heckie climbed in and turned the carriage around. The earl struck off across the snowy field toward the west side of the glen, setting a steady pace.

"Keep up, Victoria," he tossed over his shoulder.

She stuck her tongue out at his back but hurried to catch up.

"If you walk in my footsteps, it'll be easier," he said.

"I'm perfectly fine."

He headed for a group of boulders that marked the base of the path. The first part of the climb was an easy switch-back, but then the trail straightened out and began to rise at a fairly steep angle up to the ridgeline. Within a few minutes, Victoria was puffing and scrambling to keep up.

Nicholas, of course, was making it indeed look like a nice little stroll.

Soon, he stopped next to a large rock beside the path. "Take a bit of a rest. We're almost at the top."

"I don't need a rest," she gasped.

He took her by the shoulders and gently guided her down onto the rock. Since it was in full sunlight, it felt surprisingly warm. Not that she needed it, since she was perspiring from the climb and no doubt red-faced. While her feet were cold and one was damp from where snow had overtopped her boot, she could still feel her toes when she wriggled them.

"It's easy to fall on the way down," he said, "especially when you're tired. Just catch your breath for a minute."

"You're not tired at all, are you?" she asked wryly.

He shrugged. "I've been hiking these hills since I was a young boy."

From this higher vantage point, Victoria could see the tops of the mountains that marched away north and east. Craggy gray rock jutted up from glittering layers of ice and snow, presenting an imposing landscape. The slanting rays of the setting sun danced over the highest peaks, making them glow with orange fire. It was wild and fierce and altogether beautiful.

"It's breathtaking," she said softly.

Nicholas pointed at the closest peak. "That's Beinn Narnain. I climbed it with Logan when I was fifteen."

The mountain loomed impossibly large. "That must have been quite an adventure."

"It was grand," he said in a softer tone.

She smiled, imagining him taking on the challenge with boyish determination. "I'd like to hear all about it someday."

He seemed to come back to himself. "There's nothing to tell. We climbed up, and then we climbed down."

Well.

There was no thaw between them, and she'd clearly been a fool for thinking it possible.

"I'm ready," she said, standing up.

"Victoria, I didn't mean—"

She picked up her skirts and hurried past him, ignoring his aggrieved mutter. The sooner they got to Kinglas, the sooner she could stop bashing her heart against the wall he'd erected between them.

The trail was surprisingly dry, probably due to its high, exposed position. But now the wind had picked up, its gusts flapping her skirts about her legs. One blast caught her in the face, blowing dust in her eyes. She stopped, blinking to clear her vision.

"Here, let me go ahead," he said. "It's a bit tricky on the turn down."

Victoria nodded and moved aside. She was growing cold now, despite her exertions. The sun was fast approaching the horizon, and soon even the top of the ridge would be in shadow.

Nicholas glanced back and extended his hand. "It's narrow and icy here. Be careful—"

His eyes widened as his feet started to slip out from under him. He pinwheeled his arms and went down with a crash, his momentum carrying him toward the edge and the valley floor below.

Chapter Twenty-Four

Nick searched for cracks to grip in the brittle rock as his feet scrambled for purchase on the scree. With every scrape of his boots, debris plummeted down the steep slope. He'd fallen because he'd been fretting about Victoria instead of keeping a closer eye on his own damn feet. If he fell to his death off a trail he'd walked countless times, it would be the final irony of his life.

"Nicholas, give me your hand!" Victoria ordered. She knelt precariously above him on the edge of the ridge, panic lurking in her gaze.

"No, and don't come any closer," he gritted out. "It's too dangerous."

"So you informed me before you fell on your confounded arse," she said, reaching for him.

Nick almost laughed. But when he lifted a hand to seek better purchase, the movement dislodged him and he slipped again.

"If you move again I'm going to kill you," she yelped.

"Best not. You'll start to get a reputation."

The entire day was beginning to strike him as perfectly ridiculous. It was like one of those gothic novels Taffy loved to read, but without a ghost or a villain. Of course, he *did* have an old castle, so maybe he was the villain. He'd certainly been acting like one toward poor Victoria.

"Shut up," she said as she edged toward him again.

"It's all right, love. It's going to be fine."

"Not if I don't help you."

When she wriggled down, it set off a small rockfall. A few large pebbles bounced off his head, which no longer had a hat to shield it.

"Ouch," he said.

"I'm sorry. I'm sorry." Her voice quavered. "I don't know what else to do."

"There's something else we could try, but I don't want to put you in danger."

"I don't care, Nicholas. Just tell me what to do."

"All right. Get behind that rock just there and throw me one end of your muffler. If you can brace your feet against the rock and hold on to your end, I can try to pull up and get myself over the edge."

Victoria scrambled up to her knees, unwinding her scarf. As she tossed one end to him, she plunked down behind the boulder.

"All right, love. Just dig in as best you can."

"I'm ready," she said stoutly.

Nick let go of his grip on the slope and started to pull himself up. But almost instantly the fabric shredded where it passed over the boulder. He had no choice but to release it and grab desperately for a small outcropping.

Dammit to hell.

Victoria leaned over the edge again. Her bonnet was askew, and her hair straggled around her flushed cheeks. "Oh, God. I thought I'd lost you."

"I'm still here," he said, trying to reassure her. "Listen, Victoria, the trail isn't nearly as steep on the other side of the ridge. You can make it down on your own, if you're careful."

"What? I'm not leaving you! You can't hold on much longer."

"There's a crofter's hut at the bottom of the hill. Tommy Crookston lives there. He can bring a rope and pull me up."

Nick figured it would take about thirty minutes or so to make it down. With a little luck, he could hang on that long. But if old Tommy wasn't home, he was royally screwed. There was simply no way he could climb up the rockface on his own.

"I don't want to leave you," she said.

Her obvious distress broke his heart, but he couldn't afford to let her give in to it. Her life, as well as his, was at stake.

"Victoria, there's no time for schoolgirl hysterics. Get off your arse and get started down that hill."

She blinked in shock, then she sniffed and wiped her nose on her sleeve—just like a sweet, adorable schoolgirl.

"All right," she said, scrambling up. "But don't you dare fall."

"It's not in my plans, I assure you."

If he lived through this, he would do his bloody best to convince her to forgive him. After that, he would protect her from any man who tried to hurt her again.

She was just turning away when Nick heard a scrabbling noise along the path.

"What the hell is this?" a familiar gruff voice said from above him.

Equal measures of relief and irritation flooded through him. Of course, it *would* be him come to his rescue. Irony abounded.

"Mr. Kendrick," Victoria exclaimed. "Thank God! Nicholas is barely hanging on."

"I'm hanging on just fine," Nick ground out.

"Doesn't look like it to me," Logan said, peering down at him.

"Would you please stow it and just give me your blasted hand."

Victoria jabbed Logan in the bicep. "Hurry! His hands must be all but frozen."

She was right. Nick could barely feel his hands.

"Hang on, old man." Logan went prone at the edge, stretching down a long arm to reach him. He wrapped a massive hand around Nick's wrist.

Knowing his brother held him in a secure grip, Nick let go of the rock and grabbed Logan's wrist in his right hand. He gazed up into blue eyes that were a reflection of his own, fighting off a torrent of conflicting emotions. "Just get on with it."

"Ungrateful bastard," Logan muttered. He glanced over his shoulder. "Miss Knight, as delightful as you feel lying across my arse, it's not necessary. I assure you I won't fall or drop him."

"I am *not* lying across your backside," she said. "I'm simply holding your legs."

"Victoria, please do what he says," Nick snapped. He'd had quite enough of this bloody hillside.

His brother gave a mighty heave, hauling Nick close enough to the edge for him to throw his leg up and over. He let go of Logan's arm and rolled onto the path, panting heavily as he stared up at the dusky sky.

Two faces inserted themselves into his line of vision.

"Are you all right?" Victoria asked breathlessly.

"Never better." Nick sat up and eyed his brother, who'd stepped back and was now regarding him with a wary expression. "Logan, why are you here?"

"I'm staying at the crofter's cottage."

Victoria frowned. "Why aren't you at the inn at Arrochar, or even in Glasgow?"

"Because old Tommy is a friend. And because I have no intention of leaving Kinglas until I get what I came for," Logan said, a touch defiantly. "Anyway, I heard the commotion and came up to have a look. Then I heard you shriek, Miss Knight."

"You saw the avalanche?" she asked.

"We heard the bagpipes," he said dryly. "I knew that meant Angus was up to something."

"You could tell it was him?" Victoria asked while she yanked on Nick's collar.

She was obviously trying to help him stand, but was half strangling him instead. Still, having her fuss over him was a welcome change, even if he'd almost killed himself in the process.

"I would recognize the sound of my grandfather's bagpipes anywhere," Logan said. "There's nothing like it."

"He is rather dreadful, isn't he?"

"Rather." Logan flashed her one of his charming smiles. When Victoria smiled back, Nick felt like planting a facer on his brother's nose.

"What's the old fellow up to, anyway?" he asked.

"It's none of your concern," Nick said. "I told you to leave Arnprior lands weeks ago."

His brother stared at him in disbelief. "And I told you I'm not leaving until I get what I came for."

Nick began whacking grit and ice from his greatcoat. "My forgiveness? Good luck with that."

"Dammit to hell, Nick. I just saved your sodding life."

"I didn't need you to save *my* life. I needed you to save my son's life. Instead, you let him die."

The words surfaced from a grim place where all the ugly, sorrowful events of the past still held sway. For a while, the darkness had retreated under Victoria's shining light. But now that light was probably lost to him.

"You'll never forgive me, will you? No matter what I do." Logan's voice was taut with bitterness.

Nick didn't really want to hate his brother—in fact,

hating Logan was exhausting. But he kept facing that big, black wall, one that always shifted and transformed into Cameron's polished coffin. All his grief and rage condensed into that single, heartbreaking shape.

He looked at Logan and shrugged.

His brother grimaced. "Och, never mind. You never forgive anyone who hurts you, no matter how much he needs it. You couldn't even forgive Janet, your own damn wife. Well, I won't be like her. I won't break myself against your stupid stone heart."

Nick found himself going for Logan, but Victoria threw herself in his way. When she slipped on a patch of ice, he grabbed her and yanked her against his chest.

"Stop this nonsense." She glared up at him. "We're on the edge of a blasted *cliff*."

Logan, who'd pulled back a fist, muttered a disgusted curse and stepped away.

Nick carefully set Victoria back on her feet. "Sorry, but he can never shut his damn mouth."

"Oh, you shut up," his brother growled.

"You *both* shut up," Victoria said, "or I swear I will push you over the edge. I have had more than enough of the Kendrick family to last a lifetime. You are the most insanely stubborn group of men I have ever met. I am heartily sick of the lot of you."

"Tell us how you really feel, Miss Knight," Logan said in a lame attempt at a jest.

"You don't wish to hear it. All I care about at the moment is getting to Kinglas and making sure those poor girls have not been traumatized by your imbecilic brothers."

Logan sighed. "What did the lads do now?"

"Royal and the twins kidnapped three young ladies and took them to Kinglas," she said.

Logan looked at Nick, dumbfounded. "Is that true?"

"We're not sure yet what happened," Nick replied. "But

the sooner you stop pestering us with questions, the sooner we'll find out."

"Don't snap my head off. I didn't kidnap anybody."

"If you two want to kill each other, go right ahead," Victoria said. "Just get out of my way so I can get down this blasted hill."

"Fine," Logan said. "I'll go first. I know the trail better than Nick."

"Of course you do," Nick sarcastically replied.

Victoria shot him a dirty look. He couldn't blame her, since he had to admit that he and Logan were acting like boys in a schoolyard brawl.

Fortunately, the path down was in better shape than he'd anticipated. With Logan's terse but capable guidance, they tromped up to the back of Tommy's cottage a short time later.

While Nick hated to admit it, without Logan's help, he might have died. Worse yet, Victoria might have died.

Old Tommy, a grizzled widower who looked a bit like one of the shaggy Highland cattle he herded, waited for them in the doorway of the cottage.

"I was aboot to come lookin' for ye," he said, waving them in.

The three-room cottage was cozy and dry, with an expertly stacked peat fire sending out waves of blessed warmth. Nick steered Victoria across the stone floor and plunked her down into an old wooden armchair. He propped her feet up on the firedogs, then folded back her damp skirts to expose her legs to the heat.

She swatted at his hands. "Stop fussing."

"You're shivering," he said.

"I am not," she said through her chattering teeth. Her worried gaze tracked over him. "You're in terrible shape, sir. You look dreadful."

Her grumpy concern warmed him more than any fire

could. "I'm fine. Tommy, could you get Miss Knight a—thank you." He took the cup of whisky the old man was already shoving in his hand.

"Drink it," Nick ordered, handing it to her.

"We don't have time to waste on this." Still, she took a gulp and then coughed, her eyes watering.

Nick suspected the old fellow had given her moonshine, likely home-brewed. "Tommy, I must borrow your cart and horse."

"Whatever ye need, Laird. I'll go hitch up the wee beastie."

"No, I'll do it," Logan said. He slammed the door behind him.

Tommy looked at Nick. "Still at each other's throats, I ken."

"Sadly true," Victoria said.

"Ye need to get over that, laddie. It's past time."

Nick gave Tommy his best chief-of-the-clan stare. "Why are you sheltering my damn brother in the first place? I ordered him off my lands weeks ago."

The old fellow snorted. "Yer my laird, and ye ken I'd lay down my life for ye and all the Kendricks. But dinna forget I paddled yer wee bum when ye was a lad. And Mr. Logan's, too."

Victoria perked up. "You did?"

"Aye, hellions, they were. They let my cattle out into the kitchen garden. They earned that paddlin', I tell ye."

Nick winced. He'd forgotten that embarrassing escapade.

Tommy's grizzled visage softened as he studied him. "But ye were good lads, ye and Logan both. Strong, true hearts. Ye need to remember that, Laird."

Thankfully, he was spared a reply when Logan stomped back in. "The cart's ready."

Victoria rose and handed the cup to Tommy. "Thank you for your hospitality, sir. And for your words of wisdom."

The old man gave her a courtly bow. "Thank ye, mistress. I hope to see ye again. Ye seem to be a grand lass."

When she leaned over and gave him a kiss on the cheek, Tommy blushed and looked rather dazzled. Clearly, she'd won another admirer. They were all but piled around her feet.

Nick led her out to the farmer's cart. The sturdy draft horse would be slow but would do the job.

After he climbed in, Logan helped Victoria into the cart, covering her with a thick tartan blanket Tommy handed him.

"Will I see you again, Mr. Kendrick?" she asked.

When Logan shot him a quick glance, Nick kept his mouth firmly shut.

"Probably not," Logan said.

Victoria gave him her hand. "Then I thank you for your help, and I wish you most well."

Logan bowed over it. "You're too good for my pigheaded brother, ma'am."

"I'm too good for any of you," she said wryly.

Nick couldn't resist giving his brother a smirk. Then he set the carriage moving.

Logan stepped back and lifted a hand in farewell. "Good-bye, Nick. Take care of yourself."

Nick switched the reins to one hand and waved back, then stopped himself and gave a brusque nod instead. When Logan's mouth dropped open in surprise, Nick scowled and snapped his gaze forward. He sure as hell hadn't meant to wave.

"Are you cold?" he asked Victoria after several minutes of tense silence.

"No."

"Sweetheart—"

Her hand shot up between them. "I don't want to talk about it."

"You don't even know what I'm going to say."

"Whatever it is, I don't want to talk about it."

He sighed. They were tired, cold, and both on the verge of losing their tempers. Any discussion about the future was probably best left to a time when they could discuss it without yelling at each other like fishwives. They should be able to sort it all out, as long as he didn't get shot by irate fathers and she didn't get hauled off to prison.

"Thank God," she said as they drove through the arch and into Kinglas's courtyard sometime later. "I don't know when I've ever been happier to reach a place."

Nick stopped the cart in front of the tower house. "Who knows what's waiting for us, though," he said, helping her down.

"At least we'll be warm and you won't be falling off a cliff."

"Thanks to you," he said, touching her cheek.

Her gaze softened, and she started to reply when the tower house door opened. Taffy rushed out with Andrew and two of the dogs in her wake.

"Thank the heavens," she exclaimed. "When we heard about the avalanche . . ."

"We're fine," Nick said at they went into the entrance hall.

After giving the dogs a quick pat, Victoria pulled off her bonnet and gloves and handed them to Andrew. "Please tell me the young ladies are uninjured."

"The lassies are all just fine," Taffy said. "Miss MacBride and Miss Peyton are resting in one of the guest rooms."

"What about Lady Ainsley?"

"She's in Mr. Graeme's bedroom, with the others."

"Why? What's going on?" Nick asked.

Taffy grimaced. "Mr. Graeme had a fall and broke his leg."

"How the hell did that happen?"

"He was standing on the step of the carriage when that old fool—" Taffy grimaced and corrected herself. "When

Mr. MacDonald set off the slide with his pipes. The horses bolted and the lad fell to the ground."

Victoria lifted a hand to her mouth.

"Please tell me he didn't get run over by a wheel," Nick said, his gut clenching.

"No, thank the good Lord. The surgeon arrived a few minutes ago and is with Mr. Graeme now. Brody is there too."

"Your head groom?" Victoria asked.

"He's a dab hand at bone-setting, is our Brody," said Taffy. "He can help the surgeon."

Nick cocked an eyebrow at Victoria. "Can you check on the young ladies and get the lay of the land while I see to Graeme?"

"Of course. I'll take care of it."

"What would I do without you, lass? Thank you."

When Victoria gave him a troubled glance, his heart sank. Clearly, he still had much ground to make up for, but he couldn't worry about that now. He turned and headed for the staircase, impatience and anxiety driving him to see his brother.

"Your coat, sir," Taffy called.

Nick wrestled out of his greatcoat as he took the stairs, dropping it over the bannister. It had some rips in it anyway after this afternoon's adventures.

When he opened the door to Graeme's room, he pulled up short. A small mob had crowded around the poster bed, including the surgeon, Brody, a maid holding a pile of towels, Ainsley, and his brothers. With the exception of the surgeon and Ainsley, everyone stared at Nick with varying degrees of dismay.

Graeme was as pale as milk but trying to look stoic, even though he was obviously scared and in pain. He was propped up on pillows while the surgeon took his pulse.

"How is he, Mr. Dillon?" Nick gruffly asked.

"A clean break as far as I can tell, my lord," the surgeon replied, "but I'll need to set his leg without further delay."

He picked up his bag and began laying out implements on the bedcovers. Brody carefully folded back the tented bedclothes to expose Graeme's leg. The lad's boot and breeches had been cut away, exposing the ugly bruising and swelling over his calf. At least skin and muscle were intact, though, so Nick allowed himself a relieved sigh.

Now that his immediate fears were addressed, he glanced around the room. Grant ducked his head and Royal's gaze slid away.

Predictably, Ainsley glared at him before marching over to take a seat by the hearth. "It's about time you showed up. Your family is completely insane."

From the opposite side of the room, Royal scowled at her. "Yes, the sooner my brother can get you back to Glasgow, the better. Then we won't have to listen to your constant carping."

"Can his lordship wave a magic wand and clear away the avalanche that your idiot grandfather triggered?" she said tartly.

"For God's sake, you two," said Nick. "Where is Angus, anyway?"

Royal affected a casual shrug, even though Nick could read the tension in his hiked shoulders. "Hiding from you?"

"If so, for once he's acting wisely. What the hell were you lot thinking, anyway?"

Ainsley jumped up. "Please don't shout. I've had quite enough of that for one day."

"I wasn't shouting." Nick frowned, finally registering what she was wearing. "Is that—?"

"One of the maid's gowns?" she said. "Yes, your brother's chivalry did not extend to allowing me to bring additional garments on my abduction. He snatched me when I was returning home from a ball. My gown was quite ruined by the time we arrived here."

"You are a complete arse," Nick said to Royal. "I can understand the twins, but why you?"

His brother pointed at the irate girl. "She wanted me to do it."

"What rot," Ainsley said.

"Pardon, my lord," interrupted Mr. Dillon. "We'd best get started on this before the lad's muscles tighten up any further."

"Of course," Nick said.

He laid a hand on Graeme's forehead. His brother's face gleamed with perspiration, and he felt too warm.

"You foolish boy," he said softly.

Graeme gazed up at him, miserable. "I'm sorry, Nick. Truly I am. I . . . I've made a mess of everything. I always make a mess of everything."

Grant, on the other side of the bed, pressed his twin's shoulder. "It's my fault too. I'm just as responsible."

"No, you're not," Graeme said. "I'm always dragging you into horrible trouble. I'm so stupid."

Nick sighed as he studied their unhappy faces. Despite their strapping builds and brash ways, they were still so young. What the hell was he going to do with them?

He stroked Graeme's mussed hair. "Don't worry about it now, lad. We'll figure it out later."

The door opened and Victoria walked in. She blinked at the crowded room and then came to the bed.

"How are you, you silly boy?" she asked softly, taking Graeme's hand.

He clutched her fingers like a scared child. "I'm all right. I'm sorry we caused so much trouble. It seemed a splendid idea at the time."

"I'm sure that's what Angus thought too," she said dryly.

"He only wanted us to find good wives. Just like you, Nick," Grant said.

Victoria winced.

"We'll talk about all that later," said Nick. "And how are the young ladies, if I may ask?"

"Ah, they've decided they'd rather die a hideous death than marry your brothers," Victoria said.

"Really?" That was almost too much to hope for.

She gave him a slight smile. "It seemed they were initially in favor of the elopement but changed their minds over the course of the journey."

"That must have been some carriage ride," Nick said.

Grant shrugged. "It's just that they didn't get along with Grandda."

"That's because he's so horrible," Ainsley piped up.

"Not as horrible as you are," Royal said.

The surgeon made an exasperated noise. "I'm ready, my lord."

"Everyone out," Victoria ordered.

"I'm staying," said Grant in a tight voice.

"Fine, but keep out of the way." She took the towels from the maid and shooed her out, along with Royal and Ainsley.

"I don't think we have to worry about a marriage between those two," Victoria said when she returned to the bedside.

"Ready, Mr. Graeme?" the surgeon asked. "It'll hurt like the devil, but it won't take long if you stay still."

Victoria rolled a small cloth into a tube and handed it to Graeme. "Bite on this. It'll help."

Nick clasped one of his brother's hands while Grant took the other. The next few minutes made him sweat almost as much as his poor brother. When the surgeon and Brody manipulated Graeme's leg, the lad let out a groan, then clamped down hard on the cloth and held Nick's hand in a punishing grip. Through the entire gruesome process, Victoria stroked Graeme's hair, murmuring quiet encouragement. He kept his gaze fastened on her face, as if her calm reassurance was the only thing that kept him from breaking down.

Nick had never been more grateful for her presence or more convinced that he'd be the luckiest bastard in England if she could bring herself to forgive him.

"Almost there," the surgeon muttered.

He gave one more tug on Graeme's leg. The lad went limp, but his eyelids fluttered up a few moments later, and he stared blearily up at Nick.

"Well done, Mr. Graeme," Dillon said. "I'll just strap your leg, and you'll be mending in no time."

"Mr. Dillon, please give me the instructions for his care," Victoria said. "Mrs. Taffy and I will be nursing him."

"Thank you, love," Nick said, giving her a grateful smile from across the bed.

Her reply was a brisk nod.

"Brody can make some helpful poultices," Dillon said, "and I will write up my instructions."

Victoria felt Graeme's forehead. "He seems a mite feverish to me."

"Aye," Dillon said. "That concerns me a wee bit."

She and Nick exchanged a worried glance.

"How are you feeling, lad?" Nick asked.

Graeme let go of Nick's hand and covered his mouth. A moment later, he sneezed. "Actually, I think I've caught a cold."

Victoria sighed. "Of course you have."

Chapter Twenty-Five

Victoria quietly closed the door to Graeme's bedroom. Her head ached from stress and lack of sleep, but at least one of their worries was resolved.

"How is he?"

She turned to see Ainsley standing a few feet away. "Excuse me, my lady. I didn't hear you."

The girl's full mouth quirked in a wry smile. "Please call me Ainsley. After all, we've been changing sheets and mopping damp brows together for the last three days."

Victoria returned her smile. "I don't know what I would have done without your help."

Mrs. Taffy and Victoria had handled most of the nursing duties the first night, but then Grant had also come down with a heavy cold, as had four of the castle's servants. Ainsley had surprised them all by pitching in, belying her image of a spoiled society miss.

Not that she'd been the cheeriest of nurses or particularly gentle. In fact, she'd snapped at poor Graeme when he was particularly difficult or refused to take his medicine. Luckily, her stern demeanor sometimes proved more effective than Victoria's more gentle approach.

"I was happy to help," Ainsley said. "Well, not happy,

but it was better than sitting around bored in the middle of nowhere. Marginally better, anyway."

The answer was pure Ainsley. "Then you'll be happy to hear that the pass is finally clear of snow. I suspect Alec will appear sometime today. He'll escort you back to Glasgow so you can pack for your visit with your relatives up north."

"Oh, joy," Ainsley said dryly. "So, I take it that Graeme continues to improve?"

"Yes. He's still as weak as a half-drowned cat, but his fever is gone and he seems to be getting his appetite back."

"That's a relief. Things were quite tricky for a few days, weren't they?"

"They certainly were." Graeme's cold had developed into a high fever. Combined with the broken leg, he'd been sick enough for Victoria to become truly alarmed. For three days and nights, she, Ainsley, and Nicholas had nursed him in shifts, while Royal and Taffy looked after the rest of the household.

"Did you tell Arnprior the good news?" Ainsley asked.

"He was there last night when Graeme's fever broke and stayed with him until early this morning."

Victoria had been almost as worried for Nicholas, who'd been terrified that his brother might die. There were few words of comfort she could offer to a man who already knew how random and cruel life could be. But when it was clear that Graeme was finally out of danger, Nicholas had pulled her into his arms, holding on to her as if he'd never let go. They'd clung to each other for a few minutes, letting their bodies speak to their emotions, before he'd briskly ordered her to get some rest. She'd been so tired, she hadn't argued.

She and Nick had hardly spoken since they got back to Kinglas, and certainly not about their personal troubles. Their focus had been on taking care of Graeme and keeping the household from falling apart. Now everything rose before them again, unresolved.

"Do you want me to sit with Graeme?" Ainsley asked.

"Taffy just brought him some tea and toast, and one of the footmen is sitting with him for now."

Ainsley linked her arm with Victoria's. "Then let's get you some breakfast. I'm afraid you also look like a half-drowned cat."

Victoria smiled. "That bad?"

"Worse, not that Arnprior will mind. You could show up in a grain sack, and he'd still make sheep's eyes at you."

When Victoria threw her a speaking glance, Ainsley laughed. "So what are you going to do about his lordship? He's clearly mad about you, even with your checkered past."

"I truly don't know. There are so many unresolved issues, and we haven't had a chance to really talk."

"You have the chance now. And I suggest you get on it, before . . ."

"Before someone shows up to arrest me?" Victoria finished wryly.

"That wouldn't stop Arnprior. But you do need to get on it before events overtake you." She paused outside the door to the breakfast room, looking serious. "Sometimes you think you have all the control in the world, and then something happens and . . . you realize you don't."

Victoria had learned that lesson. It sounded like Ainsley had too.

The breakfast room was a cozy retreat that overlooked the loch. Decorated in cheery shades of yellow and pale green, its furnishings were comfortable rather than formal. The family generally started the day together with a hearty breakfast there, but this morning the only person present was a footman.

"Good morning, Andrew," Victoria said. "I'm happy to see you did not fall sick with that awful cold."

"Och, I'm as strong as an ox, miss. Besides, Mrs. Taffy would like to kill me if I fell ill, what with half the household down."

Then he gazed at Ainsley with an expression that could only be described as smitten. Most of the men in the household reacted the same way to her—except for Royal, who'd clearly left smitten somewhere on the road from Glasgow.

"Would ye like some fresh coffee, my lady?" Andrew asked.

"Please." Ainsley went to the sideboard and piled toast, fruit, eggs, and ham onto her plate.

It wasn't considered ladylike to display a robust appetite, but Ainsley clearly didn't care. Victoria considered it an endearing trait.

"Speaking of men and what to do with them," Victoria said after the footman departed, "have you and Royal talked at all?"

Ainsley scowled. "Why would I discuss anything with that idiot?"

"Because he kidnapped you, and you were alone with him in a carriage for hours? Unlike Miss Peyton and Miss MacBride, you were not chaperoned by Angus."

Ainsley crunched into her toast, taking her time to chew before she finally answered. "I don't care if my reputation is ruined. I'm not marrying Royal Kendrick."

"Dearest, I don't mean to pry—"

"Then please don't."

"But I'm going to," Victoria said firmly. "Why are you so unconcerned about your reputation? The damage could be severe."

Ainsley patted her mouth with a serviette before meeting Victoria's gaze. Her expression was surprisingly bleak.

"Because it's preferable to the alternative, which is having to marry the Marquess of Cringlewood."

"All right," Victoria replied. "But ruining your reputation seems rather drastic. After all, you might wish to marry someone else one day."

"Trust me, I won't." Ainsley's grim determination brooked no argument.

Victoria put down her teacup. "I'm not familiar with Lord Cringlewood. Clearly he is not very nice."

"Nice? The man's an utter pig," she said darkly. "Actually, I think I'd rather marry a pig than him."

"Why don't you simply refuse him, then?"

"Because of my blasted parents. Papa was thick as thieves with Cringlewood's father, and they arranged this long ago. Cringlewood wants to get his hands on my money—and on me." Her quiet voice sent chills down Victoria's spine.

"Is that why you're in Scotland, to get away from the marquess?"

"That's just a side benefit. My father sent me up here for punishment, thinking a winter in the Highlands will be enough to bring me to my senses." She snorted. "How little he knows me. Even if I froze to death it would be preferable."

"I'm so sorry, Ainsley. I truly wish there was something I could do." Victoria sighed. "Of course, I'm not in a position to help anyone at the moment."

Ainsley waved a hand. "I'll be fine. And I'm sure Arnprior will protect you. That man never takes no for an answer when it comes to safeguarding his family."

"Are you talking about me?" Nicholas asked as he strode into the room.

"You have no idea," said Ainsley with a wry smile.

"Yes, we were talking about how stubborn you are," Victoria said.

"I suppose I am—when I want something." He paused to drop a kiss on her head before going to the sideboard to get some breakfast.

The kiss sent a flush of heat up Victoria's neck to her face.

"I do believe I've had more than enough to eat," Ainsley said. "Please tell Andrew to bring coffee up to my room."

"You don't have to run off," Victoria said.

"Actually, I think I do." Ainsley pushed back her chair and hurried from the room, dodging Andrew, who was coming in with the coffeepot.

"That was odd," Nicholas said.

"I'd better go check on her."

He pressed a gentle hand to her shoulder. "Stay right there. Andrew, please ask Mrs. Taffy to check on Lady Ainsley. She can also bring up her coffee."

"Right away, m'lord."

Victoria sighed. "I do think I should go see her." Ainsley rarely showed emotion, but the discussion about Cringlewood had clearly upset her.

"In a bit," Nicholas said, taking his seat at the head of the table. "First, we're going to have a talk."

"Are we?"

He gave her an exasperated look. "You cannot avoid me forever, Victoria."

"We've all been busy, in case you failed to notice. By the way, how is Grant this morning? He must be relieved about Graeme."

"He's fine. Everyone is fine, so please stop fretting about them and try worrying about me for once."

"I always worry about you," she said before she could stop herself.

Nicholas gave her a slight smile over his cup. "I'm very glad to hear that."

He'd managed to shave this morning and was impeccably garbed in breeches, boots, and a dark blue tailcoat. Still, he looked a bit haggard and slightly grim.

"You're worn down," she said. "Which is why we shouldn't be discussing complicated issues right now."

"I hardly see how we can avoid them, when several of those issues will likely show up on our doorstep sooner rather than later."

"Such as a constable with a warrant for my arrest?" Just thinking about that possibility made her stomach lurch.

"I think it likely, so we should get married as soon as possible. Today, in fact. I can send a note to the vicar right after breakfast."

Her teacup clattered back into its saucer. "Um, what?"

"If you're the Countess of Arnprior, you cannot be hauled off willy-nilly before the courts. I'll be better able to protect you."

She gaped at him as he forked up a bite of ham, looking as calm as if they were discussing the weather. "That's rather a dramatic solution, don't you think?"

He swallowed before replying. "It's a bit of a rush, I admit. But it's not like I didn't intend to marry you anyway, sweetheart."

His casual attitude began to annoy her. "My lord, as I pointed out on our journey here, that was not my impression after your meeting with Mr. Fletcher."

"And as I pointed out to you that same day, I wasn't thinking clearly at the time. I was startled."

He'd been more than startled, but she had no desire to rehash that unpleasant scene. "Well, it's not a good enough reason to get married."

His eyebrows shot up. "Keeping you out of prison is

not a good enough reason? It seems like a damn good one to me."

"I do not agree."

"Oh, really?"

Actually, it was a good reason. Just not good enough, given all the other obstacles standing between them. "Yes, really."

"Do you need more? Fine. We need you. *I* need you. The Kendricks are bloody lost without you. After the last few days, I would think that's more than evident."

It was not exactly the romantic declaration of love she foolishly longed to hear. "What you needed was nursing and housekeeping help."

He blew out an exasperated sigh. "All right, Victoria. Then why don't you tell me exactly what it is you want from me?"

Might was well let it rip, old girl.

After all, what did she have to lose? "I want you to love me."

His face went absolutely blank, as if her words had knocked his wits right out of his skull. She swallowed, already feeling like a fool.

But then he gave her a rueful smile. "Of course I love you, my sweet lass. Please forgive me if I failed to make that clear. You know I'm rather thickheaded when it comes to this sort of thing."

Though not a Shakespearean declaration by any means, it considerably eased her anxiety. "I'm not a mind reader. You could have told me," she said a bit grumpily.

"I know. And I've been a brute, but I promise to be on my best behavior from now on." When he made a cross over his heart, she couldn't help but laugh. Reluctantly, of course.

"That's very kind of you, sir, but . . ."

"Another but?"

"You said some things the other night in Glasgow. About being able to trust each other."

"Are you asking me if I trust you?"

"You said you'd already had one untrustworthy wife and didn't want another." Victoria didn't think she'd ever forget how horrible those words had made her feel.

He frowned. "I don't recall comparing you to my first wife."

"You strongly implied it."

He tapped his fingertips on the table for a few seconds. "I didn't mean to. And as long as you don't lie to me ever again, it won't be a problem." He flashed her an encouraging smile, as if it were the most reasonable thing in the world to say.

Victoria was tempted to throw her scone at his head. How could he truly love her and yet say something so stupid? "So this was all *my* fault?"

"I didn't say that. You're simply misunderstanding me. Or," he hastily amended, after catching the look on her face, "*we're* misunderstanding each other."

"That, sir, is an understatement." She shoved her chair back. "And let me just say that your declaration of love was exceedingly unimaginative and lacking in . . . in everything."

"What in blazes does that mean?"

To tell the truth, Victoria wasn't sure what it meant. But her instincts had been absolutely right. They were both too tired to have a coherent discussion about their future.

"You know exactly what it means," she said.

Nicholas all but leapt to his feet. "Victoria, I forbid you to flounce out of the room. We are going to stay and finish this discussion."

"I never flounce." Of course, though, she proceeded to do just that.

However, her dramatic exit was ruined when the door opened and Alec barreled in, nearly running her over.

"Hold on," he said, grabbing her shoulders. "What's the rush?" He narrowed his gaze on Nicholas. "What's going on here?"

"Nothing," she said quickly.

"Nothing?" Nicholas echoed.

"Well, Lord Arnprior was just proposing to me," she said.

Alec's gaze shifted between them. "It obviously went as well as all the other proposals."

"Gilbride, talk some sense into your cousin," Nicholas said. "If she marries me, I can protect her."

She glared at him. "As I told you, that's not a good enough reason."

"Sounds like a good one to me," Alec said.

Victoria bristled.

"All right, don't bite my head off," Alec added, forestalling her snippy response. "At least not until I have some coffee. I was up before dawn."

Her cousin took her arm and steered her back to the table.

Victoria sank into her chair with a weary sigh. She was so tired of fighting—fighting with Angus, fighting to stay out of prison—even fighting the man she loved. She felt like she'd spent the last few months of her life in battle.

"Things have been a bit tricky around here the last few days, I gather," Alec said, fetching a cup from the sideboard.

"Yes, but we're out of the woods now, I think," Nicholas said.

"Except when it comes to Fletcher," Alec said.

Victoria sat up straight. "Have you heard something?"

"I'll get to that in a moment. First, tell me how Ainsley is."

"She's fine." Victoria gave him a brief version of events without mentioning Lord Cringlewood. "She has no wish to marry Royal and is quite unconcerned about any damage to her reputation. Ainsley doesn't care if anyone gossips about her."

Alec shook his head. "The girl is a complete mystery to me. In any event, I think we're going to be fine, since you and Arnprior managed to make it up here." He looked at Nicholas. "And you owe me a considerable debt, old son. Dealing with a pair of *extremely* irate fathers is not my idea of a jolly good time. Braden had the excellent sense to make himself scarce when they showed up, leaving me to face the heavy artillery alone."

"Oh, dear," Victoria said. "What did you say to them?"

"Not much, since they were yelling at me. Fortunately, my splendid wife showed up in the nick, and Edie yelled back just as loudly. She assured Mr. Peyton and Mr. MacBride that there was no cause for alarm, and that their precious daughters were properly chaperoned at all times."

"That's true," Victoria said. "Angus traveled in the carriage with them."

"That must have been fun," Alec said wryly.

"They all ended up hating one another by the time they arrived."

Her cousin snorted.

"And the girls' families are truly not pressing for marriage?" Nicholas asked.

"Mr. MacBride was horrified at the idea of his daughter marrying a hellion like Graeme," Alec said.

"He's a vicar. It's understandable."

"And Mr. Peyton was equally horrified at the notion of his daughter marrying a penniless younger son."

"Grant's not penniless—but never mind."

Victoria breathed a relieved sigh. "Since the girls no longer wish to marry the twins—and vice versa, I might add—I'd say we did it. Huzzah."

"Yes, we appear to have weathered the storm, thanks

mostly to you," Nicholas said, smiling at Victoria as he lifted his cup in salute.

Alec grimaced. "There's still the little matter of Mr. Fletcher."

"We'll deal with that when we return the ladies to Glasgow," the earl said.

"I'm afraid not. Fletcher arrived in Arrochar yesterday, and I suspect he'll be popping up on your doorstep any minute."

Victoria felt as if someone had just punched her in the stomach. "Are you sure?"

Alec nodded. "I'd been camped out at the inn the last few days waiting for the pass to clear. Fletcher came waltzing in last night. We exchanged a few choice words, but he remains undeterred. I managed to get a march on him this morning, so I could get here first to warn you."

"How the hell did the bastard know where we'd gone?" Nicholas snapped.

"He showed up at Kendrick House shortly after you and Victoria left. Braden tried to deal with him, but the man was quite demented in his rage." He grimaced. "He wasn't exactly sane with me last night, either."

"Is Braden all right?" Victoria asked.

"He's fine, but he inadvertently revealed where you'd gone. Fletcher made some nasty threats and then stomped off. You also need to know that he has Glasgow constables with him, and some sort of legal documentation."

Victoria pressed her palms flat on the table, quelling the urge to be sick. "Did you actually see the papers?"

"No. The idiot wouldn't show it to me, which means it's very likely not an arrest warrant." He gave Victoria an encouraging smile. "That's a good thing, pet."

She tried to smile back but couldn't manage it.

Nick shoved his chair back and stood. "All right, I've had enough of this damn nonsense. I don't care if that bastard's got a bloody regiment of Hussars with him. He's not laying a finger on Victoria." He stalked out of the room without a look back.

Alec came around to her side of the table and crouched down beside her. "I know it's worrisome, but Arnprior and I will take care of it. We'll keep you safe."

She sucked in several deep breaths. "His lordship is right. This needs to end."

Alec frowned. "What are you saying?"

"I need to tell the truth about what Thomas Fletcher tried to do to me."

"Are you sure?"

"I'm tired of lying, as if I'm the one who did something wrong. If it damages my reputation, so be it. I'm not running away and I'm not hiding anymore."

He seemed to think about that for a few moments before he rose and took her hand. "All right, Victoria. Whatever happens, we'll be there with you. Fletcher doesn't stand a chance against our united front."

As they hurried after Nicholas, Victoria sent up a silent prayer that her cousin would be proven right.

Chapter Twenty-Six

Victoria mentally ticked off the last item on her list. She'd changed into warmer clothing, packed a bag, spoken with Mrs. Taffy and Ainsley, and finally, checked on the twins. She'd done everything she could to quickly prepare for her departure, knowing Fletcher and the constables could arrive at any moment.

"Would you please cease racing about like a madwoman?" came a voice from behind her. "I'm trying to talk to you."

Victoria glanced over her shoulder to see Ainsley following her down the hall. "I'm sorry, I didn't hear you."

"That's rather miraculous, since I was all but yelling at the top of my confounded lungs."

"I'm a little distracted, as you can imagine."

Ainsley grimaced as she joined her at the head of the staircase. "I didn't mean to make light of your situation. But I've been thinking about all this, and I believe you should listen to Lord Arnprior. You should *not* leave Kinglas. Let the earl protect you."

"If Fletcher has a warrant, it would be foolish to ignore it. Besides, I refuse to bring that sort of scandal down on this family."

Ainsley waved a hand. "Who cares about a little scandal?"

"I do, and it's hardly little. I killed a man, remember?"

The girl's deep violet gaze went cold. "He deserved it. You did the world a favor."

"The world—and the law—might not agree. And they certainly won't if I'm not there to tell them the truth." She turned and started down the stairs.

Ainsley followed her. "Then have Alec go to Glasgow to tell your story for you. I'm telling you, Victoria, you have no idea what will happen once this gets out. The *ton* will tear you apart. They'll try to destroy you."

"I'm afraid of all that, too. But hiding away at Kinglas will only make things worse. If I won't stand up and defend myself, most people will assume I'm guilty of a crime I did not commit."

"But they'll probably do that anyway. People are . . . awful."

That statement made Victoria even more certain that something terrible had happened to Ainsley. She wished she had more time to find out what it was, but time had run out for her.

"You're right. But they can also be wonderful, and loving, and brave. My friends and family will help me. I will not be alone."

The girl shook her head, clearly unconvinced.

"Keeping secrets has not made my life better or safer," Victoria said. "It's time to tell the truth, no matter the consequences."

Clearing her name was the only possible way she could have a future, whether Nicholas was in it or not.

"I understand all about how secrets can poison your life," Ainsley said bitterly. "Sometimes, though, you have no choice but to drink the poison and hope you're strong enough to survive."

Victoria gave her a quick hug. "I promise we'll talk about what's bothering you when I get back."

Ainsley went as still as a hunted rabbit. "There's nothing—"

The front door opened and Andrew rushed in. "Miss Knight, a carriage is comin' up the drive. The bast—er, the visitors from Glasgow, I ken."

Victoria managed a calm nod. "All right, Andrew. I'll let the earl know."

She took off toward the library, Ainsley in her wake.

"You don't have to be present for this encounter," Victoria said. "It likely won't be pleasant."

"Oh, good. I'm at my best when people are being unpleasant."

Victoria threw her a wry smile, then tapped on the library door and went in. Nicholas stood behind his desk, talking to Alec, who paced in front of him like a caged animal. Royal had been sitting quietly by the fire but immediately hauled himself to his feet, his intent gaze going to Ainsley.

Surprisingly, the girl went to join him. Royal briefly rested a hand on her shoulder before turning his attention back to his brother.

"There's a carriage coming up the drive," Victoria said.

"Dammit," Nicholas muttered. "It didn't take them long."

"I'm sure Mr. Fletcher is eager to get it over with. As am I."

"You're not setting foot outside this castle, Victoria. I will protect you here."

"Protect me from what, my lord. The truth?" He looked torn between anger and worry and as frustrated as she'd ever seen him.

"The truth isn't always enough. We both know that."

She raised her eyebrows. "Really? If we'd told each other the truth from the beginning, we might not be in this mess."

He seemed to debate with himself for a few moments.

"All right, but I'm going with you," he finally said. "I'm your fiancé, which I will be sure to communicate to the court. That should count for something."

"But you know that sort of relationship holds no standing under the law." Besides, Victoria didn't want to expose him to scandal any more than she had to.

"I have another suggestion," Alec said. "I was just starting to explain it to Arnprior."

Victoria cocked a questioning eyebrow.

"The earl should depart for Glasgow immediately," Alec said. "If he goes by horse and changes often, he can reach the city in time to speak privately to one of the justice commissioners and to see his barrister. Then, when we arrive, we'll be well armored for anything Fletcher throws at us."

When Nicholas started to object, Alec held up a hand. "Arnprior can also send an express to Dominic as soon as he gets to Glasgow. Dominic will know how to handle this."

"He hasn't so far," Nicholas said.

Victoria couldn't help but agree with that assessment. Still, it would be more than sensible to alert Dominic. Though unlikely, Fletcher might have slipped out of London without his being aware of it.

"I think that's a sensible plan," she said to Nicholas.

"It's not, because I wouldn't be with you," he gruffly replied. "To protect you."

She took in the warmth and concern on his normally stern features, and saw in his gaze the driving need to protect those he loved. It made her fear seem to shift and settle. "You will be with me after we get to Glasgow. Then you can be an overbearing, protective old bear, and I won't mind at all."

He came around the desk to take her hands. "I cannot stand the idea of you being stuck in a carriage with that madman without me there."

She smiled up at him. "You know Alec won't let anything happen to me. And if it makes you feel better, I'll try to annoy Mr. Fletcher as much as I can."

"I might have to throttle the idiot," Alec growled.

"He's a grieving father," she said. "I'm sure he's convinced himself that I'm the villain, not his son."

"I understand his pain, but that doesn't give him the right to ignore the facts or come after you," Nicholas said.

"Grief makes us do many things we might eventually come to regret," she said softly, gazing up at him.

Victoria saw the flicker of understanding in his gaze, but then he shook his head. "Or not, which seems to be the case with Fletcher."

"She can't hide out here forever, Nick," Royal said, breaking his silence. "And it makes sense that you go on ahead."

A rap at the door ended the discussion, and Taffy came in. "The officers are here, Laird."

Nicholas glanced down at Victoria. "Are you ready for this?"

No. But she nodded.

He stepped in front of her. When Alec moved to stand beside him, Victoria blew out a breath.

"I'm fine, really," she said, wedging her way between the two brawny men.

"Stubborn lass," Nicholas murmured. "Let them in, Taffy."

They waited in silence until the housekeeper returned with two men. "Sergeant Blair and Constable Gow, from Glasgow," she announced in dour tones.

Small and wiry, with pale orange hair peppered with gray and an enormous mustache, the sergeant marched officiously into the room. The constable was considerably younger, a tall, broad-shouldered man with a diffident manner that suggested he was out of his depth. When he glanced around the room, he winced at all the scowling faces.

"I am Lord Arnprior," Nicholas said, stepping forward.

"I'll no thank ye for keepin' us waitin'," Blair said. "We're here on official business of the Glasgow Justiciary, and we'll no be put off by the likes of her." He jerked a thumb at Taffy.

"My housekeeper takes her direction from me," Nicholas said. "And you will address me appropriately, sir, is that clear?"

The man stiffened, his face turning a red several shades darker than his hair.

"Perfectly, my lord," Constable Gow said. "We meant no disrespect."

Blair shot his companion a dirty look but held his fire.

"Where's Mr. Fletcher?" Victoria asked.

Blair's contemptuous gaze swept over her. "I take it yer the one we've come to fetch."

"This is Miss Knight, and whether you take her remains to be seen," Alec said. "Now, please answer the question."

"Mr. Fletcher remained in Arrochar, sir," Gow said. "He thought the carriage might be a bit crowded if he came along."

"A more likely explanation is he thought I'd throttle him if he set foot on my lands," Nicholas said, giving the sergeant a cold smile.

"Probably not the most helpful of comments," Victoria whispered.

"Sorry," he whispered back, clearly not sorry. He held out an imperious hand. "Is that the warrant? Give it to me."

Blair scowled but handed it over.

Nicholas perused the document before handing it to Victoria. "That is not a warrant. You have no authority to arrest Miss Knight."

"No, but it is a very strong request," she said. It wasn't

as bad as she'd feared, but the short, sternly worded missive from the Justiciary officer made it clear it would not be appreciated if she failed to appear before him.

Alec plucked it from her hand and quickly scanned it. "She's right, Arnprior."

"The lass will be comin' with me if I have to bind her hands and march her out to the carriage," the sergeant growled.

Ainsley took a hasty step forward. "Be quiet, you horrible little man. If you dare touch her, I will rip off that ridiculous mustache."

"And ye'll be goin' with her, if ye try to interfere with the law," the sergeant blustered. For a small man, he had a large and annoying voice.

Royal took Ainsley's arm and reeled her back. "Your courage is duly noted, sweetheart, but we must let Nick handle this. I promise it'll be fine."

Ainsley blinked, looking a bit stunned. When Royal pulled her back to the fireplace, she started to berate him in a fierce whisper. He rolled his eyes before shushing her.

"Is there anything else, Sergeant Blair?" Victoria asked. "If not, I am ready to go with you."

The man seemed startled by her acquiescence. "We can go."

"I'll be going with her," Alec said.

"Ye will, eh?" Blair said. "And who might ye be?"

"Captain Alasdair Gilbride, Master of Riddick. My grandfather is the Earl of Riddick. Perhaps you've heard of him."

Blair raised no further objections.

Nicholas took Victoria's hand and led her out to the hall. She clung tightly to his fingers, trying to convince herself this wouldn't be the last time she would feel his touch.

When they reached the hall, he took her pelisse from the footman and helped her into it. Then he placed her bonnet on her head, carefully tying the ribbons under her chin. His warm fingers brushed against her throat before he briefly cupped her cheek. Victoria swallowed hard as she stared up into his solemn features.

"You'd best be off, Arnprior," Alec said. "Time waits for no man, especially a bastard like Fletcher."

"I'll see you in Glasgow, yes?" Nicholas murmured to Victoria.

She managed a nod.

"I won't let anything happen to you, I promise." He lifted her chin and pressed a kiss to her lips, one that held the taste of desperation. Then he released her, gave Alec a terse nod, and stalked from the hall.

Victoria watched him go with a hand pressed to her mouth, as if she could capture the warmth of his kiss.

Ainsley enveloped her in a fierce hug. "Take care of yourself, Victoria. I'll see you in Glasgow in a few days."

"Yes, I'll see you then," Victoria said, forcing a smile.

The girl hastily turned away, almost careening into Royal. "Get out of my way, you lummox," she said, giving him a shove and disappearing in the direction of the library.

"Royal, you've got your hands full with Lady Ainsley, I fear," Victoria said.

"I'll handle her. Now, you try to relax and do what Nick and Alec tell you." He bent and gave her a quick kiss on the cheek. "Everything will be fine, pet."

All she could do was nod.

Alec escorted her to the courtyard. By the time Andrew appeared a few minutes later and finally got the luggage organized and strapped to the back of the carriage, the sergeant was dancing with impatience.

"We're trying to slow things down so Nick can get a good head start," Alec murmured as he helped her into the coach, then followed.

"Is it working?"

He nodded. "He rode out a few minutes ago, hell-bent for leather, according to Andrew. He'll arrive in Glasgow hours before we do."

Sergeant Blair hoisted himself into the carriage and plopped onto the bench opposite them. He threw an irritated glare at Constable Gow, who squeezed in beside him.

As the vehicle pulled away, she glanced out the window. Royal, Taffy, and Angus stood in the courtyard, watching them go. The old man had made himself scarce the last few days, since Nicholas was still furious with him. Now he stared after the carriage with a shocked expression on his wrinkled face. When he saw her looking out the window, he raised his hand in a forlorn good-bye.

Even though she was still annoyed with Angus, she had to blink back tears. She remembered that first dreary November day at Kinglas, when she'd been appalled at the idea of spending the winter in a drafty old castle with a rambunctious group of men. Now her heart ached to have to leave the place and the family she'd come to love.

Alec squeezed her gloved hand. "Chin up, my dear. You'll be back before you know it."

"We'll see about that," Blair said in a snippy tone.

"Sergeant, unless you wish me to file a complaint with your superiors about your unprofessional behavior, I suggest you keep a civil tongue in your head." Alec's gaze shot daggers at the man.

Although the sergeant fell into a grumpy silence, Victoria noticed Constable Gow repressing a smile. When the young man was certain his superior wasn't looking, he gave her a wink.

It was a silly and entirely inappropriate gesture, but immensely cheering.

After several minutes of jostling along in uncomfortable

silence, the sergeant glanced out the window. "At this rate, we'll be lucky to make it halfway to Glasgow before nightfall."

"The horses haven't been changed since Arrochar," Gow said. "I reckon the coachman doesn't want to push the poor beasties."

More likely, someone back at the castle had bribed the coachman to go as slowly as possible.

Blair shot his colleague a dirty look. "Constable, when I want yer opinion, I'll ask for it."

"Are you familiar with horseflesh, lad?" Alec asked Gow in a friendly voice.

The young man flashed him a grateful smile. "Aye, sir. My da is a farmer outside Glasgow. I grew up around horses and all sorts of beasties."

"Really? How did you end up as a police officer?"

For several minutes, Alec and the constable had a friendly exchange about the young man's life and policing in Glasgow. Alec was clearly trying to decrease the tension in the confined space, and perhaps gain an ally. Eventually, the conversation tailed off and silence again fell over their little group. The sergeant fell into a doze, and the constable occupied himself with studying the scenery.

There wasn't much to see. They'd just gone through the pass with Victoria cravenly wishing for another avalanche, and were rolling slowly through the forest that marked the edge of Arnprior lands. She shivered, although she couldn't tell if it was from a chill as they passed into the shadow of the trees or the thought of leaving Kinglas behind.

Possibly forever.

Alec touched her arm. "Are you cold, lass? I think there's an extra—"

A massive jolt cut him off. As Victoria started to slide off the seat, Alec grabbed her. A moment later, the carriage rocked to a halt at a considerable angle. From outside they heard shouts and the thud of horses' hooves.

Victoria pushed her bonnet out of her eyes. "What's going on?"

Alec peered out the window and cursed. "Do either of you have pistols?" he asked the officers.

The sergeant, groggy from his doze, blinked in confusion. "Ah, what?"

"Are you armed?" Alec growled as the shouts outside the carriage increased in volume.

"No," Gow said. "Mr. Fletcher thought it best we go unarmed, saying it would anger Lord Arnprior if we came with pistols."

"Perfect," Alec said in disgust.

"What's going on out there?" Victoria asked.

"Whatever happens, just try to stay behind me."

She gaped at him. "Are we being held up?"

"I—"

The door to the carriage flew open, and a veritable hulk of a man loomed in the doorway. He was certainly not an appealing sight. A jagged scar ran across his face from jaw to ear, and the most deplorably dirty cap she'd ever seen was squashed down on his forehead.

Those details, however, were rendered insignificant by the sight of the large pistol he had, pointed at her face.

"Ye'll be gettin' yerself out of the carriage, wench," he barked. "And ye'll be doin' it smartly if ye don't want to be dead."

Chapter Twenty-Seven

Victoria stared in horror at the pistol, then at her cousin. "This isn't a robbery, is it?"

Alec flicked his gaze to her before returning it to their assailant. "Not on Kendrick lands. No one would dare."

Sergeant Blair bristled like a rooster. "Here, now." He jabbed a finger at the man with the gun. "Ye'll be holdin' up an officer of the law. Put that bloody pistol down and get ye out of here."

"I'll be happy to put a ball through yer skull, ye grunter, so shut it," the thug growled.

Blair flushed but held his tongue.

"Come on, you," their captor said, jabbing his pistol at Victoria.

"Best do what he says," Alec said in a calm voice.

Victoria managed to stand, even though her knees were wobbling like jelly. As she moved to the door, Alec and Constable Gow exchanged quick glances. She guessed that it meant they'd take action if an opportunity presented itself.

She hoped they would have the chance.

After carefully descending from the carriage, Victoria

cast a quick glance around. Her heart plummeted straight to the ground.

The coachman and groom were kneeling in the grass under the watchful eye of several exceedingly unpleasant-looking men. There were five in all, including her captor. They all carried pistols, but for one fellow who stood off to the side. That one had a rifle trained on the coachman.

The thug shoved her away from the carriage and toward the woods. She immediately stumbled over uneven ground and almost fell, catching herself just in time.

"Keep your bloody hands off her," Alec growled as he stepped out of the carriage.

"Or ye'll do what?" sneered her captor. "Now get ye doon on the ground and keep yer bloody mouth shut."

Alec and the two lawmen lined up against the carriage. Her cousin looked ready to kill someone with his bare hands.

"What do you want?" Victoria asked as calmly as she could.

The thug grabbed her chin and gave her a gruesome leer that showcased his rotten teeth. The sour stench of moonshine hit her like a slap, and she had to swallow hard to keep her stomach in place.

"What do ye think, lass?" She winced in pain when his grip tightened on her face. "Aye, yer a pretty piece. We'll be takin' our time with ye, I reckon'."

"The hell you will," said Alec. He launched himself at the closest brigand, catching him off guard. The man's pistol discharged as he and Alec fell heavily to the ground. Sergeant Blair staggered backward against the side of the coach, clapping a hand to his shoulder.

Constable Gow started to charge forward but came up short when Victoria's captor pointed the pistol at him.

"I wouldn't." The thug wrapped his other hand around her neck, all but choking her. She scrabbled ineffectually at his thick fingers as her vision started to blur. Desperately, she wheezed in air.

She heard scuffling and then a loud groan. When the man holding her tightened his fingers around her throat, she felt her consciousness slipping away.

"Fer Christ's sake, Mack, let her go," snapped a loud, irritated voice. "Yer all but stranglin' her."

She was suddenly released. Victoria staggered and went heavily to her knees. She braced her hands on the snow-covered ground, sucking in air as she tried to clear her head and settle her racing heart.

When she was able to look up, she wished she hadn't. Alec was sprawled facedown on the ground, still as death. The man he'd attacked, his face covered in blood, was struggling to his feet with the help of one of the other men.

Victoria started to crawl toward Alec, terror for him propelling her forward.

A massive hand clamped down on her shoulder. Her captor locked her against his side.

"It's all right, miss," Gow said. The constable was on his knees, trying to assist the sergeant. "He's just unconscious. He got hit with the butt of that fellow's pistol." He glared up at Alec's assailant.

"Aye, yer friend will wake with naught but a headache." The man then gave Victoria the most blood-chilling smile she'd ever seen. "Ye, however, willna be so lucky."

"If you harm her, we'll hunt you down and kill you," Constable Gow said in a cold voice.

He was a courageous young man, but there was very little he could do to help. Aside from the pistols pointed at him, he had his hands full with the sergeant, who was bleeding and seemed barely conscious.

"Ye'll have to find us first," the man replied. "But ye won't." Then he glanced at Victoria and her captor. "No more dickin' about now. He'll be gettin' impatient for her."

"Seems a shame we canna have a little fun with her first," said her captor. His massive hand moved down to her hip, holding her tight as he ground himself against her. Victoria had to swallow the bile that rose in her throat.

Underneath her fear, a consuming rage was building and a disbelief that this could be happening to her again. She'd killed a man for trying to take her against her will. That time, it had been an accident, but this time, if she got the chance, it wouldn't be.

"That's up to him to decide," the other man barked. "Ye ken he told us not to harm her, or have ye forgotten?"

The thug loosened his hold. "I remember." Muttering curses, Victoria's captor spun her around and began marching her away from the road, deeper into the woods.

"Where are you taking me?" she demanded in the strongest voice she could muster.

"Ye'll find out. I wouldna be in too much of a hurry to meet him. He vowed to be the end of ye."

She'd guessed what would happen at the end of this grim little march. Still, receiving confirmation almost took her out at the knees.

"You do know who I am, don't you?"

"Dinna care," he said, shoving her forward.

She recovered and glared at him. "I'm the Earl of Arnprior's fiancée. And if you harm me in any way, the earl and his *entire* family will make it their lifelong mission to hunt you down and kill you."

She saw a hitch in his step. "We ain't from around these parts, you daft bitch. No one will ken who we are."

When she started to argue, he gave her another shove. "Shut yer trap and keep walkin', or I'll pull yer skirts up and shag ye anyway."

Victoria turned her eyes forward and kept walking.

The woods were thinning, and sunlight filtered down through the feathery branches, casting dappled shadows on the forest floor. A wintry scent filled the air as her feet crunched through a thin crusting of snow and pine needles. Birds darted overhead from branch to branch, twittering away in joyous peeps.

It was a beautiful day, the Highland air crisp and invigorating. She didn't know whether to laugh or cry at the irony of it. She would never see Nicholas again or have the chance to walk with him through these beautiful woods secure in the knowledge that she'd finally found the place she truly belonged.

With him.

They walked for another minute or so before breaking through into a small glen. Though they weren't far from the road, it felt completely isolated.

No one would be coming to her rescue.

"It's about damn time," Fletcher said from off to her side.

Simply hearing that dreaded voice firmed her resolve. She would do whatever she needed to survive or go down fighting.

Turning, she faced her enemy.

Fletcher stood at the edge of the wood, dressed for riding, and several horses were tied up to trees. Her nemesis and his merry band of thugs had come by horseback.

"Do you really think Sergeant Blair and Constable Gow will not realize who is responsible for this?" she asked.

He walked forward to meet her as casually as if he were out for a little stroll. His cold, utterly satisfied smile sent a chill down her spine.

"Those idiots are barely capable of remembering their own names," he said. "Besides, Sergeant Blair already believes you're guilty. He'll think you've met a just and convenient fate at the hands of ruthless thieves."

"You know Captain Gilbride will not believe that."

Fletcher shrugged. "He will not be able to prove anything."

She stared at him in disbelief. "You were staying at the inn last night, as was Alec. You were seen in Arrochar with the two lawmen who were instructed to bring me to Glasgow to stand trial for murder. *Everyone* knows you wish to see me hang. Do you really think you'll get away with this?"

"I'm already on my way back to Glasgow," he said with a negligent wave. "The innkeeper saw me drive off in my carriage this morning, shortly after Sergeant Blair set off to fetch you. There was no point in me waiting, you see, since you had no choice but to return to Glasgow."

He circled around her as he talked, taking obvious delight in tormenting her. "My servants will swear I arrived in Glasgow well before nightfall. And in the meantime, your captors will be long gone. They know their business, Miss Knight. I made certain of that before I hired them."

Her head swam as the extent of his madness struck her. That he would take such risks and put such an elaborate plan in play was mind-boggling.

"Why?" she asked hoarsely. "You've won. Isn't it good enough for you to drag me back to Glasgow to face trial for murder?"

Fletcher leaned in, practically spitting the words into her face. "No, it is not. I want revenge for my son."

"And bringing me forward on a murder charge isn't revenge? Destroying my reputation and my life isn't enough for you?"

His pockmarked face turned a mottled red. "You already escaped justice when the magistrate refused to lay charges after you murdered my son. Even the blasted court official in Glasgow said that while he feels compelled to investigate, you'll probably escape conviction again."

Victoria shuddered at the hatred in his voice and on his face.

"You have too many friends in high places, damn you," Fletcher said.

"You mean like my father, the Prince Regent?" Victoria said, giving him as cold a smile as she could muster.

"Wut?" Mack said from behind her.

She glanced over her shoulder, taking in his consternation. "That's right. My natural father is the Prince Regent. If anything happened to me, I cannot imagine the depth of his distress."

"That's a bloody lie," Fletcher snarled, poking her in the shoulder with his pistol. "He doesn't even know you exist."

Victoria swallowed against the fear squeezing her throat. "It's the truth, and you know it."

"Listen 'ere," Mack started.

"Shut your mouth, or you won't get paid," Fletcher ordered. "And your companions won't like that, will they?"

When Mack subsided with a grumble, Victoria's small ray of hope died.

"Thomas was my only son and my heir." Fletcher's pale gaze was hollow and full of hatred. "None of my success means a damn thing now that he's dead. You took my family's future away from me, you bloody whore."

"Mr. Fletcher, I am sorry for your loss, and I truly regret your son's death," she said, struggling to remain calm. "But I assure you that what happened was an accident forced upon me by your son's behavior. He was responsible for his death, not I."

Her words were obviously falling on deaf ears. Trying to reason with a madman was a fool's errand—as his furious expression made clear.

"No, *you* are responsible. And now *I* will be responsible for your death. Only then will my poor boy rest in peace."

"Mr. Fletcher, I beg you—"

Two sharp *cracks*, one after another, echoed through the woods.

"What the hell?" Mack growled, peering back toward the road. "Ye said no one would ken about this."

"It's probably one of your men, shooting a prisoner," Fletcher said.

"You'd better hope not," Victoria said through clenched teeth. "Lord Arnprior will see you all hang." The thought of anything happening to Alec or the other men because of her . . .

"Shut yer gob," Mack said, shoving her again. "Enough of this bleedin' palaver," he said to Fletcher. "Get on with it or give her to me."

"I have no intention of watching you rut," Fletcher said with disdain. "But indeed the day is fading, so I must be on my way."

He waved his pistol at Victoria. "Move over there."

She glared at him. "No."

Mack propelled her into a nearby stand of trees and shoved her down to the ground.

"Any last words, Miss Knight?" Fletcher said as he positioned himself a few feet away. "Care to beg for your life?"

She met his lunatic gaze as calmly as she could before finally closing her eyes. She thought of Nicholas, determined that her last thoughts be of him. God, she loved him. To never see him again . . .

A pistol roared, but it wasn't his. In almost the same instant, it was Fletcher who screamed and something wet splattered onto her face. Victoria's eyes flew open to see him pitch forward, his mouth gaping and his eyes wide with shock. He went down like a felled tree, missing her by inches.

"Bloody hell," yelled Mack, whipping around to stare across the clearing.

She followed his gaze and saw Logan Kendrick charging toward them like an enraged bull, pulling a second pistol from his belt. Without breaking stride, Logan fired again, and the thug crumbled to the snowy ground.

Dumbfounded, Victoria stared at the bodies, blood staining the snow around them. Logan had shot Fletcher in the middle of the back and Mack in the center of his chest. The man's aim had been astounding.

On shaky legs, she started to clamber to her feet.

"Let me help you," Logan said gruffly. "Are you all right?"

She nodded, her mouth too dry to form words.

"You're sure." He swiftly ran a concerned gaze over her, front and back.

"Is he dead?" she finally whispered, pointing at Fletcher.

Logan let go and rolled Fletcher partway over with his foot. Then he went down in a crouch to check the man's wound and the pulse in his throat.

"No, but he will be shortly," he said. "There's nothing to be done for him."

He rose and extracted a handkerchief from inside his coat and handed it to her. "Here, lass. You've got, ah, something on your face."

He meant Fletcher's blood, of course. She swallowed hard and began scrubbing her face, sternly telling herself not to cast up her accounts.

When she got back to Kinglas, she intended to find a quiet room and have a thorough cry. Or get sick, she hadn't yet decided which.

She tried to hand him back his kerchief.

"Leave it on the ground," he said.

"How did you know?" she asked with a vague wave.

He took her arm and started walking her toward the trees. "First things first. Back to the carriage, yes?"

"Is Alec all right? There was a shot."

"Och, that was me, lass. Gilbride is as right as rain, aside from a sore head."

Her legs went weak from relief. "Thank God. And the others?"

"Some ninny from Glasgow took a shot in the shoulder, but he should be all right. Old Tommy and that young constable are helping Alec keep an eye on the men who attacked you."

She glanced up at him, taking in his calm expression. Apparently, subduing ruthless villains might be all in a day's work for Logan Kendrick. "You're quite the hero, sir."

He flashed her a charming smile, looking uncannily like his older brother. "Are you sure you don't want to marry me, instead of Nick?"

She had to repress the urge to burst into hysterical laughter—or tears. "No, thank you," she said in a quavering voice. "I only want him."

Nick leaned over the stallion's neck, letting the animal go flat out. Two grooms from the inn at Arrochar followed him, doing their best to keep up.

Victoria needed you, and you weren't there. You failed. Again.

He forced the thought of past and present failures from his mind as he rounded a curve in the road. If Fletcher *had* gotten his hands on Victoria, then succumbing to fear wouldn't help. And Nick would do any damn thing necessary to bring her back to Kinglas, including tearing the bastard limb from limb if he had to.

The forest that marked the beginning of Arnprior lands rose before him, the road narrowing as it entered the trees. Nick slowed the horse, even though he chafed to do so. But

breaking the animal's leg—or his head, for that matter—
would be the height of stupidity.

As soon as Ben Munroe, the innkeeper of the Golden
Thistle, told him that Fletcher had departed for Glasgow
instead of waiting for Victoria, Nick had known something was very wrong. Just as suspicious, Ben had spotted
Fletcher lurking behind the inn last night with a couple of
disreputable characters. The innkeeper knew almost everyone from Glasgow to Edinburgh, so he'd recognized one of
the men as a notorious smuggler. There was absolutely no
reason for a wealthy, respectable man like Fletcher to be
talking to a ruthless criminal unless he was up to no good.

Acting on instinct, Nick had asked Ben for his best horse
and two grooms, then set off toward Kinglas.

He could only ride as fast as he dared and pray he wasn't
too late.

A few minutes later, he spotted the carriage listing awkwardly at the side of the road, and his heart jumped into his
throat. The coachman was crouching down to inspect a
wheel, but the vehicle appeared empty.

Too late.

He'd just switched the reins to one hand and started to
fumble for his pistol when Victoria and Alec came around
from the back of the carriage. The shock and relief at seeing
them had Nick almost dropping the reins. Not wanting to
spook the carriage horses, he pulled the stallion to a halt
some yards back and on the opposite side of the road. He
swung his leg over the saddle and dropped to the ground,
hitting it at a run.

Victoria flew toward him, her skirts hiked up to her knees
and her face shining with joy. When she launched herself
into his arms, he swept her up, spinning once with the force
of their momentum. She peppered his face with kisses,
sobbing, laughing, and talking all at once. Nick quietly

held her, mashing her to his chest and sending a silent, heartfelt prayer of thanks to the heavens.

"I thought I would never see you again," she finally managed in a wobbly voice.

Holding her with one arm, he untied her bonnet and tossed it to the road. He smoothed back her hair. "Hush, darling. I'm here now, and I'll never leave you."

She gazed up at him, her gorgeous blue eyes bloodshot and shimmering with tears. Her nose was red and her skin was splotchy, but she looked more beautiful than ever.

"Do you promise?" she asked.

"I promise." Then he took her lips in a hot, openmouthed kiss that poured forth all the pent-up fear, relief, and love in his soul. If Nick had his way, they would never be parted again.

"Bloody good to see you, Arnprior," Alec said as he joined them in the road.

Nick reluctantly let Victoria slide to the ground but kept a firm hold around her waist. Not that he needed to. She clung to him like moss to a rock.

"You look like hell," Nick said.

Blood trickled down from under Alec's mussed hairline and a nasty bruise was starting to form around his eye. His greatcoat was covered in dirt, and his cravat was missing.

Alec just let out a sardonic snort.

"Is everyone all right?" Nick asked.

"Sergeant Blair took a bullet to the upper arm, but it was through and through so he should be fine."

"I suppose they got the jump on you," Nick said.

"I'll never live it down," Alec said. "The bastards caught us by complete surprise."

Nick glanced down at Victoria and his heart jerked. He touched her hairline. "Are you hurt?"

"The blood isn't mine." She paused, looking ill for a moment. "It's Fletcher's."

"Is he dead?"

She nodded. "He won't be bothering us again."

"Good." His only regret was that he hadn't been the one to do it.

"I can't help but feel the same," she said, "even though I know it's wrong to wish anyone dead. The poor man had gone mad with grief."

"He was going to shoot you, Victoria," Alec said.

Just thinking about what could have happened to her made Nick's gut clench. He pulled her closer, cuddling her to his side. "You killed him?" he asked Alec.

"No. You have someone else to thank for saving Victoria's life."

As he spoke, Logan appeared from behind the carriage, wiping his hands on a cloth. Everything inside Nick slammed to a halt.

"Logan?"

Victoria curled her gloved fingers into the collar of Nick's coat. "I would be dead if not for him. He arrived literally in the nick of time."

Logan casually tossed the bloodstained cloth into the open carriage boot and strolled over to join them. "I've patched the sergeant's wound, but we should get him loaded up and on to Arrochar as soon as the coachman finishes with that wheel."

"How in God's name did you get mixed up in this?" Nick peered more closely at him. "And why are you dressed in your nightshirt?"

His brother looked like he'd just rolled out of bed. His nightshirt was stuffed into his breeches and topped with a ratty old coat that probably belonged to Tommy. He clearly hadn't shaved in days, and his hair was sticking out in different directions. If a stranger had come along, they would think Logan was the villain, not the hero.

"I was dead to the world when Tommy woke me up and told me something was afoot." Logan gave Victoria an apologetic smile and scratched his bristled chin. "I might have overindulged last night, so I was a wee bit thickheaded."

"After today you can overindulge as much as you like and I will never offer a word of criticism," she said.

"So, you still didn't leave when I told you to," said Nick. "Why is that?"

Logan met his gaze with an impassive look that didn't fool Nick one bit. His brother was as nervous as a virgin on her wedding night. "I suppose I wasn't ready to say good-bye to Kinglas," he finally said.

"Thank God," Victoria said fervently. She looked up at Nick and tugged on his collar.

"Yes, thank God," he said. "You say Tommy knew something was wrong?"

"Aye, he'd been sitting in front of the cottage smoking his pipe when he spied the carriage going to Kinglas this morning and then you subsequently riding past like a madman. When the carriage came out again, heading toward Arrochar, he rousted me from bed. Said something didn't feel right, especially with the laird riding out like a demon, as he put it."

"So, you just decided to take a little ride and see what was happening?" Nick asked skeptically. "Dressed in your nightshirt?"

Logan shrugged his massive shoulders. "Not like I have anything else to do at the moment."

Except run a massively successful trading company, as Nick well knew.

"And there was the sound of that pistol shot," Logan added. "That rather clinched the deal. Tommy and I arrived to find Gilbride facedown in the dirt, and some nasty buggers holding everyone else hostage." He jerked his head toward the coach. "We've got them tied up behind the carriage, by the way. The constable is keeping an eye on them."

"Where was Victoria when this was going on?" Nick asked.

"I was dragged into the woods, to where Fletcher was waiting for me." She squeaked. "I'm fine, sir. Truly."

He grimaced and loosened his suddenly tight hold. "Sorry, love. What happened next?"

"Mr. Fletcher couldn't bear the idea that I might not be convicted, so he said he decided to take justice into his own hands." She paused, as if collecting herself, then mustered a smile. "Fortunately, Mr. Kendrick came charging out of the woods just in time, pistols blazing. He was absolutely heroic."

Logan snorted. "Yes, that's me all over."

"You *are* heroic," Victoria said earnestly, touching his arm. "I will be eternally grateful to you."

When Logan gave her that warm, charming smile of his, Nick did his best not to scowl. Apparently, he failed, since his brother glared at him.

"Stop being an idiot," Logan said. "She's mad about you."

Victoria patted Nick's chest. "Of course I am, even when you're acting like an idiot. But, sir, how did you know to come back for us? We didn't expect to see you until Glasgow."

He briefly explained the circumstances. "Ben's grooms and the coachman can help Constable Gow with the prisoners. I suggest we get on our way to Arrochar before it gets much later. That wheel looks like it's fixed now."

"I think you're forgetting something," Victoria said.

Nick frowned. "I am?"

"She means me," said Logan. "She's wondering if you're going to send me away again."

"I'll just go help Gow," Alec said, backing away.

Nick sighed. "A family discussion on top of a kidnapping and an attempted murder. What fun."

"We are not leaving until this is settled," Victoria said in a firm tone.

"But Sergeant Blair—"

"He'll be fine," she said.

Nick gave her a sheepish smile. He was being a stubborn thickhead, and they all knew it.

"Listen, Nick, I can never do enough to wipe clean my terrible failure," Logan said in an earnest tone. "I will live with it for the rest of my days. But you need to know how sorry I am." He paused. "This isn't easy for me to say, but I'm begging you one last time to forgive me—for both our sakes."

"For your entire family's sake," Victoria added softly.

Nick stared into his brother's eyes, ones that were a reflection of his own.

Those eyes were like Cam's, too. Nick's little boy had adored his big, brash uncle, and Logan had fiercely loved Cam. His brother would have given his life to save the boy—he would to save any member of the family. But for years Logan had lived in exile, separated from the people he loved.

And he'd done that because of Nick.

Victoria laid a hand on his arm. Nick saw love and acceptance in her eyes, along with a quiet understanding that smoothed the jagged edges of his soul. He breathed out a long sigh that felt like letting go of something both precious and painful.

It was time. "Of course I forgive you, Logan. I'm only sorry it took me so long."

Logan's eyelids closed for a few moments. When they lifted, tears glittered in his gaze like blue crystals. The sight of them made Nick's throat go tight.

But then the familiar, roguish smile parted his brother's lips. "You're a tough nut, you old bastard. But I'll take it, and gladly."

"And you're a complete imbecile," Nick said, jabbing him in the shoulder. Part of him wanted to grab his brother and pull him into a long hug, but he wasn't yet ready for that. He suspected it might take Logan some more time to forget all the pain and sorrow, as well.

Victoria shook her head. "I will never understand men."

"You'd better get used to it, lass," Nick said. "You'll be living with a houseful of them."

Gow approached them with a diffident air. "My lord, we're ready. And as much as I hate to say it, I still need to bring Miss Knight to Glasgow." The constable grimaced. "I have my orders."

His sergeant was no doubt still throwing his weight around, despite the hole in his arm.

"All right, Constable," Nick said. "But we'll be stopping in Arrochar overnight. I have an errand to perform."

Victoria frowned. "What errand?"

"I'm finding a vicar to marry us. When you stand before the court in Glasgow, you will be the Countess of Arnprior. And your husband will be standing right beside you."

Her eyes popped wide. "But—"

"You'll stand as witness?" he asked Logan.

His brother flashed a wide grin. "It would be my honor, my lord."

"Good. Then it's all settled."

"But—" Victoria started again.

He took her chin in his hand. "I will not take no for an answer, lass. I'm madly in love with you, and you are madly in love with me, are you not?"

"Well, as a matter of fact, I am."

"Then there is no reason to say no, is there?"

She seemed to ponder it for a few seconds before her lush mouth parted in a luminous smile that lit up the few remaining dark corners of his soul. "When you put it like that," she said, "how could I possibly say anything but yes?"

"Oh, thank God," Alec said as he returned. "You two were bloody killing me with all this to-ing and fro-ing. I'm getting too old for that sort of nonsense."

Victoria looked at her cousin and burst into laughter. The joyous, carefree sound floated up to the treetops like the call of the lark in springtime.

"All right, *Sassenach*," Nick said, taking her hand and leading her to the carriage. "Let's go get married."

Epilogue

"It's a splendid party, Victoria," Chloe said. "It almost makes up for the fact that we missed your wedding day."

Aden, sitting opposite them, gave Victoria a wink. "Arnprior did seem in quite the rush to get leg-shackled."

"There were a few extenuating circumstances, as I recall," Victoria said dryly.

"Nick would have dragged you off to the parson in any case," Logan said. "To say he was eager to claim his bride doesn't begin to describe his impatience." He waggled his eyebrows. "Especially for the wedding night."

"Logan Kendrick, behave yourself." Victoria shifted her stern look at Aden. "You too."

Her brother sighed dramatically. "We're in the dog house now, Kendrick."

"I practically live there," Logan replied.

They were seated in the formal drawing room at Kendrick House, which had been converted into a supper room. The staff had set up over a dozen tables, all covered in starched white linen and graced with the family's best silver, plate, and crystal. Huge vases filled with white roses adorned the sideboards, and dozens of candles lit the room in a soft, shimmering glow.

Thanks to the dedication and hard work of the servants, the elegant mansion looked stunning and was once more the comfortable abode of a happy family. Victoria still preferred Kinglas, but Glasgow was beginning to feel like home too.

"You and Arnprior do know how to throw a grand party," Alec said, toasting Victoria with his wineglass. "The best part is the twins can wreck your house for once, instead of mine."

"That's a regular day of the week around here," Logan said.

"Graeme can hardly be expected to wreck anything, since he's still on crutches," Victoria said. "I don't know where Grant is at the moment, but I expect he'll stay out of trouble, despite all the pretty girls here tonight." Both twins had been subdued since the elopement fiasco, and she could only hope their newfound good sense would last.

"Speaking of pretty girls," Logan said, "I'm heading up to the ballroom. Perhaps I can snag a few to dance with." He gave them a friendly nod and strolled out.

"Your brother-in-law cuts a dashing figure in his clan attire," Chloe said. "I'm sure he'll find many ladies who are interested."

"I hope so," Victoria said.

For a man with a rakish reputation, Logan led a quiet and orderly life. At her insistence, he'd moved into Kendrick House. Now he spent most of the day at his office and warehouse down at the docks. Evenings he was at home, talking to his brothers, reading his correspondence, or listening to Kade play music. Logan and Nicholas were rubbing along fairly well, although they sometimes argued.

The wounds between them ran deep, and it would take time and patience for them to entirely heal.

Still, there was no doubt Nicholas was happy that he'd made peace with Logan, and the rest of the family was overjoyed that he'd finally allowed the prodigal brother to return home.

"Logan seems like a fine man," Dominic said from his seat at the end of the table. "I'm glad he's returned to the family fold."

"Not as glad as I am," said Alec. "Fellow saved our collective arses."

"He's certainly the reason I'm sitting here," Victoria said.

Dominic grimaced. "Yes, about that, I can't tell you—"

She held up an admonishing finger. "You are not to apologize again, sir. None of what happened was your fault."

"I told you to keep secrets from Arnprior," the magistrate said, "which was a miscalculation on my part."

Aden waggled a hand. "I did too, so blame to share."

"And then I failed to realize Fletcher had left London." Dominic shook his head, clearly disgusted. "I don't think I'll ever live that down."

"Perhaps you're just getting old, my love," Chloe said with a mischievous twinkle.

"Thank you for that observation," her husband replied.

"You were out of town at the time," Victoria protested. "How were you to know the wretched man had left London?"

Dominic and Chloe had been in Yorkshire, visiting with the Marquess and Marchioness of Lendale for the holidays. Once Dominic learned that Fletcher was in Scotland, he'd set off for Glasgow, arriving the day of the attempt on Victoria's life. By the time Victoria and Nicholas reached the city, Dominic had already done much of the work necessary to have her case dismissed. There'd been some consternation regarding Logan's role in Fletcher's demise, but with Dominic's assistance, the judicial inquiry had been conducted quickly and discreetly. Since the Kendrick family was highly regarded in Glasgow, they'd managed to evade an outright scandal.

"Still, I should have anticipated that Fletcher might try something like that," Dominic said.

"It's hard for even the great Sir Dominic to anticipate the actions of a lunatic," Aden said wryly.

"Very true," Chloe said. "And why are we talking about that sad, awful man? We're celebrating Victoria's marriage."

"Correct as always, my dear." Dominic gave Victoria a little bow. "Forgive me, Lady Arnprior. I had no intention of spoiling such a splendid event."

She returned the bow. "Not at all, Sir Dominic. And I'm sorry I pulled you away from your visit with Lord and Lady Lendale. I hope I shall meet them someday soon."

"I'm sure you will," Aden said. "After all, Lia *is* your cousin."

Lia Easton, Marchioness of Lendale and the natural daughter of the Duke of York, had written a lovely letter to Victoria with a standing invitation for her and Nicholas to visit them at Stonefell Manor.

"Yet another cousin," Chloe said drolly.

"There are legions of us," Alec said. "Victoria is just getting started."

"I'm sorry the Lendales weren't able to be here," Victoria said, "but I'm so grateful that my aunts came up from Brighton," She smiled at Aden. "Thank you for arranging that."

"Of course, pet." Her brother lifted his glass to her. "After all, this is your official celebration. It's only right your family should be here."

While Victoria had intended to have only a small, family party to mark the occasion of her marriage, over the last few weeks it had transformed into a grand ball with over a hundred guests. Nicholas had insisted they open the Kendrick House ballroom, and had brought Taffy and some other castle staff down to help manage the elaborate affair. Over Victoria's halfhearted objections, her husband had arranged for a lavish supper, an orchestra for dancing, and even a card room for the gentlemen and older ladies. She'd objected, but all the Kendrick men, including Angus, had taken her husband's side.

"Ye sneaky buggers went off without us to get riveted," Angus had said, "so ye might as well let us have a grand party to make up for it."

Knowing that for too many years the Kendrick family had lacked occasion for celebration, Victoria hadn't had the heart to deny them their fun.

"It's so nice of Edie and Vivien to take my aunts under their wing," Victoria said. "I think the poor dears are feeling a little overwhelmed."

Alec snorted. "They've been getting along as thick as thieves, having a grand time racketing about town all week."

"Where are my aunts, by the way?" Victoria said, craning to look around the room.

"Edie and Vivien took them to the card room," Chloe said. "The five of them were going to form a table."

"Oh, God," Aden said with mock alarm. "I hope my wife doesn't fleece them."

"Is Vivien good at cards?" Victoria asked.

"You have no idea," Aden said.

"Perhaps I'd better check on them." Her aunt Rebecca, although a very sensible woman, was something of a gambler, though usually for low stakes.

"Don't worry. Edie will keep an eye out," Chloe said. "Your only job tonight is to enjoy yourself."

"Yes," Alec said. "You're off duty for the night, Cousin."

Kade came hurrying into the room and over to the table. "I've been looking everywhere for you, Victoria."

She took his hand. "Do you need something, dearest?"

"No, but Nick is waiting for you outside the ballroom. He says you're to stop hanging about with this group of reprobates and come talk to him."

"Goodness," Chloe said, "I hope he doesn't include me in that description."

Kade snapped his fingers. "Right. Nick said I was specifically to say that you are *not* a reprobate, Lady Hunter, and to beg your pardon."

Chloe wiped her brow with exaggerated relief. "Thank goodness. But do tell your brother that this set of reprobates is actually very nice."

"I think so too," Kade said with a shy smile.

"After you deliver her ladyship to the earl, why don't you come back and join us?" Aden said.

Kade's eyes went wide. "Thunderbolts, I'd like that. Maybe you could tell me more about your adventures during the war?"

The boy had taken quite a shine to Victoria's mysterious brother, something she found both touching and amusing. Aden had been incredibly kind to Kade, entertaining him with highly exaggerated stories of his prowess on the Continent. At least she hoped the stories were exaggerated.

She stood. "I'm sorry, everyone, but I must see what my husband wants."

"Oh, I can hazard a guess what he wants," Aden said.

"Please remember that children are present, my dear," Chloe said in a firm tone.

"I'm not a child," Kade protested.

"Of course not," Chloe said without batting an eyelash. "I was speaking of Alec."

"That's me, innocent as a babe in arms," Alec said with a grin. "Although, last night Edie and I—"

"I'll see you later," Victoria said, cutting him off.

"I like your family," Kade said as she linked arms with him and walked out to the hall. "They're jolly."

"Almost as jolly as your family." Victoria smiled at a few guests who were going into the card room.

"Not Royal, though. He's even gloomier these days. But when I ask him, he always says nothing's wrong."

"I believe he's missing his friend, Lady Ainsley," Victoria said.

Ainsley had departed a few weeks ago for her great-aunt's manor house up north. She'd refused to stay for the ball, despite pressure from Victoria and Edie. When Victoria asked Royal if he knew why she was in such a hurry, he'd scowled and said that Ainsley did whatever she wanted, whether it made sense or not.

"I thought he and Lady Ainsley hated each other," Kade said.

"No, but they do seem to have a complicated relationship, don't they?"

"Rather," Kade said in a dry tone, sounding much older than his years.

"Where is Royal?"

"He's in the ballroom with Graeme. Royal said that invalids have to sit together and keep each other company."

Victoria mentally sighed. She would have to pay greater attention to Royal. The man was clearly suffering, and his brothers didn't know how to help him. At the moment, neither did she, but she had no intention of letting that get in her way.

"You let me worry about Royal. I promise he'll be fine."

"I hope so," Kade said. "It's splendid that we're all together again, and I want him to be happy too."

"He will be, someday."

"There's Nick and Grandda," Kade said when they reached the top of the central staircase.

Hearing his brother's voice, Nicholas turned. Any worries Victoria had about Royal or the family faded under the warmth of her husband's gaze.

"About time, my love." Nicholas bent to press a quick kiss to her lips. "I've hardly seen you all evening."

"Don't be silly. It's only been half an hour since we danced." She went up on tiptoe to whisper in his ear. "But I've missed you, too."

"The Kendricks are yer family now," Angus said. "Yer the Countess of Arnprior, lass, and one of the finest ladies in the land. Yer place is by yer laird's side, not hanging aboot with a bunch of frippery Englishmen."

She almost choked at that description.

"Victoria's family is very nice, Grandda," Kade said.

"Indeed they are, and one can hardly describe Sir Dominic and Aden as frippery," Nicholas said.

"I'm going back down to join them," Kade said. "Why don't you come along, Grandda?"

Angus expelled a much-put-upon sigh. "All right, lad, if that's what ye want. I suppose I can put up with a few Englishmen for my lady's sake."

"Thank you, Grandda," Victoria said, giving him a hug and a quick kiss on his whiskery cheek.

"None of that now, lassie," he said gruffly. Still, he patted her on the back, and she could tell he was pleased.

"Another Kendrick male wrapped around your finger," Nicholas said as they watched the old man and the boy clatter down the stairs.

She rested a hand on his broad chest, relishing the feel of hard muscle under fine silk and linen. "There's only one Kendrick man I wish to wrap around anything."

His gaze smoldered like molten silver. "I think we can safely say I am wrapped around your finger, and I can't wait to be wrapped around the rest of your body, too." He leaned in close. "While I'm deep inside you."

"Hush," she said, glancing around as her cheeks flushed with heat.

"Have I told you tonight how beautiful you look?" His gaze ran admiringly over her figure.

She smoothed a hand over the flowing skirts of her creamy-white dress. Since she'd not had a proper wedding, she'd allowed Edie to talk her into splurging on a beautiful and very expensive satin and lace ball gown. The look in her husband's eyes as she'd come down the stairs before dinner had more than made up for the cost.

"You have, my lord." She cast an appreciative eye over his kilted physique. "You're looking rather splendid yourself."

"We'd look even more splendid *out* of these fine clothes," he said with a roguish smile. "Are you ready to slip away, my love?"

She blinked in surprise. "Isn't it a bit too early?"

"No one will miss us."

"But it's *our* party," she said with a laugh as he started to gently pull her down the hall.

"I asked Logan and Grandda to play host. In fact, Logan asked me what I was doing hanging about instead of carrying you off to bed."

She wrinkled her nose. "He didn't."

"He certainly did. So, what do you say, my love? Shall we sneak off and leave our guests to their own devices?" His gaze was alight with love and laughter. To know she'd helped Nicholas find happiness again made Victoria's heart fill with joy.

And even though they'd been married for almost a month, she was eager to be alone with him. In fact, love-making with her husband had become rather an obsession for her.

She faked a yawn. "Now that you mention it, I am feeling rather fatigued. Bed sounds like an excellent idea."

"*Sassenach*, I couldn't agree more," Nicholas said.

And then Victoria's handsome laird swept her into his arms and carried her off to paradise.